HER ALIEN NEIGHBOR

STRANDED ON EARTH

BOOK ONE

IVY KNOX

Cover art: Natasha Snow Designs

Edited by: Tina's Editing Services, Mel Braxton Edits, & Owl Eyes Proofs & Edits

❀ Created with Vellum

AUTHOR'S NOTE

If you don't have any concerns regarding content and how it may affect you, **feel free to skip ahead to avoid spoilers**!

This book contains scenes that reference rape, sexual harassment, eating disorders, fatphobia, racism, sexism, substance abuse, as well as graphic violence which may be triggering for some. If you or someone you know is in need of support, there are places you can go for help. I have listed some resources at the end of this book.

CHAPTER 1

VANESSA

*T*he women who buy themselves fresh flowers every week have their shit together. I am not one of them, but that doesn't stop me from perusing the flower section of the grocery store, searching for an affordable bouquet that isn't already wilting. I'm desperate to become the kind of woman who is financially stable enough to have a cart full of ingredients for healthy meals, with a bright bouquet delicately placed on its side in the upper part of the cart.

Some women rock matching sports bras and yoga pants, and some are in full Important Businesswomen attire, but all have an air about them that screams "I work hard, and I have earned this beautiful trophy cut fresh from the earth."

I, on the other hand, have a heavy basket with handles digging into the crook of my elbow filled with boxes of pasta and jars of sauce because it's the easiest meal to cook, and somehow, I'm still not sick of it. After a decade of eating it four nights a week, you'd think I'd detest this food, but it's also the cheapest, which, as a struggling thirty-eight-year-old actress living in Los Angeles, is exactly what I need. I certainly work just as hard as the women with flowers, spending my days memorizing lines and my nights mixing drinks at the dive bar down the street, but I have yet to reap the benefits.

I reach for a flimsy bouquet of baby's breath, eyeing the four-dollar price tag. I could get it if I put the jar of tomato basil sauce back, but will that get me through the week? Or will I need to eat plain pasta with butter one night? Would that be worth it? My phone vibrates in my purse, and I decide to put the flowers back. Maybe next time.

My nerves rise as they do whenever my phone rings, and I let out a sigh as "Tia - Agent" flashes across the screen. "Okay, I'm ready. Just give me the bad news. No dancing around it this time, Tia." No one ever calls with good news. If it's good news, I'd get a text filled with emojis and exclamation points.

She sighs heavily, and my heart sinks. "They decided to go another way. I'm so sorry, Vanessa."

Placing the basket at my feet, I immediately walk out of the store as tears fill my eyes. I can't go through the checkout line with this much pasta while sobbing. It's too pitiful.

"So what was the reason?" I ask Tia the moment I step outside. There's a zero percent chance the answer she gives me won't crush my spirit, but I need to hear it anyway. I wanted this part so badly. They called me in for two more rounds of auditions after the first one, and I thought I had it nailed. I was wrong.

Tia scoffs, clearly annoyed. "I can hear you crying. I'm not going to kick you when you're down."

"Just tell me."

She huffs a breath. "Fine." I hear her take a sip of something, then she says, "It was down to you and another actress. They chose her because she's…"

"She's…what?" I ask, impatient.

Tia clears her throat. When the feedback from the casting director is bad, she stumbles over her words because she doesn't want to tell me. The more she stumbles, the worse it is. "Well, she's also plus-sized, but in a way they…"

"They what?" I shout, knowing where this is going and fed up with the stalling.

"She has more of an hourglass shape," Tia finally says.

I bark out a laugh, bitter and cold. "So she's the right kind of fat. Is that what you're telling me? And I'm not. I'm just too gross for viewers to look at because I have a stomach and fat arms."

"You do *not* have fat arms," she scolds. "You're not even fat. Stop putting yourself down."

"Ugh, are you serious, Tia?" I almost scream, then realize I'm in a parking lot and people are starting to gawk. I lower my voice as I head toward my car. "I am fat, and you denying it is more of an insult than anything else."

I close my eyes and try silently counting to three as a way to calm myself. It doesn't work, though, because I'm sick of having this discussion with well-meaning people who don't understand how they've been brainwashed by society. "That's...that's like you saying you have blue eyes and me replying with 'Your eyes are *not* blue,'" I say in a patronizing tone, "when in fact your eyes *are* blue, and there's nothing wrong with blue eyes."

"I know," she replies. "You're right, I'm sorry. I have clients who still see 'fat' as an insult."

"I get it," I say, softening my tone as I gaze down at the small crown I had tattooed on my finger. It was supposed to serve as a reminder never to settle for less than I deserve, a motivating image. But now I just see it as a symbol that doesn't fit who I am. "We've all been conditioned to think that way. But I've worked really hard to undo that damage. There's nothing wrong with a fat body. Just like there's nothing wrong with a short body, or a tall one. It's just a descriptive term."

"You're right. I'll try harder."

"Thanks," I reply, not feeling any better since I didn't get the part.

"This decision came from the network execs," Tia offers. "The casting team loved you. In fact, they wanted to write a part specifically for you after the network made them choose the other girl."

"And they didn't because..." I ask.

Tia audibly gulps. You'd think she'd be used to giving me bad news by now. She's been my agent since the beginning, and I've only had a few decent roles, none of which led to anything else.

"Well, the network pushed back because they didn't want two plus-sized women on the same show," she adds. "They didn't want viewers to think it was a..." she pauses, "a show about fat people."

"Right," I say through gritted teeth. "Naturally."

God forbid the cast of a sitcom about six thirty-something friends look like normal people. It's not the first time I've lost a role because of my size, but it feels like a knife through the heart every time.

There was a short period when I first started going on auditions that I tried all the drastic weight loss tricks. I tried making myself smaller, so I stood a better chance of getting lead roles. It didn't take. Any weight I lost would come right back the moment I ate a normal meal. After I graduated from UCLA with a theater degree, I continued taking acting classes, I tried improv, took on roles in indie films that paid nothing, and networked with as many industry people as I possibly could. I have the talent to slay a comedic role or a dramatic one. That should be enough.

But after a decade of relentless disappointment, I'm starting to wonder why I continue putting myself through this. What am I still doing in a place that doesn't want me?

"Things are getting better," Tia says as she attempts to reassure me. "Shows are becoming more diverse every year in terms of race, gender, and body type. All the shows you auditioned for this pilot season had a role that was written for a plus-sized woman without her being the butt of every joke. That's progress."

"Sure," I reply, biting my lip to hold the tears back. "I just wasn't good enough to be in any of them." The wet drops fall anyway, dripping onto my teal T-shirt as I hastily unlock my car door and crawl inside. I hold the phone away from my face as I sniffle, hoping Tia doesn't hear it. I know she won't judge me for being disappointed; it's the number of times she's heard me sob over the phone that I find embarrassing. I've let her down, again, and I wonder how many more rejections it will take before she deems me a lost cause and has no choice but to drop me as a client.

"I could line up some commercial auditions for next week, if you'd like," Tia offers.

It's not an offer I have any right to refuse. Commercial spots pay well, sometimes really, really well, and there are plenty of actors who make a living off just doing ads. About six years ago, I booked a campaign with a well-known car manufacturer for their new hybrid vehicle they had just released. I had one line that was: "That stick has some power!" as I comically put the car in drive and put my foot on the gas. I felt like I nailed it. It was a ridiculous ad, and I was funny in it.

However, the line became a meme, and soon I was known as the girl in the car commercial who seemed horny for a hybrid. As humiliating as it was, the money I made from the ad covered my rent for two years. I've reached a point where I can't afford to be picky about the roles I go after. I need to try them all and hope somebody's looking for a fat girl with short brown hair and bangs who has a sense of humor.

"Yeah. Let me think about it, okay?" I ask Tia.

"Of course. Call me over the weekend if you need anything, 'K?"

"Thanks. I will," I say as I hang up.

Over the years, she's become a friend. She's a fantastic agent, too, but it's impossible to put yourself out there in this business and not have at least a few moments of heartbreak. It's a given, and Tia is always the one who sees it first. Together, we feel the disappointment, the hurt, and the betrayal.

Like the time I booked a role as a series regular on a new sitcom about a group of twenty-somethings who hated their jobs and decided to open a bookstore that sold weed in the back. It was the biggest role I'd ever gotten, and a week before we were supposed to start filming, I broke my leg, and the role went to someone else. I haven't gotten anything close to that role since.

Pressing my forehead against my steering wheel, I take a deep breath. Wiping away my tears, I ponder my next move. I need instant comfort, but what kind? The warm numbness only a bottle of wine could summon? Or should I eat my feelings?

Both sound nice, honestly, and I could send myself into a solid booze-and-sugar coma that lasts until tomorrow afternoon. However, with this type of rejection looming large in my head, I need to do something that won't make me hate my body even more when I wake up. I deserve to feel good.

Booty call it is, then.

I scroll through my recent texts until I find "Brian G." We met through a dating app, and one date turned into more of a casual hookup than a relationship, but he's not terribly boring, and his dick is nice and big, so I haven't written him off yet. He's also surprisingly okay with the fact that I never want to have penetrative sex, which is rare. Most have gotten annoyed by my hesitation and bailed the second I said no.

Me: *You busy atm?*

Brian G.: *...*

When the dots disappear, and no response pops up, I send another text.

Me: *Come over. Rough day and I want that D in my mouth.*

I add a tongue emoji and an eggplant emoji, ensuring the nature of my request is clear, and not even three seconds later, I get a reply that has my mouth falling open.

Brian G.: *Wtf? Brian's in the shower. This is his gf.*

Oh shit. Shit. Shit!

Me: *...*

I have no idea what to say. Brian certainly never disclosed that he was in a relationship. If he had, I wouldn't have gone on a date with him, and I certainly wouldn't still be hooking up with him. The knot in my stomach continues to twist until I feel like I'm about to be sick.

I can't imagine what his girlfriend must think of me. To my knowledge, I've never been "the other woman." This is a first. A horrible first.

After I berate myself for not asking Brian directly if he was involved with someone, my guilt transforms into anger. This isn't on me. Not entirely, anyway. This is Brian's fault. He's a grown-ass man, and he should've been honest with me. But he wasn't, because he's a manipulative, philandering scumbag.

Me: *I'm sorry. Truly. I had no idea he had a gf. If I had, I would've blown him off immediately.*

Several minutes pass before I get a response. And then—

Brian G.: *Tbh, I suspect you're not the only one he's cheated with.*

I don't find this the least bit surprising. Men like him often juggle multiple deceptions at once. This poor woman.

Brian G.: *How long have you been seeing him?*

My answer comes easily. Let him face the consequences of his actions. I'm certainly not going to cover for him.

Me: *Our first date was two months ago. We turned it into more of a casual thing after that. How long have you been together, if you don't mind me asking?*

Brian G.: *Just hit the one-year mark last week*

Me: *My god*

Brian G.: *...yeah.*

My phone vibrates suddenly, and my sister's name flashes across the screen as the phone continues to ring. What could she possibly want? We haven't talked in weeks. Pressing *decline* and sending her to voicemail, I return to the text with Brian's girlfriend. One piece of bad news at a time.

Me: *I know I don't even know your name, or anything about you, really, but you obviously deserve better than this. I hope you find it.*

And because this information has left me in a particularly foul mood...

Me: *Also, I hope Brian's dick falls off.*

Then I realize she might take that last comment the wrong way, and I start to panic.

Me: *Not that it will. Because of STDs, I mean. I don't have any, just FYI. So, I didn't give him any. And not that I'm saying if he had them, they'd come from you... That's not at all what I meant...*

Now I'm rambling like an idiot. I sent her a nice message, wishing her happiness, and I had to go and ruin it with a crack about Brian's dick, which I'm sure is the last thing his girlfriend needs to hear.

Brian G.: *LOL. I knew what you meant.*

I let out a breath I didn't know I was holding.

Brian G.: *Fingers crossed Brian's dick turns into a shriveled and useless paperweight someday. May neither of us ever meet another scrub like him. - Amy*

Her name is Amy, and she doesn't despise me. Not as much as she despises Brian, at least.

My phone vibrates again as it rings, and it's my sister. Again. The name "Willa" taunts me as I continue to ignore it. But then I look at the picture that appears whenever my sister calls, and it's of my nephew Jordan on his sixth birthday, holding the frosting-covered ends of the candles he had just blown out in his mouth. In good conscience, I can't ignore little Jordan.

"Hey," I say as I answer. "I've had a terrible day, Wil, so I'm begging you not to make it wo–"

"Aunt Franny died," she interrupts, her voice shaky as she delivers the news through tears. Willa pulls the phone away, the sounds of her sobs still reaching my ears. Then I hear her sniffle loudly before she says, "You have to come home."

CHAPTER 2

VANESSA

She died in her sleep. Aunt Franny, halfway through her seventy-fourth year, went to bed two nights earlier and never woke up. It's the way she always wanted to leave this world, and I'm not surprised she got exactly what she wanted. The woman had a knack for getting her way when it came to most things.

Strolling through Manchester Regional Airport, I smile at the thought of her getting into bed that night and thinking, *I'm ready. Take me away,* and God granting her wish. But my hopes are forgotten the moment I step outside, the harsh New Hampshire air hitting me like a brick to the face.

Zipping up my hot pink puffy jacket, which comes with a sack it can be stuffed into and is entirely too light for mid-March, my eyes take in the lingering signs of winter—the piles of snow that line the edges of every parking lot, containing more dirt and salt than snow at this point, the dark gray skies that make four o'clock in the afternoon look and feel like eight, and the practical boots everyone collecting a loved one at the airport seems to be wearing.

Locals are always prepared for snow. It doesn't matter if it's March or July.

I, on the other hand, am not at all prepared for this weather. Living in Los Angeles has softened my tough New England blood, apparently, because I assumed this puffy coat would be more than enough to protect me from the elements. You don't need to own a winter coat in Southern California. It's why I donated all of mine to a thrift store mere days after I arrived. The people who wear them during the winter months in L.A. only do so for the sake of fashion. Or maybe they're anemic. Who knows?

But as I stand out on the sidewalk, the same small area where departures and arrivals congregate, tucking the bottom half of my face behind the collar of my jacket, I regret not keeping at least one of my heavier coats. If only just to wear them during these family visits.

Since I moved out west, I haven't returned home as often as I should. My parents divorced two years after I graduated from college, and my mom moved to Arizona, leaving the snow, the humidity, and the borderline-unhealthy obsession with Boston sports teams behind. Willa and I tried to find ways to divide our time fairly between the two, but the distance became difficult, especially once Willa and her husband, Ethan, started having kids. We decided the easiest thing for everyone was for me to visit Mom a few times a year in Arizona, and for Willa to do the same with Dad.

She only lived a few streets away from our childhood home, so she and Dad were together all the time. It felt like it, anyway.

Then Dad got sick.

He was diagnosed with lung cancer at fifty-seven years old and died a few weeks after his sixty-second birthday. Mom never visited him and that was probably for the best, but I visited as often as I could, making short trips where I hid mostly in the house. My sister took on the role of his primary caretaker, even moving him in with her and Ethan when his condition worsened.

I still struggle with the guilt of not being by his side on his last day. He had Willa, so it's not like he was alone when he died, but I should've been there too. Just as I should've been there for Aunt Franny.

Flashing headlights to my left catch my eye and my heart skips a beat. For a split second, I think it's a cop car, and my entire body turns to stone. But instead, a silver sedan slowly pulls up in front of me. "Welcome back," Willa says with a solemn grin.

After tossing my suitcase in the trunk, I hop in the passenger seat.

That seems to be her calling in life. Since the day my nephew Jordan was born, Willa has spent every moment caring for others. Jane was born two years later and only added to the chaos. It seems to make her happy, and that's all I ever wanted for her.

Though, today, the mood is anything but happy. She pulls me in for a tight hug as soon as I shut the door, and I instantly break down. It was easy to direct my grief toward a to-do list: packing, booking flights, and the various logistical details that go with travel. Now that I'm here sitting in front of Willa with her familiar laugh lines and the smell of generic lavender hand cream, my emotions have nowhere to hide.

"Shh. It's okay, Van," she murmurs softly as she rubs my back.

I chuckle at the sound of my nickname as I wipe the tears from my cheeks. "I can't believe she's gone," I reply, sitting back and buckling my seat belt. "I didn't get to say good-bye."

Willa grabs my hand, giving it a squeeze, before releasing it and turning her blinker on. "Aunt Franny knew you loved her." Her tone turns slightly resentful when she says, "And she certainly loved you. The woman hated just about everyone." She turns to me. "But not you."

I try to hide my smile but fail. Willa's right, and I don't even bother to offer any placating words to refute her claim. I have no idea why Aunt Franny adored me as much as she did, but it was clear I was her favorite niece. She was always pleasant to Willa, but her warmth never went beyond that. When she saw me, however, her face would light up as if I were her daughter.

Willa used to take it personally, and when we'd return home from visiting Aunt Franny, she'd run up to her room in tears. My mom would then turn to my dad and say, "You need to do something. That sister of yours is pure evil for choosing a favorite. Go console your daughter."

My dad would roll his eyes and agree, his steps heavy as he trudged up to Willa's room.

Later, he'd pull me aside and said, "I can't control how Aunt Franny acts, kiddo. God knows I tried when we were younger. But you can control how you respond to her gifts and endless praise. Don't gloat in front of Willa, okay? Do me that favor?"

I would say, "Okay, Dad," and quietly go to my room so I could play with my new toys in private.

My sister merges onto I-293 North, singing a song from Taylor Swift that I know but can't name. I take that as a cue to turn the volume knob on the radio.

"Really?" she asks without taking her eyes off the road.

I scoff as I turn the dial, trying to find the right station. "I'm doing you a favor. Ahh!" I squeal when I find it. "Now you don't have to waste your energy creating a soundtrack for our drive."

"But I like to sing," she replies, her tone curt.

"That's what your shower is for. There's no better venue to showcase your vocal talents."

She shoots me a familiar glare, then lifts her top lip in a snarl.

"So what are the plans for the funeral? Can I help with the planning, or have you already taken care of everything?"

Willa taps her thumbs against the steering wheel, following the beat of the song. She shrugs. "Nothing to take care of, actually. No funeral. Aunt Franny left very specific instructions for what she wanted, which was cremation. We should get the urn in a few days. And she wanted her ashes to be spread around the outside of her house in various spots and on specific dates and times. That, you can do."

"Seriously?" I ask, not surprised by my late aunt's detailed demands because that's just like her. What I do find surprising is the *specific dates and times* part. Why not just spread her ashes all at once? I can't imagine what the point of doing it over an extended period is.

"We have an appointment to meet with her lawyer tomorrow at nine in the morning, so set your phone alarm," Willa says in what I'm pretty sure is her stern mom voice. "You're on the couch tonight, by the way."

I look over and her teeth are clenched in an *oops, forgot to mention that earlier* expression.

I sigh. "I thought you had a guest room."

"That's Jane's room now."

"Your kids don't share a room?"

She shoots me a judgmental side-eye and says, "Jane is five and Jordan is seven. Or have you forgotten how old your godchildren are?"

"No," I reply sheepishly. "I don't know how old kids are when they get their own rooms. It's not like I have any frame of reference."

"Huh," Willa says, her brow furrowed as she merges onto 93 North from 293. "I figured you didn't want kids. Like Aunt Franny."

While I appreciate the comparison because I always admired how Aunt Franny didn't bend to society's expectations, I'm also offended by the assumption. "So, because I haven't had them yet, you figured I didn't want them?"

"I mean, you are thirty-eight."

I smack her arm. "How dare you? I have plenty of time." I point to my stomach. "Plenty of eggs waiting for their gravy."

Her lips flatten in mild disgust as she holds up her hand to block a potential second slap. "Don't attack the driver, dumbass." Then she sighs. "What's the plan, then? Wait to have kids until after you've gotten your big break in Hollywood?"

My eyes roll toward the passenger window, away from her assessing gaze. "I don't know. I'm still working on that."

"Acting is going well, then?"

"Yup," I reply quickly, hiding my tightened features from her. "Great."

"You plan on seeing Beth and Caitlyn while you're in town?" Willa asks suddenly. My teeth clench at the sound of their names.

"Probably not," I say, hoping that's the end of it.

"Huh," Willa mutters as if surprised, though I know I've told her more than once that Beth, Caitlyn, and I are no longer friends. "I see them all the time," she adds with a smile. I don't turn away from the window to see it, but I can hear the smile in her voice. "Their kids are the same age as Jordan."

"Wow, interesting."

I'm glad Beth and Caitlyn have gone on to lead fulfilling lives, but that doesn't mean I want to hear about it. I haven't spoken to either of them since graduation. Not even a like or a comment on social media since then, and that's how I prefer to keep it. They broke my heart when The Incident occurred on prom night, and they didn't have my back. They abandoned me when I needed them most. After the worst night of my life, they called me a liar and pretended not to know me at all.

The four of us were inseparable throughout high school: me, Beth, Caitlyn, and another girl, Sam. Beth liked to think of herself as the ringleader of our little group, though the only one who actually took orders from her was Caitlyn. I'm not surprised to hear she and Beth are still close. I can't picture Caitlyn putting on a pair of socks without seeking Beth's approval first, even in her late thirties.

Sam, on the other hand, was the best. We've drifted apart over the years, the distance between us making it easy to lose touch, but I have only fond memories of her.

Willa and I ride the rest of the way in silence, letting the pop hits of the eighties, nineties, and today fill the car. Warmth fills my chest as we pass exit signs for neighboring towns—towns that I couldn't drive to fast enough to escape the dullness of my hometown once I got my license. Back then, driving forty minutes to stroll around the mall or the park was the highlight of my week. I hated every moment I was stuck in Sudbury.

There are too many painful memories I was sure would follow me everywhere once I left for good. Luckily, that wasn't the case. I was able to put Sudbury, and the trauma of my youth, behind me. For the most part.

Even on visits home, I could block it all out. By following a strict itinerary of going to my parents' or my sister's house directly from the airport and never venturing outside until it was time to fly home, I avoided running into anyone from high school. Anyone who could remind me of the things that happened during those terrible years.

This time, however, I'm not sure how lucky I'll be.

* * *

"Her collection of hats?" Willa asks Mr. Albert Dennings, my late aunt's lawyer. "She's leaving me her collection of hats. You're serious?"

He clears his throat and pushes his small round glasses up the bridge of his nose. "And her limited-edition Christmas bunny ornaments."

Willa rubs her forehead, looking utterly confused. "It's not that I expected her to leave me a bag of money." She turns to me to make sure I'm paying attention. "I want to be very clear about that. I know Aunt Franny didn't have much. But…hats? Really? I don't even wear hats. Why would she think I would want her damn hats?"

"What's the big deal?" I ask. "Just throw them out."

Willa looks between me and the lawyer. Her hazel eyes are wide and filled with shock at my suggestion. "She wanted me to have them, Vanessa. I can't just throw them out." Her hands flop into her lap in a defeated gesture. "Now I have to find a place to store them, and it's not like we have the room for it."

This is silly. I can understand waiting maybe a week after inheriting an heirloom, however ugly or unwanted, out of respect, but beyond that? It's just stuff. And these hats will weigh on her. I know how her mind works. "Want me to throw them out?" I offer. "I don't mind doing it."

"No, no," she mumbles, her eyes unfocused as if she's trying to hatch a plan on how to get rid of the hats without the ghost of Aunt Franny ever finding out. Then she fusses with her long chestnut-colored hair hanging perfectly straight around her shoulders. "Well, what did she leave Vanessa?" she asks Mr. Dennings.

"Ah," he says, an eager grin stretching his thin, chapped lips. "Yes, here it is. Vanessa Bradford will inherit the deed to Francesca Norton's house located at 210 Clarke Lane in Sudbury, as well as her car, which is a 2012 Toyota Avalon, color: obsidian, parked in the garage at 210 Clarke Lane."

I shout, "What!" the same time Willa yells, "Are you fucking kidding me?"

Turning to look at Willa, I say, "You want the house? The car? Take them. I certainly don't want them."

She slaps her hands on the arms of her chair. "You live in a shitty apartment. How could you not want your own house?"

"Because I have no interest in living *here*," I instantly reply. Then the guilt hits me as Willa jerks back slightly. "No offense. It's just not where I want to settle."

She twists her body toward me, her knees bumping against the side of my chair. "So you'd rather struggle to pay your rent in a place that, while beautiful, you'll never be able to afford without a million-dollar paycheck?"

I insulted her by saying I didn't want to live here. That much is obvious. While I feel bad, it's the truth, so I don't take it back. This place has too many memories. I square my shoulders and face her. "That's an extreme exaggeration and you know it." I huff a breath.

"Oh, so you think you'll buy a house out there?" she asks, knowing that the housing market in Los Angeles is insane, and that no, I probably won't.

"Why do I have to buy a house? I can just keep renting," I bite back. "Besides, maybe I'm happier out there than I ever was here."

Her face softens, and she tilts her head slightly. "You are?"

I sit there, saying nothing as Willa's piercing gaze sizes me up, making me remember how I lost that part to the other plus-size woman and the previous roles I lost for not having the "right" kind of body.

I bite my lip to hold back the tears while I think of a clever retort. Something that will make it clear to Willa that I'm doing just *fine* out there, but Mr. Dennings interrupts.

"Pardon me, ladies. I can see there are some family issues to be worked out here, but I have other appointments after yours, so if you could take this," he waves his hands in a shooing gesture, "elsewhere, I would appreciate it."

Really? This is the guy Aunt Franny trusted with handling her estate? I'm sure the majority of appointments he has are unpleasant, as family members of the recently deceased attempt to process their grief in the divvying up of riches, but still. You'd think he'd be so used to it that he'd have some manners. Although, that might be why Aunt Franny chose him. She appreciated directness, which he certainly has.

I lean forward, propping an elbow on the edge of his desk. "May I ask what your relationship was to Aunt Franny?"

He stops fiddling with the stack of papers in his hands, and his face falls. He removes his glasses and rubs his eyes. "She was a dear friend. That's why she asked me to be the executor of her estate. Eccentric woman. Misunderstood, I think." Mr. Dennings chuckles softly, gazing at something off in the distance. "Lovely, though. Damn shame she's gone."

They were friends. I wasn't expecting that. I didn't think Aunt Franny had any friends. She'd email me once a month, updating me on which stores went out of business and which restaurants were moving into town. She never went to said restaurants, but I think she found the infrequent changes to the town thrilling to share with me.

Mostly, her emails were written in a rambling, stream-of-consciousness format, and covered the latest gossip on neighbors and other townspeople she didn't like but ran into at church, how the weather was awful no matter what time of year it was, and which trees surrounding her house needed to be cut down.

I didn't devote enough attention to them at the time, and right now, I hate myself for that. I will never again receive one of Aunt Franny's emails, and I'd give my left arm to hear her complain about those damn trees again.

She would also slip in a mention of the "beefcake brothers" who moved into the big house next door to her, how she thought they were around my age, and how I needed to visit her immediately so I could make one of them my husband. I thanked her, of course, but declined the setup.

If these brothers were anything like the guys I grew up with, it's likely they had a limited vocabulary, owned pickup trucks they cared way too much about, found racist jokes funny, and considered thick work pants tucked into steel-toed boots proper date attire. That's not the kind of man I'm interested in. I had my fill of them in high school, and they left a rancid taste in my mouth.

Mr. Dennings hands Willa and me manila folders with copies of Aunt Franny's will, and other things I don't bother to read at the moment. He stands, a clear signal for us to leave. "Oh, Willa," he says, rubbing the white scruff on his chin, "the hats and ornaments are in the basement of her house. The boxes should be labeled with your name on them. Vanessa can show you." Then he presents me with a set of five keys dangling from a yellow keychain that says, "Gave my last fuck in a previous life."

I bark out a laugh, and the two of them give me a strange look. Running my fingers over each key, I determine their uses. The silver key with the Toyota logo is obvious, and I assume one of the four bronze keys goes to the front door of Aunt Franny's house. But what are the other three for? "Excuse me," I ask Mr. Dennings as Willa reaches for the door to his office to leave, "do you know what these keys go to?"

He gestures to the folder tucked inside my arm. "It's all in there."

Clearly, he doesn't wish to waste any more of his precious time on us, so I nod good-bye and follow Willa out the door. It takes ten minutes to drive to Aunt Franny's house, and when we pull into the driveway, I suck in a breath at the sight before me.

"What the fuck happened to the view?" I shout.

Aunt Franny's house has never been the nicest on the block. It felt outdated and shabby the moment she bought it, with a strange layout no one but her could appreciate. But the view of the sprawling hillside leading from her property and far-off cornfields surrounded by towering trees that turn rich shades of yellow and orange in fall, with a river cutting through the middle, has remained the prime selling point.

Now, though, there's a wooden shed blocking that view. What is it doing there? When did it get there? Why would Aunt Franny allow this eyesore to be constructed? I throw my hands up, the weight of responsibility I've been handed suddenly wearing me down. "How am I going to sell this place now?"

Willa's chin dips as she shakes her head. "You can't sell this place, Vanessa. She wanted you to have it."

I chew on the inside of my cheek, frustrated that I've been put in this position. "Wil, I don't live here. This isn't my home anymore. What do you want me to do? Just abandon my life in L.A. and move back here?" She turns her head forward, facing the view that's now practically non-existent. "What would I do for work in Sudbury? I can't imagine there's a dire need for actors."

Willa sighs, tipping her head back until it hits the headrest. "I don't know. Just don't rush to sell it, okay? Promise me that."

It's a promise I can't make. My boss at Lou's Bar gave me two weeks off, and that's it. Plus, I need to see if Tia can line up more auditions for me. I need to get back to my life, which means I need to sell this place and the car immediately, and head back west.

I can't bring myself to say any of this to Willa, though. She looks so tired. I imagine she must be after her daughter, Jane, woke up screaming at three in the morning, and demanded Willa and I read her two books each before she'd try to go back to sleep. I'm pretty exhausted, myself.

"Okay," I finally reply, "I'll take my time. See if I can make Aunt Franny's place my home." It's a lie. Every word of it, but it seems like what Willa needs to hear right now. And I can't think of anything beyond going inside and taking an epic nap. I open the passenger door, but then I stop. "You want to come in and get your hats?"

Willa's mouth curves up on one side. "Why don't you hold onto them for me? I'll pick them up another time."

Nodding, I grab my folder and my purse and hop out of her car. Pulling my suitcase from the trunk and waving good-bye, I take in the front yard, *my* front yard, I guess. It should be an emotional moment, standing here and gazing at the house I was always excited to visit as a kid. I'd give my left arm for Aunt Franny to come rushing out the front door with arms outstretched, telling me there was nothing to stress about. That everything was going to be okay.

But that's not going to happen. She's gone, and her house is now mine.

I sigh heavily as I trudge toward the front door, too tired to cry over all I've lost and the burdens that now weigh me down.

CHAPTER 3

AXILSSANAI "AXIL"

"*I* cannot believe she is gone," Zev, my younger brother, says of our late neighbor as he leans against the doorway to my shed. I spend most of my time in the shed, which I built by hand a year ago, on the edge of Lady Norton's property.

I let out a heavy sigh as memories of her flash through my mind. "Neither can I." I know she was of advanced age, for humans, anyway, but she seemed healthy. Her death came as a surprise to me and my brothers despite how many times she told us she was ready to pass on. It is a comfort knowing she had no unfinished business, apart from the stack of love books on her bedside table she was eager to read. "I miss her laugh."

"As do I," Zev says, nodding as a smile lifts the corners of his lips. "She had such a kind and generous heart."

We spent many hours in her little home, helping her unclog drains, raking the leaves on her lawn or trimming the grass, and fixing her meals, but my favorite time with Lady Norton was when we would watch TV. She would put on some love story she had seen dozens of times, and we would ask her questions about the women onscreen, and why the man's actions made him a heroic figure within the story in an effort to gain a better understanding of human behavior. My younger brother, Mylossanai, would then ask countless questions about the human courting rituals displayed before us.

"She could tell we were different," Zev adds. "Did she ever ask you? Where we came from, or what we are?"

"No," I reply with a wistful laugh. Perhaps our obvious otherness was why she enjoyed our company so much, as she seemed to have little tolerance for others. She never outright asked if we were not human, but I am certain she suspected as much. "I am not sure what my response would have been if she had."

"True," Zev says, chewing on the inside of his cheek. "It is not as if you could say, 'Yes, we are draxilios from the planet Sufoi. Our ship exploded just outside of Earth's atmosphere thirteen years ago, and our pods crashed in the middle of the woods in eastern Massachusetts. We were genetically modified at birth to change our appearance at will, giving us the ability to hide our horns and transform the color of our skin from a shimmering cerulean to whatever shade we desire in order to blend in.'"

I chuckle at his hypothetical revelation, adding, "There is no need to fear us, Lady Norton, even though we can shift forms into massive fire-breathing beasts. We request that you do not alert the authorities."

Zev runs a hand through his wavy, dark brown hair. "No, we certainly could not say any of that."

We trusted Lady Norton, of course, more so than any other human we have come across, except maybe for Harper, our brother Lukassanai's human mate, but our presence on this planet is supposed to remain a secret for as long as we live, which is a very long time in earth years.

My brothers and I fled Sufoi in search of new opportunities, freedom, and most importantly, mates. Though, the latter has taken a rapid descent on my list of priorities. Since Lukassanai fell in love with Harper, and their courtship was anything but smooth, I have ceased looking for my mate. If she even exists, that is.

Our handlers on Sufoi made it clear that no genetically modified draxilio, or "podling" as we were often referred to, deserved a mate, and was prohibited from taking one. The tampering with our cells rendered us ineligible and unworthy of the loving bond that natural-born draxilios are promised.

It was a lie, of course, that was used to control us, just as it was used to control the many podlings that came before us. Some were told mates simply did not exist for podlings. We were told taking a mate was not allowed. Our handlers shifted the lie however they saw fit in order to keep us focused on protecting the king.

The podlings that came before us were given much simpler genetic modifications than the many my brothers and I have, such as the manual calcification of a certain part of the brain rendering them incapable of feeling a particular emotion.

The original podlings were notorious for their battle skills, as the four of them together lacked fear, awe, trust, and remorse. But our handlers got greedy with the options at their disposal, and began adding more alterations to our cells, blood, and brain tissue. My siblings and I were batch thirteen, which meant our handlers had tried and failed more than ten times to design the perfect assassins for the king.

My heart squeezes at the thought of the twelfth batch of podlings. Those poor souls were doomed from the moment of their creation. Given the modifications of intense strength, a thirst for blood—any kind of blood—and an uncontrollable libido, they were used in battle only once. When they attempted to fornicate with the warriors on the opposing side, the king quickly removed them from his guard and those draxilios spent years constantly sedated before they were shipped off to an unknown planet. I do not know if they still live.

Being surrounded by the other podlings on Sufoi was a comfort. Natural-born draxilios did not see us as equals, but the podlings understood what it meant to be seen as a freakish, disposable draxilio by the rest of society. Once we realized our common goal of seeking freedom and mates, the podlings worked together to find another planet where we could live freely. Earth was not our top choice, but it ended up being the place we selected when it came time to flee.

We are lucky we crashed where we did. Luka is lucky he found

Harper when he did. And after we left the city of Boston, we were lucky the house we bought was next to Lady Norton's.

"I must go to work," Zev says as he checks the time on his phone.

I nod. "Farewell, brother. See you for dinner."

Zev closes the door to my shed, and memories of Lady Norton's low and crackling laughter continue to fill my mind. She had quite the odd sense of humor, quite dark, at times, but endearing.

I grab a block of red oak from the stack beside me, and glide it toward the blade of the table saw, smiling as it slices through the wood like butter, then turn the block around so it may carve the roughened edge of the other side the same way. Once I have the trim removed, I turn off the motor and inspect my work.

Impeccable, as always.

Not that there was ever any doubt. It is the reason my custom furniture business has taken off since we arrived in this quiet town over a decade ago after leaving Boston.

Switching out the clean block of wood with a second piece I must cut, I turn the table saw back on and resume my work. The blade has sliced through half the block when the door to my shed flies open and a wild creature stumbles in.

No. Not a creature. A human female.

Her hair is a dark brown, so dark it is almost black, and cut in short, choppy pieces that frame her round face. There is also a section of shorter hair that obscures her forehead. It is matted in the back and sprouting up in chaotic waves on one side. She is shouting something, but as I am wearing my safety headphones, I cannot hear a word.

What is she thinking, entering my shed? On my private property, no less. Thankfully, my hands stilled the moment she came in, but I could have easily injured myself on the saw's sharp blade had I not noticed her right away.

I have no idea how she ended up here, but looking at her disheveled state and uncontrolled rage, she must be in need of professional care I cannot provide.

"What do you want?" I bark out once I cut the engine on the saw and remove my headphones.

"The noise!" she shouts back, her chest heaving. My gaze drifts down to the area, following the movement. She is wearing a pale-yellow T-shirt that is practically molded to her lightly tanned skin, the bottom hem tied in a knot at her hip, exposing a narrow patch of skin along her stomach just above the waistband of her soft black pants. Her shoulders and arms are plump, ending in slim wrists and small hands. Her breasts appear big enough to fill my palms, and I feel them begin to sweat as I envision squeezing, massaging, then feeding the hardened tip of one into my mou—

"Do you have to be so fucking loud?" she yells, running a hand through her tousled hair. "I was trying to sleep."

I direct my gaze at the window, taking in the light gray sky of the early afternoon. "Do you often sleep in the middle of the day? Do you not have a job?"

Her mouth falls open, surprised by my curt tone, and I notice how lush her lips are. They are shaped perfectly. I could not envision changing a thing about the thickness or shape if given the chance.

"Uh, not that it's any of your business," she practically hisses, "but the last few days have been total shit and I haven't slept well. I finally got a moment of peace this morning and climbed into a soft, warm bed. Next thing I know, I'm awoken by the sound of power tools." The mysterious woman puts her hands on her wide hips, then pinches her eyes closed as if reliving the event against her will. "Like nails on a goddamn chalkboard. Do you have to do that right outside my window? Isn't there anywhere else you could," she waves an open palm at the block of wood, "do your little crafts?"

Little crafts? The nerve of this woman coming in here and dismissing my work simply because she chose to nap the day away. She has no idea how much time and care are put into every single one of my pieces. It is not as if I slap a few blocks of wood together and sell them at an obscene markup.

I take my time, adding intricate carvings into table legs, the backs of chairs, along the length of walking sticks, and so on. All I ask is that clients include three of their most cherished hobbies or interests when placing an order. The artistic freedom this arrangement allows makes the work enjoyable. And she just wandered in off the street and mocked it.

My patience, what little there was to begin with, has evaporated. "I do not know who you are, or how you ended up here, but I suggest you leave. And maybe sleep at night like everyone else."

As I put my headphones back on, she says, "I told you already, I live next door." The pieces of this puzzle start to fall into place. Lady Norton's bedroom window is just outside the shed, and her glass panes are quite thin.

If this woman was in Lady Norton's home, that must mean... "So you are the niece. From California. Vanessa, is it?"

She jerks back, surprised. "Aunt Franny told you about me?" She shakes her head. "I mean, she mentioned she had neighbors my age she wanted me to meet, but I didn't think you actually knew her."

Her age. How adorable. If only she knew there were centuries between our ages. Draxilios age slowly, allowing us to maintain our youthful appearance for a very long time.

"My brothers and I were quite close to her," I tell her, leaning forward and pressing my fists into the table, my knuckles cracking under my weight. "Lovely woman. We spent a lot of time at her, er, I suppose, now it is your home."

"That's kind of weird, don't you think?" she spits out, crossing her arms beneath her ample chest. "Why would a group of guys hang out with an old woman?"

I do not understand her question. Why would we not hang out with an old woman? It is not as if we were seeking an old woman to befriend when we moved here, but the friendship we built with Lady Norton did not seem strange or inappropriate. It felt natural. I suppose this is something uncommon among humans, though I do not understand why. We revered our elders on Sufoi.

"We liked Lady Norton," I tell her plainly. "She was funny."

Vanessa's nose scrunches up as if she inhaled a horrid stench. "Lady Norton? Why on Earth would you call her that?"

"Well, she—" I begin to explain, but Vanessa puts up a hand and groans.

"Know what? I don't even care," she mutters impatiently.

Why is this woman so unpleasant? She cannot even let me finish a sentence. All because she is sleep-deprived? If Vanessa was Lady Norton's favorite niece, then I cannot imagine how rude the other one is. Willa, I believe. I hope I never meet her.

"I'm selling the house, so I'll be out of your hair soon."

She grins in a smug sort of way and turns to leave.

"Wait!" I shout. She turns to face me and lifts her brows in a questioning glance. "Why would you sell it? Lady Norton wanted you to have it. She said as much to me." It was Lady Norton's wish for Vanessa to inherit her home and create a life here. She thought it would make Vanessa happy to be given a house and a car and not have to struggle financially anymore, as she has done for so many years on the other side of the country.

"Because I have a life in L.A. I'm not just going to it throw away."

Though I have spent a significant amount of time studying humans and their odd choices—both before we fled Sufoi and after we crashed—there is still much that puzzles me. Like refusing to honor a late relative's wishes simply because those wishes are inconvenient. "So you are selfish," I say with a nod. "I see."

That certainly keeps her from leaving. She plants her feet where she stands, her eyes blazing with fury. "Excuse me?"

I keep my eyes trained on her, saying nothing.

"You think I'm selfish? Why? Because I don't want a house I never asked for?" Her neck reddens, the color traveling up to her cheeks in her rage. "A future I never, not once, said I wanted." Her lips flatten, then she lifts them, exposing her teeth. "I'd gargle broken glass before I'd live here again."

"And Lady Norton was aware of your disdain for this town?" I ask, not offended by her feelings toward Sudbury, this is not my homeland to defend, after all. But Lady Norton loved Vanessa as if she were her own daughter. I am certain she had nothing but her happiness in mind when she was drawing up her will. Vanessa's vitriol does not make sense. "Why would she leave you the house then?"

Vanessa throws her hands up. "The fuck if I know." Her chin dips, and her large, light blue eyes swirl with sadness. "It's not like I don't appreciate the gesture. She wanted to take care of me by giving me the house. She always took care of me." She sighs, her eyes locking on mine. "But I don't believe in ghosts or heaven or any of that, so I'm not convinced Aunt Franny is watching over me, disappointed by my decision. I'll honor her wishes by sprinkling her ashes where she wants me to, but I'm not keeping the house. I'm meeting with a listing agent tomorrow at ten a.m. to see how quickly I can sell it. Then I'm going back to L.A. the moment it closes."

"Very well," I reply, scratching my beard. "Then I suppose this is good-bye."

She nods, and I could swear there is a flash of longing in her expression. "Yeah, guess so." She steps forward, offering her hand. I take it, knowing this is a gesture of politeness among humans. "It was entirely unpleasant, but nice knowing ya."

A chuckle bursts from my lips at her sardonic tone. I let her go, and only then do I notice the tingle that lingers in my hand. It feels as if she branded me.

Before she steps outside, she turns, "Oh! I didn't get your name."

Though my given name is Axilssanai Buunii iy Xen Dwai, surely Vanessa would find that suspicious, so I offer the shorter, human-sounding name I chose after we crashed, "Axil," I say, my voice dropping low. "My name is Axil Monroe."

Her gaze travels from my lips down to my hands as I roll the cuffs of my flannel shirt to the middle of my forearms. Her lips part, looking almost…frazzled by my newly exposed skin. A scent hits my nose, ambrosia breaking through the harshness of the metal, wood, and chemical scents that fill my shed. My mouth waters, and I feel my heartbeat quicken.

It is her. Vanessa. Though, it is not her normal scent, which is also quite pleasing. This is different. Heady. She is aroused.

By *me*.

When her mesmerizing pale blue eyes lift to meet mine, she shakes herself free of the trance she was in, and says, "Right. Okay, bye," then slams the door shut behind her.

I continue to breathe in the sweet scent she left behind, hoping it remains for the rest of time. As I turn the table saw back on, my eyes land on the love book Lady Norton gave me the day before she passed. She said it was a *romance* story that was good to learn from, and my purpose becomes clear.

Lady Norton wanted her home, her sanctuary, to go to Vanessa, and for it to remain in her name until Vanessa's last breath. It was a gift—a generous one. A gift Vanessa should not be so quick to discard. If Vanessa intends to sell Lady Norton's house, then I intend to stop her.

CHAPTER 4

VANESSA

"*D*enise! So great to see you." I greet my former biology lab partner at the front door, stepping aside so she can enter. "I didn't realize you had gotten into real estate."

The front door of Aunt Franny's house opens into the dining room with a small office off to the left and the rest of the house on the right. I take Denise into the hallway and a few short steps inside the living room. She tells me about how she got a business degree at Plymouth State, which is about forty minutes north of here, and felt lost afterward until she helped her mother sell her house. It was then that she found her calling. She tells me about her four kids, and their asshole father she finally divorced last year.

"Can I get you something to drink?" I ask as she takes a seat in the oversized accent chair with the faded pine-green upholstery.

I spent all yesterday afternoon cleaning, and continued into the night, trying to get this place ready. Especially after that horrible encounter with the neighbor, Axil, I'm more eager than ever to get the hell out of here.

"Do you have orange juice?" Denise asks, placing her purse on the floor beside her feet.

"I do," I reply. "Be right back." I scurry into the kitchen and pour her a large glass. Handing it to her, I take a seat on the deflated cream leather sofa across from her.

"So," I say with a smile, patting the tops of my thighs, "I need to sell this house. And I need to do it quickly. How can we make that happen?"

She takes a long sip of juice, draining half the glass, and makes that satisfied "ahh" sound. "Well," she begins, pulling out her phone. She swipes across the screen a few times and opens a blank note page. "Let's have a look around, and I'll see what I can do about expediting the process."

Denise doesn't ask questions about how the house came to be mine or why I want it sold so quickly, and I'm grateful for that. It's the last thing I need right now.

The backdoor that opens into the kitchen crashes against the wall as it's swung open, and Axil strides right in. "Hellooo," he calls out in a cartoonishly high-pitched tone. "Vanessa? Are you at home?" When his eyes land on me, his smile is wide. Far too wide for my comfort.

I shoot Denise a tight smile. "Excuse me for a second." Then I race into the kitchen and block Axil's path before he can make it into the living room where Denise is. I have no idea what he's doing here, but I can't imagine the encounter going smoothly.

"What do you want?" I whisper, barely concealing my wrath. "The listing agent is here right now, so you need to leave."

"Oh," he says, looking over my shoulder at Denise, "what terrible timing." He lifts one shoulder in a half-shrug and it's obvious the intrusion is intentional. "Since you so rudely entered my private space unannounced yesterday, I thought I would return the favor." He looks past me and waves at Denise. "Is that orange juice? I love orange juice!" Then he steps around me with surprising grace for a man so large and plops himself down on the couch.

"I am Axil," he says to Denise, laying on the charm. "Pleasure to meet you."

Denise's cheeks turn beet red as she chuckles shyly. "Denise Watkins," she finally mutters, sticking her hand out.

Axil leans down and presses a kiss—an actual kiss!—to the back of her hand and gently shakes it. Denise's mouth falls open and I don't see her blink for almost a full minute. She's completely entranced by my intruder.

I get it. In a purely physical sense, Axil is a total fantasy come to life. With his wavy light-brown hair that looks perfectly coiffed even though he clearly put no product in it, his thick, veiny forearms covered in tattoos, and boyish smile, he could probably make anyone swoon. He's also way over six feet tall and has intense gray eyes, so you really have no choice but to focus all your attention on him when he enters a room.

But in terms of personality, he's extremely lacking. He's arrogant, rude, and he acts like he's smarter than me, which I'm certain he isn't.

"Vanessa," he says, turning to face me. "I would love a tall glass of orange juice." He twists around, facing Denise. "I am quite thirsty after hours of working with my hands." He lifts his hands in front of Denise, showing them off in an absurd way. "I make furniture, you see."

You've got to be fucking kidding me.

But Denise just laps it up with enamored gasps and flirty chuckles.

"Sorry," I say, clearing my throat and entering the living room. "Denise got the last of the orange juice, so it's probably best if you run on home now."

He stands, smoothing his hands down the front of his green-and-gray flannel shirt. "Very well. Lovely meeting you, Denise," he says in a low purr. He stops in front of me, and his lips curl up into a calculating grin. "By the way, my brothers and I are having a party right now. You are welcome to attend, if it pleases you."

I shake my head before he's even finished speaking. "We can't. We have important business to attend to here. Besides," I look at the clock above the stove, "it's ten fifteen in the morning. What kind of party takes place at ten fifteen in the morning?"

"Well, I have invited several of my woodworking friends over, so we will be trading tips and doing some work in the shed," he nods then adds, "with power tools, of course."

I roll my eyes. "Of course."

"And my brother, Zev, is an aspiring DJ, so he will be mixing the greatest hits from The Beatles with contemporary yodeling, as well as some death metal." He chuckles, and I want nothing more than to break his perfectly straight nose. "It is sure to be a full day of entertainment." He leans down conspiratorially near my ear, but still speaks at full volume. "Probably going well into the night."

This fucking guy. "Late into the night, huh?"

He nods, then claps his hands together. "Well, I must be going. Have a lovely day, ladies." As he passes me, he adds in a whisper, "This is for Lady Norton." Then lets the kitchen door slam shut behind him, whistling as he goes. He actually had the nerve to whistle.

Unbelievable.

Why is he acting like I'm disrespecting my late aunt? This kind of thing happens all the time. People die, they leave their house to a family member, then said family member sells the house. It's a common occurrence. Plus, Aunt Franny wanted me to be happy. I know she did. And there's no way I'll be happy living here, so wouldn't she ultimately want me to sell it, then use the money to settle down somewhere that doesn't remind me of my painful past?

I brush off Axil's infuriating interruption with a deep breath, then clear my throat as I approach Denise. "How about I give you the tour?"

She sucks down the last of her orange juice, then follows me around the house as I show her my aunt's bedroom with its questionable baby-pink wallpaper with large black tulips, the two guest rooms on either side that are too narrow to fit a queen bed and a nightstand, so there are only twin beds in each, and the bigger of the two bathrooms, located all the way at the end of the hall, nowhere near the primary bedroom, but larger than the two guest bedrooms combined, with a massive bronze claw-footed tub in the corner that could fit an entire family.

There's also a gilded birdcage hanging between the two sinks, with a human skull lying at the bottom of the cage. It's not a real skull. Aunt Franny liked to load up on skeleton decor the day after Halloween when everything was half-price. Her bedroom dresser is covered in little skeleton figurines.

I tried removing the birdcage this morning after I showered, but there was no way to remove it without yanking it down and taking part of the ceiling with it. I couldn't even open the cage to take the skull out.

As Denise pokes at the cage using the tip of her pen, I anxiously chew on the inside of my cheek until I taste blood. "Obviously, there are some interesting design choices here, but that shouldn't really matter to prospective buyers, right? I mean, anyone interested in buying would want to do their own thing entirely." I hope. I hope, I hope, I hope.

Denise sighs. "Well, it's important to remove anything unusual. You want people to be able to picture themselves living here, so the decor should be as bland as possible. Nothing intense or strange. Nothing offensive."

"Okay…" I trail off, taking in the uneven brushstrokes in the purple paint covering the bathroom walls. "Well, I can definitely remove the birdcage." I just need to find a pair of wire cutters first. I'm not even sure she has a toolbox. "And maybe the wallpaper in the primary bedroom." Not that I know how to remove wallpaper. I've never done it before. That's something I'll have to look up online.

Denise scratches her forehead, looking weary, and says, "There's a basement, right?"

I nod.

"Why don't we give that a look?"

The basement is a total disaster. A sea of boxes covers the floor, and tall stacks of books and photo albums practically touch the ceiling. I didn't realize Denise would want to look down here, but that was a foolish assumption. Obviously, she would want to see the entire house.

When she asks to get a closer look at the water heater, I have to kick aside several boxes just to clear a path.

"Oof," she grunts when she looks at the water heater's manufacturer label. "This thing is pushing thirty. You're going to need to get it replaced before you sell."

"Uh, even if it's working perfectly?" I ask, my voice breaking on the last word.

"Oh yeah," Denise mutters, typing something into her phone. "It's on borrowed time, and it's something that prospective buyers won't want to deal with. If you get a new one, it'll help sell this place faster."

Nodding, I try to remain calm. "Okay, that makes sense. So, how much does a new water heater cost?" I'm embarrassed to ask the question, but I need the answer.

"Could be anywhere from eight hundred to two thousand dollars."

A squeaky gasp tumbles out of my mouth in response. "That's something I'd have to pay upfront?" The last time I checked my bank account, I had seventy-nine dollars. There's no way I can afford to buy a new water heater for a house I don't even want to live in.

Denise looks at me as if I've grown horns. "Yes."

She continues pointing out less urgent flaws I should cover up as we go back upstairs, but I'm not really listening. The chipped paint and dents in the walls are hardly a priority when I need to drop at least eight hundred dollars on a water heater.

The moment we step outside for an exterior peek at the house, our ears are assaulted by the combination of a power drill, blaring music that's shaking the thin windows, and the boisterous laughter of men, one of whom has become my sworn enemy.

Denise has to yell her questions at me, and storms ahead with a deep scowl when I ask her to repeat herself a third time.

"What. The fuck. Is this." I ground out, mostly to myself since I know Denise can't hear me. We make it to the part of the property that borders Axil's and I find a pile of trash next to the shed, spreading out over his property line onto mine—three half-full beer bottles are spilling onto the soil beneath the primary bedroom window.

Denise shoots me a look of disgust, and I mirror it, knowing Axil is responsible for this. There wasn't even a stray napkin here this morning when I opened the blinds. He must've just dumped this here.

I am going to kill him.

Stepping in front of Denise, I take the lead the rest of the way to ensure she's protected from any tripwires or animal traps Axil may have set. I shoot a lethal glare at his stunning, four-story mansion, even though I know he can't see me. When we make it back to the front lawn, we're both grumbling about the noise. Out here, it's quieter, and we can hear each other, but the symphony of dude sounds is still very clear.

"All right," she says with an upbeat smile, though I know she's about to give me some good news before the bad news, and I know the bad news is going to be extremely bad. "Storing the personal items and covering chipped paint are easy fixes that will greatly improve the overall look of the house. Unfortunately," she says, her eyes dropping to the ground, "there's the water heater, the roof seems to be in need of repair in a few spots, and the layout might be an issue. I suggest we stage those smaller rooms, at least, to give the place a fresh look."

More costs that I'm sure will need to be covered upfront. Fantastic. "How much would it cost to do the staging?"

"Uh, well," Denise starts, her head tilting side to side as she mentally prepares an estimate, "if we staged the whole house, which I recommend, maybe around fifteen hundred? But if money is tight, we could just do the bedrooms, and it would be around four hundred."

I can't seem to swallow the lump in my throat. I haven't added up the total in my head yet, but I know it's way more than I have. More than I've ever had, actually. It seems I can't sell this house without spending a ton of money, and if I do spend the money, I might not get very much for the house, if I get a buyer at all.

Denise tells me she'll email me a more detailed summary of our meeting with names of repair men she's used before who can help me with the roof. We say our good-byes, and I storm back inside and into the bathroom, grabbing all the toilet paper I can carry, save for three rolls I leave for myself.

Then I sneak out into the trash-covered path between my bedroom window and Axil's shed. I hear laughter coming from the other side of his house, so, knowing he's elsewhere, I grab one end of the toilet paper and launch the rest over the roof of his shed. I grab the second roll and launch it from the other side of the shed and continue on until I'm racing around the tiny shack and wrapping it in white. Part of me hopes Axil's inside, and only discovers my act of revenge when he opens the door and tears through several layers of Aunt Franny's discount one-ply toilet paper.

I drop the bare cardboard rolls onto the top of the trash pile and smile at my work. Then I march back inside and pull a bottle of vodka from the freezer. Dumping the rest of the orange juice into a tall glass, the orange juice I told Axil was gone, I add the vodka in with it.

I'm tempted to mix a more sophisticated cocktail, but Aunt Franny's fridge and cupboards are sparse, and I'm too impatient to get creative. Dropping a few ice cubes into my former signature drink—before I could legally imbibe—I make my way into the large bathroom and climb into the empty tub.

The music Axil's brother is playing is just as horrid as I imagined it. I can almost make out the words to a Beatles' song, but then a screeching yodel breaks through and I can't hear anything else. The window above the tub rattles, and I wonder when the glass will shatter. Probably while I'm lying in the tub. That seems on pace with my luck lately, and the kind of nonsense that seems to follow me around in Sudbury.

I sit up enough to take another sip of my drink when a folded piece of paper beneath the soap dish catches my eye. Leaning forward, I tug the paper free to examine it. It's a folded envelope with my name on it.

Did...Aunt Franny leave this for me?

I set my drink on the floor outside the tub and tear into the letter. It only occurs to me after the envelope is ripped in half that I should've saved it, but oh well.

Across the top of the paper in capital letters, it says "WHO" and it reads,

My Dearest Vanessa,

If you're reading this, I'm most likely gone. Dead. Passed. Expired. Gleefully skinny-dipping in a pool of chocolate syrup with Bruce Lee, if heaven is how I've always imagined it.

If heaven is not precisely that, I intend to start a letter-writing campaign and badger the powers that be until I am given what I deserve. Because I certainly deserve a pool of chocolate syrup and some quality time with Bruce Lee, don't you think?

I know life hasn't always been kind to you. It wasn't kind to me, either. Life is often unkind to those who live outside the lines of society.

Boundaries put in place hundreds of years ago by men who owned slaves and decided that life should only be lived one way. Their way.

You and I have not followed that path. Perhaps if Victor and I had grown old together, I would've had children, I would've attended their sports games, their recitals, and their graduations. I might have been a completely different person if my husband had not died young. Alas, daydreaming about "what-ifs" is a fool's game, because the person I was... I liked. The life I lived was a good one.

I want the same for you, my dear. The path you follow doesn't matter as long as you're happy on that path.

A tear falls onto the paper with a splat, blurring the "essa" of my name. I didn't even realize I was crying.

It may surprise you to learn that I believe you can find happiness right here within these very walls. It may not strike your heart like lightning the moment you unpack your bag. I know you better than that. In fact, it might take a long time for you to truly see its potential, to see the beauty and strength and support this home will provide. But I do believe you will be here long enough to see it.

I know how much you enjoy treasure hunts and solving puzzles. Remember that Easter when you refused to come inside until you checked the entire yard for eggs? Your curious spirit has always been my favorite thing about you, so I have pieced together a fun treasure hunt just for you.

What the...?

Solve the riddles. Find the treasure. Sell the house.

I suck in a breath.

Yes, my dear. There is a pot of gold at the end of this rainbow, and it should cover all the repairs this old home requires. I didn't have time to fix everything that needs repairs, but I've been saving money for quite some time, knowing I would need to eventually.

Oh my god.

If, after you uncover your prize, you decide to sell the house, please know I will understand. Your eternal joy is the only thing I want. But I'm quite certain this journey will make you see your hometown, even this house, a little differently. You may even grow to love it.

I can't believe she did this. She left me the house knowing I'd find her clues. She didn't leave me with a broken-down pile of wood that I'd go broke trying to fix up in order to sell. In her final days, Aunt Franny wanted to give me a gift. A gift she hid from everyone.

She's wrong about growing to love the house or Sudbury. That's never going to happen. But at least I'll have some fond memories before I leave this town in my rearview mirror.

In order to find what you seek; you must enter the dwelling of the beast with a beak.

Okay, it's a riddle, and with "WHO" being all in caps across the top, I'm guessing she must have left five clues around the house for who, what, when, where, and why. So I need to solve five of these riddles before I find her secret money stash. I'm so excited, I practically knock my drink over as I scramble out of the tub.

Then I read the bottom of the page.

If you have trouble locating these clues, there is someone who can help: Axil. Have you met him yet? He lives next door.

Fuck me.

CHAPTER 5

AXIL

My lips seem to be stuck in a proud smile as I continue adding ridiculous song choices to Zev's playlist. This morning could not have gone any better. Vanessa's meeting with the listing agent, Denise, went terribly, I assume, and even if she has Denise list the home for sale in the coming days, I plan on making myself a spectacular nuisance at each showing, scaring away any potential buyers.

"You have still not explained why we are torturing our new neighbor with terrible music," my brother Mylo points out as he leans over my shoulder and inspects the playlist.

"It is for Lady Norton," I reply, not knowing how else to articulate my desire to irritate Vanessa. No one will want me and my brothers as neighbors if we continue to throw loud gatherings, ensuring Vanessa will remain the owner of the home, just as Lady Norton intended.

That is the only reason I am eager to sabotage the sale of the house. It has nothing to do with keeping Vanessa nearby. In fact, my life would become much easier if she were not so close. The woman is maddening.

"Are you certain, Axil?" Zev asks, opening a can of beer and sniffing it. His face twists into a look of disgust before he puts it down. "It is not like you to provoke humans in such a way."

I let out a frustrated breath. "What kind of person chooses to reside in the most expensive corner of the country when she is clearly not happy there? She says she is, of course, but her frustration with whatever it is she lacks out there is written all over her face." Her soft, animated face with her striking pale blue eyes, her small, upturned nose with the freckle on one side. I have seen every emotion flash across that face in the mere hours I have known her. And her lips... Lips that could send a man to his knees and offer eternal devotion in exchange for a single kiss.

I will admit she is tempting. Her presence elicits feelings inside me that I have never felt. But they are nothing more than fleeting bouts of desire.

It has been many years since I have been with a female. Ten, to be exact.

My brothers and I had our fun after we first landed on Earth. We were seeking mates, but when none of the women we bedded seemed to fit that description, we thought it best to continue honing our communication skills as well as other areas of expertise until our mates came along.

"Is she your mate?" Mylo asks, pulling my shoulder until I turn around to face him. "Have your eyes turned?"

I push him off immediately. "No!"

An unfortunate modification our handlers had given us was our eyes turning a horrifying blood red when we discover our mate. Though podlings were prohibited from mating with natural-born drax-ilios or other podlings, that did not stop a few that came before us from trying. Our eyes turning red was a way for our handlers to maintain control over us. If our eyes turned red, we were to be executed immediately as our focus would no longer be on serving our king, but instead, on worshiping our mate.

It was a new modification our handlers had never used before, so we were not sure what to expect when it finally happened to one of us. Luckily, it happened here on Earth with Luka and Harper. Unfortunately, his eyes turned red at the worst possible moment during their courtship, frightening Harper to the point where she almost ended it with Luka.

Luka described the feeling as an intense itching sensation around his eyes, and Harper has told us that his eyes were red for several minutes before the red started to blink, similar to a turn signal inside a car. The blinking continued until Harper accepted him as her mate. But his eyes did not turn upon first meeting Harper or even the first time they had sex. It was later when his flightless form and draxilio form became aligned in the knowledge that Harper was the only one for them. It was the syncing of the two halves of Luka that caused his eyes to change.

Since then, Zev, Kyan, and I have avoided sexual intercourse, in the chance that our eyes would turn red while buried deep inside a woman's cunt, frightening our mate in a moment when she should feel anything but fear. There is no telling precisely when our two halves will agree on a mate. It can happen at any moment.

Mylo has chosen not to conduct himself as cautiously. As a librarian, he has read more on the human race, and more stories written by them, than any of us. He is convinced humans see what they want to see and remember what they choose to remember. He also believes humans can be convinced of anything, and should he find himself red-eyed while in a compromising position, he remains confident he can talk his way out of it. And while his job requires him to be of service to the public, he does not hold humans in high regard. He finds them amusing in a harmless sort of way.

I, on the other hand, hesitate to underestimate them. I keep them at a distance by rarely leaving my home and not showing my face anywhere in relation to my business. Where humans are concerned, I prefer to remain as anonymous as possible.

"Do you ever miss Sufoi?" Kyan asks, staring off into our backyard. "Specifically, the work we did for the king?"

Mylo scoffs. "You mean, killing anyone who wronged him? What is there to miss about that?"

Kyan shrugs, still facing away from us. "It was part of our identity, to kill. Sometimes I find it hard to forget."

I watch the muscles in Kyan's back tighten, and I imagine he is currently lost in the memories of our former lives on Sufoi. He is right, it is hard to forget the things we did during our time as the king's assassins, but being on a different planet eases the pain. It does for me, at least. "Are you well, brother?" I ask, not knowing what else to say.

Finally, Kyan turns to face us. "Do you think any of you would do it again? Kill, that is?"

"A human?" Mylo asks, aghast. "Of course not. They pose no threat to us."

"No, but they pose a threat to each other," Zev says, shaking his head. Then he turns to Kyan. "Is that what you mean? Would we kill a human to defend another?"

Kyan nods.

Mylo wrinkles his nose. "It seems like it would be quite messy, but I suppose I would. If the human I am defending is my mate."

"As would I," I reply easily.

"Agreed," Zev adds.

Kyan remains quiet and turns to face the yard once again. Despite the strange, unpleasant sounds coming out of Zev's speaker system, I am too distracted by Kyan's question to enjoy it. I find myself annoyed at how quickly he soured the mood.

Eager to extricate myself from Kyan's darkness, I make my way around the back of the house toward my shed, but stop short when I find it covered in white paper draped loosely over the roof and around the exterior. Stepping closer, I realize it is toilet paper. Lifting the end of one roll, I find myself impressed. Annoyed, but also fascinated by Vanessa's chosen method of payback. This must be for the trash I left beneath her window or my intrusion during her meeting with Denise. Or, most likely, both.

"Son of a bitch," I hear someone grumble on the other side of my shed. "How did she even," then a strained groan, "get you...up here?"

Stepping around to the front side of the shed, I find Vanessa scratching and clawing her way up the trunk of the large red oak tree that grows between our houses. "What are you doing?" I ask.

She turns, panting from exertion, and sneers. "You again." As she resumes her—I guess you could call it a climb though her feet remain on the ground—she hollers, "Pick up your damn trash, by the way."

"I believe you left some trash as well," I reply, pointing toward the mess behind me, "all over my shed, in fact."

She chuckles, the sound spiteful. "Yeah, well, you deserved that."

I shove my hands into the pockets of my work pants and lean back on my heels. "So we are even, then?"

She ignores me and starts jumping as she tries to reach the bird-house that I made for Lady Norton that sits two branches up. There is no way Vanessa will reach it. Her jump is not high, and she is far too short.

"What do you want with the birdhouse?" I ask, coming to stand behind her.

"None of your business," she mutters, brushing the hair out of her face in frustration. When she seems to accept defeat, her shoulders sag, and I find myself compelled to help her. "I just need it, and clearly, I can't reach it. I tried to find a step stool, but I don't think Aunt Franny has one."

"Yes, she does," I reply quickly. The layout of Lady Norton's home is as familiar as my own. I know where she kept almost everything. "It is in the dining room closet."

Vanessa's brows lift as her eyes widen. She was not expecting me to know that. I have a feeling Vanessa does not expect me to know anything at all. Just in the way she looks at me, I can tell she has written me off as some provincial simpleton. But this seems as good a time as any to prove her wrong, if only to keep those eyes of hers wide and locked on me.

"You do not need it, though. Move," I tell her, stepping around her. With a short leap, I grab the lowest branch with one arm. Then, swinging my legs, I am able to propel my body to the next branch, planting my feet on the lowest one. I carefully remove the birdhouse from its nook and hop down, landing quietly next to a gaping Vanessa. "Here."

She takes the birdhouse from my hand without dropping her gaze from mine. "Uh, thanks."

I should probably say "You are welcome," or "my pleasure," or something else polite, but I cannot seem to form words when she looks at me in such a way.

Eventually, the trance is broken, and she turns the birdhouse over in her hands, inspecting it closely. She runs her fingers along the hand-carved woodland scene I etched into the roof. "Wow, this is beautiful," she says.

"Thank you," I reply, eager to acknowledge her praise.

"You made this?"

"I did," I reply, my voice low and suddenly hoarse. Her astonishment at my skill level is mildly insulting, but the way she looks at it feels like a compliment. Then she turns it on its side, dumping out the birdseed, and yanks the little door open, almost tearing it off its delicate hinge. "Careful!" I shout. "You are going to break it."

"I'm sure the birds will find another house," Vanessa mutters under her breath as she uses two fingers to poke around the inside of the small box. When she lifts the corner of a piece of paper with her pointer finger, she yells, "Aha!" and hops in place. She shoves the birdhouse back into my arms as she frantically unfolds an envelope with her name written across it.

She shoves the torn envelope into the pocket of her jacket and then reads the letter silently to herself. Her lips move as she reads. She is unaware that I can read lips, even at a great distance, so I could follow along easily, but I do not. I am far too distracted by her scent as it creates a thick cloud around my head. She smells like freshly bloomed freesia, and I breathe it in while she reads.

When she is done, she purses her lips, and her eyes dart back toward her house.

"What is it?" I ask.

Vanessa gives me a look I cannot decipher. "You think I'm going to tell you what it says after the shit you pulled today?"

Ah, rage. This is her rage.

I shrug. "Fine. Do not tell me. But if it has anything to do with the large amount of money she left for you, just know it is not exactly a secret."

She jerks back. "You know? She told you she was going to send me on a treasure hunt throughout the house, solving riddles?"

"Uh, no. I was not privy to the riddles or the treasure hunt. Lady Norton only told me she was going to leave money for you that her lawyer did not know about."

Vanessa's spine straightens and a determined glint appears in her eyes. "She said you could help me."

Me? What could I possibly do to help other than pluck items down from high surfaces?

"She said if I can't figure out the clues, you'd be able to help." Vanessa stares at me as if waiting for something. "Well? Will you?"

I suppose I do not have much else on my task list for the day. Vanessa's meeting with the listing agent has been ruined. That was all I set out to accomplish. My work can wait until tomorrow.

Though, it seems this vexing female needs me, which means I have the upper hand. "What happens when you find the money?"

She sighs, looking so tired, I wonder how she still stands. It is as if she has been awake for years. "That money will be used to fix all the problems around here that Denise said would keep this place from selling. I can't afford to buy a new water heater or repair the damn roof. I'm barely able to make it now, living paycheck to paycheck."

I hate the nagging, twisting feeling that settles in my gut. Her pain affects me in ways I was not anticipating, and it is clear she has felt deep, suffocating pain. From what, I am not certain, but I am sure I want nothing more than to ease it.

Despite her frustrating behavior, she is too magnificent a creature to look as weary as she does.

"I will help," I tell her when the silence becomes too heavy.

Her face lights up in pure, unbridled joy. "You will? Really?"

"Yes," I reply, clearing my throat. Bracing myself for the fury she is bound to unleash upon me. "But there is a catch."

As quickly as her expression lit up like fireworks across the night sky, Vanessa's face falls into a vengeful, cunning expression. "What?" she demands through gritted teeth.

"You will give me something I want."

"I'm not giving you any of the money. I need it. I ca–"

I hold up a hand, stopping her. "I do not want your money." My brothers and I spent our entire first year on Earth swindling investment bankers and hedge fund managers out of their fortunes so we could build our own. We each have enough money that we never need to work, we simply choose to do so.

"Then," she says, clearly shocked that I am turning down cash, "what do you want?"

I tilt my head, giving her a half-smile. "I have not decided yet. But I will let you know when I do."

She folds the letter carefully, then crosses her arms. "Let's see if you can solve the riddle first."

I chuckle at that. Perhaps Vanessa is smarter than I thought. "Very well."

Vanessa pulls the letter back out and reads from the bottom of the page.

It was here that my ankle did twist, a short tumble led to a sprained wrist. But oh, it could've been worse, had the good ones not gotten there first. Take a trip through faces and places and see if wistfulness blooms in traces.

"And she wrote 'WHERE' across the top, so this is the clue for that," Vanessa adds. But the context she provided was not necessary, because as soon as I heard "twist," I knew the answer.

"The basement. Lady Norton fell down the stairs when she was going to get a photo album she wanted to show us."

"What? When did that happen?"

"Two years ago," I tell Vanessa.

Her chin dips. "She never told me that."

"I took her to the emergency room," I say with a sigh. "It was just a sprained wrist." Vanessa looks as if she is on the verge of tears, which I am not sure I can handle. "But the 'faces and places' is definitely the dozens of boxes filled with photos. I would start there."

"Okay then," she says, now focused on her task, "let's go." She tugs the sleeve of my flannel, but then stops after taking one step. "Just to be clear, I'm only letting you help so I can find the cash, fix this place up, and leave town the moment it sells." She stares at me, her eyes blazing. "This isn't a friendship."

I have no idea what this is, but I agree that friendship is not the proper word to describe it. "Certainly. I understand." I gesture for her to take the lead. "Shall we?"

She smiles, but then immediately tries to hide it. "We shall."

CHAPTER 6

VANESSA

*I*t takes three hours for us to dig through ten boxes of photos, and still, we've found nothing. Two boxes contained photo albums, which were much easier to inspect than loose photographs despite the occasional silverfish scuttling between pages and scaring the bejesus out of me. But at this point, I'm beat, hungry, and also slightly buzzed. I've been sucking down OJ and vodka since this morning when I should've been drinking water.

However, most of these photos are of my past here in Sudbury, so the booze is helping to numb the pain.

Where is the next clue? How did she manage to bury it among this mess?

I hear Axil laugh quietly from where he's sitting on the bottom step, a stack of photos in his hands. "Is this you?" he asks, rising to his feet and taking large, careful steps into the narrow path we made through the basement. The photo is of me and Willa, both of our faces covered in whipped cream as we sat at Aunt Franny's kitchen table, wearing dresses made out of trash bags, and playing a homemade version of the pie face game. The only part of our faces exposed is our smiles.

"Yep," I say with a giggle. "That's me on the left, with three missing teeth. And that's Willa, my sister."

"Very cute indeed," he says as I hand it back to him. "Your aunt never spoke much about Willa."

I nod. "I think it's because Willa was the model child, always polite, well-behaved, and bubbly. Then she grew into the perfect teenager who got good grades and never did anything wrong. The girl all the boys chased."

I sigh, thinking about how many times my mom said, "Why can't you be more like Willa?"

"Then Willa got married and had kids and followed the exact path my mom wanted her to. Willa likes her life, so it's a path she willingly chose. But I think Aunt Franny could tell I was different. Not in a bad way. I wasn't some rebellious little brat," I quickly add, "but more reserved. I kept to myself for the most part until I got to high school."

"And then?" Axil prods.

"And then things got better when I joined the Drama Club. Everything just felt easier to navigate," my eyes go unfocused as the memories hit, "until it all fell apart."

Axil's gaze is intense. His eyes swirl with a mix of anger and pity, but pity is the dominant emotion.

Eager to forget that look, I put my almost empty cup beside me on the floor and lean up onto my knees. It's then I spot a smaller unopened box in the corner directly behind Axil. "Ooh," I say excitedly as I rush to get to my feet, but sitting on the hard floor for such a long time has sent my feet into a restful slumber, and I stumble the moment I take a step. Suddenly, I'm hurtling toward Axil's crotch, and I'm terrified I'm going to headbutt his junk. But his strong arms come around me, and the next thing I know, he lands on the cement floor with me draped across his lap.

I feel his warm breath fan my cheek before I realize how little distance is between us. When I turn, he's smiling a lopsided, shy grin that catches me off guard. It's hard to imagine him shy and humble in any situation, but the way he's looking at me right now, as if he's honored just to have me in his arms…it sends goose bumps over my skin.

I could get up. I *should* get up. Axil is certainly not my favorite person. I can't stand him, in fact. But his lips are *right there*, and I can feel the heat radiating from his body. It's comforting, and I want more of his comfort.

"I have decided what I want, Vanessa."

My gaze drops to his lips. He notices, and leans in, just an inch, maybe not even that. The tip of his nose brushes against mine, and my stomach does a nervous little flip. I expect him to close the distance between us, but he stays where he is as if daring me to do it. Closing my eyes, my lips part as my head dips forward.

But then, there's nothing. Just air.

My eyes fly open, and I find him jerking back, frantically rubbing his eyes. "Are you okay?" I ask.

His eyes are watery when he stops rubbing them. He looks at me strangely.

"Yeah, just uh," he stammers, "something in my eye." He quickly lifts me as if I weigh no more than a piece of paper and plops me down on a wide box filled with photo albums we've already looked through. Then Axil gets to his feet and runs a rough hand through his hair. His shoulders are tight, and his fingers are clenched into fists at his sides.

Something else is going on here.

He leans on the banister at the bottom of the stairs and hangs his head. "I should go," he says in a guttural rasp, sounding nothing like himself, and more like a demon with a sore throat.

"Um, okay. Sure," I say, not knowing how to respond to his obvious discomfort. I don't understand what just happened. Is he freaking out because we almost kissed? It seemed like he wanted to. He even said he knew what he wanted, and I was certain he was ready to cash in his favor for a kiss. Most likely, one or both of us would've regretted it later. We don't exactly get along. But it's just a kiss. A kiss that didn't even happen.

How much can an almost-kiss even mean? With the way Axil

aggressively shakes his head to himself and then storms up the stairs, I guess, a lot.

Is it me?

I breathe into my hand, checking my breath. It's not the best, given how many screwdrivers I've had to drink, but it's also not terrible. That can't be it.

A quiet voice in my head, an insidious foe I was certain I'd vanquished years ago, pipes in, *It's because you're fat.*

No, I reply forcefully in my head. I refuse to go down this path again. It's a path filled with quicksand and rattlesnakes, and no one gets to the other side unscathed. It has taken decades of therapy to silence that voice, which sounds like me, but is really the voice of society telling me to work out more and eat less, or actually, don't eat at all because starvation and suffering will lead to happiness, and maybe work out one more time today because summer is coming, and you'll get the life you've always dreamed of if you're thinner.

No. It's a lie. I will not listen to it.

I'm finally able to look at my naked body in the mirror without recoiling in horror. I even like my rolls, dimples, and spider veins as they are. My rolls are cute. My cellulite adds texture and character to my body. And the spider veins, well, I haven't found a way to embrace them quite yet, but I no longer Google "spider vein removal" every week, so that feels like progress.

Sure, Axil has the kind of beauty that feels reserved for A-list actors, but I've dated hot actors in the past. My body is not the problem here.

Or...maybe it is, but if that's the case, Axil can go lick rust. I don't even like him anyway. It's not as if I'm in the market for a boyfriend, and certainly not one who lives in Sudbury.

Pulling the small box toward me that I was trying to reach before we almost kissed and Axil's panties got all twisted, I start flipping through the loose photos. When I break the stack in two, a folded envelope slips out and lands on my foot.

Tossing the photos back in the box, I rip open the letter, my breath lodged in my throat. My eyes immediately go to the top of the page, looking for the type of clue, then the bottom, for the riddle. But neither are here, despite the letter being addressed to me.

My Dearest Vanessa,

Did you think every letter I left you would contain a clue? How silly!

Seriously, Aunt Franny? You sent me down here.

Did it occur to you that perhaps I have more to say to you than can fit in five letters?

Although... I suppose I did direct you toward the basement, didn't I?

Uh, yeah. You did.

Ah. Anyway, where was I?

Did I ever tell you how Victor and I first met?

This is a story I'd been meaning to ask her in the last few years. I hate that I didn't get to hear it from her lips and see the way her smile curls up slightly on one side at the mention of her late husband's name. They were deeply in love and had only been married for seven years when he died. My father adored Victor and often described him as the older brother he never had.

I was strolling down Yawkey Way (now known as Jersey Street) in Boston after a game with a girlfriend of mine. We had just left the game and were in high spirits from their victory over New York (that wretched team).

The last line has me chuckling. I can practically hear the disdain in her voice. The rivalry between the two teams has fizzled in recent years, but most, if not all, New Englanders would wholeheartedly disagree. The hatred remains, and that flame shall burn for eternity.

It was a windy autumn night. I had just purchased a new ball cap outside the park, but it flew right off my head the moment I put it on. When I turned around, with every intention to chase that hat across the city, I saw a man standing there, clutching my hat in his hand, and smiling at me as if he'd just won the lottery.

"This yours, miss?" he asked me. His voice was like water and velvet, if the former didn't have the capacity to ruin the latter. It was smooth, and the way it wrapped around me was thrilling. I never

wanted to stop listening to that voice. He asked me my name, and if he could take me out sometime.

I said yes.

That was it. We were inseparable from that point on. We married a year later.

The reason I share this is not for you to mourn your Uncle Vic, though it's a tragedy you never got to meet him.

I tell you this story because if it weren't for that hat and the wind, my life could've been completely different. Maybe I would never have met Victor. My happiness with him didn't last long, God rest his soul, but the time we had was filled with magic. It was big and bright and loud like the pride parade Axil and the boys took me to last year.

Aunt Franny went to a pride parade? And Axil took her?

Something as simple as losing a hat can lead you toward your destiny, Vanessa. The universe will show you the way, but you must pay attention to the signals.

All my love,

Aunt Franny

P.S. - Your next letter is hidden in my bedroom. No, I will not tell you where.

I hate that Aunt Franny had done so much in the final years of her life that I had no knowledge of. Her injury, the time she's spent with Axil and his brothers, and even attending a pride parade. We emailed each other once, sometimes twice, a month, and she never hesitated to invite me for the holidays, but I didn't take her up on it.

There was always an audition or a callback or a shift at the bar that I prioritized over seeing her. It's clear to me now that my priorities were all wrong. At the time, it felt like I was making the right decision staying in L.A. instead of flying back to New Hampshire. None of those auditions or callbacks ever led to a job, though, and I could've easily gotten my shifts at the bar covered by someone else.

I should've put her first. I should've come back here more than I did.

The fear of running into Beth and Caitlyn, or the man responsible for The Incident, was what ultimately kept me from booking a plane ticket, but it shouldn't have.

I know, now, that I will have to face the people who hurt me. The longer I'm here, the more inevitable that becomes. And when it happens, I will handle it.

Tears fill my eyes as I carefully fold Aunt Franny's letter. I hold it against my chest, praying silently that she's watching over me. Without knowing if the next letter will actually contain a riddle to solve, I decide to take a break from the treasure hunt and eat.

My stomach growls as I climb the steps from the basement into the hallway. Standing in front of the open fridge, I ponder my meal options. The fridge contains multiple jugs of orange juice, iced green tea, prune juice, and eggs that have expired. The freezer has chocolate chip cookie dough ice cream and more vodka.

So far, my options are limited unless I want to keep drinking until I fall asleep, which seems like a needlessly destructive idea.

In the cupboard, I find a single can of country vegetable soup and half a sleeve of crackers, which, I decide, is good enough for tonight. Tomorrow, I'll go to the grocery store and restock this kitchen, but for now, soup will do.

* * *

The morning sun shines through the steam-covered windows in the bathroom as I blow-dry my hair. My hair is fine, and I keep it short, but I have a lot of it, so it takes me approximately six minutes for it to go from soaked to completely dry. Once I use my straightener on my bangs, I rub a few drops of anti-frizz oil over my part, then fluff my roots with some finishing spray.

I tend to keep my makeup minimal most days, with just a layer of concealer, a spot of blush that I blend in, and some tinted lip gloss in bubblegum pink, but since I might come face-to-face with one or all of my nemeses while running errands, I add some mascara and a thin stroke of gold eyeliner across my upper lash line. I'd prefer to not see these fools at all without the help of a full hair and makeup team, but since I have limited resources, I know I'll at least feel confident enough to engage in tight, forced small talk for a few minutes.

If I'm lucky, I'll go to the grocery store and the bank and return home without a single sighting. That would be ideal.

Once I get the seat and mirrors adjusted in Aunt Franny's Avalon, I stick the key in the ignition and hope for the best. The engine revs, but it doesn't start.

Whatever. It's fine. Probably just needs extra time to get going, I think to myself. It's an older car.

After three attempts to start it, I slam my head against the headrest, defeated.

"In need of assistance?"

A high-pitched scream rips from my throat as Axil pops his head against the outside of the window. "How are you able to sneak up on people when you're the size of a damn tree?"

He laughs. "I suppose I have a light tread." He looks down at my hand, still wrapped around the key. "Lady Norton's car giving you trouble?"

"Yes," I reply, sighing heavily. "I can't get it to start."

"Mmm. That is probably because she never drove it," Axil says. He looks back in the direction of his house, and when he faces me, there's a hint of smugness in his eye. "I shall drive you. Come." He opens my door and offers a hand.

A surprisingly chivalrous gesture for someone who dumped a bunch of trash beneath my window not twenty-four hours earlier.

I consider his offer to chauffeur me around town. It would certainly be easier to deal with those I do not wish to see with a giant, beautiful man by my side. But then I'd have to explain my obvious tension following any interactions to Axil the moment we're alone, and I'm not sure I'm ready to put that past pain into words. "What's in it for you?" I ask, skeptical of his intentions.

He huffs a breath, his gaze dropping to his brown steel-toed boots. "Consider it," he pauses, "a peace offering for my behavior yesterday."

"So you're apologizing for making me look bad when Denise was here?"

He shakes his head. "No. I am not sorry for trying to delay the sale of Lady Norton's home. I just..."

"You just what?"

He looks off in the distance as if he's trying to carefully select his next words. "I realized it is unnecessary. She is keeping you occupied enough for now with this treasure hunt, and even when you do find the money, it will take time to get the house repaired enough for it to sell. Lady Norton has already found a way to keep you here and keep the home from going to someone else. I do not need to waste my time trying to sabotage you."

As much as I'd like to slap the smug grin off his beautiful face, he's right. I'm not getting out of here anytime soon. I guess I didn't realize until now that there's no way out. And I can't even feasibly fly back to L.A. and return when it's time for repairs to be made. I haven't found the money yet, and then I'll need to oversee the repairs since the house is mine now. "Well," I say, resigned, "thanks for not making my life worse, I guess."

"I am quite the generous fellow," Axil mutters, nodding proudly.

"Why do you talk like that?" I ask, following behind him as he leads me along the path next to the garage.

"Like what?" he asks, not turning around.

Maybe I shouldn't have asked him that. It's rude to question the way a person speaks, but it's something I've wondered since I first met him. "It's so...formal. Where are you from, again?"

"Near Boston," he replies quickly.

I'm surprised he doesn't have an accent, but okay. "It's more in the words you choose, I guess. Like how you call my aunt 'Lady Norton' as if she's a duchess or something from the Regency era."

A man slightly taller than Axil appears out the back door of the house, taking a bite of a Granny Smith apple, and chuckles when he sees us. "If Lady Norton were a duchess," he says as he chews, "we'd call her Duchess of Norton. Right, brother?"

"Uh, I believe so, yes," Axil replies.

"Have you not seen *Bridgerton*?" the man asks. His shoulders are broader than Axil's, but tragically hidden under a light blue button-up shirt and a white cable-knit sweater vest. The shape of his body is lean but cut. Not as bulky as Axil. His navy-blue chinos are clearly tailored, given how they cling to his thick thighs and neatly brush against the top of his brown leather dress shoes at his height, which I would guess is almost seven feet tall. He wears glasses with a square frame in a tortoise-shell color that fit his sharp, angular features perfectly. "I have had the pleasure of watching it three times now."

"I'm sorry…" I trail off, having trouble understanding what's just been said. "You guys have seen *Bridgerton*?"

"Yes," Axil replies easily. "Have you not?"

"Of course, I have!" I practically shout. "Every woman my age, er, every woman of any age, I'm pretty sure, has seen it. But I'm surprised you have. And multiple times?"

"I have seen it only once," Axil corrects, "but I did enjoy it."

"A delightful story," the man says, rocking back onto his heels. "Lady Norton wanted us to see it. Then I simply couldn't stop at one viewing. So I kept going. And then I read the books."

I was not expecting that.

"There are books?" Axil asks as if his entire world has just been thoroughly rocked.

"Why, yes," the man says. "Several, in fact."

Axil throws his hands up. "Why did you not tell me this?"

The man shrugs and continues eating his apple.

Axil gestures to the newcomer. "Vanessa, this is my brother, Mylo. Mylo, this is Vanessa, Lady Norton's niece who inherited her home."

"Ah, yes," Mylo says, extending a hand. "Axil has spoken about you many times since you arrived." His large hand wraps around mine, and I'm amazed at how soft it is, whereas Axil's is rough and calloused, though the latter is clearly due to Axil's work.

"I'm sure it was all bad," I say with a laugh.

Mylo doesn't disagree. He only smiles as he rubs the scruff on his chin. He adjusts his glasses and gives us a slight bow. "I must be off to work. Lovely to meet you, Vanessa. I am sure we will be seeing much more of each other." He shoots me a wink before crossing through the backyard and onto the long paved driveway.

"Where does he work?" I ask Axil.

"He is a librarian at the Sudbury branch," Axil replies.

My eyes remain fixated on Mylo's back as he makes his way toward the compact hybrid vehicle parked near their mailbox. A male librarian who binge-watches *Bridgerton*, wears sweater vests, and drives an electric car? Who *are* these guys?

"Are you coming?" Axil yells from several feet in front of me. "Or would you prefer to ogle my brother all day?" His voice drops to a low growl, and instinctively, I quicken my pace as I run to catch up with him, while trying to ignore the jolt of electricity that shoots through me upon hearing that voice.

He leads me into the large detached garage, which has six parking spots. All but two are empty. There's a black Cadillac Escalade parked in the far corner with dirt covering the bottom half, and an older navy-blue F-150 in the spot closest to us.

"Let me guess, yours is the truck," I say, moments before he unlocks the doors from the fob in his hand.

"Yes," he replies, his tone hesitant. "Why? Do you not like trucks?"

I chuckle. "No, trucks are fine. I could just tell you drove one. You're that type of guy."

He opens my door and offers a hand as I climb into the passenger seat, which I wasn't expecting. I'm not used to manners from men who dress like they're about to install aluminum siding.

When he climbs in on his side, I wonder briefly how his giant body will even fit inside the truck. "And what *type of guy* is that?" he asks, settling into his seat with surprising grace.

"You know," I begin. "The kind of guy who works with his hands and is always covered in sap or dirt, and who drinks cheap beer. The typical rural man who hunts and fishes and all that."

Axil's brow furrows as he looks at me. "This is who you think I am? This typical rural guy?"

I tilt my head as I take in the sharp line of his jaw and the enticing shape of his lips. "Am I wrong?"

He backs out of the garage, and the garage door shuts the moment we're in the driveway. Axil remains silent for several minutes, his intense gray eyes focused on the road. "Does it matter?" he asks, and it takes me a moment to remember what we were talking about. "You have already decided what kind of man I am. Why argue?"

I'm...stunned. I expected him to fight back, to list all the ways he's not that guy, or even to embrace the stereotype and explain why hunting and fishing are thrilling ways to pass the time. At least join in on the banter and tell me the kind of woman he thinks I am. But he doesn't. He's letting me sit with my assumptions of him, of this idea that he's just like all the guys I grew up with around here.

My gut twists as a disappointing thought pops into my head. What if I'm wrong and Axil isn't like them? What if he's unlike any man I've ever met?

CHAPTER 7

AXIL

*V*anessa does not speak the entire ride to the grocery store. She seems distracted. By what, I am not sure. She is probably tallying the many ways I am clearly a "typical rural man." I could correct her. Perhaps I *should,* as making blanket assumptions about anyone is a dangerous, cruel gamble, but what is the point? She sees me as this one thing, nothing more.

It is not as if I seek her approval, anyway. I had hoped, after hearing Lady Norton describe her as a kind woman with the beauty of an angel, that I could become friends with Vanessa. Much in the same way I was with Lady Norton. While there have been a few passing moments with her that have not been utterly infuriating, I would hardly describe us as friends.

Though, it is starting to seem impossible to avoid her. She is so very loud. And with all the time I spend in my shed on the edge of her property, it is easier for me to hear her than any of my brothers.

She does not like us, my draxilio grumbles.

I suppose that is true.

He adds, *We cannot trust her.*

Also true.

The bond between me in my flightless form and the fire-breathing creature I shift into is a sacred one. It is for all draxilios. My draxilio is a cautious, fearful thing. I suspect this is due to the mistreatment and neglect from our handlers.

He is timid and offers the worst-case scenario whenever I am pondering the outcome of a bold endeavor. He is also restless most of the time, which I cannot blame him for. Though I am able to cloak myself with invisibility the moment I take flight in my other form, there is still not enough room to shift freely on our land without being seen.

We might not be detected as we soar through the clouds, but those first few moments when we stretch our wings, swing our tails, and adjust to the much larger body on land—we remain visible. And being seen is too great a risk to take.

We have built a closed-off area on our property with tarps and ropes tied to trees as a way to shift in privacy, but we must only do so under the cover of night, so my draxilio does not get enough time to exist in his skin. It is an issue I am constantly trying to remedy.

"Ready?" Vanessa asks. It is only then that I realize we have arrived at the grocery store. I even parked, though I do not remember doing it. Vanessa looks at me expectantly as she stands outside the truck with her door open.

"Yes," I reply. "Yes, of course."

I notice her taking deep breaths as we cross the parking lot. I am about to ask her what is wrong, but when we enter the store, she stops. She pulls her phone out of her bag and her mood shifts.

"Okay, most of my stuff is in the pasta section," she says, staring at the list on her phone with intense focus. "Shouldn't take long."

She goes to reach for a basket, but I stop her. "I need things too." Grabbing a cart, I return to her side. "Plenty of room. Now, let us begin with produce."

Vanessa's teeth sink into her bottom lip, looking uneasy. She eventually agrees and follows at my side. I do not understand what about grocery shopping could make someone so tense, but it is not my place to prod into her personal life. We are not friends, after all.

By the time we venture down the pasta aisle, the cart is half-full of only the products I have chosen. But once we reach the sauce section, she starts grabbing as many as her small arms can carry from the shelf to the cart.

"This is all you plan to eat?" I ask as she tucks a stack of four boxes of rotini beneath her chin. "Just noodles and sauce?"

"Yes," she says, dropping the pasta into the cart with a huff. She runs a hand through her short hair, then fiddles with the short pieces on her forehead. "I like pasta." Her tone has a defensive edge to it, which I do not understand. It causes my muscles to tighten as if Vanessa requires my protection from a looming battle. Perhaps not the type of battle I am used to with fists, fangs, and fire, but something that causes her to resort to these odd food choices.

"I forgot something," I tell her, "in produce. We must go back."

She shrugs. "Okay."

Casually, I grab two red peppers and a white onion, place them in the plastic vegetable bags, and drop them into the cart. I notice Vanessa grab some carrots as we leave the produce section and smile as her eyes light up the moment she sees bread and potato chips. Then I guide her toward the refrigerated meat alternative section, and pick up a package of firm tofu as well as crumbled seitan, the latter a delectable addition to the pasta sauce I make once a week for my brothers. The very sauce I plan to make for Vanessa since she refuses to make balanced, nutritious meals for herself.

"You like tofu? And seitan?" she asks, her brows raised.

I meet her gaze. "What? Your typical rural man does not practice Meatless Monday, I gather?"

Her mouth falls open, and my cock hardens at the sight of it. "You're serious?"

I think to tease her more about her misguided assessment of me, but I am interrupted by a sharp, most unpleasant voice.

"Oh. My. God. Vanessa? Is that you?"

Vanessa and I turn toward the voice. The source is a woman of average height, slightly taller than Vanessa, but with a leaner frame. Her body and face are made up of harsh lines and pointed angles, and she gives off a cold energy, whereas Vanessa is nothing but warm softness.

"Wow, it *is* you," the woman states without inflection, crossing her arms across her chest.

"Hey, Beth," Vanessa says, her body stiffening. "It's, uh, good to see you."

I notice Vanessa's scent changes in an instant. It goes from the rich scent of freesia to acrid, and it burns my nose. It is fear I am detecting from Vanessa. She clearly does not wish to be interacting with this woman.

Beth just nods as her eyes travel from the top of Vanessa's head to her toes. "Been a while." Her pointed red nails drum against her arm as she waits for Vanessa's reply.

"Yeah. You look great," Vanessa says, attempting her best, bright smile. I can tell it is not genuine, but I am not sure Beth can. "Still doing yoga, I see." Vanessa gestures to the clothing Beth wears, a bright yellow top that leaves her lean stomach exposed and matching yellow pants that seem molded to her skin.

"You look," Beth looks up and down, once again, "the same. How's acting going? Famous yet?"

"Well, uh—"

"Of course, you're not," Beth interrupts. "If you were, surely you wouldn't be back here. In this 'shitty little town.'" Her fingers curl in the air in a gesture I have seen but still do not understand. "Isn't that right?"

Vanessa clears her throat, her lips forming a tight line. "Actually, I'm here because my aunt recently died."

"Oh, that's right. I heard," Beth says. "So sorry for your loss." Though she does not sound sorry at all. Then her eyes drift to me. "Who's this?"

"Right. How rude of me. Beth, this is Axil, my aunt's neighbor," Vanessa says. "Axil, this is Beth, an old friend of mine from high school."

Friend? I cannot fathom a world where Vanessa considers Beth a friend, but perhaps the explanation rests in the word "old" Vanessa used to introduce her.

"Hello," I say, summoning my manners when I wish to just walk away. "Pleased to meet you."

I do not like the way Beth looks at Vanessa, as if Vanessa is beneath her. I have spent a significant amount of time studying human behavior, mostly between males and females, and I have yet to understand the peculiar ways in which women interact with each other. It is a verbal minefield unlike anything I have ever witnessed.

"Oh, right," Beth says, recognition flashing in her small, green eyes. "You're one of Mrs. Norton's gigolos. I've seen you around."

It is not a word I have ever heard used, but I do know what it means. I would be insulted if the assumption were not so amusing.

"No, he's not," Vanessa quickly replies. "I thought it was weird, too, at first, that my aunt was friends with her young, hot neighbors, but that's genuinely all it was."

Hot? Vanessa finds me pleasing to look at? That is an interesting development.

Of course, she has only seen the version of me that I allow her to see. The one that blends in with her kind. She has yet to see the *real* me. With my ability to change my skin color and hide my horns, the only version of me she will see is the one I chose to maintain when we crashed here.

The humans with the pale skin seem to be least wary of other humans that look like them, in fact, they seem to have built an entire political philosophy around such an arbitrary thing, so that is the shade we chose for ourselves.

If Vanessa were ever to see me in a state of rest, when I am unable to hide my horns and blue skin, I wonder if she would find me attractive at all, or if she would see me as nothing more than a monster. An outsider who does not belong here.

"Come on, Vanessa," Beth pipes in. "You really believe that? Why would *they* be friends with your aunt?"

She speaks of me and my brothers as if I am not here, listening to her mockery. What an astounding boldness, or a dangerously misguided ego.

"That rumor has been flying around for years," Beth adds. "There's no other explanation."

Vanessa straightens her spine, and I see the muscle in her jaw tick. "Fascinating which rumors you choose to believe and which ones you automatically assume are lies. It's whatever keeps you comfortable, isn't it?"

Something in her words rattles Beth because she begins to fidget with the keys in her hand and her chin dips. "I really should be going. Can't leave Trevor alone with the girls too long. They haven't warmed up to him yet."

This female's soul is hideous, my draxilio hisses. *Get away from her this instant.*

Vanessa sucks in a breath quietly enough that Beth does not notice, but I certainly do. Then Vanessa's posture changes completely as if a cement block is tied around her neck, slowly pulling her to the ground.

Beth smiles at this, then turns on her heel and leaves without saying another word.

I grab Vanessa by the shoulders before her knees buckle. "What happened?" My voice comes out raspy and panicked. "Tell me."

Slowly, Vanessa pulls herself together, standing, but on legs that remain wobbly, a haunted expression still on her face. She stands there, rubbing her forehead and looking off in the distance. "I'm fine," she finally says. "Let's just go."

We finish our shopping within minutes, Vanessa grabbing some other food items, then pulling the end of the cart toward checkout with a newfound sense of urgency. We pay for our food separately, despite my offer to pay for all of it. Vanessa waves a dismissive hand at me without looking as she puts a divider between our items on the conveyor belt.

I drive her to the bank, and she tells me to stay in the truck because she will not be long. I do not argue since I would prefer some space to figure out what I witnessed in the pasta aisle. There were no obvious insults in Beth's words. Something about her mate being alone with her children. What was it that struck Vanessa so deeply?

Then it hits me. The name. It was when Beth uttered the name of her mate that Vanessa's face turned white, and her eyes widened. What was the name? Something with a T?

"Okay," Vanessa says as she climbs back into the passenger seat. "Told you I'd be quick."

"Who is Trevor?"

Vanessa's hands freeze, her seat belt an inch from being buckled. Then she blinks a few times, and her lips purse. "No one. Can we go?"

I move her hands away and buckle the seat belt for her. "That is what hurt you. When Beth said the name, you changed. Tell me why." I take her hand in mine, merely to offer her comfort, but my skin prickles with something I cannot place the moment my skin brushes hers. "Who is Trevor? What has he done to you?"

I follow her eyes as they drop to our hands. For a moment, she looks as if she wants to tell me, as if this story about Trevor is burning her from the inside.

Then she rips her hand away. "Just…" she trails off. "Just don't worry about it. He's one of the many aspects of Sudbury that I hate and do my best to avoid every time I'm forced to come here." She sighs as she rests her head against the window as I start the truck.

It is clear Trevor has caused her great pain, but what kind? Is it heartbreak? Did he abandon Vanessa to be with Beth? It is a scenario that does not make sense given how frigid and unpleasant Beth is, but not impossible, especially considering how fickle humans are with their romantic entanglements. They seem to discard the ones they love almost as often as they launder their bedsheets.

Divorce is not something that exists on my home planet of Sufoi. When a draxilio finds their mate, the bond is eternal. Though, without the guidance of mate signals and the unwavering strength of a mate bond once it is formed, I suppose we, too, would wander aimlessly through life looking for our perfect match.

"I merely wish to help you, Vanessa," I finally say when I can no longer stand the quiet.

She turns, her expression puzzled. "Help me? How?"

I turn down the country road that will take us most of the way home. "Clearly this Trevor person has hurt you. Perhaps I can speak with him. Make it right."

Vanessa barks out a laugh, then covers her mouth when she sees I am serious. She clears her throat. "That's a nice offer, Axil, really, but that would be a complete waste of time."

I open my mouth to protest, to tell her that Trevor is probably a reasonable man, and if he knew how much pain he has caused, he might apologize. That would be something, would it not? But Vanessa stops me.

"Don't worry about it, and please don't get involved. I'd like to forget about this whole thing."

I nod, my muscles tight. "Very well." I do not understand why, but knowing Vanessa is in pain rips at my insides. Also, knowing the person who caused this pain still roams the Earth and she refuses to do anything about it frustrates me to no end. She is a stubborn female.

I turn down Clarke Lane and pull into her short gravel driveway. I hop out and come around to her side to help her out of the truck, but by the time I get there, she is already down, with her grocery bags in hand. I offer to take them from her and carry them to the door, but she shakes her head. Vanessa is not used to being on the receiving end of manners, it seems. Why is chivalry so common among the love books I have read, but not done in real life? What has happened to men of this planet that they continue to fail at basic decency?

Suddenly, I am unsure what to do with my hands, so I clasp them behind my back. "Will you be looking for more letters today?"

She scratches the side of her head as if it is the furthest thing from her mind. Given how desperate she is to repair the house and sell it, I find this odd. "Yeah, probably."

I decide I am tired of waiting on her to rely on others when she needs help. I reach into her purse and pull out her phone.

"Hey! What th— You can't just reach into a woman's bag," she shrieks as she tries to snatch the phone out of my hand.

I hold the phone to her face in order to unlock the screen, and once

I am in, I add my contact info and call my phone so that I may have her number as well. Handing it back, I say, "In case you come across a riddle you cannot solve."

She takes it while still staring daggers at me. "Will do," she adds with a nod.

When she is almost to the front door, I call out, "If you would like me to destroy this Trevor person for you, do let me know."

Vanessa turns, a silent chuckle lighting up her heart-shaped face. "Don't offer me a happy ending you can't deliver, Axil."

The door slams behind her, and I find myself eager to give Vanessa exactly what she wants, and more. So much more.

CHAPTER 8

VANESSA

I finish spreading peanut butter and jelly on slices of white bread, my mouth watering as I reach for the final ingredient of my beloved childhood snack. Tearing open the bag of potato chips, I place six chips atop the peanut butter, then gently place the jam-covered slice on top. Then I flatten my palm on top of the sandwich and press down, careful not to crush the baby carrots I've spilled onto the plate. The crunch of the chips in the middle of the sandwich is so satisfying, I moan at the feeling of those delicate chips snapping in half.

A frustrated groan follows when there's a knock at the door.

I expect it to be Axil, too eager to hunt for treasure to stay away, but instead I find Willa, holding a tall turquoise box with a square wooden top. "Aunt Franny's urn," she says, lifting it and turning it slightly to show me.

"That's an urn?" I ask. I expected a giant vase with a loud floral pattern.

"It's the most expensive one they had, apparently," Willa replies, dropping her purse on the dining room table and making her way into the living room. "Guess she wanted to go out in style."

She pulls down a dusty fake floral arrangement from the middle of the mantel above the fireplace and puts the urn in its place.

I stare at it, not knowing what else to do. It's hard to believe that my aunt, with her bold spirit and open defiance against anything considered "the norm," is nothing but ash inside a wooden box now. How can such a dazzling soul just vanish when a person dies?

I've never believed in heaven. It has always seemed like a lovely idea, and I understand why it comforts so many, but I couldn't wrap my mind around the existence of a place no one alive has ever seen. But now, I wish I did believe in heaven. I want Aunt Franny to have a place to go, a place where at least part of her still exists.

"Should we say a few words?" I ask, hoping Willa says no because I have no idea what to say.

She wipes a smudge off the front of the urn with her thumb. "I think that's what the scheduled ash-spreadings are for."

"The what?"

"Remember? I told you Aunt Franny wants her ashes spread in various spots around the property at scheduled times."

"Oh," I reply, somewhat dumbfounded. I remember the conversation, but I still find it such an odd choice. "Do you have the schedule?"

"Huh? Oh, sorry. No," Willa mutters. She lets out a yawn that seems to go on forever, and it's then that I notice just how tired she looks. The messiness of her bun is not intentional, there's an unidentified pink stain across the chest of her heather-gray sweatshirt, and her eyes are puffier than usual. She always looks a bit disheveled, but in an adorable way a mom dropping her kids off at school in the morning would. This is different.

"You okay?"

"Mmm," she grunts, nodding. "Yeah, it's just... Jane was up all night with a fever. She's fine, it broke this morning, but I'm running on no sleep."

"Aww, poor little munchkin," I say, feeling terrible that I have yet to spend quality time with my niece since I've been back. Though, I wasn't planning on being here more than a day or two. That plan has certainly changed.

"Um, where are those hats Aunt Franny left me?" Willa asks, eyes closed as she rubs them. "Ethan cleared a space in the basement. I can take them."

She's half-asleep standing up. As hilarious as I still find it that Aunt Franny left Willa hats and Christmas ornaments, I can't kick my sister when she's down. "I'm still cleaning things up around here. Why don't I hold onto them for a bit?"

Willa smiles, and it looks like she's about to attack me with a hug. "You sure?"

"I'm sure."

Then she summons the energy of a rabid bat and pounces. "Thank you! Thank you thank you thank you!"

"Ugh," I groan as she knocks me to the ground. "We're old women now. You can't just tackle me, ya fuckin' dingus."

She crawls off me and gets to her feet. "There's that New Hampshire accent! I knew you still had it."

"Yeah, well, it only comes out when *you* piss me off. If I start saying 'wicked' again, please just punch me in the face."

"Oh, come on!" Willa says, placing a hand over her heart as if I've wounded her. "It's part of our charm."

"Sure, sure."

"Okay, so I'll be here in two days, at noon," she says. "For my scheduled time to spread Aunt Franny's ashes."

"Uh, okay. That works. Can I get a copy of the schedule?"

She turns to me, her nose scrunched. "I don't have a copy. I just know when my time is. It was with the pickup instructions for the urn."

I stare at her, confused. "So there will be people just showing up to spread Aunt Franny's ashes? And there's no way for me to know when they'll be here? What if I'm not home?"

She pauses at the door, leaning against the frame. "Well, it's not like you're out and about all that much when you're here. She probably figured you'd stay in, and it's not like she had a ton of friends, so I can't imagine it'll be that many."

I suppose that's true, and with the treasure hunt, it makes sense for Aunt Franny to throw this unexpected wrinkle my way. She seems to enjoy doing that. "Yeah, okay. Give Janey a smooch for me?"

"Yep," Willa says, waving at me without looking back. "Later, kid."

I return to the kitchen to eat my sandwich, and once my belly is filled with carbs and sugary goodness, I climb into bed for a nap. Lying there, I expect the sound of a power saw to blare from Axil's shed, but it doesn't. Perhaps the work he's doing today doesn't require obnoxiously loud tools. He could be sanding the rough edges of a chair or whittling a design into a coffee table. Or maybe he's not in the shed at all.

It takes several more minutes of pondering what he could be doing, and why I care how he spends his time before I nod off.

When I wake up, it's to the sound of my phone vibrating on the nightstand. There are texts from my agent, Tia, about an audition for a "supporting role: goofy, unattractive/fat best friend type for rom-com." The project is for a major streaming service, which would be good exposure, but the audition is next week, and there's no way I'll be able to leave and come back. There's too much to do around here.

Plus, the part sounds insulting. I'd be willing to bet the last few dollars in my bank account that there's at least one fat joke in that script.

Me: Pass. Can't make it back in time, I text Tia.

She responds immediately.

Tia: Totally understand. Sending you hugs!

Then there's a text from my mother.

Mom: You're at Aunt Franny's right? Can you see if that hussy stole my emerald necklace? The one your father gave me for our eighth anniversary.

My eyes continue a steadied roll for a full minute. Mom and Aunt Franny never got along, Aunt Franny even took a bottle of champagne to Dad's house the day the divorce was finalized, but the woman *just* died.

Me: IDK, Ma. Haven't seen it. I'll keep you posted, though.

There's no use trying to point out her lack of tact. She'll just get defensive and start listing the ways Aunt Franny treated her poorly. Then it'll turn into a whole thing and I'm not in the mood to deal with it.

The final unread text is from my boss, Pamela, from the dive bar back in L.A.

Pamela: Hey honey. Just checking in. Are you back in town next week? If so, can you take the closing shift on Tuesday?

Ugh, I forgot to tell her I needed more time here. The problem is that I have no idea how much time. Pamela's understanding, and incredibly sweet, but I doubt she'll be okay with me requesting an extended leave with no end date. But I can't leave her hanging either.

Me: Hi Pam! I'm so sorry, but it looks like there are some loose ends to tie up here. My aunt left me her house, and it needs tons of repairs before I can sell it.

Me: I have no right to ask this, but can I let you know when I'll be coming back? I'm not sure how long it will take to get everything done, but I can't leave until it is.

I take a deep inhale.

Me: Totally understand if you want to fire me. I'm not exactly Employee of the Month material right now.

The three dots appear, indicating that Pamela is typing, and my heart feels like it's climbing up my throat. I start typing too, unable to stand the anticipation, offering to work doubles when I come back with several more apologies peppered in just as her response pops up.

Pamela: Girl, relax. I'm not going to fire you. You're one of the best bartenders I've got. Take all the time you need.

The breath I didn't know I was holding whooshes out of me, and I start laughing at the intense peak of nerves my anxiety just took me to.

Me: Thank you so much! I'll be back as soon as I can. I appreciate you.

Pamela sends me a kissy-face emoji, and for the first time since I arrived, I feel relieved. At least this aspect of my life hasn't gone to total shit.

I pull myself out of bed and start looking through Aunt Franny's dresser drawers for the letter she said was in here. It feels weird rifling through her bras and underwear, but what else am I supposed to do? The sneaky old bird refused to give me a hint.

In the bottom drawer of her dresser, there are no letters, but also no clothes. Just VHS tapes, and tons of them. She still has a VCR on the shelf beneath the TV, which I find adorable. I bet it still works.

In fact, putting an old movie on in the background that I'll most likely have to rewind first sounds rather lovely. When I make my selection, I pull out the tape, snap a picture of it, and post it to Instagram with the caption "An underrated classic."

Within a few seconds of posting it, I get a DM from Sam, the fourth member of our group in high school, and the only one I still like and communicate with.

Sam: *Now and Then! OMG, I haven't seen this movie in ages. Remember when we'd watch it after school at your aunt's house?*

Me: *Haha, of course I do. Those were good times.*

I mean every word. Sam and I spent the majority of our time sophomore year in this very house. It was closer to the school than either of our parents' houses, so we'd leave school and come here. We'd tell our parents that we were doing our homework, but Aunt Franny would make us Shirley Temples and cookies and we'd watch movies instead.

Sam: *Yo, I'd recognize that floral quilt anywhere. Are you at your aunt's place?*

Me: *Yeah, she passed away a few days ago and left the house to me. So I guess this is my old-ass floral quilt now.*

Sam: *Oh, wow. I'm sorry. Truly. She was an amazing woman.*

Me: *Thanks. Means a lot.*

The majority of the communication that occurs between Sam and me these days is on social media. She'll post a photograph from her latest assignment as a freelance photographer, or one that has won an award, and I'll shower her with praise in the comments. We'll reminisce about old inside jokes over DM, or we'll tag each other in a funny meme.

Normally, I'm fine with where our friendship has settled. We've gone in different directions, quite literally, but have always remained in contact, even if it's a single like on a post. But now, I wish she were here. Besides my aunt and my sister, Sam is one of the few things I actually like about this town. None of the memories I have of her are painful.

She never let Beth boss her around like Caitlyn did, and whenever those two were off doing their thing, Sam and I did ours. Or, more often, we would leave them and hang out, just the two of us. And when The Incident occurred, Sam supported me, and that support never wavered, no matter what was said about me in the hallways at school.

Sam: *I'm in town visiting Mom between assignments. Give me ten minutes. I'll stop and get wine on the way.*

The moment I finish reading the message, I leap off the bed with childlike excitement coursing through my veins. Sam's coming over with wine, and it's like the ugliness of this morning's encounter with Beth has been wiped off the map.

I change into a pair of gray sweats and an oversized teal hoodie with the words "Caught Feelings for a Fictional Hero" across the chest in white cursive letters, grab the movie, and head toward the kitchen.

If Sam's bringing wine, the least I can do is make her something to eat. Luckily, wine and pasta are a picture-perfect pairing. I've just dumped half the box of rotini in the pot of boiling water when the doorbell rings.

I throw it open and spread my arms wide. "Samwich!"

"Vanillaaaa!" she squeals back as I pull her in for a tight hug.

We laugh and sway in a circle as I nudge the front door closed behind her. "I was kind of hoping that nickname was dead."

She pulls back to give me a sideways glance that is classic Sam. "Well, that's your fault for bragging about being distantly related to Columbus when we were in fifth grade." She tugs her large brown leather messenger bag over her head and drops it on the dining room table. She shakes her head, an amused twinkle in her eye. "Silly white girl."

"Ugh, it's a holiday we used to celebrate," I say, throwing my hands up in surrender. "I didn't know the truth then." It was not one of my finest moments, but I was also a kid. In my defense, there was no mention of genocide in the history class we both took.

Sam runs a hand through her long, tight brown curls, then lifts her nose. "Ooh, do I smell dinner being prepared?" She saunters through the house, wine in hand, then adds over her shoulder, "What are you making me, Vanilla? Mayonnaise sandwiches on white bread? With a side of unseasoned chicken?"

"Ha-ha," I say in a sarcastic tone. "Actually, how's a giant bowl of pasta sound?"

"Mmm, sounds lovely," she says with a pleased sigh as she takes a seat at the kitchen table.

I pull out two wine glasses and then get back to stirring the pasta as Sam pours the wine. We clink our glasses together, then take simultaneous long sips. Dumping the sauce into the pot, I turn and lean against the edge of the sink with my wine glass in hand.

"It's so good to see you," I say to Sam as she looks around wistfully.

"You too," she replies with a smile. "I can't believe this place is yours now."

"Uh, ditto."

"Wait," she says, putting the glass down a little harder than was necessary, "does that mean you're moving back here? Permanently?"

"Fuck no," I reply instantly. Though, the strength in that sentiment has waned. I find myself feeling unsure about where my future is set. "The house is old and needs to be fixed up before I can sell it, so I'll be sticking around for that, at least."

"Okay, I know this is all happening because Aunt Franny died..." Sam pauses to make the sign of the cross out of respect, "but selfishly, I'm thrilled you're stuck here because I don't have another assignment until next month. So I'll be here too!"

Sam has built a brilliant career as a freelance photographer. She started out by shooting her favorite bands at concerts and then finagling her way backstage to show off her work. Eventually, a band signed her as their main photographer, and she went on tour with them. Her ex-husband even joined her on tour with the band after they got married. His work as a journalist allowed him the ability to work on the road. Now, the work she does is mostly commercial shoots for food and beverages, but she's paid well, and she never has to settle in one place, which was a fear of hers growing up.

"You're crashing at your mom's?"

"Yeah," she nods. "Plus, Jackie and Marty have been handling the bulk of Mom's care, so it's my turn. They'll get a break, and I won't feel like such a shitty daughter."

I had completely forgotten about her mom's Alzheimer's until now. "How's she doing?"

Sam's eyes drift to the array of old magnets on the fridge. Her hands still, and I can tell this is a tough subject for her. Normally, she's so animated, but when her hands aren't moving, Sam is too inside her own head. "She has good days and bad, exactly like the doctors said she would." She rests her elbow on the table and drops her chin against her palm. "They just didn't say how bad those bad days would be."

I place my wine on the counter and kneel in front of her, putting my hands on her knees. "I'm sorry, it sounds awful." I don't know what to say, or if there's anything I could say that would comfort her. I can't imagine watching my own parent forget who I am. Or who they are. That must be absolutely terrifying. "I'm here. You can come over here whenever you want, and I'll be here."

"Thank you," she mutters through a choked sob as she crushes me to her chest. I rub her back as she cries against my shoulder, her tears seeping through the worn fabric of my sweatshirt.

Once the pasta is done, we grab our shallow bowls, piled high with noodles, sauce, and Parmesan, and settle in next to each other on Aunt Franny's old leather couch. *Now and Then* is already cued up in the VCR.

We eat, chat, and drink, not really watching the movie, but reciting the dialogue at certain parts, and when I pause it to take our dishes into the kitchen, Sam makes a rather disappointing discovery.

"We're out of wine," she says. When I come back in, she's frowning dramatically as she tips the empty bottle upside down.

"Welp," I say, opening the freezer. "I have vodka and orange juice, but that's about it."

Her eyes light up. "Let's walk down to Tipsy's. That new bar on the corner of Hobart Street."

I scrunch up my nose in disgust. I'm all cozy in my sweats and full of pasta and going out into the cold sounds about as fun as getting a pap smear. "Boo. No, thanks."

Sam rolls her eyes. "It's two blocks away! And remember Izzy H. from biology?"

"Yeah."

"She owns it. Oh, wait. I'm sorry. *They. They* own it."

An Instagram post from about two years ago pops into my memory. "Ah, she came out as nonbinary, right?" I ask.

"Yes, and *they* make the best cocktails in town."

I scoff. "Well, that's an easy competition to win. What are there, like, three bars total in Sudbury now?"

"Um, actually," she says in her snottiest, haughty voice, "there's four. And this one is the best."

I groan, not wanting to go anywhere outside this house after seeing Beth, but reluctantly accepting how pushy Sam can be when she wants something. "I don't wanna…" I pout.

"Nope," she says, getting to her feet and nudging my side. "Go put on your big girl panties and then put some actual pants over them."

"Ugh, you're in town for how long?" I ask jokingly as she skips behind me, practically herding me toward the bedroom.

I grab the twill cropped pants in black that I packed just in case I needed to attend Aunt Franny's funeral and change out of my sweats as Sam rifles through my suitcase looking for a shirt. She tosses the one I planned to wear with said pants to said funeral: a short-sleeved, flowy black top with balloon sleeves and open V-neck with ties. It's the dressiest outfit I have with me since everything else is loungewear. Not that I need to look dressy. I'm sure most of the patrons at this bar will be in extremely casual attire.

"Well?" I ask Sam, giving her a spin.

"Gorgeous," she replies, mimicking a chef's kiss.

She steps in front of the mirror, straightens the oversized red cable-knit sweater with cream stripes, and tugs slightly at the waist of her dark jeans, rolled expertly at the cuff. Sam has always had the kind of confidence with fashion that I've envied. Everything looks good on her. Everything. And the girl takes risks. She isn't afraid to rock a cropped tee with a bodycon skirt and platform heels.

The best part is that she's my size, if not slightly wider in the hips, so even though the majority of clothing made for our larger bodies is hideous, she finds the gems that fit as if they were made for her. It doesn't matter if she's wearing a skintight dress or a baggy sweatshirt and even baggier sweats. The rise of her chin and the straightness of her spine remain the same.

"Ready?" she asks, her eyes meeting mine in the mirror.

I huff out a breath. "Guess so."

We have a few close calls with patches of black ice on the sidewalk, but we make it to Tipsy's in under ten minutes. Sam and I fix our windblown hair, rub our wet noses once we're inside, and grab seats at the bar.

The bar itself is small with only ten stools, but the rest of the space is open with a few four-top tables occupying the center of the bar and a couple pool tables in the back.

"Hey, Izzy!" Sam exclaims when the bar's owner emerges from the kitchen.

"Sam!" Izzy replies with matching enthusiasm. "And Vanessa Bradford too. Well, this is a surprise."

"Good to see you, Izzy. Congrats on this place." I make a sweeping gesture with my arm. "Looks fantastic in here."

Izzy nods, proudly. "Thank you. I'm happy with it."

"So, are you going to the reunion next weekend?" Sam asks Izzy.

My jaw drops. "Good god, reunion? Has it really been twenty years since we graduated?"

Izzy sighs while opening a fresh jar of maraschino cherries. "Well, it's supposed to be in June, so it lines up with the actual twentieth anniversary, but with all the event cancellations during Covid, the gym got booked pretty quickly. This was as close as they could get it. That's what Maggie said, anyway."

"Oh, Maggie's running it?" I ask, not surprised. She was our class president and loved planning these kinds of events. I haven't seen her in two decades, but I doubt that's changed.

"Yup," Izzy replies, "She's putting together a slideshow of 'graduate success stories' that, apparently, I'll be featured in for the bar."

"Yeah, I'm in it too," Sam says with a shrug. "She asked permission to use one of my photos for it."

Then Sam turns to me with a grin curling her lips. I know that look. It's not good. "You can be my date!" She grabs my hand and squeezes when she sees my obvious reluctance. "Come on, please? Don't make me suffer through this nightmare alone. Plus, Maggie will be so excited if you come too."

I don't give a fuck about Maggie's level of happiness. Dressing up to spend an evening with several people I'd love to never see again sounds like pure torture. "I don't know, Sam. I can't imagine how I'd survive that."

Sam and Izzy start chatting about who is planning to attend the reunion, and how terrible it will be, even though they both plan to attend. Then they move on to talk about the bar, how long construction took when Izzy first bought it, and how it used to be a dental office. I continue looking around, but when my eyes land on the guy lining up his shot on the pool table in the back, my heart stops. My breath freezes in my lungs. I don't have to look down to know my knuckles are white where they grip the edge of the bar. I can't look down, even if I tried.

It's...him.

The figure from my nightmares.

The one whose face occasionally pops into my head, reminding me of the trauma I still have not processed.

The source of all my pain tied to this place.

The sole party responsible for The Incident.

My senior prom date.

Trevor Burton.

He's here.

CHAPTER 9

VANESSA

*I*zzy slams a drink down in front of me, pulling my attention from him. I find myself grateful for the distraction.

"Um, what's this?" I ask, staring at the tall glass of red liquid, still dazed and not sure what to do. Should I leave? I'm tempted to leap off this stool and run and run and not stop running until I get home. But isn't that what I've been doing for twenty years? Running?

I figured this day would come eventually; I just didn't expect it to be today.

"It's a Shirley Temple with a shot of coconut vodka and chili salt around the rim. Remember?" Sam says, giving me a strange look. "You made these all the time when we were in high school. You even gave it a name too."

"Th—," I swallow, my throat suddenly dry, "the Baby Spice." I get the words out, but I don't recognize the hoarse tone coming out of me.

"Everything all right, Vanessa?" Izzy asks, leaning on the bar.

Sam looks over my shoulder, and I know when she spots him. Her eyes widen and I see her jaw clench, but almost immediately, her features soften and return to a neutral expression. I find it odd. She knows what he did to me, but something about how quickly she masked her reaction puts me on edge even more than I was.

She smiles and turns to Izzy. "Uh, Izzy, can you give us a moment, please?"

Izzy nods and heads to the other end of the bar to check on the older man snacking on peanuts and nursing what looks like a dark beer.

Sam wraps her hand around my forearm once we're alone. "You have every right to be here. We can leave if you want, okay? I'll go with you. But you shouldn't let him run you out of here. Fuck him. This is your town too."

She's right. Rationally, I agree with her. But the sweat covering my palms and the way my heart is beating like a hummingbird on cocaine are not reactions tied to rational thoughts. They are rooted in fear, in sheer panic, that what he did to me once, he will do again.

"Just keep looking at me," Sam says with a warm smile. "Follow my lead." She takes a few deep breaths in and out, and I breathe along with her. "Good. See? You can do this."

Maybe if I don't turn around, I can pretend he's not there at all. It seems like an insane thought when everything inside of me is screaming "Run! Get out while you still can," but I have to try.

It doesn't matter if I leave here and go back to L.A. in a few weeks, I need to do this. If only to prove to myself that I physically can.

"Has he noticed us yet?" I ask Sam before I take a big swig of my drink.

She looks over my shoulder again, a slight wince flashing across her face. "No, I don't think so. He's playing pool. Hopefully, that will keep him occupied and over there for the rest of the night."

I nod, not comforted by her observation because he could spot us at any moment and decide to come over. I wouldn't put it past him to greet me with a smile as if nothing happened, but I'm glad I'm facing the door and won't have to look at him. All the same, I can't help but take a cautious glance his way.

Trevor is still tall and lanky, just over six feet tall, though he seems to have filled out a little in the midsection. His jeans still hang off his bottom half, his belt working hard to hold them up as if he still has no clue what size he is after twenty years of wearing clothes. His brown hair is styled the same way it was back then, spiked up with too much gel with the front pushed forward, and shaved on the sides. I remember his inability to grow facial hair back then, and it seems the only progress he's made in that area is a trimmed goatee that makes him look like he owes child support in Tallahassee.

I wouldn't put it past him. I wouldn't put anything past him, in fact.

Sam looks down at the drink in my hand and starts laughing. Then I realize my glass is empty. I place it on the bar and look at Izzy. "Another? No rush, just when you get a chance, please."

Izzy smiles and immediately comes over. Sam's jack and Coke is still half-full, so she waves away Izzy's offer for a refill.

With my new drink in hand, I look up to find Axil entering the bar with a guy who looks very much like him (one of his brothers, no doubt). Instinctually, I wave him over the moment his eyes meet mine. His lip curls up on one side, pleased, giving me a single nod.

It's weird, I realize, to randomly spot him in a public place. So far, I've only seen him on my property or his, and they were tense interactions, if not all-out confrontations. But now, I find myself thrilled and relieved he's here. This is likely due to the fact that Trevor is here, and with Axil at my side, I feel safer. Or maybe my irritating neighbor is starting to grow on me. Or, a third option, it's the wine and vodka pumping through my blood.

"Vanessa, here you are," Axil says, coming to stand next to me.

That's a strange way to greet someone. "Were you looking for me?"

He looks like he's about to say yes, but then changes his mind. "Uh, no. Of course not."

The man to his right clears his throat, and Axil appears grateful for the interruption. "Vanessa, this is my brother, Zev Monroe. Zev, Lady Norton's niece, Vanessa."

I shake his hand. "Zev, nice to meet you."

He's a lot shorter than Axil, and also leaner, like Mylo. His hair is a darker shade of brown and pulled back in a tight, small ponytail at the nape of his neck. He's wearing a black AC/DC tee shirt beneath a black leather jacket. He has two different colored eyes, one green, one blue, and a slightly crooked nose. With the exception of his face, every speck of exposed skin I see is tattooed, including his long neck and slim fingers.

"Zev, Axil, this is my friend Sam Rodriguez," I say.

When Sam shakes Axil's hand, she pauses, looking between the two men. "You...look like someone. Have we met?"

Axil looks surprised. "No, I do not believe so."

She shakes Zev's hand, and he says, "Perhaps you have met one of our brothers. There are five of us in total."

"Ah, that must be it," she replies, though not looking convinced.

"Five?" I ask. "I thought only four of you lived next door."

"That is true, but one of our brothers lives south of here in Salem," Zev says. "Luka."

I realize I still haven't met the fourth brother who lives next door. "Who haven't I met? Besides Luka."

"Kyan," Axil says with a shake of his head. "He is always working. That is why you have not seen him."

"Very important boss man, that Kyan," Zev says, his tone mocking.

Sam chuckles at the clear disdain for the corporate office structure. "What do you do, Zev?"

"I am a tattoo artist," he says proudly. "I work at a shop in Tilton."

"Very cool," I say. It's been years since I got my last tattoo. I've been eager to get another since getting a crown tattooed on my right ring finger and a pine tree on the inside of my left wrist but haven't been able to afford it. Tattoos, as beautiful as they are, get as pricey as they are addictive.

"And you, Axil?" Sam asks.

"I build custom wood furniture, most with carved, detailed accents," he replies, his voice quiet. Unlike the bold declaration Zev made about his job, Axil seems, not embarrassed, but humble. "I sell it on Etsy."

Sam nods, then a moment later, lets out a gasp. "Wait, are you Forest Furniture Fella?"

I swear Axil blushes as his chin dips.

Sam slaps a hand on her knee. "My sister will not shut up about the end table you made her. She's obsessed with it."

"Well, I am gra—"

"Is that Sam?" a loud, grating voice shouts from across the bar. "It is!"

My hands start to shake as I hear his feet shuffle toward us. I watch Sam swallow hard before plastering on a fake smile.

It's happening. He's coming over here and there's nothing I can do about it.

"Trevor," Sam says coolly, "hello."

Axil's entire body tenses. His fists ball at his sides as his gaze moves over Trevor. Zev notices Axil's shift in mood and lifts a brow in my direction. I shrug, not knowing how to quickly explain the history that links me and Sam to this monster.

"Wow, been a while, eh?" he says, and I hear him lean against the bar, directly behind me. "Hey, I'm having a Cinco de Mayo party this year. You're going to love it. I got excellent decorations for it. *Muy auténtico.*" Except he hits "muy" too hard and puts a pause in the middle, so it sounds like "moo eee."

"Cool," Sam replies, unenthused. "But I'm Puerto Rican, not Mexican. So..." she trails off with an eye-roll.

How long can I sit here before turning around? Maybe if I stay perfectly still, he won't notice me at all.

"Who's your friend?" he asks.

Fuck.

He taps me on the shoulder obnoxiously hard, as if he's offended I'm not paying attention to him. I flinch at his touch. "Hello, there."

Fine. Let's get this over with. I grit my teeth as I turn, refusing to smile. I'm not giving him that. He gets what he gets. "Trevor," I say, the word practically burning my tongue.

He jerks back, but not in genuine surprise. More like he discovered an old toy he used to play with, which is not unlike our situation. "The famous Vanessa Bradford, gracing us with her presence. What a treat."

I say nothing because I have no idea what to say. If I were to open my mouth, I'm worried I'd either scream like a banshee or wretch all over his North Face jacket and ill-fitting thermal shirt.

He snags a peanut from the old man's bowl two stools down and tosses it into his mouth. Then he smiles, and it sickens me. "Doesn't Hollywood need you? I mean, shouldn't you be walking the red carpet for your new movie?"

"New movie?" I ask, not knowing what he's talking about.

"Oh, that's right," he says, slapping the bar top. "You're more of a hybrid-car-loving girl for commercials, aren't you?"

I turn around and take a sip of my drink, hiding my reaction from Trevor. My eyes are hot with unshed tears, and it's a struggle to get the straw into my mouth with the way my hands are still shaking.

"I think it is time for you to leave," Axil says to Trevor, his voice low with a frightening edge to it.

Shifting in my seat, I turn to find Axil stepping into Trevor's personal space. Trevor straightens his spine and puffs his chest out, though being several inches shorter than Axil, his attempt to look tough is rather comical.

"Is that right?" Trevor asks, shoving his hands into his jean pockets. "Why the fuck is this any of your business, bro? These two," he says, pointing to me and Sam, "are old friends of mine."

Friends. I'd laugh if I weren't struggling to breathe.

Axil's eyes bore into mine. He doesn't look away as he says, "They do not seem happy to see you. That tells me it is time for you to go."

Trevor doesn't say anything; he just stares at Axil. Axil returns the glare, and the two of them continue their staring contest for I don't even know how long. Then Trevor's hand goes to his jacket, my eyes following the subtle movement. He pulls back one side, revealing the grip of a handgun shoved into the waistband of his jeans.

Axil's eyes drop to the gun, but other than that, he remains perfectly still, his muscles bunched. Then he laughs. "You plan to use that tonight?"

"I will if I need to," Trevor replies, leaning closer to Axil.

Men are so dumb when they behave like this. If I were an outsider, I would think Trevor was about to kiss Axil, but no, he's threatening his life because Axil asked him to simply walk away.

Trevor tilts his head, his beady eyes narrowing. "Guess the rest is up to you, friend."

Axil smirks. "You think that can hurt me?"

Sam and I exchange a puzzled glance. Bravado can only take a man so far. Is Axil actually implying that he's bulletproof? That seems foolish.

Zev notices our reaction and steps to Axil's side. "Let us rethink this, yeah?"

Trevor sends Axil a mocking smile. "Yeah, maybe listen to your boy."

"Okay, that's enough," Izzy shouts, coming around the bar then pushing through all three guys until standing in the middle of the group. "Take your penis-measuring contest somewhere else, 'K? There's no fighting in my bar."

Trevor quickly pulls his shirt over the gun, hiding it as he throws his hands up, trying to look like the victim. "Of course, Izzy. I would never."

Izzy gives each of them a stern look before grunting annoyance and going back behind the bar.

"Should I make the owner of this establishment aware of your little toy?" Axil says to Trevor.

Trevor scoffs. "As if Izzy would actually believe you."

Suddenly, I can't feel my fingers, as numbness spreads through my hands and wrists. I try flexing them, but there's nothing. My breath comes out in short pants as a wave of dizziness washes over me. I feel like I'm falling, or about to fall off this stool.

"Vanessa, what's wrong?" Sam asks, concerned, as she grabs my shoulders.

"I," I can't get the words out. I want to tell her I think I'm having a heart attack, but I can't get them out. "I—I, um," I stammer, sweat soaking my hairline.

Then I'm no longer in the bar mere inches from the man who changed my life forever in a single night. I'm there. In the past, sitting in Officer Burton's office, in one of his cheap, plastic chairs as he sits on the edge of his desk, looking at me in my torn prom dress as if I'm a bug he's about to squish beneath his shoe.

"I understand, you know," he says, his tone softer than I expected.

"You're kids. You're at a party with no adults, and the booze is flowing. Things can get out of hand quickly. And, hey," he says, putting a hand on my shoulder. I wince at the contact, being touched by him of all people is the last thing I want right now. "I've been there."

He stands and strolls slowly around his desk, his head tilted back. "I know you're a good kid, Vanessa. Your parents seem like nice folks. Maybe, now that you've sobered up a bit, you regret the choices you made with my nephew tonight."

"No," I quickly reply. "I didn't even have that much to drink. I remember everything, and what happened." A sob wrenches from my throat as I relive it. "I didn't want it to happen. He didn't listen. I said no and he didn't listen."

"Now, now," Officer Burton says, putting a hand up as if that will calm me. "There's no need to get so upset." He hands me a tissue, but it's clear by the look on his face that he thinks I'm overreacting. Or lying.

"I'm telling you the truth. Trevor raped me."

He sighs. He actually sighs at my words.

"I know he's your nephew, and I'm sorry. I don't want to cause any trouble," I stammer, trying to figure out how to get him to believe me. It's not like I even wanted to press charges. I called my mom right after it happened, and she and Dad picked me up. They saw me crying, and I told them everything. I didn't even pause to breathe. The words just fell out of my mouth as tears ran down my face. My mom insisted we come straight here and that I tell the cops what happened.

"Well, it's a bit too late for that, now, isn't it?" Officer Burton says, his tone hardening. "You come in here and accuse my nephew of such a heinous crime and then say you aren't looking to cause trouble?"

Goose bumps cover my skin as I begin to realize what a colossal mistake this was. I should've just gone home.

Officer Burton rubs his forehead, exasperation clear on his face. "I want you to think about this two, even three, steps ahead, okay? Let's say," he pauses, "you decide to press charges. That means we'd need to open an investigation. Everyone who was at the party will be ques-

tioned, so your classmates would find out about this. Then it comes down to evidence."

I nod, staring at the black smudges of mascara on my fingers from trying to wipe away my tears.

"In most rape cases, there isn't enough evidence to proceed, because it's a situation of he-said she-said, so charges are dropped. Imagine," he says, lowering his voice to a whisper, "going through all that, the comments from kids at school, for nothing. Is that really how you want your final days before graduation to go?"

My vision blurs as the scenario plays in my head—ostracized, talked about everywhere I go while wearing a cloak of shame. It's the last thing I want.

"Or, if the case goes to trial," he adds, "you'll be condemning my nephew to a miserable, stunted life. He'll lose his scholarship to UNH, and he'll have trouble even getting a job. The kid has so much poten-tial. I know you two are good friends. Is that really how you'd treat a friend?"

I did consider Trevor a good friend. We've been in a lot of the same classes since freshman year. We usually partner up on projects, and he always pulls his weight. He doesn't leave me to do all the work. He makes me laugh, and we spend a lot of time together outside of school since he's Beth's neighbor.

But then...tonight happened. I certainly wouldn't wish a miserable future on any of my friends, but could Trevor say the same? If he saw me as one of his close friends, why would he violate me? What about what he did? What about my future?

"Think about it, Vanessa," Officer Burton says with a huff. "You were seen drinking tonight. People saw you follow Trevor into that bedroom, but then, suddenly, he's a monster who attacked you? Do you think people will actually believe you?"

"Vanessa! Hey!" Sam shouts, snapping her fingers in my face. She sits facing me in the backseat of an SUV, her seat belt unbuckled as we speed down Clarke Lane. Zev is driving, and Axil is facing us from the passenger seat, his face pinched in concern.

"Hmm," I grunt, nodding my head to let her know I'm listening. I have no memory of leaving the bar and getting into what I assume is Zev's car, but with how weak my entire body feels, I imagine someone carried me. "Yeah, I hear you."

"Thank god," Sam says, pulling me in for a hug. When she pulls back, her eyes are wet. "You okay?"

I nod again, my mind still hazy. We pull into my driveway, and Axil races to open my door and help me out. I let him guide me toward the house, grateful to have Sam on my other side, ready to catch me if I collapse, which I feel on the verge of doing.

We get into the living room, and Axil sets me in the middle of the couch, then kneels in front of me. He looks as if he's in physical pain, and I wonder if he and Trevor got into it while I was having a breakdown. Sam sits on the edge of the coffee table at Axil's side, putting her elbows on her knees.

"What was that?" Axil asks so quietly; I almost didn't hear him. He looks terrified. "What happened?"

Before I can answer, Sam says, "Panic attack." Then she looks at me. "Right?"

"Yeah," I reply, wiggling my fingers and toes, amazed the numbness is gone. I sigh loudly. "Yeah, it was a panic attack. Brought on by something Trevor said."

"What did he say?" Zev asks from where he stands in the corner of the room.

"I don't know, something about," I try to remember, "not believing Axil's side, about Trevor having a gun." My voice sounds so small even to me. As fragile as glass. "It just took me right back to that night."

Sam nods, knowingly, her eyes swirling with sympathy.

"When Officer Burton told me," I continue, "no one would believe me."

"Believe you about what?" Axil asks.

Sam, as if she didn't hear Axil, asks, "You never went to the hospital that night, did you?"

"Nope," I reply solemnly. "I should've, but after what Officer Burton said, I don't know." I put my face in my hands. "It just felt pointless to do anything other than go home and try to forget it happened."

"Forget what?" Zev asks.

"It's not like that did any good," I add, "because by Monday, everyone knew what happened, and I was 'the slut who tried to ruin Trevor's life.'"

Sam rolls her eyes in solidarity. "So fucked. The whole thing was so fucked."

Axil rises to his feet. "Please," his voice barely containing his obvious frustration, "just tell us what you are talking about."

"Trevor raped me on prom night," I say in a blunt tone. It's probably the third time I've uttered the statement out loud, and it still feels strange to my ears. As if part of my brain knows it happened and is desperate to accept the truth, while the other part of my brain scrambles to protect me from it with unyielding denial.

Axil and Zev react to my words simultaneously with waves of rippling fury coming off their strained bodies. "He…" Axil begins, his teeth gritted, "he did that to you? And he still walks free?"

"Happened to me too," Sam says as she looks down at the carpet beneath her feet. "About a year after graduation. Way before Trevor and Beth started dating."

I swallow, praying she's just saying this to offer me some kind of temporary comfort. That this isn't trauma we share. "Are you serious?"

Her demeanor changes, the sadness she felt on my behalf now gone as she shuts down. Her lips form a flat line, and her tone is wooden as she says, "There was a house party. I don't remember whose house it was. At some point, I was drunk and found a room upstairs to pass out in. I woke up to Trevor on top of me."

All I can do is gasp; the horror of what Sam is telling me prevents me from forming coherent words.

She stares at the pillow next to me, her gaze unfocused. "My memories of that night are spotty, but I do remember saying 'no,' and him saying 'shh.'"

Axil explodes. "Why! Why does he still live? Why has no one rid this Earth of his twisted soul?"

Sam turns to him. "You expect us to kill him? Believe me, I'd love to. But that would just create more problems for us, and he'd be seen as the victim. Just like he would if either of us had pressed charges in the first place."

Zev shakes his head. "I do not understand. How is he able to get away with these violent crimes?"

"Um, because he's a white guy whose uncle is a cop," I reply, annoyed that we have to spell this out for them. Axil and Zev are in their thirties, they should know this by now. Of course, it would be just as easy for them to not pay attention to how hard it is for women to exist. They have the luxury of remaining blissfully ignorant until something like this affects them personally.

"A man's potential will always outweigh a woman's suffering," Sam adds. "After what happened to Vanessa, there was no way I was going to report him to the cops. So I did nothing."

Axil's chest is heaving, his face a tight grimace. He looks around the living room helplessly. I have no idea what he's looking for. "We must stop him. He does not deserve to breathe another day." He turns to Zev and repeats himself, this time louder and angrier.

Zev nods and places his hands on Axil's shoulders. "Relax. Axil, you must calm yourself."

"No," Axil growls, "I will not relax." He runs a rough hand through his hair, cursing under his breath. "The way women are treated on this planet is unacceptable."

This planet? Why did he phrase it like that?

"I know," Zev says, trying to gain Axil's attention, but failing. "There is nothing we can do about that tonight."

Axil shakes off Zev's touch and begins pacing back and forth in front of the coffee table. He's speaking quietly to himself, and I can't understand a word, but if I had to guess, I would say he's forming a plan. I eventually pick up "obliterate" and "broken bones" and my suspicions are confirmed.

"You can't do anything to him, Axil," I say. "It's not worth the trouble you'd get into."

He ignores me. Zev grabs his arm, and Axil shoves him, hard, and he goes stumbling into the wall.

"Calm yourself!" Zev shouts, righting himself and cracking his knuckles.

I cannot have these two buff giants throw down in the living room. The damage would be too expensive to fix.

"I will not!" Axil yells back. "You expect me to do nothing? To allow this savage beast to continue attacking women?"

Axil looks like he's two seconds from punching a hole in the wall, and though his temper scares me a little—god help anyone who finds themselves on the business end of it—I also find it comforting that he's this angry on our behalf. It's kind of hot, actually. I can't speak to Sam's experience, but there wasn't much anger after I was raped. I expected more than I got.

My parents seemed heartbroken when I told them, but not angry. They weren't even angry when I told them I wasn't going to file a police report. They seemed relieved that I wasn't going to drag them through a lengthy litigation.

Willa supported me by letting me cry on her bed for several days in a row. Hers was a quiet, composed anger she never expressed outwardly.

Beth refused to believe it was true. She didn't think Trevor was capable of hurting anyone, and that the incident must've been a miscommunication between me and him. Caitlyn followed her lead and remained silent whenever someone brought it up in front of them.

It took about a week for the gossipmongers at school to move on to another scandalous story, at which point, what happened to me was forgotten.

Sam thought it was bullshit that Trevor got away with it but wasn't surprised. She didn't leave my side after it happened, but I think she could tell I wanted to put it behind me, so we didn't talk about it at all.

Aunt Franny knew something had happened but wasn't sure what. When she asked, I said I didn't want to talk about it. I think eventually my dad told her, long after I moved to L.A., but she never broached the subject with me again.

Seeing Axil on the verge of losing control, it makes me feel...cared for. Like I'm worth protecting. It's the reaction I wanted right after it happened—for someone, anyone, to be as furious and emotionally shredded as I felt. When I didn't get that, it made me think what happened wasn't a big deal. That any lingering pain was an overreaction on my part, and I just needed to get over it.

Clearly, I haven't, though, because a mere string of words put in a particular order turned me into a trembling, sobbing mess. In L.A., there were no reminders of him, of what happened. I've seen a therapist for several years, but I've never discussed this part of my life. Not with anyone. I was able to shove it all into a deep, dark corner of my mind and forget about it. But now that I'm back, the wound feels fresh.

"What if he attacks someone else?" Axil yells, getting in Zev's face. "What if he hurts Vanessa again? We cannot allow this to stand. We must do something."

"Enough!" Zev shouts, getting behind Axil and shoving him toward the back door through the kitchen. Zev looks back at us as he opens it, then gestures to Axil. "He needs a bit of fresh air. We shall return."

I sit there, sagging back into the couch as, now completely sober, and Aunt Franny's face appears in my head, and I'm angry. Angry at her for not letting me run back to the life I know three thousand miles away. She's the reason I'm stuck here, why I need to show my face around town, and why I've had to see the very people I hoped I never would again.

It's not fair to feel this way. I know that, and I know that my resentment is misplaced. Trevor is the one I hate. Him, Officer Burton, and Beth too. They are the ones who broke me apart and stomped on the pieces.

At some point, I would've had to come back here after Dad's death, I realize, whether for Aunt Franny's death or for Willa. There are parts of me that remain in Sudbury, as much as I hate to admit it. I suppose it's better to deal with this now than to let another decade pass with this trauma waiting to rise to the surface.

And if it's going to happen now in the wake of Aunt Franny's death, I guess it's a good thing I'm not alone.

Zev enters through the back door, then holds it open for Axil. Axil does look calmer, but in a way that makes it clear he'd much rather be severing Trevor's head with his bare hands than remaining composed in my kitchen.

His fiery gaze meets mine and softens as he walks toward me. He kneels in front of me and sighs. "I do not know how to comfort you in this moment," he reaches into his back pocket, "but I thought this may help. Women seem to like it." He places a peanut butter cup in my hands.

A laugh escapes me as I look between the treat in my hands and Axil's face. He didn't know what to do with his anger, so he got me chocolate. I can't imagine a more perfect distraction from my past. "Thank you," I say, tears falling once again, but these are happier. "It's perfect."

He smiles, and it knocks the air out of my lungs. I never realized he had dimples hidden beneath that beard, but there they are.

"What else can I do?" he asks, taking one of my hands in his.

I toss the candy to the side and crash into him as I wrap my arms around his neck. He chuckles, surprised by the contact, then splays a hand on my lower back. "Just stay," I say with a sniffle. "Stay."

CHAPTER 10

AXIL

She wishes for me to stay, and I shall grant her wish. For a little while, at least. My fury has not waned, but I will hide it for now because that is what Vanessa needs. Zev reminded me the moment we stepped outside that Vanessa is scared and hurting, and while I want nothing more than to find Trevor and pummel him so badly that he can taste his own spine, that would require me to leave Vanessa's side. She does not want me to do that, so I will not.

Trevor cannot remain free, though. I will not allow this injustice to continue. The sentence for rape on Sufoi is death by flame, the attacker kept alive as their victim shifts into draxilio form and slowly burns the attacker's skin off their bones. The sentence, while brutal, mirrors the brutality of the crime committed, and thus, has made rape an infrequent and rare crime.

Humans may see this option as too barbaric for their delicate sensibilities, but is not allowing these attackers to remain free even worse? When a rapist is made to pay for their crimes immediately after said crimes have been committed, they can no longer harm others. The structure the humans have put in place to hold rapists accountable makes no sense. There is nothing stopping these wretched beings from causing more pain.

Vanessa's grip tightens around my neck as she sobs into my shoulder. She tries to muffle her cries using my shirt, but the more I rub her back, the more she lets go. Sharp pain slices through my chest at the thought of her being on the receiving end of an attack like this, from someone she once considered a friend. I cannot imagine a more vile betrayal. It is becoming clear to me why she was so eager to abandon this town.

After a while, Zev pats me on the arm to tell me he is going home. I lift Vanessa as I stand, and her legs instantly wrap around me, her feet crossing at my lower back.

This causes friction between our bodies, and my cock hardens in response. I must ignore this, however, because it is the worst possible time to want her.

"I'm going to stay in case she needs anything," Sam says, grabbing her shoes and carrying them to one of the guest rooms. "Not sure I'd be okay driving home now anyway."

"I wish you a restful slumber," I tell her in an attempt to acknowledge the pain she, too, has carried without actually mentioning it.

She shoots an amused smile my way. "You too, Axil."

As I turn off the lights around the house with Vanessa still attached to my front, I notice her sobs have ceased. She still trembles, but she is quiet as her breath tickles my neck. When I pull back to look at her, I find her cheek mashed against my shoulder and her eyes closed. I chuckle at the sight of her asleep as pride fills my chest.

It is entirely possible that the stress of the confrontation and the crying that followed has exhausted her. But I want it to be me. I want to be the reason she was able to reach this place. I want the warmth and strength of my body to make her feel protected. Because that is what I plan to do: protect her.

I also find it deeply concerning that such a sinister creature possesses a gun. Bullets will not hurt me, but I have seen enough human news to know how easily they can harm or kill other humans. Hurting others seems to be something Trevor enjoys, as he continues to do so.

Whether the end result means Trevor lives or dies, it does not matter. With every part of me, I will do what is necessary to keep Vanessa safe. It is what Lady Norton would have wanted. It is also what I want. In fact, there is nothing I have ever wanted more.

"Mmm," Vanessa mumbles sleepily, nuzzling closer. "Jussa lil' longer."

Once the front door is locked and the house is dark, I carry Vanessa into the bedroom and pull back the covers. I gently place her on the bed and tuck her in. She makes a few nonsensical protests when I release her, and I do my best to remain silent. It is difficult, however, with how adorably displeased she looks, even when unconscious.

I brush a hair off her nose and tell myself to turn off her bedside light and go. Yet, my feet remain planted. I...cannot leave her. I lean down and press a kiss to her forehead, wishing there was more I could give her—Trevor's head on a stake, for instance—wishing there was more I could do to ease her agony.

The moment my lips leave her skin, her arms wrap around my neck. Surprised, I say, "You are awake."

"I am now," she says before lifting her head off the pillow and pressing her lips against mine.

My draxilio purrs in response. *She wants us.*

Her actions leave me stunned. I am frozen in place as she kisses me, unsure if it is appropriate for me to respond at all. Pulling back, I stroke her cheek. "We should not."

"Why not?" she whispers, tilting her chin up, reaching for me with those dangerous lips of hers.

"After what happened tonig—"

She puts a finger to my lips. "I don't want to think about it anymore. I want to forget." She traces my bottom lip, then her finger trails down my chin, along my throat, until she reaches the top button of my shirt. She undoes the first button, then the second. "Axil," she moans, "make me forget."

I cover her hand with mine, stopping her from undressing me further. It takes a tremendous amount of willpower, and my draxilio growls incessantly at my actions, but I must resist, if only so I can do this right. Lifting her hand, I press my lips to her palm. "You have been drinking tonight," I point out, "I will not take advantage."

She gasps the moment she feels the tip of my tongue flick against her skin. "You wouldn't be taking advantage," she whispers. "I sobered up after…you know."

"Yes," I say, nodding. "And we will not speak of it again." My lips move to her wrist, then the inside of her forearm, then her elbow. "It would be my honor," I whisper, dropping her hand, and leaning over her as I plant a kiss just beneath her ear, "to help you forget."

Vanessa groans as her head lolls to the side, giving me better access to her neck. I feel her reach between us as she rips the covers off her body and pulls me closer. She cups my face in both hands, turning me toward her. Her eyes search mine, and for a moment, my heart lodges in my chest. Are my eyes red? They do not feel itchy, but is itchiness something we will all experience? They felt itchy for a brief moment when I came close to kissing her in the basement. It was a frightening moment in which I was sure my entire world had turned upside down. Have they turned…for her? That worry fades when her mouth curls up on one side into a smile. I do not know what she sees in my gaze, but I am relieved it is something that brings her joy, and not fear. She deserves nothing less this night.

I kiss her slowly, savoring every little sound that escapes her. Her tongue slides along my bottom lip, and I meet it with mine, eager to explore the depths of her wicked mouth. The taste of her drink lingers from earlier, but it cannot match her natural sweetness. No, hers is a flavor too rich, too lovely, that it compares to nothing else in this world. In this universe, even.

Her arousal scent fills the air like a cloud around my head, making me dizzy with want. But this is about Vanessa and seeing to her needs. My desire can wait.

"You should know…um," she trails off, her voice shaky. "I can't have sex. I mean, I can," she quickly amends, "technically, but I won't enjoy it. Everything but actual sex, though, I can do. I don't know what it is, but ever since…that night, my body just sort of shuts down, um, down there when things get close to the main event." She points between her legs, though I knew what she meant without the gesture.

"It is fine, Vanessa," I tell her reassuringly. "We will not do anything that makes you uncomfortable."

She bites her lip. "It's not that I don't want to…"

I tilt her chin up until her eyes meet mine. "We will go as slow as you need. I am in no rush."

She chuckles, her expression skeptical. "Every guy says that at first, but eventually they get tired of waiting for me to come around. Then they bail."

I plant my hands on either side of her on the mattress and hold myself above her. "I am not like other men."

She sucks in a breath as she parts her thighs for me.

Reaching out, I cup her breast, a growl rumbling through my chest at how perfectly it fits in my hand. I acquaint myself with the weight of it, the softness, and smile against her mouth the moment I feel her nipple harden into a stiff peak. Kissing down her chin, then her neck, I push up the fabric of her shirt, exposing the smooth, tanned skin of her stomach. Vanessa is soft everywhere, but particularly here, and I deem myself a spoiled male with such a splendid canvas to worship. My tongue traces the silver lines surrounding her belly button as my hands work to undo the clasp of her bra, situated between her breasts.

Thirteen years on this planet, and I have yet to find a reason these mystifying contraptions exist at all. They are difficult to remove, and they hide, trap, and tame the most magnificent part of a woman's body. Shameful.

With enough fumbling, her heavy breasts spill free, and my mouth waters at the sight of them. I make it a point to watch Vanessa as I look up at her through my lashes, my mouth hovering above one dusky pink tip, less than an inch away. "I want to kiss you here. May I?"

"Mmm," she moans. Her mouth is pink and swollen from my kiss, and her hair wild. She is the most stunning creature I have ever laid eyes on.

I do not move my head, I merely part my lips, and with a frustrated, impatient groan, she arches her back, feeding her nipple into my mouth. The taste of her is divine, the salty sweetness of her skin causing my cock to throb against my thigh. My pants continue to tighten to an uncomfortable degree, but I ignore it, focusing my energy on sucking and nibbling her nipple, as her body begins to tremble.

"Axil?" she whimpers as if asking a question.

I release her nipple with a final flick of my tongue. "You like that?"

She doesn't reply, but her breath quickens.

Skating my lips across her rib cage, I pause at the underside of her other breast. "I am afraid I did not hear you, Vanessa." Using the tip of my tongue, I trace the outside of her nipple in a small tantalizing circle, and then repeat, "Do you like that?"

"Yes!" she gasps, throwing her head back. "Yes. Feels so good."

Male pride surges through me at the sight of her coming unraveled. I did that. I can make her moan and lose control. And I have only just begun.

"Good girl," I say before taking her into my mouth once again. She gives me a strange look, but the moment my teeth brush against her nipple, it is gone, and she remains lost to the sensations of my lips on her skin.

It is not something I have ever uttered during a romantic encounter with a female. But with Vanessa, knowing the struggles she has faced, the pain she has endured—the words just came out.

When I decide her breasts have received equal attention, I move down to her stomach. A groan escapes my lips as I grip her sides, my fingers sinking into her supple curves. My hands move down, reaching the waistband of her pants. I look up, a question in my gaze.

"Touch me," she mewls, her tone husky. "Please."

I glide her pants off her legs, leaving a pink scrap of fabric covering her core. She spreads wide for me, her hand lightly resting on the lower part of her stomach. I want nothing more than to taste her here, to shred the cloth barrier that stands between me and her pussy. But she is not ready for that. When that day does come, and it will, I plan to make her writhe and scream my name so loud that all of Sudbury hears it and knows she is mine.

In pleasure only, my draxilio pipes in. *We still cannot trust her.*

I ignore his words of caution, reminding myself that I must go slow with Vanessa tonight. I must show her how I plan to care for her. How willing I am to give her all that she desires. "Turn around," I say, kicking off my boots. I move deeper onto the bed and pat my chest. "Lean against me."

Vanessa crawls to me on her hands and knees, a sight that robs me of breath with her breasts exposed and swaying as she moves. She gets into position, the back of her head pressed against my chest, and asks, "Like this?"

I kiss her hair, then dip my head and kiss along her cheek, moving to her ear. "Yes, just like that." I wrap my arms around her, then gently nudge her knees apart. "You are doing so well. Good girl," I say it a second time, the words feeling true and right.

She sucks in a breath, and I am not sure if it is because of my praise, or because of my hand inching up the inside of her thigh. With my other hand, I play with her nipple, rolling it between my fingers, and giving it the slightest pinch at the end. She arches back, and I continue licking and kissing along her neck. When I slide my hand beneath the thin fabric that shields her from my eyes, she groans, and I am met with the wet heat of her folds.

So slick. So perfect.

Saliva fills my mouth as I picture her pussy, glistening and begging for my mouth. I simply cannot wait another moment. Greedy for a taste of her, I run a finger along her slit and bring it to my lips. She quivers at my touch. The moment her juices hit my tongue, my entire body tightens with pulsing, aching need. It is as if I have come alive at the taste of her, but teeter on the verge of death simultaneously if I do not get more. She is sweeter than the ripest mango; a fruit I cannot seem to get enough of when it is in season. I imagine I will no longer mourn the lack of available mangos, and I shall simply feast on Vanessa instead.

Turning her chin toward me, I kiss her, hoping she can still taste herself on my lips. She releases a strangled cry, my mouth trapping the volume of it as I move my hand back to her mound and explore every dip of her center with my fingers. "May I?" I ask against her lips.

"Yes," she pants.

Then I stroke into her, first with one finger, before adding a second. "Tight," I growl against her earlobe. "So tight and wet."

Her only reply is a short, panting breath.

I let go of her breast, and rub against her clit with my middle finger, using both hands on her cunt. And I continue to pump into her hot channel as I curl my fingers into a hook shape. When I find the patch of flesh deep inside that causes Vanessa's eyes to roll back into her head, I feel as victorious as I did in the arena on Sufoi after defeating another draxilio in a brutal exchange of fire and claws.

Her breath stops the moment I pick up the pace, circling her clit more rapidly, adding pressure as I go. She is close. "Yes, like that," she demands hoarsely. I do not have to see her face to know her skin is flushed and her lids heavy with lust.

I comply, giving her what she needs as I kiss up and down her neck. She gasps, and I feel her entire body shudder. Her fingernails bite into my forearms as she holds on for dear life. A moment later, she shatters, the walls of her cunt flexing around my fingers as she throws back her head and screams.

"That is it. Come apart for me."

Then suddenly, she turns her head toward my bicep, and I feel her teeth sink in through my flannel, not hard enough to draw blood, but enough to go through the fabric and leave a mark on my skin.

For a moment, I consider asking Zev to trace the mark in ink, a permanent acknowledgment of the night my heart was unexpectedly stolen from my body by my former neighbor's niece. Because nothing, no previous encounter on Earth or Sufoi, could ever compare to this. I have not even reached release, and yet, as I continue to hold Vanessa in my arms as she comes down from hers, I feel completely fulfilled.

She is not ours, my draxilio grumbles. *Do not get attached. She is still planning to leave.*

Knowing the hour grows late, I release her, reluctantly, guiding her onto her back on the bed. I press a final, soft kiss to her lips before rising to my feet. She smiles at me, her eyes still glazed, but her entire body visibly relaxed. She pulls back the covers on the other side of the bed, a silent invitation for me to join her.

"I must go," I tell her, "and you should sleep."

"You're leaving? Really?" she asks, clearing her throat, trying to seem unbothered, but failing. "Do you have a wife or girlfriend you haven't told me about?" She chuckles as if trying to cloak her fear of rejection with humor.

If only she knew how badly I wanted to stay. How my entire body is fighting me with every inch I put between our bodies. But I cannot fall asleep at her side.

The mask I don at will, the one that hides my horns and changes my blue, otherworldly skin to a light cream color, cannot hold while I am asleep. If she were to wake before me and catch me in my natural state, it would ruin everything. My brothers and I would be exposed. We would need to flee Sudbury, just as we fled Boston after Luka met Harper. I would like to think I can trust Vanessa to stay quiet about our existence here on her planet, but I do not know for certain.

My draxilio growls, fervently agreeing with my hesitation. *It is not worth the risk. Protect the family.*

If she were my mate, it would be different. We would be forever linked by the mate bond. But my eyes have yet to turn, and though I can no longer imagine my days without her, I cannot risk my brothers' safety over an infatuation with a beautiful human.

"There is no one I desire but you," I tell her honestly. "I promise I shall return in the morning." I take her hand and kiss her knuckles. "Sleep now, Vanessa."

I steal one last glance at her before I leave, going through the kitchen and out the back door.

As I stride along the narrow path between her house and mine, I hope I was successful tonight in helping her forget. Judging by the smile I cannot seem to wipe from my face, and the ache in my chest that appeared the moment I left her, this night will be burned in my memory for centuries, and I know there will be no sleep for me.

CHAPTER 11

AXIL

"There you are," Zev mutters from the recliner in the living room the moment I enter. He gets up and races over to me, grabbing my face in his hands.

I shove him off. "What are you doing?"

"I was certain you would come home with eyes blinking the color of blood," he says, leaning back against the kitchen island. "She is it, right? Your mate?"

Staring at him for several seconds, I finally say, "My eyes have not turned, so no. I do not believe so." It disappoints me to be so unsure, especially when, in many ways, Vanessa feels like the one I have been searching for. The one I gave up on ever finding.

My draxilio disagrees. *We cannot trust her. She is leaving soon.*

I cannot argue with that. The latter is still of concern.

Pulling my phone from my pocket, I quickly type a message to Luka.

Me: *Need your help. When did you know Harper was your mate? How long did it take for your draxilio to agree with your feelings about her?*

I hope he answers me. Outside of our annual family visits with him, Harper, and their two children at Christmas, he keeps his distance from us as we are "troublemakers."

Kyan strides through the front door, loosening his tie and grumbling something under his breath.

"How was work?" I ask out of politeness. His answer is always the same. "It was work" he will say each night before pouring himself a large glass of water, tossing a bag of kettle corn into the microwave, and taking both up to his wing of the house. His obsession with kettle corn, particularly as his nightly snack before bed, has puzzled all of us since we arrived.

"It was work," he replies, right on cue. He tosses his blazer over the back of the couch and comes into the kitchen to begin his evening routine.

After taking a large sip of water, he asks, "Why do you both look strange? What has happened?"

"We are draxilios pretending to be humans," Zev says with a smirk. "Do we not always look strange?"

Kyan glares at Zev, then shifts his narrowed gaze to me. "Dish. Now."

Zev rolls his eyes at Kyan's demand. It has become a catchphrase of sorts for Kyan, ever since he discovered that "dish" can also mean "reveal your secret." Kyan is also the one we deliberately hide things from since his temper is the least predictable, and the most likely to get us into trouble with the authorities.

It is why I cannot tell him about the earlier events of the evening. The moment he discovers a rapist living in our vicinity, he will kill him. And he will do it in a messy, spectacular fashion that will lead the police directly to our door.

Although, the thought of severing Trevor's head while he sleeps and mounting it to the wall does sound appealing...

My draxilio purrs in agreement.

For now, I must keep Trevor's crimes hidden from Kyan. He will be angry when he finds out, but I can handle Kyan's wrath. Getting locked in a human jail for who knows how long, I cannot. "We went to Tipsy's bar earlier, and met Vanessa and her friend there," I say, simplifying the events of the evening into a single sentence that will bore Kyan. "It was enjoyable."

Kyan grunts as he grabs a bag of kettle corn, rips it free of the plastic, and puts it into the microwave. He is quite ornery for a draxilio posing as a human. It must be the eighteen-hour days he spends at his office. He turns to face us. "Is the niece still trying to sell the house?"

So much has happened since the last time Vanessa spoke of it, I genuinely do not know. Though, after seeing Trevor, I cannot imagine her wanting to stay. Until she says otherwise, I will assume that is still her plan. "Yes, I think so."

"If you should require assistance in keeping her here, do let me know," Kyan says conspiratorially. "I have a guy I can send over."

Everything about that sounds alarming, and I do not like the way he is scratching his chin as he ponders this plan of his. "To do what, exactly?"

"You said the house is in need of repair, yes?" he asks. "Repairs she cannot afford to fix."

"Yes," I reply. "I did say that."

None of my brothers know about the treasure hunt or the cash Lady Norton left for Vanessa. They would have no interest in trying to claim it for themselves, of course. But currency is important to Vanessa, and her story to share if she wishes.

The microwave beeps, signaling the popcorn is done, and he takes a deep inhale as he opens the top of the bag. "Well, my guy can create more areas in need of repair, if you know what I mean."

"No," I say, my tone firm.

"To which part?" Zev asks, his tone bored as he traces the lines of the snake tattoo he recently added to his right arm. "No, you do not know what he means? Or no to Kyan sending a strange male over to Vanessa's to destroy her house?"

"That," I practically shout. "The second one." My fists ball at my sides as I look at Kyan, playfully tossing kettle corn into the air before catching it in his mouth. "Do not send anyone to Vanessa's. Do you hear me? If anyone she does not recognize takes a single step on her property, I will end you."

He smiles as he looks between me and Zev. "Ah, so we have found another human mate, have we?" He pauses. "What is the expression?" his brow furrows, "two down, three to go?"

"Yes, I believe that is how the saying goes," Zev replies, his tone mocking. "Right, Axil?"

Feeling outnumbered, I growl low in my throat and snag the bag of kettle corn out of Kyan's grasp, knocking it to the floor. He roars grumpily as it spills onto the kitchen tiles.

"Now I need to pop another bag!" he shouts.

"You do not *need* to do anything," I point out. "What kind of drax-ilio eats popcorn before bed?"

"Splendid, you are all here," Mylo mutters as he descends the stairs. "We must have our monthly meeting."

The three of us collectively sigh.

He holds up a hand, rejecting our displeasure. "We have not had one this month, and now is a good time to do it." He grabs his tablet off the TV stand and gestures for us to follow him into the living room. We do, dragging our feet, and take our seats: Mylo in the center of the couch in the middle of the room, Kyan and Zev on opposing loveseats, and me in the recliner in the corner. Mylo starts tapping on the screen of his tablet and Kyan lets out a loud groan.

"You do not need to keep the minutes," he says, rolling his eyes. "Really, it is entirely unnecessary."

Mylo pushes his glasses up the bridge of his nose as he stares intently at the tablet, then shouts "Ah!" triumphantly. "Actually, Kyan, you complained about me keeping the minutes two meetings ago. Do you know how I know that?" Mylo asks him, smiling. "Because it is in the minutes."

Kyan shakes his head, annoyed, as he crosses one leg over the other. "Very well, then I would like the record to reflect that these meetings are a waste of time, once again."

"Your complaint is noted," Mylo says as he adds a note to the document on the screen. "Now, who wishes to share their learnings first?"

Kyan uncrosses his legs and leans forward. "I will."

Zev and I sigh at the same time, mentally preparing for another battle between him and Mylo. They have butted heads for as long as I can remember.

"I would like to trade my media assignment," Kyan says. "Reality TV is not something I find enjoyable, and it is riddled with human slang, which is difficult for me to grasp. I do not understand why I was assigned this, and why I cannot change my assignment for a full calendar year."

Mylo clears his throat. "Unless there is someone who wishes to trade with you, you must keep it. We have been over this."

Kyan leans back and pouts.

"Besides, it is crucial for us to rotate these forms of media, so we all grow to understand them equally," Mylo adds, looking at each of us. "Unless someone is willing to trade, reality TV will remain yours, just as scripted stories shall remain mine, music will remain Zev's, and news and documentaries will remain Axil's."

"I do not like the news," I say. "It is extremely depressing what these humans do to one another on a daily basis." Kyan's eyes widen with hope. "But I would rather have that than reality TV."

"Yes, it is tragic they fail to see the beauty in their kind," Zev notes. "Especially when they have no knowledge of what lies just outside their galaxy."

"What a thoughtful observation, Zev," Mylo says enthusiastically. Then he looks at me. "And, Axil, what have you learned from the news?"

"That human bodies are shockingly frail," I say, picturing just how satisfying it would be to break Trevor's jaw.

Mylo swipes his pointer finger across the screen of his tablet. "Uh, you said the same during last month's meeting."

I nod. "I am still surprised by it."

Mylo sighs and turns to Kyan. "Kyan, anything you would like to add? About reality TV?"

Kyan rises from his seat. "No. Now, if you will excuse me, I need to make more popcorn." He shoots me a deadly glare before stomping toward the kitchen. Then he whips his body around to face us. "Actually, yes. If you are a bachelor, it seems important in human courtship to give your mate a single rose when you decide to keep them forever."

We all nod, stunned by the insight.

"That is excellent information, Kyan," Mylo says, making a note of it. "I shall look deeper into this."

Mylo dismisses us, and we each meander toward our respective wings of the house.

It takes five minutes to brush my teeth, splash cold water on my face, and strip my clothes off before climbing into bed. It takes another four hours for me to fall asleep.

* * *

Two hours of sleep. That is all I was able to get before my eyelids popped open and I remembered I promised Vanessa I would return to her this morning. What she does not know is that I plan on making her breakfast, a feast fit for a king, in fact.

Since I abhor the lack of room, tools, and ingredients in her kitchen, however, I shall prepare the feast in mine and take it over, which is usually what I would do when I cooked for Lady Norton. With a surge of energy at the thought of seeing her again, I shower as quickly as I can, throw on clean clothes, and race downstairs.

It seems Mylo is the only one awake this early. It is just after seven, and the rest of the house is silent. Kyan is either still asleep, or more likely, already at work. Zev will not rise until after ten, but this is where I typically find Mylo at this time, munching on his usual blueberry bagel with cream cheese, sipping a cup of English breakfast tea, and reading a book.

"Brother!" He greets me, chipper as ever. "Lovely morning, is it not?"

I shrug as I open the refrigerator and gather the ingredients I need. "I do not know. I have only experienced a small fraction of it thus far."

"Well, I had a very restful slumber, and I saw the weather will not be too cold today, so I have a good feeling about it. And," he replies, holding up a finger as if he just had a brilliant idea, "I am reading to the children later for Storytime Corner."

"Oh? Have you picked out the story yet?" I ask, tossing a dish towel over my shoulder and rinsing a few potatoes before putting them on the cutting board.

"I usually let one of the children choose between two options," he says, his tone focused and thoughtful. "Though they will probably select Dr. Seuss again."

When Mylo told us that he wanted to become a librarian, as it is a public-facing job that requires extensive knowledge of literature, we were not shocked, exactly—not a day passes without his nose in a book—but it was not what we expected. He is passionate about his work helping the community here, however, and I cannot imagine him doing anything else.

"Why do you include Dr. Seuss as an option, then?" I ask, tossing the cubed potatoes into a bowl. Then I add olive oil, pepper, and garlic salt, and spread it all on a sheet pan before sticking it into the oven.

"Dr. Seuss is a crowd pleaser, and I aim to please."

I look up at him from the bowl I have cracked an egg against. "These are children, though. How hard could they be to please?"

He gives me a sideways glance. "Extremely. And they are vocal about even an ounce of displeasure. They have their parents trained well too. It is quite astonishing to watch, really. If they do not enjoy Storytime Corner, they will cry and scream and their parents will never bring them back again."

"Wow," I mutter. Here I thought they would mostly stare blankly at Mylo as they soiled themselves or fell asleep.

He takes a final bite of his bagel, throws back the rest of his tea, and grunts his good-bye. He stops before he reaches the front door and grabs his glasses, putting them on and giving himself a final check in the mirror before stepping out. Mylo's vision is perfect, as is the rest of ours, but with the many films we have seen featuring an intelligent character who wears glasses, Mylo insists on wearing a fake pair of his own as a way of leaning into his human role.

Without any distractions, I move about the kitchen quickly and efficiently as I continue preparing Vanessa's meal. Once I am done, I lay everything out on two plates, wash my hands, and head toward her house.

Carefully, I open the back door and close it quietly behind me with my foot, all without dropping the plates. The door to Vanessa's room is ajar, and when I nudge it open, the door makes a loud creaking sound, and she pops up with a gasp.

"Oh! Oh, hi!" she says, her voice hoarse from sleep. "You scared me," she says with a sigh, but then her gaze drops to the plates. "Wait, did you bring me food?"

"I did," I reply. "Told you I would return."

Vanessa licks her lips as she scoots up into a seated position on the bed. I place her plate on her lap, then sit on the edge of the bed, facing her as I hold mine. "Oh my god, breakfast burritos?"

I nod, chuckling at her excitement. She dips half of the burrito into the pile of salsa on the plate and takes a bite. She moans as she chews, her eyes pinched shut, and I am mesmerized. She takes several more bites with me gawking at her before I snap out of my trance and take a bite of my own.

"This is amazing," she says. Then reaches out and places her hand on top of mine. "Thank you."

My skin buzzes at the contact long after she removes it.

"What is that incredible smell?" Sam says as she barges into the room. Her mouth falls open at the sight of plates in our laps. "Where's mine?"

I feel terrible. I genuinely forgot she was here, or I would have made enough for her too. Getting to my feet, I offer her my plate. "Here, there is still half a burrito left."

Out of the corner of my eye, I catch Vanessa staring at me as if I failed to mask my horns. But since I know for certain they are not currently jutting out of my skull, I ignore it.

"No, no," Sam says, brushing away my offer. "I have to be heading home anyway." She walks over to Vanessa and picks a few potatoes out of the top of her burrito. "That should do," Sam says, her mouth full.

"Hey!" Vanessa yells in protest, but it is immediately clear she is not angry.

"Text you later, Vanilla!" Sam shouts back as she walks out of the room.

Vanessa shakes her head and giggles. "Bye, Samwich."

I take my place at the foot of Vanessa's bed, and we continue our meal. There is not much chatter, but only because we are focused on our food. The lack of conversation does not feel uncomfortable.

When we are finished, Vanessa takes our plates into the kitchen and refuses to let me wash them. "You cooked," she says with an adorably stern tone. "So I'll clean. That's the deal."

"Is that the deal?" I ask. It certainly does seem like a fair way to divide the tasks. I know after I have cooked a meal, the last thing I wish to do is clean up. "Can you tell my brothers about this deal?"

She laughs, and warmth spreads through my chest at the sound. It is a light, musical, unburdened sound. I long to hear it again.

Vanessa decides to shower after the dishes are cleaned, and I putter around the house while I wait. I fall into the old habit of checking little things like I used to for Lady Norton. I test the batteries in the smoke detector, look behind the blinds for spiders in the living room where the plants are kept—I find one and kill it, and check the wood pile in the basement to make sure she has enough chopped wood should the temperature drop. Once those tasks are completed, I slump into the thick, deflated cushions of the couch and scroll through emails on my phone regarding new furniture orders.

I look up from my phone the moment Vanessa strides into the living room wearing nothing but a beige towel. "Hi," she says in a shy voice, her cheeks rosy from the shower.

"Hello," I reply, tossing my phone on the couch next to me. Work holds no interest for me anymore. At least, not while Vanessa's skin is completely bare beneath that towel. One flick of the wrist could have her naked before me. "Enjoy your shower?"

She bites her lip. "I did." Her hair is brushed back and off her face, hanging in short wet strands that curl around her ears. Her skin looks so smooth, my hands flex with the need to touch her as she comes closer. "I thought, um," she mumbles, her knee bent on the couch at my side as she climbs into my lap, "we could pick up where we left off." She straddles my thighs, giving me a small peek at her pussy as she lowers herself, pressing her core against my cock. The only thing between us are my pants. I hate my pants, I realize. Hate them.

Then she drops the towel.

My lips fall open at the sight of her on display, so round and soft, her dusty pink nipples already pebbled, begging for my mouth. I swallow hard, my throat suddenly dry. I reach for her, but she bats my hands away, one eyebrow raised in an arch. "You want to touch me, Axil?"

I cannot speak. Words evade me. All I can do is nod.

She lifts just enough that her nipple almost brushes against my nose, then grinds down. A groan rips from my throat as my eyes fall closed.

"You can use your mouth, not your hands," she says, trailing a finger along my jaw. "Do you understand?"

I grunt in response as I lean forward toward her chest with my mouth open, but she stops me.

"Do. You. Understand?" she asks again.

"Yes," I eventually reply, my voice rough, pleading. "I promise."

Her eyes are heavy-lidded as she grins at me, and I take that as permission to proceed. My mouth is on her, licking and sucking one stiffened peak as she threads her fingers through my hair. Without thinking, I put my hands on her back, pulling closer, but she jerks away.

"Uh, uh, uh," she says with a tsk. "No hands." She grabs my wrists and places each arm along the back of the couch. "Keep them there. Or we stop."

I find it surprising that she is commanding in a sexual scenario, given her discomfort with actually having sex, but perhaps it is the control that makes her feel safe. Knowing I will only do what she tells me to do, and nothing more. If this is what she needs, I will gladly play along as I continue to show her that she can trust me.

Breathing hard, barely able to keep from crawling out of my skin, I say, "Okay. I will not move them."

The moment the words leave my mouth, I am on her again, this time, kissing along her collarbone, then moving down the center of her chest. She rolls her hips as she tips her head back, moaning.

While I enjoy the taste of her skin, and the floral scents of the shampoo and soap she used in the shower, not being able to put my hands on her is pure misery. There is so much of her to hold, to grip and caress, and I can only use my mouth. She deserves all I can give her, and she will only allow me to give a little. I try adapting to her rules. I really do try. But after using my tongue and lips and teeth all over her top half, I grow frustrated.

"Please, Vanessa," I groan, rubbing the coarse hairs of my beard against her nipple, causing her body to jerk. "Let me touch you."

She looks down at me, her hair starting to dry, the front pieces falling in waves. "But I'm not done torturing you," she whispers.

"That is the goal? To torture me?" I grit, my tone harsher than necessary, but this female has me dangling on the edge of my control.

Vanessa chuckles, a look of pure mischief on her face as she starts unbuttoning my shirt. She places a kiss on every new inch of exposed skin. When she reaches my chest, she looks up at me through her lashes. "How else could I repay you for that disastrous meeting with the listing agent?"

My grip on the back of the couch tightens. "So you are punishing me?" I ask, aghast at her words. This was all to wind me up? To what end? "I thought we moved past that."

She continues undressing me, then slides between my legs until she is kneeling on the floor. The final button is released, and she opens my shirt, her eyes widening as she takes in my bare chest. "We have moved on," she says, her eyes traveling down my stomach. "Water under the bridge. Especially after last night. That orgasm you gave me settled the score."

I am confused. "Then what are you doing?"

She finishes unbuckling my belt, and I watch as her hands swiftly undo the button at my waist and pull down the zipper. Then she reaches in, her small hand wrapped around my cock as she frees it. Her hand moves up and down my length, gently at first, then adding more pressure. I suck in a breath. It is one thing to see Vanessa naked and kneeling before me. It is quite another to have that, plus her mouth, so close to the head of my cock; precome already pooling at the tip.

I have no idea what she is planning, but I am willing to wager I will not last more than a minute. Most likely, thirty seconds.

When she does reveal her plan, it is not at all what I expected her to say.

"I'm thanking you for the burritos," she says, then flattens her tongue against the base of my cock and drags it slowly up to the tip.

My hips buck before I can ask a follow-up question, lost to the feel of her smooth, hot tongue on me.

"No man has ever brought me breakfast in bed before," she mutters, then wraps her lips around the head, sucking hard.

I can hear my heart thundering through my chest as a rumbling growl climbs up my throat.

"So good too," she says, lapping at the head as if it were a lollipop. The wooden frame of the couch begins to creak as my knuckles turn white. "And big. It was the tastiest, juiciest, biggest burrito I've ever had, to be honest. I'm still full."

"You should stop," I say through gritted teeth, a sheen of sweat now covering my brow.

She removes her tongue to ask in an innocent tone, "Why would I do that?"

My chest heaves as her breath fans my cock, her lips moving closer...closer, without touching me. "Because your mouth feels too good, and I do not know how much longer I can hold back."

She sticks her tongue out, giving it a single lick. Her eyes glazed with desire. "So don't."

Then she takes me deep, stroking me with her hand while her head bobs and her lips move around my cock. "Vanessa," I groan, throwing my head back. She swirls her tongue around me, and the moment she uses her other hand to massage my sac, I erupt. My hips jerk forcefully, then erratically as I pour my hot seed down her delicate throat.

She reaches a point where she can take no more, and I watch in awe as it dribbles down her chin, droplets of white landing on her breasts. The sight of my come on her skin unlocks something within me. A primal desperation to rub my seed into her flesh, to cover her entire body in it until she is thoroughly marked as mine. I have never felt this with another. It is unexpected, and the intensity of it is…unsettling.

I expect my draxilio to say something, to encourage me to stop, or to keep my heart protected from Vanessa's clutches, but he remains quiet. Is he starting to like her? Or even, see her as ours?

My ragged breaths start to even out, and it is then that I realize she is laughing. "What? What is it?"

She points to the back of the couch, now uneven and forming a strange shape. "You broke my couch."

Incredulous, I crane my neck to inspect it, and sure enough, the wooden frame is cracked in two parts along the back of the couch where each of my hands were. I could apologize. I certainly *should* apologize, but ultimately, if Vanessa let me touch her, the couch would still be intact.

When I turn to face her, ready to tell her this is her fault, she has wiped my come from her chin, and still looks playfully amused at the fact that I destroyed her furniture. Before she can protest, I lift her off the floor and toss her onto the couch next to me where she lands on her back, her breasts bouncing. "Hey! I didn't say you could touch me yet!" she squeals as I remove my shirt and shove my pants down to my ankles.

Then I cover her body with mine and whisper, "You had your fun" before pressing my lips to hers. "It's my turn now."

"Oh fuck," she groans in mock irritation. "You're going to torture me now, aren't you?"

"Of course not, love," I murmur against her neck as my hands roam her body freely. "No torture. Just pleasure." I reach between us and find her pussy soaked, her folds swollen and hot against my fingers. "Mmm."

"Yes," she gasps, her blunt nails digging into my back. I move down her body until my shoulders push against the inside of her thighs. I look up at her once more, checking to see that she is still with me.

Vanessa gives me a nod, and I flatten my tongue against her seam, giving it a long, deep lick. Her fingers tangle in my hair as she holds my head in place. Her hips jerk when I do not immediately lick her again.

I spread her folds, marveling at the beauty of her, the scent of her. I cannot believe her body is mine to cherish. Then I thrust my tongue deep into her center, and she lets out a scream I am certain the neighbors will hear. I pull back and look up at her as she thrashes beneath my tongue. "Good girl," I tell her. "Let go. I have you."

Then I resume feasting on her core, lapping up every drop of honey her body provides as I suck and lick along her folds. I uncover the swollen bud of nerves at the top of her seam and focus all my attention on it. Her mouth falls open in a silent scream.

It takes only two laps around the outside of her clit before her thighs begin to shake against the sides of my head.

I slide two fingers inside her as I whisper, "Yes, love. Come for me."

She does. Vanessa's body freezes, and her face contorts into blissful agony as her cunt flutters around my fingers, her feet kicking up in the air. I continue thrusting my fingers in and out of her body as I climb up until our lips are almost touching.

As she starts to come down, her eyelids open in a mere sliver, but when she sees how my body is positioned, and that my cock is mere inches from her entrance, they fly open in alarm. "No!"

I release her entirely, and back away on the couch, holding up my hands. "It is okay, Vanessa. I was not going to proceed without your permission." I would be offended by the horror and disgust on her face at the idea of me taking her how I wish, but her past pain is too thick to break through. Patience is what she needs.

Her chest is heaving as her breaths come out in rapid pants. She flattens her palm against her forehead, and then I see tears sliding down her cheeks.

"Vanessa?" I want nothing more than to gather her in my arms, but will the embrace be welcomed?

"I'm so sorry," she whimpers, shaking her head. "Fuck, I hate this. I'm s-so embarrassed."

Shame is not an emotion that should be anywhere inside her mind right now, and I hate Trevor even more for putting it there. "It is okay," I tell her in a soft tone. "Truly. There is nothing to be embarrassed about." I rest my hands lightly on her thighs, and once she feels my touch, she grabs me by the shoulders and pulls me in until I am on top of her.

She sniffles against my neck, trying to compose herself. "I wish I could do this. I *want* to do this, and usually the *want* isn't even there. But with you..." she trails off as she pulls back to look at me.

Even with her cheeks stained with tears, Vanessa is the most angelic creature I have ever seen. This world does not deserve her.

"It is okay," I whisper again before pressing my lips against hers. "There is no rush."

She nods, unconvinced, before wrapping her arms around my neck and pulling me back down against her body.

Eventually, once her tears have dried, I turn us until we lay side by side.

She falls asleep in my arms as I continue placing gentle kisses along her hair and temple. Though the cushions are a tight, uncomfortable fit, and the couch itself is broken beyond repair, there is nowhere I would rather be.

CHAPTER 12

VANESSA

*T*he doorbell jolts me awake, and immediately sends me into panic mode when I look down and realize Axil and I are still naked on the couch. He's chuckling quietly as I scramble to my feet, looking for my towel. "What's so funny? Someone's here!"

"I have never seen you so skittish. Does the doorbell always illicit this kind of reaction?" he asks, putting his hands behind his head in a carefree way that makes him look irritatingly smug, but also shows off his massive biceps covered in tattoos, making me want to crawl on top of him and trace the lines with my tongue.

"Somebody is waiting for me out there," I whisper. "Cover yourself up."

He shrugs. "So make them wait."

I stare at him, blinking rapidly. How is he so calm right now?

Axil grunts as his eyes land on my breasts. He shakes his head. "You are so beautiful. You must know that already, though."

My stomach flutters at his words, and I can feel my cheeks turning red. "I certainly don't mind hearing it," I say, my words coming out low and quiet. "Yes!" I shout when I find the towel. Grabbing it off the floor, I wrap it around myself, and then take a moment to de-sex my hair, because I have no doubt its messiness reveals exactly what we were doing. "It's not just the doorbell," I reply to his earlier question. "The phone too."

"The phone?" he asks, lifting a brow. "When someone calls, you turn jittery? Or text messages as well?"

"Just when someone calls."

"Why is that?"

"Because the only phone calls I get nowadays are when someone has bad news," I explain. "The second my phone rings, every part of my body clenches with anxiety. Besides, the majority of communication now is digital, so phone calls feel strange, too intimate, I guess. It's why I prefer texts, like most people." I fiddle with my bangs in the hallway mirror, trying to get them somewhat straight using sheer force of will, which is pointless. "Being my age, you must understand that."

He tilts his head. "Am I your age?"

"You're..." I trail off as I stare at him, trying to come up with a guess. He might be older than me, but not by much. "Forty-one?"

He gives me a strange look at first but eventually nods. "That is correct. Good guess."

Is he lying about his age? No. That couldn't be it. Men never do that.

Axil gets to his feet, stretching his arms over his head. His manhood, even though no longer hard, is still too magnificent to look away from. I could've had that thing inside me earlier, gloriously stretching my insides, and I ruined it. The moment I saw how close it was to my pussy, I completely freaked out.

I can give head, and love doing it, I can be eaten out, do sixty-nine, play with toys—I can do everything with another person except for sex. Once it reaches that point, my pussy dries up like the desert. I can't think straight, and the only thing I know is that fear has consumed me, and I need to get out, out, out before things go any further.

Axil feels different, though, compared to other sexual partners I've had. When he says there's no rush, it seems like he means it. And the problem is that I want things to go further. He's the first person I've actually wanted to have sex with since The Incident. I want to figure out a way to make my body cooperate because I know he'd give me the kind of orgasm that would melt my brain.

The doorbell rings again just as Axil starts pulling on his pants. I don't realize I'm still gawking at him until he looks up and says, "I thought you were eager to answer the door."

"Right! Yes, that," I stammer, rushing through the hall and into the dining room. I swing it open to find Zev leaning against the door frame, a boyish smile on his face as he reads something on his phone. A text perhaps? "Hi, there, Zev. What brings you by?"

His eyes finally leave his screen and widen when he sees what I'm wearing, or more accurately, how much I'm not wearing. "Apologies, Vanessa. Am I interrupting something?"

"Not at all, little brother," Axil replies for me as he approaches from behind. "We were just having a lovely mid-morning snooze." He managed to put his pants on, but not a shirt, and with me still wrapped in a towel, it's abundantly clear what we were doing. The only thing that could make it more obvious is if I had Axil's dried come all over my chin.

Oh god, do I? I wonder as I reach up and feel along my chin, trying to make it look casual. I find nothing on my face, but I doubt the action looked as natural as I intended. Luckily, Axil and Zev don't seem to be paying attention as Zev gives Axil a knowing smirk and says, "Is that so?"

Axil ignores his teasing and asks, "What are *you* doing here?"

"I am here to spread Lady Norton's ashes with you, Vanessa," he says, pulling out a piece of paper and mouthing the words as he silently reads. "Just beneath the bench swing in the garden, apparently."

"Ah, right. Okay, well, come on in. I'll get changed really quick," I say, stepping aside so Zev can enter.

As I leave the dining room, I hear Zev say, "Axil, a word?" followed by Axil sighing, and the front door shutting behind them. I try not to think about it as I go into the bedroom and put clothes on. Whatever they're discussing is not my business. The timing of it, however, makes me wonder if the thing they're discussing is me.

Is Zev telling him not to get involved with me? I can't imagine that's it, as Zev has no reason to say those things, but that doesn't stop my mind from wandering down that path. Does Zev not think I'm good enough for his brother? Not pretty enough? Or does it have something to do with my weight?

No. Not doing this.

I step in front of the mirror and lean in, so my face is almost touching the glass. Then I point at my reflection. "Your fat ass is fine just the way it is. Not everything is about you. Let it go."

Then I recite the words "it's not about you" silently to myself as I add a stroke of blush to my cheeks and put on lip gloss before striding down the hall. This is just a casual fling with Axil, anyway. He's no longer insufferable to be around, and he stood up for me when Trevor started acting like a dick at Tipsy's. Then he got me out of there when I had a panic attack. So he cares about me, that much is clear. I'm starting to care about him too.

And the things he does to me...my god. His body is somehow a finely tuned machine as much as it is a work of art. His hands, the strength and warmth of his arms, and that mouth... a shiver rips through me at the memory of last night when he first called me a "good girl." It was definitely strange, at first. It's never happened before with previous partners. But beneath the initial shock was something else, something I didn't realize even existed in my mind: elation.

Words spoken in that low, rough voice of his as he showered me with praise made my toes curl, all while giving me the best orgasm of my life. I have to think that part of the reason it was so amazing is *because* of the "good girl" thing. It felt embarrassing, and I didn't know if I was embarrassed to hear the words or embarrassed for Axil for saying them. Then it felt good. Very good. A tingling sensation that started in my belly and spread to my fingers and toes, and suddenly, I wanted to hear him say it again. I became desperate for it. I wanted his smoldering gray eyes on me as he told me how good I was.

Maybe it's something my sex life has been missing. Or maybe it's only with Axil, and it would feel weird and wrong with anyone else. But as much fun as I've had with him, I know this is not a relationship of any kind. It's a temporary, casual thing. I'm going back to L.A., eventually, and he's made no mention of wanting anything more serious, so I'll enjoy it while it lasts.

As I grab Aunt Franny's urn from the mantle in the living room, I hear Zev and Axil come back inside. "Shall we?" I ask Zev as I meet them in the dining room.

"We shall," he says, gesturing for me to lead the way.

Axil has an odd look on his face, a mix of nerves and stress that must have come from the talk he and Zev just had. "I must, um… I must make a call. I shall return after you spread Lady Norton's ashes."

I nod, holding back the many questions I have about the shift in his mood.

Axil leaves, and Zev and I head outside, going around the right side of the house, past the garage, and down a small hill to where the garden is. A thin layer of snow covers the garden with dead fallen leaves trapped in the pile and peeking out. I wish I could see the garden in the summer when her plants and flowers are in full bloom. Though, the way it is now certainly matches the tone of what we're doing.

We sit on the bench swing as Zev reads a letter he wrote to my aunt, thanking her for being such a thoughtful neighbor and a loyal friend. He thanks her for introducing him to coleslaw, which seems an odd thing for a grown man to never have tasted before, but I brush it off. Overall, the letter is incredibly sweet.

I didn't realize how close each of the brothers were to Aunt Franny. But when Zev's voice begins to crack with emotion at the end, I find myself impressed and even a little jealous that Aunt Franny, a sassy woman in her seventies, was able to become besties with all her extremely handsome neighbors.

Zev gives me a hug after he spreads some of her ashes beneath the bench swing, and says he has to head to work. Axil reemerges from the path between our houses a few minutes after with a soft smile tugging at his lips. I brush away the urge to analyze the possible reasons for the smile and who he needed to call so urgently because it's none of my business. He could be sleeping with other people and that would be fine with me. Perfectly fine. Not at all irritating. Not at all.

Axil takes my hand in his and brings it to his lips and all thoughts leave my head. "What do you say," he kisses my knuckles, then takes the tip of my pointer finger into his mouth and nips, "we look for your next clue?"

"Uh, yeah," I mumble, breathless.

"Yeah?" he repeats, taking my middle finger into his mouth and giving it a flick of his tongue.

"Yes," I reply, clearing my throat, trying to break free of his spell. "That sounds like a great plan."

He chuckles, noticing his effect on me, and nods toward the house before pulling me along by the hand.

"She said the next letter was somewhere in the bedroom," I tell him once we get inside. "I've looked around but..." I shrug, "nothing." We kick our shoes off by the door, and before I turn to face him, he has his arms wrapped around me, my back against his chest. His hands roam my breasts and stomach as he kisses just beneath my ear.

"I missed you," he whispers, palming my breast.

"Mmm," I moan as he squeezes it. "You were gone for what, ten minutes?"

He grunts. "I do not care. Any amount of time spent away from you, not touching you, is wasted."

I can't argue his logic. I'm growing addicted to his touch, and I certainly don't mind being on the receiving end of his affections. My last few relationships were not great. They lacked emotional intimacy and loving touches. But with Axil, every touch is loving. I can feel it.

Turning in his arms, I wrap my hands behind his neck and pull him down for a kiss. "I thought we were going to look for clues," I mutter against his lips.

He growls in response. "Fine." Then he sighs. "I suppose we should." Axil looks around the dining room, then down at me. "This house deserves to be cared for."

We go into the bedroom, and he starts searching the closet as I continue with the dresser drawers. After that yields no results, I decide to check under the bed. I sneeze as I lie on my side, noticing all the dust beneath. As I reach for a plastic storage container, Axil yells, "Found it!"

He tosses the paperback book it was hidden in aside and helps me to my feet. I tear open the letter and see "WHAT" written across the top. "It's a clue!" I shout, doing a triumphant hop in place.

My Dearest Vanessa,

In my black velvet jewelry box, you will find my engagement ring in the top compartment on the left in a royal blue ring box. Keep it, it's yours. Or sell it. I don't care what you do with it, honestly.

Can I let you in on a little secret? It's not my favorite piece of jewelry. My most prized possession is the ruby necklace with black diamonds on the thin white gold chain. That can be found on the bottom level of the same jewelry box in the gray drawstring jewelry bag.

I must insist you keep this piece, and I would be oh so delighted if you would wear it, as it holds a special memory from my past. Not long after we married, Victor and I got into a terrible argument. He was spending too much of our money on things we didn't need. Specifically, things I didn't need. He would come home from work every day with flowers, perfume, jewelry, or a pretty dress for me, and I kept telling him to stop.

We were saving for a house, as we lived in a small apartment at the time, and I had not asked for any of these gifts. When I would tell him to stop, and we needed to be more mindful about how our money was spent, he would brush it off with, "I make good money, and I want to spend it on my wife."

This may sound sweet to you, and I found it romantic as well, at first. However, we had goals we couldn't reach, goals we both thought were important, and his spending was setting us back. It frustrated me to no end. I was not working at the time (few wives did, it was a different era), so there was nothing I could do to help.

I refused to speak to Victor for two days after he brought home a stunning pair of leather gloves. That's how angry I was. He tried begging me, he brought home more flowers, and he attempted to bake a cake for me (and almost burned the apartment down). On the third day, Victor came home with a gift for me to open, and I threw a book at his head and walked out.

He ran after me and got down on his knees on the sidewalk and said, "I returned every gift I could to get you this. No new money has been spent in order to buy this necklace, and I wanted to show you that I am listening. I don't know how to love you the way you deserve to be loved without showering you with gifts. But I know we can't afford for me to keep doing this, and I want a house just as badly as you do."

My arms were crossed as he spoke, loving the sweet words, but skeptical about how serious he was.

Then he said, "Please, let me show you I can be the kind of man worthy of your love."

He promised to curb his spending, and stick to a budget, and from that day forward, he made good on his promise.

This necklace is a symbol of the kind of marriage we had. It was not perfect, but it was exquisite, nonetheless. He kept the promises he made. He made me laugh. When I cried, his arms were there in an instant, holding me until I felt better. We fought, but we always forgave each other.

Even though many claim that marriage is "work," ours did not feel that way. If it was work, then it was work we were both eager to do. Loving him always felt as easy as breathing, even when I wanted nothing more than to throw a book at his head.

I hope one day, should you decide to marry, that your marriage is like ours was. May this necklace serve as a reminder that you should settle for nothing less.

It was here we all sat, with wine in our glasses as we had a good chat, laughing about love and life and this and that. Axil played a prank, that sneaky rat, causing Zev to trip over his own feet and fall flat. These rascals are my family, even when they behave like brats. "I'm going to get him," Zev said. "Lady Norton, please hold my hat."

All my love,

Aunt Franny

"The dining room," Axil and I say simultaneously as we finish reading the letter. Even without Axil's help, Aunt Franny front-loaded the answer to the riddle in the first sentence. I doubt the next clue will be as easy to figure out, though. Aunt Franny's too clever for that. She wants to tease me just as much as she wants Axil to help me solve each riddle.

I race into the dining room, Axil close on my heels. I look beneath the vase of fake sunflowers in the middle of the table. Nothing. Axil pulls out all six chairs and starts looking beneath the table as I check between the stack of folded cloth napkins. When Axil comes up empty, I check the armoire next to the table, filled with fancy china that I know has almost never been used. There are centuries-old teacups in here that I know are extremely delicate, so it takes me a while to check beneath and in each one.

"Found it!" Axil shouts, tearing through the scotch tape that held Aunt Franny's next letter to where she hid it beneath the chair.

I rip it open as soon as I get my hands on it, and after a quick scan, I find no clues or riddles to solve. I'm disappointed, and I'm sure Axil can tell by the sigh I let out, but then I feel guilty for the disappointment. Like a letter from my late aunt isn't enough of a reward. Although, she did raise my expectations by telling me there's a pile of cash at the end of this treasure hunt, so I suppose I shouldn't feel too bad.

"My dearest Vanessa," I read aloud.

"You do not have to share it with me, if you do not want to," Axil reminds me. It's then that I realize how differently I see Axil compared to when we first met. Because I don't mind sharing these letters with him.

"It's okay," I say. "I want to."

He ducks his head shyly, his cheeks turning a bright pink shade as his lips curl into a smile. I thought he was mesmerizing before... Shy Axil is a sight I never want to forget.

I clear my throat as I continue reading the letter. "Yes, it's just another letter. No, there is no riddle to solve. There are two clues left, and I have no doubt you will find them soon and reach the end of this treasure hunt. I thank you for humoring me. I had a delightful time putting it together and hiding the letters around the house. I hope you've enjoyed it too. Or at the very least, I hope this has provided enough of a distraction to dull the pain of my passing, and the deeper pain you've felt since coming back here."

My voice breaks on the last line, but I take a breath, trying to mask it.

"Now, my dear girl, I sincerely hope the boys next door have been kind to you." I notice Axil chuckle at that. "I know they have because they are good, decent fellows. But they are different, as I'm sure you've noticed. They are not like other men you've come across."

Axil's face hardens, and his posture turns rigid. I shift my position slightly so I can continue watching his reactions as I read on.

"I'm sure you've found that the majority of the male race to be lacking. I, too, have noticed this. It's why I never remarried. How could I possibly go from having the perfect male specimen to an ignorant, lazy fool with a face like a boiled turnip?"

Laughter escapes me in a loud, undignified howl.

"The Monroe brothers, you see, are not and will never become the boiled turnips of the male race. They are abundantly curious about the world around them, always learning as much as they can about others in order to understand them. This curiosity is a profound and unique quality in a person. Do not dismiss them as 'just like the rest' because they are not. They are more. All my love, Aunt Franny. P.S. Perhaps your next clue can be found there, next door. Ask Axil where he keeps his goodies."

"Goodies?" I ask Axil the moment I finish reading. "What kind of goodies are we talking about here? Sex toys?"

He scratches the back of his neck, looking embarrassed. "I believe she is referring to my stash of candy. I shall show you where it is. Come," he says, gesturing for me to follow. We leave out the back door and head toward his house.

"I can't believe I haven't seen your place yet," I mutter as he opens the front door. My mouth falls open when I step inside. It's huge. I mean, you can tell it's a mansion from the outside, but a house filled with grown men... I never expected it to look so nice, or so clean. The interior is a dark wood color much like a log cabin. The front door opens into the living room, and the design is an open floor plan with the humongous kitchen directly behind the living room. There's a wide, curved staircase that leads from the edge of the living room to the upstairs hallway, with a room at the top of the stairs, and more off to either side. The first floor is similar, with rooms to the left and right of the living room and kitchen.

"Wow, this place…" I trail off.

The decor in the living room is minimal, but intentional, and with a classically masculine feel. There are wood carvings and framed photographs on windowsills, the coffee table, and the mantle above the fireplace. Thick plaid blankets are draped across the backs of all three enormous couches that face the TV in the far corner of the room. There is one worn brown leather couch in the center, and the other two couches are a deep burgundy. All three are overstuffed and oversized— the perfect couches for napping, I assume.

"It's so…"

Axil laughs as he takes my hand. "I hope the ends of these statements are good," he says. "Come. I will show you my goodies."

I stop, planting my feet. "You know that sounded sexual, right?"

"I do," he replies casually. "You did not think I brought you over here just to read a letter, did you?"

I let out an exaggerated gasp. "You sneaky, beautiful giant."

He leads me to the walk-in pantry in the kitchen and pulls out a drawer along the bottom with "Axil" written in marker on a piece of tape. The drawer is filled to the brim with candy, and none of the filler garbage candy either. This is high-end gourmet candy. He's got individually wrapped peanut butter cups with organic ingredients, dark chocolate-covered ginger, sour gummies, sour peach rings, chocolate-covered raisins, and an entire sandwich bag filled with pink Starburst. Just the pink ones.

"Holy shit. You've got a bit of a sweet tooth, eh?" I mutter, seemingly unable to let go of the Starburst.

"You can have that," he says when he sees it. "I only like the red ones."

"Are you serious?" I ask in shock. I've never heard of anyone preferring red to pink.

"Yes," he replies. "Mylo only eats the yellow ones, and Kyan likes orange. Zev does not like them at all. That leaves the pink."

"Are you sure? You've tried the pink ones, right? You've actually tasted them?"

His brow furrows. "Yes, Vanessa. I have tried them, and I do not like them."

"Wow, you might be the perfect human," I say under my breath as I open the bag and start unwrapping the pink ones.

"Here it is," he says, uncovering a folded letter beneath the pile of candy. Axil holds it in front of me, but when I go to reach for it, he holds it above his head. "While this is certainly pressing business, I have other ideas," he says, his voice dropping to a low purr.

I shoot him a smirk. "Such as?"

He turns on his heel and heads down the hall, and my stomach flutters as I follow. Axil pulls me into what I assume is his bedroom at the far end of the hall. He tosses the letter onto a bookshelf by the door and wraps me in his arms. Then his mouth is on mine, hungry and desperate, as his hands roam my body, eventually settling on my ass. He grips me there as he groans against my mouth. "I love your body," he whispers, then I feel his tongue against the seam of my lips. I let him in as I unbutton his flannel. If only he would wear a shirt that I could remove quicker.

He pulls my shirt over my head and gets to work on my bra clasp as I pull down my leggings. With a triumphant cheer, he unhooks it in the back, and I let the straps fall down my arms slowly as my breasts are bared. Axil grunts as he shakes his head, his gaze moving over my body in such an intimate way, it feels like he's touching me. "Beautiful."

Pulling me close, he kisses my cheek, then my neck, and over to my ear. "Get on the bed," he commands. He steps back to give me room, and when I hesitate, he says, "Now, Vanessa. Do not make me wait."

A shiver rips through me at his tone, husky and rough as if he's already on the edge of losing control. I don't move. "What happens if I do make you wait?" I ask, my hands going to my breasts. "What if I just…" I trail off, my eyes closing as I play with my nipples.

I hear him swallow, then a growl starts to build in his chest. "You would defy me?" My breath catches as he unbuttons his pants and steps toward me, closing the distance between our bodies. He pushes his pants down his legs and steps out of them before he lowers his head, his lips hovering less than an inch above mine. "Are you sure that is what you want?"

If it means he'll refuse to touch me, then no, that's not what I want. Not at all. I want his hands all over my body, and I want it right fucking now. Did I think I could be in control here? That I would even want that? Not letting him put his hands on me this morning was thrilling, and it made me feel powerful to have a giant man like Axil quivering under my mouth, but that was different. I had a plan. Now, I don't, other than to see how he reacts when I refuse to obey.

I can't exactly bend to his will now, though. Not after making it seem like I'm in a rebellious frame of mind. Keeping one hand on my breast, I let the other travel down my stomach, and between my legs. My clit throbs as I swipe a finger over it.

Axil's breath is hot on my neck as he inches closer, still not touching me. "Are you wet, Vanessa?"

"Mmm-hmm," I reply, nodding as I continue running my fingers through my folds.

"Feels good?" he asks, his nose brushing through my hair as he inhales my scent.

"Yes," I say, sucking in a breath. My chest is heaving as I work my clit faster, harder.

His tongue traces the shell of my ear and I moan. "And you do not want me to touch you? To fulfill your needs?," he whispers, then bites down on my earlobe. I can't take it anymore. I turn and throw my arms around his neck, but he stays perfectly still, not touching me.

"Please, Axil," I beg, no longer worried about how I look or who's in charge (it's him). I just want his hands on me.

"Get on the bed," he says again.

This time, I obey and crawl into the middle, looking over my shoulder at him, seductively. "How do you want me?" My eyes land on his cock and widen, still in disbelief over his size. He's just... wow, he's big. Even his balls are impressively large, hanging heavily behind his cock. I'm surprised by how desperately I want that cock inside me.

My body should be frozen in fear at the idea of having sex with Axil, but it's not. I want him, and I trust him.

"On your knees, leaning back on your heels," he says as his cock bobs in front of him, as if it's reaching for me.

Axil keeps his gaze locked on mine as he strides toward me with the grace of a predator hunting its prey. Then he sits on the bed and opens his arms. "Come."

My pussy clenches at the command, knowing I will soon. I throw my leg over his, and he puts his hands on my hips, guiding me until I'm straddling him, the head of his cock inching closer to my entrance.

"Do you wish to try?" he asks, reaching one hand up to cup my cheek when he sees my gaze widen at his size. Then his thumb moves along my bottom lip, tracing it.

"Yes," I reply in more of a whimper than coherent words. I part my lips and wrap them around the tip of his thumb, sucking on it.

"Would you like to pick a safe word?" he asks. Why have I not considered this before? Because it felt like I didn't need one, simply because there was nothing too kinky about my encounters? Only now do I realize how dumb that was. A safe word helps two people keep boundaries in place. It doesn't matter what activities are involved.

I nod, "Let's go with," my eyes drop down between our bodies, and "banana" flies out of my mouth. Ugh, banana? Really?

He laughs when he sees how red my cheeks are.

"Very well," he says, still smiling. "You say 'banana' and we stop. It is that simple. Say the word at any moment you feel uncomfortable, okay?"

Words evade me because I'm so nervous I'm going to fuck this up, so I just nod again. I don't want to have to say *banana* at all. I just want this to work, and for this frustrating, embarrassing sexual hang-up to be a thing of the past.

Leaning down to kiss him, I jerk back as a thought pops into my head. "Do you want a safe word too?" He probably doesn't need one, but it can't hurt to ask.

He tilts his head to the side as he thinks. "I will use 'banana' as well."

A grateful smile tugs at my lips. He's humoring me, I know he is, but I don't care. It puts me at ease.

"Mmm," he groans, his eyes locked on my mouth. He wraps his arm around me, splaying his fingers at the small of my back, and pulls me closer until my nipples graze the top of his chest. "Good girl," he says as I slowly lower myself until his cock brushes against my pussy.

My eyes instinctively pinch shut as I push the images of Trevor from my mind. I can feel my heartbeat start to race.

No.

No, I need to fight this.

"Hey," Axil says, crooking a finger beneath my chin. "Do you wish to stop?" he asks.

"No," I automatically reply, opening my eyes to look at him. "I don't, but what if I can't do this?" The memories continue to flood my mind, of Trevor's rancid breath on my chest that night as he held me down, the hateful look in his eyes as I cried.

"Keep your eyes on me," Axil says, his tone soft but firm. "There is no one here but us."

I feel my breaths start to even out the longer I keep my gaze locked on him. The sight of him is comforting. The feel of his arms around me makes me feel safe. I adjust my body slightly, so my pussy is directly above his cock, and I reach between our bodies to guide him in.

The moment our bodies are connected, he presses the tip of his nose against mine and whispers, "You can do this. Just me and you, Vanessa. No one else."

Axil doesn't move. He keeps himself perfectly still as I continue a slow, agonizing descent down his length. His expression becomes strained as he struggles to keep his eyes open. The man deserves an Olympic medal in restraint.

With Trevor absent from my mind, I decide to take that next step in ridding myself of this pain by slamming my hips down until I'm speared on him, and our bodies meet hip to hip.

He groans as his fingers dig into my back. "Hurts?" he asks, brushing the hair off my forehead.

"No," I reply, panting. In truth, it hurts a little. I would be amazed if it didn't after twenty years of zero dicks inhabiting the space, but it's nowhere near as much pain as I expected to feel. There's a slight burn, but as I continue breathing, my muscles relax around him, and I start to get comfortable. "More."

He thrusts upward slowly. A muscle in his jaw ticks as sweat forms on his brow. "You feel so good, Vanessa. Fuck!" he grunts, his voice shaking.

He's trying so hard for me.

I take his face in my hands and lean down, planting a gentle kiss on his lips. "Harder, please. I want more of you."

Just as the words leave my mouth, Axil's fingers bite into the skin of my hips as he slams me down on his cock. Warmth pools in my belly, slowly curling and spreading throughout my body as my muscles grow taut. I put my hands on his shoulders and hold on as he continues his thrusts, taking me along for the ride.

My eyes fall closed, briefly, and the terror comes rushing back. Axil notices immediately.

"Eyes on me," he commands, his fingers getting tangled in my hair as he presses his forehead against mine. "Don't let the memories take you away, my love. Stay here."

I do as he says, and relief washes over me as I continue to gaze down at him, and the images fail to return.

"Good girl, Vanessa," he says as he nuzzles my neck, "So good. Take all of me." His tongue moves down to my chest until his lips close over my nipple.

When his teeth brush against the hardened tip, I throw my head back and scream. I have no idea what I say, or if I even formed words, I just know it's impossible to stay silent with what his body is doing to mine.

"Wait," he says, pulling all the way out. I whimper at how empty I suddenly feel. Axil reaches down and runs two fingers along my slit, then puts them directly in his mouth, obscenely licking off my juices as he watches me. "There is nothing sweeter than you," he says as he reaches down, going for more. I assume he's going to lick his fingers clean again, but he doesn't. Instead, he just pulls me close and slides back in.

"Yesss," I whisper, scraping my nails lightly against his scalp with each pump. I feel myself getting closer, my back arching as everything inside me tightens like a bowstring about to snap.

He kisses me, his lips brutal and rough as he swallows my screams, my muscles tightening as my release edges closer. Then I feel something... else. Something pressed against my asshole, circling it. I jerk back to look at him, a question in his eyes. "Banana?" he asks.

"No," I reply quickly, surprising even me. It's not something I've ever done, or even thought I could do, given my reluctance in the front. My backdoor has been locked up tight, and I hadn't really considered changing that policy. Maybe I *am* vanilla, as Sam's nickname for me suggests, including in the bedroom. Or maybe I haven't been with anyone I felt safe trying new things with. I guess it doesn't matter. All I know is that with Axil, I want more. I want it all.

He uses my come to lubricate the area before slowly entering me with his finger. Instinctively, I hold my breath, not knowing if what I'm feeling is good or bad. It just feels tight. My entire body feels tight.

"Shh, relax. You must breathe for me," he says. I take a few shallow breaths, and I feel myself let go. As the breaths get deeper, Axil's finger continues to push deeper inside me, and I start to feel full. So utterly filled by Axil as he fucks me in both holes. I never expected to enjoy this, but when he eases the second finger in, I clench around him. My hips writhe as I chase my release, and within moments, my entire body is shaking.

He removes his fingers and holds me in place, my body boneless as he pounds into me. Axil roars his release, his forehead pressed against my chest as his hips jerk erratically.

We exchange soft words and gentle kisses as we come down, then Axil tosses me onto my back on the bed, my head bouncing against the pillow. Then he wraps me in his arms and pulls me close until we're on our sides. Our legs entwine as we lie there, and he presses a gentle kiss to the tip of my nose before rubbing it with his.

We grow silent for several minutes, just holding each other close. "I liked that," I tell him.

"Yeah?" he asks, brushing a lock of hair behind my ear. "You would do it again?"

"I think so," I reply honestly, realizing this is the most vulnerable I've ever felt with another person. Not during sex, or even when he stuck a finger in my ass—those were intimate moments, but I didn't feel as exposed as I do right now, talking about sex after the fact. "I trust you."

His lips curve into a lopsided, boyish smile. "I know this is a gift you do not give freely, so I am honored."

I chuckle, agreeing with him. There are very few people I trust, and Axil is the only man in the bunch. He's the only one who was willing to wait for me to be ready to have sex, and it turned out, he didn't need to wait all that long. I wanted this, probably from the moment I met him, if I'm being honest with myself. There's just something about him.

Moments later, I shoot up in bed at a startling realization. "We forgot to use protection." I drop my head in my hands. "Fuck, oh fuck, oh fuck."

I hear the bed shift next to me, and when I look up, Axil's gone. I hear the sink turn on in the adjoining bathroom, and when he returns, he places a black box on the nightstand next to me. Condoms. The biggest ones I've ever seen, in fact.

"It was a thoughtless mistake," he says with a sigh. "I am deeply sorry, Vanessa."

"It's okay," I mutter as I examine the box. "Jesus, were these made for dinosaur dicks?"

He chuckles as he takes a wet cloth and wipes the inside of my thighs.

"I forgot too," I remind him. "It should be fine. Not that I've ever had to worry about it, really. I don't know what happened."

I suck in a breath as he moves the cloth over the seam of my pussy, cleaning off the come that continues to spill out of me. Then he tosses the cloth into the hamper and climbs back into bed. "Whatever comes of this, if anything comes from it, I am with you. Fully. I shall do whatever you want."

Leaning in, I kiss his lips, deep and quick. "Thank you," I tell him. He didn't need to say those words, but I appreciate that he took the time to do so, knowing I was anxious about it.

"What are your plans for tonight?" he asks.

I search my mind, trying to remember everything I haven't gotten done. "Well, I—"

"And tomorrow? And the next day?"

Laughing, I push against his chest, playfully, as he tries pulling me closer. Then he rolls us until I'm lying on top of him, my chin resting above his beating heart. "Well, I have to go dress shopping at some point with Sam for this stupid reunion."

"Reunion?" he asks, running his fingers through my hair.

"Yeah, it's our high school reunion," I say, sighing. "Twenty years. Can you believe it's happening right when I'm home? What kind of twisted sorcery is that?" I truly do not want to go, but Sam feels like she has to go since they're including her in some slideshow they made, and I can't let her go alone. Especially knowing Beth and Trevor will be there, and knowing what he did to Sam…I would never forgive myself if she had a panic attack like I did, and no one was there to carry her out.

There's also a chance that upon seeing Trevor again, I'll have another panic attack. I really don't want that to happen, but there's also a part of me that wants to face these assholes and show them I'm okay. That they don't own me. I'm sick of feeling like I can't go anywhere in this town because I might run into Beth or Trevor or even Caitlyn.

"I shall accompany you," Axil says, "as your date."

Um. Okay. It's not what I expected him to say, but I suppose I shouldn't be surprised. He was there the last time I saw Trevor, and obviously, it didn't go well. But if he's there, Sam will feel like a third wheel, and I really need to be focused on her, just as I know she'll be focused on me. If Axil comes, my attention will be split between Sam and Axil while also worrying if Axil and Trevor will throw down, and I'm definitely not in the mood to deal with that.

"That's really sweet of you to offer," I reply, choosing my words carefully so as not to hurt his feelings. "But I've already told Sam I'd go as her date, and it's already going to be stressful enough with Trevor there. I think it's probably best if yo—"

"Trevor is going to be there?" Axil shouts. "No. You cannot go."

"Excuse me?" I spit back. "I can't go? You're actually telling me I'm not allowed to do something?"

Axil's jaw clenches. "I do not want that monster within a mile of you. After what he has done? Why would you even want to go?"

"I don't want to go, actually. Sam is going and wants me there for support. I'm doing it for her."

"Fine," Axil says, throwing his head back on the pillow, exasperated. "I will have Zev go as Sam's date, and I shall be yours."

"Well, no," I stammer. "That's not... I wasn't suggesting we just stick one of your brothers with Sam. She doesn't know Zev that well, and I doubt she wants him present on a night that's bound to be filled with awkward small talk and traumatic flashbacks."

"All the more reason for Zev and me to be there. We can assist both of you during your temporary bouts of insanity."

Immediately, it's clear that Axil regrets his words. "No, that is not what I meant. I am sorry. I was simply saying that—"

"You know what?" I say, interrupting. Now I'm annoyed. He apologized, but he still let the words out, and they hurt, especially from him. "It's fine. But I'm telling you that Sam and I are going to the reunion alone."

"That is preposterous," he replies, getting to his feet. He circles the bed and grabs his pants off the floor. "A reunion is a formal event, is it not?"

"I mean, yes," I say, not knowing where he's going with this, but finding it odd that he feels the need to confirm what a reunion is. Has he never been to one? Or heard of them?

"Then I should be there. I have seen it many times when a woman is invited to a formal event, and her man goes with her," he stammers, pulling his pants on.

Seen it many times? What is he talking about? Like, in the movies? Has he never been to a wedding or school dance before?

"Men, if they are good men, accompany their women to such events. And you are my woman, so I must—"

"Whoa, what are you talking about?" I ask, holding up my hands. "Suddenly I'm your woman? Axil, we've never discussed labels."

"Labels?" he asks, creases forming on his brow. "I am not following."

I stand and pick up my clothes from the floor. If he's getting dressed, I'm not just going to lie here naked like an idiot. "I'm not your girlfriend. Or your woman. Whatever you'd prefer to call it."

He jerks back as if he's been slapped. "How can you say that? After all that has passed between us... You cannot tell me you do not feel what I feel."

"Look, I don't know what you're feeling, and I really like spending time with you." I put my bra on, backward at first, then I grumble under my breath until I get it right. "Sex with you is also a good time," I continue, "but that's all this is. It's just a casual arrangement that allows both of us to have fun while I'm still in town."

"Still in town?" he says so quietly I almost didn't hear him. When his eyes find mine, they're wide and wounded, filled with emotion he's trying to contain. "You are still planning on leaving?"

I tug my shirt over my head, and my mouth falls open, but the words don't come. I hadn't decided to stay, exactly, and give up on my life in L.A., but I've also reached a point where I'm not particularly eager to go back. "I...I don't know," I finally reply, giving him the most honest answer I can.

He rubs his eyes, then runs a hand through his hair as his gaze drops to the plush, light gray carpet that matches his eyes. Except that, right now, his eyes are much darker, stormier gray than usual. He turns away from me and leans his hands on the windowsill, his head hanging in defeat. Eventually, he opens the window and deeply breathes in the cool air filling the room.

I want to go to him. I want to wrap my arms around his middle and tell him it'll be all right, that I'll stay, and we can be together. But that would be a lie. There's nothing I can do to comfort him right now and I hate it.

When he lifts his head, he turns and looks at me over his shoulder. "So leave."

"What?" I ask, unsure I heard him correctly.

He stands, grabs the letter off the bookcase by the door, and shoves it into my hands. "You wish to go? Then go."

His face hardens, the warmth in his gray eyes from earlier now completely gone. There's nothing left but resentment and disappointment. "Axil," I begin, but nothing follows, because I have no clue what to say. I just know I don't want him to keep looking at me like I'm his worst enemy.

"Go!" he shouts, the sound so deep and threatening I can hardly believe it came from his mouth. My body springs into motion, grabbing my shoes off the floor and running out his door and down the hallway.

Tears stream down my face as I pass Mylo, who offers a friendly wave, but then asks, "What is wrong?" as I reach for the front door. I don't stop to put my shoes on. I just run barefoot through the wet snow until I make it home. Then I collapse on the kitchen floor and cry into the doormat.

CHAPTER 13

VANESSA

*E*ventually, the tears stop falling, and I pull myself to my feet. I strip off my clothes as I walk toward the bathroom, my bare feet tracking snow and mud through the house. Aunt Franny would kill me if she saw what I was doing. She would probably also kill me for hurting Axil the way I did.

Turning on the shower, I wince at the memory of his face when I told him what we have is casual. He looked so confused, so heartbroken, but how? Why? Did he really assume that because we had sex, that automatically makes me his girlfriend? He can't be that naive. He's had sex with several women, I'm sure of it.

Though I can't deny how incredible the sex is with him. It was also meaningful, given that I was unable to have it with anyone else before him. I'm not sure if we're extremely compatible in bed, or if there's more to it.

I do have feelings for him, but it's not like I'm ready to tell him I love him. That would be insane. We've known each other a handful of days. That's it. Nobody falls in love that fast.

Stepping into the shower, I let the water rinse the tears from my cheeks and the dirt from my feet. As I shampoo my hair, flashes of Axil appear in my mind—of his lips on my neck, of his hands gripping my ass, then I see his heated gaze as he watches me. Every touch, every shuddered breath, he watched me, learning my body based on my reactions. And he kept me focused on him the entire time. He guided me through my trauma in a moment I did not think it possible.

I've never had a guy give me so much focused attention. It's almost overwhelming.

"Ugh," I mutter aloud as I lather my cheeks with foamy face wash. Maybe I'm a dumbass for reacting the way I did. Really, all Axil wanted to do was come to the reunion with me and protect me from Trevor. Is that so terrible?

But he also refused to listen when I told him I preferred to go with Sam, so I could be there for her. He insisted on bringing a date for Sam, a person she doesn't know or trust, just so he could be my date. He clearly didn't care about Sam's needs, and that's fine, he doesn't need to. But I do, and he needs to respect when I say I need to be there for her.

Then he was shocked when I said I wasn't his girlfriend as if that's a decision that can be made without my input. I don't know what the fuck that was, but I found it unsettling. How can he make an assumption like that without asking me how I feel? Did he expect me to drop everything and move here for him? Just because he's the first guy to stick a finger in my ass, he thinks he owns me now?

I run a bar of soap over my body, fuming at the thought of him trying to boss me around. Does he think I want to be told what to do just because I liked it during sex? That feels like something I shouldn't have to explain—that during sex, it's totally different.

Maybe he's more inexperienced than I thought. Just because he's had sex with other women doesn't mean he has a grasp on how to date. Speaking of which, he hasn't even offered to take me out on a date. There has been no wining and dining. I deserve to be wined and dined.

I step out of the shower, towel off, and leave the bathroom, dirty clothes in hand, without looking in the mirror. I can't bring myself to do it right now.

Tugging on an oversized T-shirt and comfy cotton panties that are not at all sexy, I climb into bed and bury myself beneath the covers. All the lights are still on, and it's not even seven p.m. yet, so it's likely I won't be able to fall asleep. Then I remember the letter from Aunt Franny that's still in the kitchen.

I throw off the covers and head toward the kitchen. Tearing open the letter, I stand, frozen in place. I can't bring myself to unfold the paper.

"Come on," I whine, my hands starting to shake. "I could really use a mind-bending riddle to solve." Ultimately, I can't do it. My hands refuse to cooperate, and I can't bring myself to read this letter without him.

Axil should be here, I realize. He should be finishing this treasure hunt with me. I want to feel his presence in this house, to feel his warmth as he stands by my side. I want to hear his laughter, all deep and rich, and watch the dimples form in his cheeks while he does.

I can't believe I didn't tell him what he means to me. That maybe I do feel what he feels. Because if what he feels is this profound burning hunger to feel his skin on mine, this ache in my chest the moment we say good-bye, and a blinding desire to spend every waking minute breathing in the same air as him, then yes, I do feel what he feels.

Suddenly, I'm grabbing Aunt Franny's warmest bathrobe, shoving my feet into boots I found in the coat closet that are definitely too big, and stomping toward the back door. The cold night air bites at my bare legs, giving me an incentive to run.

I walk past the front door and around the side of the house. If Axil's window is still open, or at least unlocked, I can sneak into his room and apologize with my lips wrapped around his cock.

Trying to avoid any sensors that could set off lights or alarms, I take wide, careful steps until I make it to his window. The room is dark, but the window is cracked open about an inch and the shade is up. I can see the outline of his legs on the bed. He's in there, but possibly asleep.

I consider knocking, but the idea of being able to wake him with my body instead of scaring the shit out of him seems much better to me. I press the buttons on either side of the screen inward, then lift it until it locks at the top. Then I grab the bottom edge of the window and push up slowly. The window is low enough that I can climb inside without having to pull myself up, which is convenient since I couldn't do a pull-up to save my life.

I don't get inside gracefully, but I do get in there quietly. And I'm pleased to find Axil still asleep with his back facing me, so there's no chance he caught me in any of those unflattering, spread-eagle-like poses as I shimmied inside.

Toeing off my boots, I drop the bathrobe to the floor and crawl onto the bed. I notice Axil's wearing loose sweatpants, but no shirt, so I cautiously lie down behind him and press my lips to the middle of his back. His skin feels dry here, and I make a mental note to give him a back rub with some of my moisturizer. He groans, not fully awake yet, so I place my hand on his arm and let my fingers trail over his shoulder—hmm, dry here too—and up his neck as I continue kissing his back. "Axil," I whisper. "Axil, wake up."

He turns, his arms coming around me without ever opening his eyes. "Mmm," he groans, "my love."

I bring my hand to his cheek. I can't see him well in the dark, but I can just make out his most striking features. Letting my fingers explore him, I trace along his sharp cheekbones with feather light touches, over the long, proud slope of his nose, and along the creases in his forehead, before circling the base of his horns.

Wait, *what*?

My hand stills as I blink my eyes rapidly. Maybe I'm seeing things. Yes, that must be it. Because if I'm not hallucinating, that means Axil has two horns curling out of his head. The horns are dark, probably black, and end in sharp points. My hand shakes just above the part where horn and head meet, and I wonder if I reach out, will they just disappear? Holding my breath, I drop my hand, inch by inch, until the tips of my fingers land on the smooth, velvety exterior of his thick, black horns.

A choked scream escapes me, and I throw my body backward, scrambling on my elbows until I fall off the bed completely.

Axil hears my scream and awakens, lunging toward the lamp on his nightstand. It clicks on as Axil turns, and as he sinks into an attack stance, his eyes widen in horror as he sees me seeing him for what feels like the first time.

He stands in front of me, but he has cerulean blue skin and thick, black horns jutting out of his head.

Axil is not human.

It's unclear what happens after that. I'm certain that I scream my head off, but only because Axil chases me around the room and begs me to stop. I scoot past him and get the bedroom door open, which feels like a victory, but I'm caught by Mylo and Kyan, and carried into the living room with both of them restraining me. They sit me down in the middle of the brown leather couch, and plop down on either side of me, preventing me from escaping.

"Are you going to kill me?" I whimper through panting breaths, the moment Axil steps in front of me with his arms crossed, still in his... whatever version of him this is with the horns and blue skin.

He winces at my words. "Of course not, Vanessa. I would never lay a hand on you in anger. Never."

I want to believe him. God, I want to so badly, but it's difficult when he looks like an actual monster. I mean, he has dry, coarse scales rather than soft human skin, and frightening horns that end in points as sharp as a knife.

However, the shade of blue is rich and lovely, and his scales look like they contain multiple shades of blue and a hint of silver. They also have a shimmery quality to them. The horns look deadly, sure, but unless he plans to gore me to death, which I doubt he does, I don't think he'd ever use them to hurt me. He's actually really beautiful in this form. Terrifyingly beautiful.

What does it say about me that I just discovered my sort-of boyfriend is an alien and I can't stop thinking about how pretty he is? Shouldn't I be afraid? Shouldn't I be trying to call the authorities and report him? Shouldn't I want to do something other than run my hands over his bare chest?

Mylo nods vehemently. "We are not dangerous. I promise you," he says in a soft voice. "And we have no intention of causing you or your kind any amount of pain. We're just trying to live our lives. Quietly. Undetected."

My next question comes easily. "So, what are you, exactly?"

Axil sighs, rubbing a hand down his face.

"Shall I do the explaining, brother?" Mylo asks since Axil is still as worked up as I am.

"No," Axil replies, looking down at the floor. "It must be me." He moves the coffee table back about three feet and grabs the recliner from the corner of the room, lifts it above his head as if it were a pillow, and places it on the carpet in front of me. Then he sits, his knees almost touching mine. Axil clears his throat, and rubs his palms together, preparing himself for what he's about to tell me. Or, more likely, preparing for my reaction.

"We come from a planet called Sufoi," he says. "I suppose that would make us 'aliens' to you. We are born with blue skin," he gestures to his bare chest, "and horns. We..." he trails off, looking at Mylo nervously.

"You what?" I ask.

"We have another form," Mylo replies.

"The one that looks human?" I ask, knowing that's probably not the answer, given how hesitant they are to say it.

Axil shakes his head solemnly. "No, that is our mask. It is an ability we were given at birth to mask our natural form to blend in with other races."

"See, now you've lost me," I say, looking around at the three brothers.

Kyan leans forward, putting his elbows on his knees and steepling his fingers. "I think we need to go outside. Showing is much easier than telling."

"That is not a good idea," Axil says in protest. "She is already afraid of me. I do not wish to make it worse."

"Well, now you have to show me," I say. I have no idea what they intend to show me, but there's nothing more irritating than someone telling you they have a secret and then not sharing. I would wager the not knowing would haunt me more than any kind of monster would.

I turn to Axil. "Please?"

He runs his fingers over his beard, pondering my request. "Fine."

They drape a puffy winter coat over my shoulders and shove my feet into someone's boots before Axil leads us out the back door, quickly masking his skin and hiding his horns the moment we step outside. My heart squeezes at the sight of him hiding his horns and natural skin tone to fit in with other humans. I understand it, but it's also sort of heartbreaking to see how quickly and easily he hides his true self. Mylo and Kyan flank me on either side as we walk through their backyard, stopping when we get to the edge of the wooded area that spans about half an acre wide.

"If you murder me out here, I'm going to be very upset," I tell them as we get deeper into the woods.

Mylo chuckles. "If we wanted to kill you, we would've done it inside. Anyone could spot us out here."

"I disagree," Kyan adds. "Why would we kill her in the house? Her blood would get everywhere. All over our nice furniture. Out here, we could slice her throat and not worry so much about the mess."

"Huh," Mylo replies, tilting his head to the side as he considers this. "That is a good point. Then we could bury her body in the dirt. It would probably take years for her remains to be discovered."

I swallow the lump in my throat that's starting to form. Is it too late to turn back? How do I escape these freaky aliens without getting caught?

Axil whips around and growls at his brothers. "You. Are not. Helping. Stop scaring her, or I will rip your throats out."

Kyan laughs, unbothered by Axil's threats. "And that would not scare her?"

We reach a small clearing in the middle of the woods with three black tarps strung up on the surrounding trees. Hanging at least fifty feet up, the massive tarps could cover the outside of a three-story building. The edges of the tarps come together, forming a large triangular shape. There appears to be nothing behind the tarps.

"What's this?" I ask.

Mylo nudges Axil with his elbow as he walks past him toward the tarps. "Watch your girl. I shall provide the show and tell here."

Axil steps back until he reaches my side, and looks down at me with sad, remorseful eyes. I feel the back of his hand brush against my knuckles, a request to take my hand. I pull my hand away, instinctively. All I wanted was to give him an apology blow job, to maybe admit that I felt something for him too, something I didn't know what to do with. Now I have no idea what's going on. His lips flatten into a thin line, and I feel like a jerk, but I still don't understand why they're here and what they're planning, so for now, I need to protect myself. Particularly, my heart.

Mylo pushes the tarp aside so he can enter the covered space. A moment later, the air changes, the hair on my arms standing on end as the temperature rises.

I keep my eyes on his feet, the only part of him that I can see behind the tarp. Then a flash, and his feet are no longer the feet of a human, but the enormous dark blue paws of a beast with curled claws scraping the dirt beneath. He ducks his head beneath the rope holding up the tarps and emerges.

A long, steady gasp falls from my lips as I take him in, this massive, winged blue creature with even bigger black horns, a long tail with spikes running down the center, and a head the size of a jeep, with so many sharp fangs I feel faint just looking at them.

"We can transform into what you call *dragons*, Vanessa," Kyan says low into my ear. "Though the correct term for our kind is *draxilio*."

I step back, putting as much distance as I can between me and Mylo, barking out a laugh at the thought of calling this *thing* by name when it looks like it's about to eat me alive. I turn to run, but Axil catches me by the waist, keeping me right where I am.

"Please," Axil begs, his arms still wrapped around me. "Will you let me explain? Please, Vanessa. Let me try."

Mylo shifts back before my eyes, going from dragon, or *draxilio*, rather, to the goofy guy who wears glasses and sweater vests, in a cloud of what looks like dust. "How?" I ask, pointing at his clothes, wondering how he was able to keep his clothes intact, despite shifting into a much larger body and back down to this. "H-how?"

He can't read my mind, so my stammering causes him to tilt his head, waiting for me to finish my question.

"Come," Axil interrupts. "Let us go back to the house and we will answer any questions you have."

I walk back with them, not paying attention to my surroundings, or even noticing how cold it's gotten. I'm in a daze, and I still don't have the full story. I can't believe this. Aliens are real! And I have four living next door to me!

"Did Aunt Franny know?" I ask the moment we return to the living room. It's not the most pressing question I have, and I suppose, ultimately, the answer doesn't matter. I can't bring myself to put any other question before it, though.

"No," Axil replies, clasping his hands together. "She knew we were different, but she never asked specifics and we never told her exactly how we differ from the average human male."

That sounds like her. She's extremely judgmental of most people, but not when they may be part of a marginalized group. She hated most of the people around here because they revealed themselves to be bigots or just plain cruel.

"How are you able to speak English?" I ask.

Mylo scratches his chin, stopping to trace the adorable dimple in the center. "We learned as many human languages as we could before we left Sufoi. We can also read in your language."

Kyan hands me a glass of water and I chug it down. Between sips, I ask, "What happens to your clothes when you shift?"

Mylo smiles. "It is a contraption that is surgically implanted in our arms, right here," he says, pointing to the inside of his left bicep. "We get it before our first shift. It removes our clothes as we shift into our draxilio form and puts them back on our bodies as we shift back into this form."

"But," I shake my head, "that doesn't make sense." My brain can't seem to grasp how such a thing is even possible.

"We Sufoians are quite proud of our technological advancements," Kyan replies, somewhat smugly. "There are many things we are able to do on our home planet that humans could never even fathom."

I roll my eyes. As if bragging about how much better their planet is than ours is the focus of this conversation. "And yet, here you are. Slumming it on Earth," I add, not trying to conceal the ice in my tone. "Why is that? What exactly is your plan? Are you trying to overthrow our government and take over our land?" My mind drifts through several events throughout American history. "Because it...wouldn't be the first time that happened, actually."

"No, we have no interest in that," Kyan says. "Your government is, uh," his gaze lifts to the ceiling, "how shall I say it?"

"A mess of horrors," Mylo says, finishing his thought.

"Yes!" Kyan exclaims. "A mess of horrors. We do not want it."

"We came here for the freedom to find mates, Vanessa," Axil says with a sigh, clearly sick of his brothers being part of this conversation. Or he's exhausted by the events that took place this evening. I'm not sure which. "Love. That is all we wish for," he says, his voice lowering to a whisper. "We are not like natural-born draxilios, you see. Each of them is guaranteed an eternal mate, a partner to spend their days with. But we were genetically modified in a laboratory, so by societal standards, we were considered peasants. On a completely different plane of existence."

I want to focus on the love part, but the mention of genetic modifications causes my mind to spin.

Mylo nods, adding, "Our handlers were given free rein to tinker with the makeup of our cells, giving us abilities that natural-borns do not have. These abilities made us fierce warriors for our king. We were his special little army," he says, his tone darkening at the end. "We served our time as the king's henchmen, and at a certain point, we were allowed to retire. But retirement for the podlings," he turns to me, "that is what we were called by everyone else because of our otherness. Retirement for us simply means entering a life of isolation and very few rights. In order to earn enough credits to retire comfortably, we needed to showcase our talents differently. The podlings who came before us mostly fought in an arena for sport. The battles were broad-cast, and the crowds were huge."

"These abilities," I begin, "you mean it's more than just changing into a dragon?"

"Draxilio," Kyan corrects haughtily.

"That is correct," Axil replies to me. "The masking we mentioned before, our ability to change our skin color and hide our horns, is an ability we were given."

"And all of you have that ability?" I ask, looking between the three of them. They all nod. "So the natural-borns can't mask, but you can. Can the other podlings mask as well? Or is it just you guys?"

"The podlings are birthed in groups of four, five, and six," Axil explains. "There were four original podlings: Nirossanai, Bexossanai, Alussanai, and Kulissanai, and each underwent a calcification proce-dure where part of the brain that processes emotions is destroyed. For example, Alussanai was modified to lack fear, so the part of her brain that registers fear was calcified, making her incapable of feeling that emotion."

"Jesus" is all I can say. It's too much to process, and I can't imagine what it would even look like to live without fear.

"We were the thirteenth group of podlings to be birthed, so our modifications were quite different," Mylo explains calmly. "Our handlers did not alter our emotions in any way but focused more on our physical abilities: enhancing our speed and agility, allowing us to become invisible when we take flight, and being able to camouflage, in a way, to match our environment."

A smile tugs at my lips. "Wait. Is that why you turn into white guys when you mask?"

Axil seems surprised by my amused tone. "Yes, when our pods crashed on Earth, we landed in the middle of the woods in a suburb outside Boston. A quick flight above the city indicated the population was largely white. We chose that skin color in order to hide more effectively."

I can't help but chuckle at that. "It is one of the whiter cities in America, that's for sure." Then I think back to one of the first conversations we had. "So when I asked you where you're from and you said 'near Boston,' that's why? Because that's where you crashed?"

"Yes," Axil replies, his cheeks darkening to a navy blue. "It was not a lie, technically."

The taste in my mouth turns bitter at that comment. "Compared to all the other lies, it was certainly one of the smaller ones." A lie by omission is still a lie, and for him to have sex with me without giving the slightest indication that he's an alien from another goddamn planet is a major red flag. With this, my plan for make-up sex feels completely foolish, and I can't begin to see what this means for us.

"We were sentenced to a life of loneliness on Sufoi by existing just how we are," Axil says through gritted teeth. "That is not something I would wish on anyone."

Adding to that, Mylo says, "The podlings, all of them, got together in secret and began searching for planets we could travel to with inhabitants we are capable of procreating with to begin our lives anew. Once Earth was chosen as the destination, the five of us immediately volunteered."

"How did you land here? In New England of all places?" I ask.

Axil shakes his head. "Our ship exploded just outside your planet's atmosphere. We had no control in choosing where our escape pods crashed. If we had, we probably would have chosen a warmer climate." He holds up his hands. "No disrespect meant, of course."

I laugh. "None taken. Why do you think I moved to Los Angeles?"

"And you like it there? In terms of the weather?" Kyan asks, resting his chin in his hand.

"No," I admit. "I found the constant sunshine kind of boring. It hardly ever rained, and it never snowed. I missed that about this place," I say, remembering the hopeful change I felt during the first snow of the season. "There's a special kind of magic in unpredictable weather patterns. It reminds you to respect nature, to give it room. It's humbling to exist around the weather rather than assuming it will stay the same and accommodate you."

"That's a lovely way to look at it," Mylo says with a grin as he pushes his glasses up his nose.

"Do you actually need those to see?" I ask.

"No," he chuckles. "It is part of my human costume."

And I laugh along with him. It's not long before Kyan joins in too. Axil doesn't, though. He gives me a half-smile, but his gaze still swirls with sorrow.

"Vanessa," he says, taking my hands in his. "You are my mate. You are the love I never thought I would find."

I can see Mylo shaking his head out of the corner of my eye, silently telling Axil to stop.

But he doesn't. "I know this is quite a shock to you, but the man you have gotten to know is me. The color and texture of my skin does not change that. It does not change what has happened between us. I am yours, and you would honor me by becoming mine."

"Is that...are you...proposing to me?"

Axil nods. "Yes, I suppose I am."

I don't want to reject him, especially considering that I came over here in the first place to tell him how much he means to me. He's being incredibly sweet right now, but I have to ask the question that seems to get louder in my head. I give his hands a squeeze, a sign to let him know I've heard him. "If I say no right now... If I decide to end this, this thing between us, what will happen to me now that I know the truth?"

Mylo coughs, Kyan rubs his palms anxiously over his thighs, and Axil's mouth falls open, but nothing comes out. It's not a comforting reaction, that's for sure.

"Nothing," Mylo eventually says. "Nothing will happen to you."

Kyan looks like he wants to argue that point but changes his mind.

"Admittedly, this is new territory for us, Vanessa," Mylo continues. "When Luka's human mate, Harper, learned the truth, she and Luka were already very much in love. Practically mated. It scared her, but she quickly accepted him as he is."

"Having a human out there who knows what we are and is not one of our mates puts us at risk," Kyan says. "We cannot be exposed. If the authorities learn about us and what we can do, they will surely apprehend us. I fear we will never again see the light of day."

I rub my eyes, the stress of tonight starting to weigh on me. "So what does that mean? Are you going to silence me if I refuse to be Axil's mate?"

"No!" Axil yells, rising to his feet. "Absolutely not. I promise you, Vanessa. I will not force you to become my mate, and I will not say a word, none of us will say a word, should you decide you never wish to see me again." He looks between his two brothers. "Agree to this."

They nod enthusiastically as they stand. "Agreed," Mylo says, shoving his hands into his pockets.

"If Lady Norton had discovered the truth, we would have done nothing to keep her quiet because we trusted her." Axil's eyes meet mine. "I trust you, Vanessa. I know you do not wish to hurt me or my family."

"I don't," I agree, the last one to stand. "I would never tell anyone, I swear." My chin dips. "It's not like I have a great history with trusting the authorities anyway. Fuck them." I take a deep breath. "They will never find out about you guys."

A yawn escapes me, which is odd, considering the ground-breaking discovery I just made. "This is going to sound weird, but can I go home?" I ask shyly. They've vowed to let me live my life, whether I end up with Axil, but I'm still outnumbered in a house that belongs to four dragons, so it seemed only appropriate to get permission.

"Of course," Axil quickly replies. "I shall see you out."

He masks as he follows me to the door. The two of us step outside, and he follows me down the path toward my house, keeping a respectful distance.

When I reach the back door, I turn to face him. "I'm not saying no," I tell him. His expression lightens with hope. "But I'm not saying yes either." Then it falls, just as fast. "With everything that's happened tonight… it's a lot to process."

"I understand," he mutters, but his voice breaks with emotion.

"Give me some time?" I request. "I just need time to think."

He leans down, placing a single kiss on my cheek. It's chaste and quick, but my skin tingles long after his lips leave my skin, making me question why I'm asking for time when what I could be doing is riding him like a prize bull.

"Take all the time you need," he says with a small smile. "I will wait."

I melt at his words, knowing he's telling the truth. I muster the courage to bid him farewell before shuffling inside and locking the door behind me.

He's willing to wait. But am I?

CHAPTER 14

VANESSA

The sound of rain pelting the roof wakes me far earlier than I care to be awake, especially after tossing and turning most of the night. There's a lot to think about, and that's what I've been doing: thinking. But this has proven to be a worthless use of brainpower because I still haven't figured out what to do.

First, there's the whole *aliens are real, and they live among us* thing. I find it shocking, and while I know I'd never tell a soul about Axil and his brothers, I still have no clue what to do with the information. It's not as simple as keeping it to myself. That, I can do.

But this isn't a tiny secret, like, how Willa steals soy sauce packets from restaurants and empties them into a bottle at home so she never has to buy more, or, how Sam gets her armpit hair lasered off. This is a whopping, monumental, iceberg-sized secret just waiting for the Titanic to hit it and for all hell to break loose. This could, no, this *would* change the world if it got out.

How many more aliens are currently living among us? Are there more alien shifters? Do alien wolf shifters exist? What about alien bats? Or cats?

I suppose ultimately it doesn't matter because I'm not telling anyone my neighbors are aliens. This is a secret I'll take to the grave.

Which leads me to the second conundrum: One of those alien dragon shifters happens to be my sort-of boyfriend who just asked me to marry him. What in the wide world of fuck am I supposed to do with that? I hate myself for noting how Axil didn't have a ring when he proposed, but the thought persists, and I can't shut it down. That's society's fault, really, with their obsession with diamonds and marriage and procreation.

Even if he did have a ring, however, and it was the most stunning ring I've ever seen, would I have said yes? Probably not. We had just had our first fight, a fight that we didn't technically make up from since he told me he was a dragon. So the issues of Axil not listening to me and telling me what to do still persist. We haven't solved that one yet. And now he wants to marry me?

I no longer care that he hid his true form from me. It makes sense, and he was just trying to protect his family. I get that, but I can't help but wonder if he'd be proposing if I hadn't caught him unmasked. If I hadn't discovered his family's secret. I don't think he would've, and that crushes me a little. It was a beautiful proposal, if not poorly timed. He said all the right things. I've never been proposed to, but I know I'd want to hear those precise words. I'd want every promise Axil offered me last night.

But would I want to hear it from anyone else's lips? I'm not sure. There's a lot about Axil I don't understand, and with what I've just learned, I have several more questions I'll need to jot down so I don't forget. I feel like I know the important stuff, though. He's kind and thoughtful; he knows how to make a mean burrito, which is very important. He's excellent in bed, but it's not about skills, it's more in the way he makes me feel, like he's worshiping my body with every kiss, every touch. That's rare.

Pulling myself up in bed, I peer out the window, trying to get a glimpse of the view with the rolling hills, the river, and the cornfields in the distance. I don't see any of that because of Axil's damn shed. He's not even in there, so I don't get a view of him either.

Grumbling under my breath, I climb out of bed and head to the kitchen to make coffee. I mindlessly scroll through emails while I wait, finding nothing important other than links to casting calls from Tia, all of which are for one- or two-line guest appearances that pay terribly.

After the coffee is done, I add "too much cream" and "too much sugar" as my mom lovingly described it the last time we had breakfast together, and pop two pieces of bread in the toaster. Then I add butter to one slice and jam to the other, and then take a seat at the round kitchen table with only one chair, and watch the birds fly from one tree to the next in the side yard.

I shower, change, tidy up around the house, then thump down on the broken couch with a sigh. What now? I want to see Axil, but he's going to ask me what my answer is, and I don't have one for him yet. Plus, space is good. It's what I need right now.

My gaze goes unfocused as I stare in the direction of the dining room, and when I spot the chair that had the letter taped beneath it, I remember I have another clue! Axil and I found the next letter in his candy drawer, and I brought it home with me last night.

With renewed excitement, I slide into the kitchen on socked feet and grab it from the counter, unfolding the now-wrinkled paper frantically. The top of the paper has "WHEN" written across it.

My Dearest Vanessa,

I smile at the sight of the familiar words, silently thanking Aunt Franny for giving me this distraction. It didn't feel right opening the letter without Axil, but a lot has changed since I had that thought. Right now, I need this.

The year was 2018. I can't recall the exact date, but it was early winter, which means the calendar still said autumn, but the first snow had already come and gone. I was sitting in bed, reading a romance novel I'd read several times before, when I spotted movement outside my bedroom window. The sun was high in the sky, and while a thin blanket of snow covered the ground, it had already melted in the cornfields across the river, making it look like the crop was refusing to yield to the changing seasons. The faded yellow of the neatly manicured rows had a defiant glow about it that I found quite appealing.

The view of my rebellious corn was suddenly blocked by a behemoth of a man in a red and black flannel shirt, wearing a navy-blue quilted jacket. He was drinking his coffee and staring off in the distance. I'm sure you can guess who it was...

Oh, I think I can.

It was Axil.

Of course, it was.

He came over that morning and asked if I would mind terribly if he built a shed on the edge of their property. The shed would be facing the aforementioned cornfield and would likely block the view of it from my bedroom. The boy wanted to take away the view of my mutinous corn! How dare he!

I wondered how he convinced her to let him put the shed there. I assumed it was bribery.

He started talking about woodworking and how he was getting the hang of it, and I swear, his face lit up like a child on Christmas morning. His plan was to build the shed and use it as a space to continue making custom furniture, and he said the view of the cornfields inspired him. He looked at it each morning and wanted to make things that took his breath away like that view had.

He wanted to turn his beloved, humble hobby into a successful business, and he'd even met a man in Loudon who had become his mentor. Rick Olsen, or something. Perhaps his last name was Oliver. Or Overland. I can't recall. He's in the phone book, though, should you care to meet him.

Come on, Aunt Franny. Who still uses a phone book? I didn't even know they still existed.

Anyway, the boy was excited. He was so eager to have a space for his work, how could I refuse? I have spent many mornings admiring that view, but I wasn't using it to inspire my work. I was using that view to help me relax. Does an old woman really require more of an incentive to relax? I think not.

Still, the view was hers, and she knew it would be mine, and she gave it to Axil anyway. I don't get that.

Then he told me he built something for me and ran outside to get it. What he made me, dear niece, was a cedar rocking chair with the view of the hills, the river, and the cornfields carved into the back. He gave me my view in the form of a truly spectacular and thoughtful gift.

Ah, so it was bribery. Sort of.

I could not say no, so I said yes. It's not lost on me that the view was a selling point for the house. I know this, and I know you are probably cursing my name for allowing Axil to build his shed right in front of it.

I mean, yeah.

But perhaps you could consider the new view all the more spectacular? Sure, it's not a cornfield, desperately clinging to life before the frost annihilates it, but it is Axil building furniture with his hands. And on hot summer days, there is much, much more of a view to enjoy.

Aunt Franny, you creepy old bird!

I'm a widow. Don't you judge me.

Fair enough.

All you have to do is open your eyes, sweetheart. You don't need the Pacific Ocean by your side in order to pursue your art. Your life begins now, just be brave enough to start. Be willing to put yourself together as well as fall apart. I dare say, this kind of stupidity is actually quite smart, especially when a forever kind of love has been sparked.

All my love,

Aunt Franny

That's it? That's the riddle? How am I supposed to solve that? It doesn't include even a hint at a location or even a general area. It's just a confusing poem telling me to stay.

Granted, Aunt Franny deserves some serious props for playing matchmaker. She knew Axil and I would hit it off, which we did, eventually, but a "forever kind of love"? I'm not sure about that.

I fold the letter and shove it into the front pocket of my hoodie. Having no clue where to begin looking for the final clue, the "WHY" of this treasure hunt that will hopefully lead to the cash, I decide to set the hunt aside for now.

Plus, the wording of the riddle left me feeling unsettled. It was too… pushy? No, that's not the right word. Intimate? Yeah, it was too intimate and on the nose, given what happened last night.

I wish there was someone I could talk to about this whole thing. Aunt Franny would be the best choice, given that she knows Axil, but she's the one person I can't speak to. Sam might be a good sounding board, but I wouldn't be able to share many details. That goes for Willa too. There's also part of me that's in dire need of comfort right now. Sighing, knowing I might regret it later, I grab my phone and call my mom.

She picks up after two rings. "Did you find it?" she asks before even saying hello.

"Find what?"

"The necklace. The emerald necklace I told you about. Was Aunt Franny hiding it from me?" she replies in an impatient tone.

"No, Ma, I didn't find the necklace," I tell her. "I was actually calling bec—"

"Bev! Bev!" she pulls the phone away from her face and yells to someone in the background. "Would you grab me another towel?" And then, "Sorry, sweetie. I'm at the pool," she says to me, "what did you need?"

Her lack of attention throws me off, and I completely forget what I wanted to talk to her about. Or why I thought to call her in the first place. "I, um…"

"Vanessa?" she shouts into the phone. "I'm having trouble hearing you. Why don't I call you a bit later, yeah?"

"Uh, sure. Okay," I mutter, knowing she won't call me back. It'll be days before I hear from her again.

"Okay, bye, sweetie."

She hangs up before I can say good-bye, and I stand there, staring at the phone. Here comes the regret.

Luckily, I have no time to wallow in my disappointment because the doorbell rings. I don't think it's any of the guys. They don't want to push me while I'm in such a delicate state, and I expect them to follow Axil's lead. If he's not coming over to see me, which I highly doubt he is, they won't either.

When I open the door, I find a very cranky Willa, whose presence I'm surprisingly delighted by. "Move! It's fucking freezing out here," she shouts, pushing me aside so she can get out of the rain.

"Morning, sis," I say cheerfully. "How goes it?"

She hangs up her raincoat and gives me a deadly side-eye. "What's wrong with you?"

I shrug, maintaining my smile. "Nothing, why?"

"Because you're not a morning person," she says, slowly turning to face me. "And you're all," she scrunches her nose in disgust, "happy and shit. What's going on?"

"Nothing," I repeat.

"Are you on drugs?" She puts her hands on my shoulders, then grabs my face. "What is it? Edibles? Cocaine?" She yanks on my eyelids, peering into them. "Acid? Ecstasy? What?"

I push her off, rubbing my now watery eyes. "The hell? I'm not on anything."

She crosses her arms and huffs a breath. "Okay, I believe you."

"Is that why you came over here? To interrogate me?"

"No," she replies, "I'm here to spread Aunt Franny's ashes with you. It's my day, remember?"

I definitely did not remember, but that's fine. She's here now. "Of course, I remember. Where does she want you to spread them?"

"Um, by the mailbox."

My brow furrows. "The mailbox. Really? Why the mailbox?"

"It's none of your business," she hisses, and the expression on her face makes her look like she's ten years old and yelling at me to stay out of her diary. "Can we just go?"

"You want to do this in the rain?"

She looks at the weather app on her phone. "It's supposed to do this all day, turning into sleet overnight. We might as well do it now."

"Ugh, fine," I grumble, grabbing an old poncho from Aunt Franny's coat closet. I also take an umbrella to hold over Willa as she carries Aunt Franny's urn.

We reach the mailbox, our teeth already chattering, and Willa hands me the urn before taking the umbrella. Then she pulls out a folded piece of paper from her pocket and clears her throat.

"Aunt Franny, I know we weren't always close. I have a theory that you didn't like me as much as you like Vanessa because I look like my mom, and you hated her." She chuckles, and I notice her eyes filling up with tears.

"But there is a memory I have of you that will always hold a special place in my heart. I was six and came here to visit you with Dad. Vanessa was home with Mom, and Dad brought me here to practice riding my bike. Your street is so quiet and is a perfect straight line until that big hill at the end. So I was going back and forth along the road, practicing turning and using my brakes, and I took a sharp turn to avoid the mailbox and fell right over."

Willa laughs as a tear runs down her cheek.

"My knee was scraped up pretty badly, and the gravel from the driveway cut up my hands. I remember Dad running over from the car, and you put a hand up and said, 'I got this.' Then you ran toward me at full speed and lowered into a crouch with your foot out. I can still feel the bits of dirt and gravel hitting my face as you slid in next to me like you were stealing home plate."

That pulls a giggle from me as I can totally picture her doing something kooky like that.

"You showed me your scrape, and it was much worse than mine. You said we were tough girls, and tough girls deserved to be pampered. We spent the rest of the afternoon on the couch, with ice packs on our scrapes, and Dad running back and forth from the kitchen to refill our lemonade."

Willa lets out a choked sob. "It's one of my favorite memories. I felt loved, and the scrape didn't hurt anymore, once I knew you felt it too."

I can't watch my sister cry without getting choked up. Especially after hearing that. Hot tears sting my eyes as she folds the letter and puts it back in her pocket.

"Thank you for making me feel less alone," Willa whispers to the air. "I know it was only one day, but I'll never forget it. I love you." She wipes the tears from her cheeks. She hands me the umbrella and takes the top off the urn. Willa sprinkles Aunt Franny's ashes at the base of the mailbox in a gravelly spot right next to it where Aunt Franny's epic slide must've taken place.

We're both quiet as we walk back inside. We remain quiet as we take off our coats, remove our shoes, and return the urn to the mantle. Willa strolls around the living room, then the kitchen, looking closely at the various knickknacks Aunt Franny placed on every shelf. She peeks out the window on the back door and turns. "How's it going with the neighbors? They giving you trouble?"

I don't know if it's the mention of Axil and his brothers, or because I'm still emotional from hearing Willa's letter to Aunt Franny, but I immediately break down. Sobs rack my body as it all sinks in, and Willa wraps me in a tight hug as she leads me over to the couch.

I hear her mumble, "The fuck is wrong with this thing?" as she looks at the misshapen back of the couch that is cracked in several places, but then her eyes are back on me. "What happened, Van? Tell me everything."

But I can't. There's so much to tell, and I can't share any of it with her without exposing what the guys really are. Though, I suppose I can minimize the events over the last twenty-four hours to a mere sentence or two. That should be enough because I definitely have to give her something. "I've developed a bit of a...a thing with one of the neighbors. And now there are feelings involved. I'm really confused, and I don't know what to do."

Willa pulls me in for another hug and rubs my back. She whispers "It'll be okay" over and over, and after a while, I start to believe her, if only because I'm too tired to argue. She pulls back with a wide smile. "Hey, why don't you come over for the day? You can hang with the kiddos. I know they're dying to see you. Ethan is home. We'll have dinner." She looks around with a slight grimace. "It'll be good for you to get out of this house for a bit."

"Yeah," I reply, confident that seeing my niece and nephew will be a nice change of pace. They are tiny balls of energy and trying to keep up with them will occupy my mind enough so I don't spend the entire day overanalyzing my situation with Axil. "Yeah, that sounds good."

Willa claps, excitedly. "Yay! Okay, let's go."

* * *

The rest of the day passes by quickly, due to the endless chaos of being in a house with two kids. We eat lunch, we play dress-up, the kids play tag, Jane convinces me to join her tea party—which is really just a gossip session about her other dolls and the scandalous activities they've been up to in her dollhouse—there's a brief nap, then they wake up and want to do it all again. I'm completely exhausted by the time dinner is served. How does Willa do this every single day?

"Auntie Nessa, you sit here," Jordan says, patting the back of the chair to his left.

"I'd be honored, little dude," I reply, putting my plate of spaghetti and meatballs next to his.

Ethan, Willa's husband, comes in carrying two plastic plates with Disney characters on them, and puts one in front of Jordan, and one in front of Jane. "Here you go, nuggets."

"Ethan, how's work going?" I ask my brother-in-law as he sits across from Willa and next to Jane. A wave of guilt washes over me at how I've been in town for days and only asking this now.

"Eh, it's accounting at a law firm," he says with a half-shrug. "It's not thrilling work, but it pays the bills, and I'm home by five thirty every night, in time to have dinner with these hooligans," he says, leaning his face next to Jane and pretending to bite her cheek. She giggles, the sound like a tiny, tinkling bell. Willa smiles at him, her gaze lingering in a way that feels too intimate for my eyes.

He's a good man. I'm glad she married him.

"How are things at Aunt Franny's place?" he says after taking a bite of spaghetti. "You still planning on selling?"

"Uh, yeah," I reply, deciding to continue using this as my standard response until something, or someone, changes my mind. "I think so. I just need to get enough money together to make all the necessary repairs first. But after that..." I trail off, using my fork to cut the meatballs into smaller pieces. "After that, I'm outta here." I huff a breath, not totally believing my own words anymore.

I notice Willa and Ethan sharing a look filled with skepticism, and I don't have it in me to deliver a witty retort.

"Will you come see my play, Auntie Nessa?" Jordan asks.

That certainly gets my attention. "Play? What play is this?"

"Peter Pan!" he shouts with glee, then gives me a smile like he's about to reveal a secret. "I'm gonna be Captain Hook."

"Wow! That's so great, Jordy! Excellent casting too. I can see you being a stellar pirate."

He puts a hand over his heart, flattered. "You mean it?" It's so cute I want to cry.

"Indeed," I reply.

"Yup, he's wicked excited about it," Willa says in a cautious tone.

I wait for her to explain further, but she doesn't. "What is it?"

Ethan chuckles. "Well, Wil here has volunteered to direct the play, and she's...uh, not so thrilled."

"You're directing? Oh my god, how fun!" I cheer. I'm sure trying to keep a group of seven-year-olds focused long enough to memorize lines would be a headache, sure, but also unbelievably cute. They're bound to go off-script, or just stand there frozen in place, but since it's children, any screw-up will be seen as adorable. It's a win-win.

"You offering to help?" Willa asks, handing me a piece of garlic bread.

"I didn't say that," I reply, putting the slice on the side of my plate and keeping my eyes on it. "I'm just excited for you."

"Listen, I have no friggin' clue what I'm doing directing this play, okay?" she says, taking a big sip of red wine. "I agreed to do it with one of the other moms, but she backed out last week. Now it's just me." I can feel her eyes burning into the side of my head. "I could use your help."

"Okay," I say, after sitting silently and twirling my noodles, which doesn't seem to work. "I'll help you with the play while I'm still in town. How long do you have to prepare?"

"We have two months," Willa says, lifting her chin and closing her eyes as if trying to remember the date. "It's the spring play, so end of May is when we'll put it on for the whole school."

"Hmm," I grunt, regretting what I just agreed to. "That's not bad. We should be able to get the kids ready by then."

"The roles have already been assigned, and scripts have been sent home with the kids so they can practice."

"And I'm Captain Hook!" Jordan says again.

"That's great, kiddo," I tell him.

"I'm Tinkerbell!" Jane shouts with a piece of spaghetti hanging out of her mouth.

"Really? You're in it too?" I ask, surprised.

"Yeah, Janey has a very important role," Ethan says, shooting me a wink. "She's going to play Tinkerbell at home to help Jordan practice his lines. Isn't that right, princess?"

Jane nods proudly, as she shoves the end of the noodle into her mouth with a single, sauce-covered finger.

Willa gives me a sideways glance. "You sure you want to do this?"

"I mean, no," I tell her honestly, "but I can't be the second person to bail on you, so…"

Willa drops her fork. "Yay! Oh, this is such a relief."

Ethan, still chewing, adds, "Wonderful! Glad you'll be helping her, Vanessa. That way I don't have to."

I swirl the wine around in my glass. "Kinda seems like you owe me one, dear brother-in-law."

He smiles. "Hey, I'm fine with that."

"Van, I know it's not Hollywood," Willa says, her tone placating, "but this is your area of expertise. Use that talent."

I wouldn't say directing a group of kids in a school play is the best use of my talents, but it isn't a waste of my talents either. It's *acting-adjacent*, I guess.

After dinner, and a scoop of mint-chocolate ice cream—one for each of us, so it's fair—Willa drives me home. She grabs my arm unexpectedly as I go to get out and pulls me in for a hug. "I love having you home," she says quietly.

"Yeah," I tell her as she releases me. "I'm glad I'm here. I think."

She laughs. "G'night, kid."

As soon as I get inside, I start turning lights off and shutting the place down. It's only eight-thirty, but those kids wore me out. I go to lock the back door, but a flash of pink on the cement step catches my eye. When I open the door, I find a plastic bag filled with pink Starbursts with a note attached.

I believe these are yours. Enjoy.

Sweetest dreams,

Axil

Ugh, why does he have to be so damn cute? Can't he just be terrible so that I can forget about him? It would certainly make my life easier.

I quickly eat three, then four more before brushing my teeth and climbing into bed. I tell myself not to think about him anymore tonight, and even though I do fall asleep rather quickly, Axil follows me into my dreams.

CHAPTER 15

AXIL

*T*wo days. Forty-eight whole hours have gone by since I last spoke to Vanessa. Since I last saw her bewitching smile. I have had no contact with my mate aside from leaving her the pink candies she seems to covet. I am trying to give her the space to think. It is what she asked for, and I am powerless to deny her wishes.

Yet, my brothers have seen her, and it makes my blood boil with jealousy that they have spent time in her presence when I cannot. Mylo visited yesterday to spread Lady Norton's ashes, and to read his letter to her. He said that all seemed well, and Vanessa was willing to continue assisting with spreading Lady Norton's ashes despite the awkward tension that remains between us and her, now that she knows what we are.

"She was curt, at first, but she seemed to warm up by the end," Mylo said of Vanessa once he returned home.

"Did she say anything about me?" I ask. I know I sound like a desperate, lovesick fool, but I do not care.

She is not ours, my draxilio reminds me for the fourth time today. *She has not accepted us.*

He seems to think that because Vanessa has not yet agreed to be my mate that I should forget about her. An idea I continue to disagree with him on. I thought spending more time in my draxilio form would improve his mood, so I have spent each night flying all over the state of New Hampshire. Still, he is restless, agitated, and stubborn as ever. He is seeking something more. What, I am not sure.

"No," Mylo says with a pitying sigh. "But it felt like you were off-limits, in terms of topics for discussion. I did not ask, and neither did she."

How can she not wonder how I have been? Is she not thinking about me at all? Because I am certainly thinking about her. I cannot sleep. I cannot eat. I cannot even breathe without attempting to suck the scant remains of Vanessa's floral scent into my lungs and keep it there.

What information does she not have? She knows everything there is to know about me now. What else does she need to determine before agreeing to spend the rest of her life with me? I need no further proof. I am certain she is the one for me. My eyes have not turned red, but I no longer care about that. Vanessa is mine. I feel it in my bones.

My draxilio grumbles, *Not yet.*

"Kyan is there now?" Mylo asks, watching me stare out the window at Vanessa's back door.

"Yes," I say, my voice thick with frustration. "He left forty minutes ago. What is he doing over there?"

"Maybe he is fucking your mate," Zev says, coming down the hall from his wing of the house.

I launch myself at him before he makes it to the final step. My hands are wrapped around his throat, and I am quite enjoying the panicked look on his face.

"Kidding," he chokes out, holding up his hands.

I release him and pull him to his feet. "Not funny."

"I respectfully disagree," Mylo says from his stool at the kitchen island, munching on dry cereal straight out of the box and reading a book.

Kyan walks through the door, his face a blank slate.

"Well?" I ask, following on his heels as he grabs a bottle of water from the fridge.

"Well, what?" he replies, not looking up.

I knock the unopened bottle out of his hands. "You know what. How was Vanessa? Is she well?"

He groans as he picks up the bottle from the floor and twists the cap off slowly, intentionally trying to get under my skin. "She is fine." He takes a sip, then notices I am still staring at him, waiting for more. "She seems a bit sad," he continues, "and anxious, though I did not ask why. Other than that, she was perfectly pleasant as I said my final farewell to Lady Norton."

"You were there forty minutes. You must have talked about other things," I point out.

He tilts his head from side to side, cracking the bones in his neck. "You asked a human female to marry you after how many days of knowing her?"

Without looking up from his book, Mylo answers, "Four."

"Four days," Kyan says, feigning shock. "You have only known her four days. Outside of reality television, that does not seem common practice among their kind."

"What was I supposed to do?" I shout, throwing my hands up. "Let her run off with our family's secret without letting her know how much she means to me?"

He sighs. "She has your number. She knows where you live. When she is ready to speak to you, she will," he adds, running a hand through his hair and grabbing his brown tweed blazer off the back of the couch. "Now, I must return to work." He does not say good-bye, just walks out the front door, letting it slam behind him.

I am tempted to spend the rest of the day destroying his closet full of suits with neon pink spray paint, but my phone rings, and Luka's name flashes across the screen.

"Finally," I say when I pick up. "Why has it taken you this long to get back to me?"

"Perhaps because you fools bring nothing but trouble with you," he replies instantly. "I got your text; I just did not want to involve myself with your messy pursuits. So, what is it? What is so pressing? You found your mate?"

"Well," I say, swallowing the lump in my throat. If he thought we caused trouble before, he will not be happy with what I am about to tell him. "I am not certain, but I also am certain, in other ways."

"Huh?"

I stomp toward my room, seeking silence to find the best way to articulate this. "You see, my eyes have not turned. Not yet anyway."

"Okay," Luka says, drawing out the "ay" as if waiting for me to explain.

"Vanessa, her name is Vanessa. She is Lady Norton's niece."

"Ah, your elderly neighbor who passed away?" he asks.

"Yes, and Vanessa is in town to settle her aunt's affairs. She plans to sell the house, and I was originally determined to stop her, to keep her here, because I know Lady Norton did not want her house to be immediately sold off to a stranger. But then, we started spending more time together, Vanessa and I." I pause as the memories of the last several days come flooding in. "She has the most beautiful laugh, brother, and her smile stops my heart. And...and this bold spirit. She is magnificent."

"I fail to see the problem here," Luka says in a bored tone. "She is your mate; make it so."

"I started to think she returned my affections, but then we had a disagreement of sorts. She snuck into my room that night, to apologize, I think, but she caught me...in my natural form. I have not seen her since that night."

I wince as I know Luka will unleash his wrath over my careless-ness. His continued silence makes every muscle in my body clench. He is the eldest brother, and for some reason, I struggle with the idea of disappointing him.

"You mean to tell me," he growls, his voice low and ominous, "you allowed your mate to learn our secret before you could make her your mate? And now she is just...just out there with this knowledge, and can do whatever she wants with it?"

"She will not. I trust her, Luka," I vow. "She will not tell a soul what we are."

"How can you be so sure?" he shouts. "Do you realize it is not just you that she could hurt if she tells even one person? It is all of us. Axil, I have a wife, children." He huffs a breath. "This is why I keep my distance from you all. I must protect my family."

"We are your family!" I roar. "You do not get to leave us behind. I know that is your wish, brother, but you cannot. We came to Earth together, knowing the risks. You are quite lucky to have found Harper," I say, softening my tone. Harper is not the source of my anger, and I do not want it to appear that way. "You found your mate before the rest of us. That does not mean you can pretend we do not exist. We are all seeking the same thing: what you have. We cannot mingle among the humans and assume something like this will not occur."

"Yeah," he says, and I can tell he is nodding on the other end. "You are correct."

"I know she is my mate, Luka. I do not need my eyes to turn in order to be certain," I tell him, scratching the back of my neck nervously. "Is it possible they turned, and I was not aware of it? They did not feel itchy…"

"No," Luka replies confidently. "Vanessa would have told you. Harper said it was more terrifying than seeing me in my natural state because she was worried I was sick or injured."

Then I ask him a question I did not care to hear the answer to before now. "How did you know Harper was your mate? Was it the moment your eyes turned? Or did you know before?"

He sighs, and I can practically hear the smile forming on his face. "I knew it before they turned. Looking back, I think I knew it immediately. The moment I first saw her, I was drawn to her. It did not make sense at the time. I remember asking myself why *this* female? I had bedded so many before her, and none of them captivated me the way Harper did."

I cannot help but smile as well, hearing him speak of his wife, my sister-in-law. She is a lovely woman with a kind heart, and we saw the changes in Luka immediately. We knew she was different. "What else?" I ask, now desperate to hear every detail of their story despite being present during their courtship. I was happy for my brother, of course, but I did not pay close attention while it was happening.

"There was something about her scent..." he trails off. "Most human females smell divine, but when Harper's scent hit me, I felt it in my blood, deep within my cells. It was this intense, primal reaction that had my feet moving in her direction before I realized I had started walking. It pulled me."

It is as if Luka is reading my mind. I have felt the pull he describes.

"Everything that followed only strengthened that pull," he continues. "Her fear scent made me want to turn an entire city to ash. Her arousal scent intoxicated me, and her pleasure became my reason for living. Making her come felt like...like I could slaughter the king of Sufoi and his entire army with only one hand. It was a powerful, all-consuming type of pride."

"Did you stop caring about your own pleasure?"

"Yes," he replies instantly. "My pleasure was secondary. She did not let it remain secondary, though, which made me love her even more."

"I, um, I am not sure I fully understand what love is," I confess as blood rushes to my cheeks in embarrassment. "I am familiar with the definition of the word, and all of us have spent hours and hours watching expressions of this love in movies and on TV with Lady Norton, but how do you know when you have it?"

"I do not wish to sound too much like a human, brother, but you just know."

"So it is this pull, then? Is that what you are saying? The pull that tells me Vanessa is my mate—that is love?"

"Not precisely."

"Then what? What am I supposed to feel? Because what I am feeling now could only be described as pure chaos. I feel sick, but it is a nervous, excited sickness, and it is constant. She is all I think about. All I care about. I want nothing more than to make her happy and keep her safe. When I cannot be by her side, it feels as if my organs are being twisted and yanked apart from the inside."

"That," he replies simply, "is love, but it is merely the beginning of love. The start is thrilling and unexpected, and you never know what will happen next."

"Right, and I do not like it. I want to know what will happen next."

"You cannot, brother. That is not how it works."

I sigh as I hang my head in my hand. This is so confusing. How do the humans live this way?

Luka chuckles at my obvious distress. "The best part of love comes later."

"Later?"

"Yeah. When you look at your mate, and not only see her as the center of your world, but a partner to take on the world with. A friend. That is love, and it is the only kind of love that will last."

His words make sense. We only see Luka and Harper once a year, but when we are in their company, it is clear they have that kind of love. A love that is also a friendship. "I envy you."

"Why?" he says, sounding surprised. "It sounds as if you have found what I have."

"I have not yet moved beyond the nervous, excited sickness, I am afraid."

"Well, go win her back."

I shake my head. Of course, he would make it sound simple. "How am I supposed to do that?"

"You have seen the movies, Axil. Woo her."

That, I believe I can do.

CHAPTER 16

VANESSA

Sam pulls into the driveway, and we both sigh in unison. Neither one of us is looking forward to the reunion tonight, but there's no turning back now. We spent the entire day shopping, and at least we now both have dresses we'll look cute in. I grab mine from the backseat and lean in through the passenger window. "So you're going to pick me up in three hours?" I ask, looking at the time on my phone.

"Yup, go shower and get dolled up," she says, trying to give me an encouraging smile. "Tonight is just one night. Then it'll be over, and we'll never have to do this shit again."

"Ugh, fine," I grumble dramatically. "See you later."

"Bye, Vanillaaaa," she shouts as she backs out onto the street.

I go inside and make myself a peanut butter, jelly, and chip sandwich with baby carrots on the side, just to calm my nerves. Plus, I have no idea if there's even going to be food at this reunion, and I can't face my rapist and my ex-friends on an empty stomach. There's only so much trauma a woman can handle.

I check the weather on my phone, and it says we're supposed to get snow tonight, hopefully one of the last storms of the year, but it isn't expected to start until around ten. I'm planning to be home and drinking wine in my pajamas by then, so that's fine.

Taking a peek outside the back door, I can't help but smile when I discover Axil's latest gift. We still haven't spoken or seen each other since the night I saw him in his natural form, and that was four days ago, merely six days after first meeting him. After he left me the bag of pink Starburst, I started finding other little gifts on the step just outside the door.

There was a teddy bear holding a giant heart, then there was the basket of freshly baked bread, and last night he left me a tray with a piping hot burrito, homemade salsa, and a stack of peanut butter cups for dessert. I came very close to texting him after my delectable feast, but then deleted everything I had written and decided against it entirely.

I still don't know what to say. *Thank you for the burrito! I'd like to continue having sex with you, and maybe we could go on a date, but I'm going to pass on the marriage thing for now. Cool?* doesn't seem like the kind of response that would sit well with Axil.

I don't want to hurt him by ignoring his sweet gestures, but I also don't want to give him false hope either. I'm trying to see this from his point of view, though it's difficult since he's an alien. I have no knowledge of his culture or how things were done on Sufoi, but it's clear by his proposal that relationships move quickly, and I should know by now whether I want to be his mate-slash-wife.

So what does it say about me that I still don't know? Does it mean I don't love him? That we aren't meant to be? Or is my reluctance perfectly reasonable because no one in their right mind would marry a man they met only six days prior? The latter feels right, but when I think about saying no to marrying him, there's a chunk of my heart that feels like it's breaking. Axil is unlike anyone I've ever met. If we were to go our separate ways, I know I'd never forget him, and I doubt I'd ever find anyone who makes me feel the way he does.

A dull headache blooms in the center of my forehead, and a cat nap seems like the ideal cure, especially since it will give me a break from thinking about this. I finish my snack and head to the bedroom, grab a throw blanket from the foot of the bed, and crawl underneath it as I sink into the mattress.

Kyan's words from two days ago continue to play on a loop in my head. *"You do not have to know if you love him right now. You just need to decide if you can live without him."*

When he came over to spread Aunt Franny's ashes on the edge of the patio in the side yard, he finished reading his letter to her, and I just blurted out, "I don't know what to do about Axil."

He lifted his head, blinked at me several times, and asked, "What do you want to do?"

Then he told me all about Luka and Harper, and what falling in love looked like from Kyan's perspective. He seems to take himself very seriously and has the air of a corporate douchebag, but that day, he was anything but. He was thoughtful, an attentive listener, and genuinely seemed to care how I felt without expecting an answer from me on whether I'd marry his brother.

I didn't expect him to put me at ease the way he did. And considering how terrified they must be knowing a human knows their secret and could easily blab to the entire town about it, I'm surprised he was nice to me at all.

Turning on my side, I let my gaze go unfocused as I look out the window. All I can see is Axil's shed, which he doesn't appear to be in at the moment. I watch the bushes planted around the exterior rustle in the wind, slapping against the side of the shed. My eyes start to feel heavy, and just as I'm about to let them close, I notice a piece of plastic sticking out from behind one of the shutters of Axil's shed. It looks entirely out of place, given how tidy Axil keeps his little woodworking hut. What's it doing there?

Hauling myself up, I lean against the nightstand, trying to get a better look. Then I realize it's not just plastic. It's a plastic bag, maybe? Or a strip of plastic wrap, but there's something white inside of it.

Shoving my bare feet into my sneakers, I throw on my puffy jacket and race to the back door. Looking around for wandering neighbor aliens, I deem the coast clear and jog over to Axil's shed to get a better look. The shutter is just for decoration. It doesn't actually move, so it's a struggle to yank the plastic out from behind it. As quietly, but also as quickly, as I can, I wiggle the plastic out from behind the shutter, and sure enough, there's an envelope inside with my name on it.

A letter!

All you have to do is open your eyes, sweetheart.

She was telling me exactly where the next clue was. Right in front of my face!

Your life begins now, just be brave enough to start. Be willing to put yourself together as well as fall apart.

Could she really have predicted this entire thing? Me falling for Axil. It doesn't seem possible unless she was a witch. "Were you a witch?" I ask aloud once I get back inside. Then I kick off my shoes and rip open the envelope. "WHY" is written across the top.

My Dearest Vanessa,

I'm afraid we have reached the end of our journey together. It has been such a delightful journey too. Wouldn't you agree?

I feel myself nodding in response.

Now, back to the business at hand. You'll notice I followed the format of Who, What, When, Where, and Why, and though the ones in the middle were out of order, I chose to feature the Why as the conclusion of this treasure hunt.

So, my dear, why? Why did I do all of this? Why did I arrange for you to turn my house upside down in order to find money I had been saving for repairs I simply did not have time to complete?

Perhaps it's because I adore a spectacle. Perhaps I was concerned Heaven would be a bore and wanted to secure a bit of afterlife entertainment for myself. Would that be such a terrible thing?

Nope, and I would expect nothing less.

Or perhaps...it is because I have watched you struggle from afar for too long. We did not have to be in constant contact for me to know you were unhappy. You are unhappy.

Tears sting my eyes. My head is shaking no, but if she were wrong, would I be crying?

I have seen you happy, and I have seen you unhappy. I know the difference, and you are unhappy with your life in its current state. That is easily remedied, however.

Oh yeah, Aunt Franny? Let me guess, I can just move back here?

You simply need to decide that you will no longer settle for less than you deserve. Let me be clear, I am not implying that any sort of deeper melancholy can be cured by making a single decision. I am not a doctor, and there are medications to handle such things.

Thank you, Lexapro.

However, I have watched you face rejection after rejection to land parts that are not even worthy of the talent you possess. I have watched you struggle to afford your rent payments, and I am aware of how often you eat pasta for dinner in order to maintain a strict budget.

How the fuck did she find out about that?

(Blame that mother of yours. Her social media page is a mess of conspiracy theories and gossip about you and Willa.)

Well, now I need to add "Call Mom and tell her to cut the shit" to my seemingly endless to-do list.

I am giving you a way out of that life, Vanessa. You could sell this house, return to L.A., and continue on as you have, should you so choose. I promise not to haunt you over that choice. You could also stay here and see what lies ahead in a place that has changed a great deal since the last time you were here.

Really? Seems pretty much the same to me. Trevor still acts like he owns the town.

If only for the four strapping young men who now live next door. You can't tell me you haven't enjoyed their company. Or, specifically, the company of just one of them?

Yup, definitely a witch.

Do not give me too much credit, my dear. This was not the elaborate, mystical scheme you think it to be. I spent enough time with Axil to know him well. He became my dear friend, and in that friendship, I discovered a man who truly seemed worthy of getting to know my favorite person in the world: you. The two of you make sense together. At least in my head.

Man, she's good.

Of course, there is a chance that, by the time you read this, you still have not met Axil at all, or you did meet him, and you hated him. Or maybe you figured out you are better suited for Mylo or Zev. Not Kyan. I'm certain you and Kyan would be awful together.

A loud cackle escapes me at the idea of me with Kyan. Absolutely not.

In any case, my final wish is not that you end up with Axil, or anyone else. It's not even that you keep the house and remain in Sudbury. All that I ask is that you consider it. Ask yourself if you truly are happy in L.A., and if you're not, what will you do to change that?

The tears return, and this time, they fall as soon as they form.

I want happiness for you, my dear. That is all.

The words begin to smudge as my tears land on the paper. I have to hold the letter up so I can keep reading. Though, with everything blurred, it's not easy.

At the end of this rainbow, find your pot of gold. Bring your gloves, as you're bound to get cold. The earth will be stiff, I have been told. Take the shovel from the basement and be wary of mold. At the top of the hillside, where there's a view to behold, that is where you'll spread the last of me and share your thoughts untold. Bid me farewell, my dear, and step into your future with a heart that is bold.

No. No, I'm not ready to say good-bye. Not yet.

All my love,

Aunt Franny

At the bottom of the paper is tomorrow's date with two o'clock underlined, which is the time and place I'll need to say good-bye to Aunt Franny, and presumably, also where I'll find the money for the repairs. Based on her final riddle, it seems her treasure is buried.

Logically, I know that Aunt Franny has been dead for over a week, but with the letters and the clues, it felt like she was still here. I wondered why I hadn't cried that much after arriving, considering I was staying in her house without her there. I've been constantly surrounded by her possessions and mementos from her past, and I wasn't sad. Not as sad as I expected to be, anyway. And tomorrow, I'll have to let her go.

I don't want to. I'm not ready. She's been here, guiding me through this strange purgatory that my life has turned into. What am I supposed to do without her?

Axil's face pops into my head, and I realize he hasn't shown up to spread Aunt Franny's ashes. Surely, he was given a time and date to do so, right? Since he seemed to be her favorite of the Monroe boys. Maybe his is tomorrow, as well, but before mine.

That means I'll have to see him, talk to him, and he'll be wondering if I'm ready to give him an answer. I look down at Aunt Franny's letter again.

"You are unhappy with your life in its current state. That is easily remedied, however."

She's right. I can change my situation. I don't have to go back to L.A. and throw myself back into auditions with the constant stress over whether I'll book a part I don't even want just so I can pay my rent for another month. I could try something new with a fresh start some*where* else. I could stay.

For the first time since I arrived, I realize that I…want to stay. This house could use some serious repairs, and the current decor is not my taste, but over time, I could turn it into an inviting, cozy space. I start looking around with fresh eyes, envisioning bold accent walls in the living room, wallpaper in the bathroom, and turning one of the small guest rooms into an office.

My phone buzzes in my pocket. It's a selfie of Sam in her outfit for tonight, sticking out her tongue as she looks in the mirror. She chose a sleeveless silver swing dress that hits just above the knee and has a large cut-out from the base of her throat all the way to the top of her ribs, so there is major cleavage and side-boob action. She's going to pair the dress with a black velvet bow tie, a black tuxedo jacket, and platform oxfords.

When she came out of the dressing room, she looked like a celebrity about to walk the red carpet.

Sam: *This night is ours, Vanilla. You'll see.*

I smile at her confidence. It puzzles me how she can be so nonchalant about being in the same room as Trevor. Everyone handles trauma differently, but with Sam, it's as if what Trevor did doesn't even phase her. I'm envious of that.

But maybe tonight, facing both Beth and Trevor in the same place will help me get there. I'd like to reach a place where the very thought of running into one or both of them doesn't make me dizzy. I know I'll probably never fully recover from what Trevor did. Part of me was taken that night. My body was no longer my own. It was a vessel to be used and harmed and tossed aside. That will stick with me.

It's taken me a long time to feel comfortable during intimate, sexual encounters. For three years after that night, I was completely celibate. I didn't even kiss anyone, because I was too afraid that I'd be paralyzed with fear the moment someone touched their lips to mine. Then I got back into it slowly, moving from one base to the next like an inexperienced teenager until I could go no farther.

Now, I've had sex. I've slid home, and my body feels like it's completely my own. I get to decide what happens to and with it. Then came Axil with his adoring words—which felt over the top at first, but once I let the compliments settle, I felt like a goddess.

I can't let him go. He's become too important to me. I can't say for sure whether I'm ready to marry him, but, as Kyan said, I know I don't want to live without him. I *could*, but I don't want to. A life without Axil would be an unhappy, bland life.

Part of me wants to text him or run next door and say all this to his face. I'm sure he would love to hear the words, and he'd also love to accompany me to the reunion as my date. But I need to do this on my own. I need to know that I can be in the same room as these people without them emotionally destroying me. Once I know I can do that, I'll tell him everything, and hope he still wants me.

A half hour later, I'm standing in front of the bedroom mirror, applying blood-red lipstick that perfectly matches Aunt Franny's ruby necklace that hangs around my neck. My mascara is on, eyeliner has been neatly applied into a sleek cat-eye, hair is done, and my dress clings to my body in all the right places. It's a black, floral mesh midi dress with spaghetti straps and lace accents in a mermaid silhouette. I couldn't do a split in it to save my life, but hopefully there won't be flexibility contests tonight and I can just look hot.

I hear a car pull into the driveway, then my phone buzzes.

Sam: *Your chariot awaits.*

I take a deep breath and shove my feet into my red, ankle strap pumps.

Here goes nothing.

CHAPTER 17

VANESSA

"Why didn't you bring a jacket? Did you forget where you are?" Sam asks as we get out of the car and run toward the entrance of the school.

I'm rubbing my arms frantically to warm myself up despite the twenty-four-degree temperature. "I don't know. Because I'm an idiot?"

"You know it's supposed to snow tonight, right?" she asks, tying the belt of her peacoat tighter around her waist.

"It's muscle memory," I explain, trying to justify my own stupidity. "Remember when we'd drink really fast and then walk from one house party to the next? That was in the dead of winter, and we never wore coats."

"We were also in high school and thought we were immortal."

"Excellent point, Samwich," I say, accepting defeat. I run ahead of her and yell, "Come on!"

When we make it into the gym, the lights are off and it's completely empty. "Don't tell me I spent the entire day psyching myself up for this and we got the date wrong," I groan, crossing my arms.

"Hello there!"

We turn around to find Maggie, the class president and organizer of this event, poking her head in through the gym doors.

"The heat's not working in here, so we've moved the reunion to the cafeteria," she explains, holding up pieces of paper with "Event in cafeteria" on them. "Just putting up these signs for people coming in."

Maggie and Sam make pleasant small talk while we walk to the cafeteria. I can't hear any of it over the sound of my heart thumping like a war drum. The music bumping from the stereo is also quite loud. We reach the edge of the cafeteria, and Maggie runs off to greet someone. I grab Sam's hand, keeping her from moving deeper into the room.

"You okay?" she asks, looking down at our joined hands where I'm squeezing hers way too tightly.

I swallow, and picture Axil's face. The way his light brown hair falls across his forehead. I focus on the dimple in his cheek, and how the skin next to his eyes crinkles when he laughs. By the time I envision his lips, my heartbeat has steadied. "Yeah, I'm good," I tell her, letting go.

We grab our name tags and drink tickets off the front table, and head toward the bar. "Only two tickets each? Fó," Sam grumbles once we get in line.

"What does that mean?" I ask.

"It's *ew*, basically," she says. "As in, I find it disgusting that we get so few drink tickets, considering how much I pay my therapist to talk about my high school days."

I chuckle, feeling extremely grateful that she's my date. "Perfectly reasonable."

Izzy finds us in line and cuts several people to stand with us. "Whatever, I'm queer and nonbinary living in a small-ass town," Izzy says, justifying the action.

Nobody behind us says anything. They must know not to mess with Izzy.

"Good for you," Sam says encouragingly. "You've earned it."

Izzy orders our drinks, which is how I end up with a whiskey sour, a drink I never would've ordered for myself. After a tiny sip, however, it's not that bad.

We head for a table where a few members of the old Drama Club are gathered. They get to their feet when they see me approach and run up to me, cheering. It's not the reaction I expected from anyone here, quite the opposite, actually. It catches me off guard.

"Vanessa! So glad you came back for this!" Henry Campbell says as he traps me in a dance-y type of hug where we sway side to side. He pulls back to look at me. "We've been following your career and just, wow. That car commercial? Amazing! You must be having such a blast in L.A."

"You've been following my career?" I ask, noticing the nodding heads of other drama kids and their spouses standing around us. "Well, it was really just the car commercial. I haven't done much since," I explain, not wanting to disappoint them. If they were hoping for inspiring stories on how to make it in Hollywood, they've come to the wrong person.

"No!" Jenna Smythe adds. "You had that line in that rom-com a few years ago. Hilarious!"

"Oh, yeah," I say, having forgotten all about it since it only paid $400, and it was one of two gigs I booked that month. "That."

"You had that other commercial too. What was it?" Emily Rosenberg pipes in. "For the, um, the pizza toppings?"

"Right," I nod. "It was a new recipe for a spicy chicken pizza for a frozen food brand." That job paid $2,000, which felt like I had won the lottery. I was finally able to pay off one of my credit cards with that paycheck.

We take our seats at the table, but even then, all eyes remain on me.

Henry sighs. "We are so proud of you."

I look around, genuinely confused as to who he's talking to.

"You, Vanessa," Emily clarifies with a giggle.

"You just went for it," Henry says with a wide smile. "Packed your bags and chased your dreams."

"Yeah, we're all a bit jealous, I suppose," Jenna adds.

I feel Sam nudge me with her elbow, and she gives me a wink when I look over.

"You know, if you're back in town for a while, a few of us are starting a community theater group. You could join if you want," Henry offers.

Jenna nods with so much enthusiasm, she's practically bouncing in her seat. "It'd be great to have a seasoned Thespian to guide us."

Seasoned Thespian? Me? I'm one of thousands of women my age and shape trying to get a steady acting job in L.A. that pays well. It's incredibly hard to find, especially when you don't fit into a size zero. How could they find what I've done impressive? Are they messing with me?

I look around the table, and though I'm inclined to dismiss this as a prank because my career doesn't seem worthy of their praise, their expressions are genuine. These are my old drama club friends. They were, and still seem to be, lovely human beings.

Maybe this night won't be so bad.

"You know," I begin, "it's not all glitz and glam. I mean, I've spent over a decade desperately hoping to find a job with a steady paycheck."

"But at least you're out there. You're trying," Jenna replies. "I loved acting. I still love it, but I'd be terrified to go on a real audition."

"Yeah, we've all settled for boring desk jobs," Henry says. "We get together once a month to workshop manuscripts or just do improv, and it's fun. It scratches the itch, you know? But it's not the real thing."

My fists unclench, and the muscles in my body start to relax.

"Oh my god, is this Britney?" Emily shouts, then everyone goes silent as we listen to the lyrics. It takes less than a second to determine that yes, it is Britney, and everyone at the table gets up in a hurry to dance to the rest of it.

Sam, Izzy, and I are the only ones who remain.

"See?" Sam says. "Not everyone from high school is a total schmuck."

"Not everyone, but most," Izzy adds with a laugh.

I ease back in my chair and sip my whiskey sour, watching people I used to know jump around the dimly lit cafeteria. I can almost smell the French bread pizza and canned green beans that they served us every Tuesday.

Happy memories, ones I haven't thought of in years, start to fill my mind as I watch the crowd. Then Beth walks in on Trevor's arm, Caitlyn following behind them, and the breath leaves my body. "Fuck," I whisper, subtly gesturing over my shoulder when Izzy and Sam shoot me concerned looks.

Sam sighs heavily. "Well, it was fun while it lasted." She looks down at her watch. "All of twenty minutes."

Izzy's eyes dart between us and Beth and Trevor. Then Izzy stands. "I'm gonna hit the restroom."

I don't blame Izzy for bailing. This is my battle, and I'm sure there's enough high school drama at the bar every night.

Sam puts her hand over mine. "We're just not going to look over there, okay? Their table is on the other side of the room, and as far as we're concerned, they're not even here."

"How do you do it?" I ask, not meaning to, but the words just come tumbling out. "How are you able to block it out? What happened?"

Her gaze drops to her lap, and her voice softens. "I don't know. I honestly don't know." She takes a big swig of her drink, then continues. "I saw him about a month after it happened, and, I don't know, it's like, in my mind, I was able to pretend it happened to someone else."

She begins mindlessly fiddling with her nails, examining the pale pink polish closely. "I don't break down in front of him. I never have. But it usually hits me the next day."

"Really?" I ask, putting a hand on her arm.

She barks out a laugh, the sound bitter. "Yeah, usually when I'm in the shower. It's weird. I'll step in, the memories and the pain hits, and then a half hour goes by and I'm sitting beneath the spray, shaking from the freezing cold water that's replaced the hot."

"I'm so sorry," I say in a solemn tone. Not that "I'm sorry" feels like enough in this context, but it's all I can say. I hate that I share this particular trauma with her. Neither one of us deserve to suffer this way, and here we are, twenty years later, still struggling to hold it together. Because of *him*.

Sam and I decide to avoid the dance floor. The last thing we need right now is to end up doing the Macarena next to Trevor and Beth. We remain in our seats, far away from them, just chatting with our table mates for the next hour. When I notice Maggie climbing up on the small stage, my teeth clench.

"Hey, class of 2002! Let me hear you!" she shouts and gets a deflated response from the crowd, but it's better than nothing. She shakes it off and looks down at the notecards in her hands. "Okay, so in honor of our incredible graduates coming together after two decades, I've put together a little slideshow to celebrate how far we've come over the years." She looks at the DJ. "Hit it!"

She steps off to the side as the lights go out and the light from the projector fills the room. Vitamin C's *Graduation (Friends Forever)* starts to play, and the words "Class of 2002 Superstars" appear on the first slide.

There's occasional laughter and applause from the crowd as Maggie clicks through photos of our fellow graduates in their respective jobs. Out of three hundred people, there are only about fifteen featured, and I suck in a breath when a still from the car commercial I was in pops up.

I look at Maggie and see her waving to me and pointing to the screen. Feeling oddly compelled to thank her, though she must've added me at the last minute once she knew I'd be coming, I give her an awkward thumbs up. Most people clap, but I hear Trevor's sharp and mocking laughter across the room, and my muscles tighten.

Sam gives me a knowing look and claps louder, lifting her arms over her head to do so.

She always knows the right moments to be obnoxious. It's an art, really.

Following the superstar slideshow is another slideshow with candid photos from senior year. The song changes to Green Day's *Good Riddance (Time of Your Life)* and there are hoots and hollers from people in the crowd who are featured in the photos.

The song is coming to a close when a photo of Trevor and me at prom fills the screen, and my stomach turns at the sight of me smiling next to him, of his hands on my hips, knowing what's in store for me that night.

Maggie grabs the mic again once the song ends, and she introduces the 2002 prom king and queen for a slow dance. Nate Timmons, the star of the soccer team, and his ex-girlfriend, Quinn Wright, the valedictorian, rise from their seats and meet each other on the dance floor. They're both married with kids now and dated for only two months at the end of senior year, but both are good sports about the whole thing.

Before Celine can begin her heartbreaking ballad about love lost on the Titanic, Wyatt Young, aka Trevor's best friend, trips as he runs up the stage, and grabs the mic from Maggie. "Hey! We should all get on the dance floor! What do you say?" he slurs into the mic, a bottle of beer clanking against the mic in his hand.

The crowd gives him a placating cheer, just enough applause to not make him feel bad, but no one gets up to dance with Nate and Quinn.

"Trevor!" he shouts, "Get off your ass, bro."

I throw my head back and empty my glass. The whiskey burns as it slides down my throat.

He coughs, not holding the mic away from his mouth while he does it. "Ask Vanessa to dance with you! Come on, for old time's sake!"

Everyone in the room turns to look at me. What the *fuck*?

Wyatt notices and finds this hilarious. "Be careful, though," he warns. "Watch where you put your hands!"

Laughter follows. People actually laugh at that. It's only male laughter that I hear, which, sadly, doesn't surprise me. Then Trevor puts up his hands in an "Okay, okay," gesture and approaches me.

The spotlight follows him across the room, and when he stops in front of me and bows, the crowd goes quiet. "Vanessa, what do you say? Shall we dance?" he asks, holding out his hand.

Suddenly, it feels like I'm drowning. My mind spins and my breathing turns shallow and labored as the object of all my nightmares waits for my response, while everyone else just sits there, watching.

He leans closer, causing me to jerk back. "I forgive you, by the way." He must see that I'm confused, so he adds, "You know, for the whole thing back then."

He forgives me? *He* forgives *me*?

Is this really happening?

My eyes land on Beth, her mouth twisted in an angry grimace and her gaze narrowed at me as if this is somehow my fault. Caitlyn leans close to Beth and whispers something, causing Beth to nod vengefully as they glance back in my direction.

"N-no," I say, the word barely making its way out of my mouth.

"What's that?" Trevor asks, dramatically putting a hand to his ear.

My cheeks turn hot, and my palms sweat as I repeat, "No. No, thank you," I say in a louder, more forceful tone.

His feet remain planted as he stares at me, still holding out his hand. It's like he didn't hear me. Or he chose not to.

It's too much. I can't take it anymore. Why did I come to this? What was I thinking? I continue to blame myself for this situation as I launch myself off my chair and race to the bathroom, tears staining my cheeks.

Sam finds me leaning over the sink at the far end of the restroom about a minute later. She comes to stand at my side, then grabs a handful of paper towels, holds them under the faucet, then presses them against my forehead. "That sucked," she says quietly. "Wanna ditch this bitch and eat ice cream at your place?"

Chuckling, I sniffle, wiping the snot from my nose. "Yeah. Yeah, that sounds good."

She uses the paper towels to wipe the tears from my face before throwing them away. "We just have to grab our bags, then we can leave."

"Ugh," I groan. "We have to go back in there?" My heart starts beating rapidly again, and I lean against the wall, pressing my hand against my chest, willing it to slow down. "I don't know if I can."

She nods, understanding. "I'll run back in and grab our stuff, okay?"

"No," I reply immediately. "I don't want you to have to face them alone."

She looks around the bathroom as if realizing how bad that would be. "Let's just stay in here for a bit." Sam comes to stand beside me against the wall, and we slide down it together until our butts hit the cold floor.

Sam sighs, leaning her head on my shoulder. "Too many memories in this place."

"Indeed," I agree, wishing Axil were here. At the very least, he'd serve as a giant shield, so we wouldn't even have to look at Trevor. His massive body would just block him out. But I suppose this is rock bottom. I had a public meltdown when Trevor asked me to dance. All my fears about coming back to Sudbury have been realized. There's nothing left to fear. That's something.

Several minutes later, Beth storms into the bathroom, and I'm back to rock bottom. Caitlyn trots in on her heels. Beth crosses her arms as she juts out a hip. "Well, that was fucking embarrassing."

I struggle to get to my feet with the heels and tight dress restricting my movement. When I do, I ask, "What was? Your trash bag of a boyfriend asking me to dance in front of everyone? So sorry I didn't consider your feelings, Beth. I really should work on my priorities."

Sam laughs.

Beth scoffs. "You couldn't just dance with him? For even a minute? You made everyone uncomfortable with that little scene."

Sam and I exchange a glance that says *Is she for real?*

"You embarrassed Trevor," Beth adds.

I can't believe there was a time when I felt guilty about the way my friendship with Beth ended. And how I was eager to talk it out with her, to figure out what I did wrong.

"Oh, what an absolute tragedy that Trevor felt a moment of discomfort," I bark out, my tone dripping with disdain. "Believe me, that was nothing compared to what I went through the last month of high school. He'll be fine."

"What should embarrass you is how you both smell like a couple of musty towels," Sam add with a snarky touch. "Though I suppose it is kind of on-brand for your whole," Sam gestures in a wide circle toward Beth, "deeply vile, scummy couple vibe."

Beth rolls her eyes. "Always a pleasure to see you, Sam. Tell your mom I said hi, if she can remember me." Then she laughs. "Does she even remember you at this point?"

Sam grits her teeth so hard; I swear they're about to break, but before she can launch herself on top of Beth and rip her hair out, the bathroom door swings open, and Jenna and Emily step inside, holding our purses. The moment they see Beth, the two of them grimace and plant themselves between us and Beth and Caitlyn.

"Hey, Beth. Your boyfriend just left the party. Pretty sure he's about to score his third DUI," Jenna spits out in an ominously sweet tone. "Might wanna go check on that."

Beth's cheeks turn beet red, and I hear her mumble something about me under her breath as she turns on her heel and leaves, Caitlyn following.

Jenna turns, letting out a relieved sigh once they're gone, and hands over our bags. "You guys okay?" she asks.

"Oh, you know," I reply, exhaustion setting in. "Just another day in paradise."

Emily steps forward, reaching her hand toward me, then pulling it back at the last second. "I, um, I'm sorry about everything."

"It's fine," I say, waving a dismissive hand as I take my bag from her. It's certainly not Emily's fault Beth and Trevor are assholes.

"No, I mean, about back then," she clarifies in a quiet voice. "I believed you, and I should've told you that."

"Yeah," Jenna adds. "Me too. I believed you."

Sam and I look at each other, stunned by the support. It doesn't matter how late it is.

"We were kids, you know? We didn't know what to do, or what to say," Emily says with a shrug.

Jenna nods. "But that's no excuse for saying nothing. Our silence was part of the problem. Henry agrees, and he would tell you himself if we weren't in the ladies' room."

I've spent so much time wondering if going to the police was the right decision. It felt like it wasn't, given how I was treated, how Trevor didn't face any consequences, and how the entire school found out about it anyway. It seemed like a complete waste of time that only hurt me. But I don't know, maybe it was the right choice.

The four of us share a loaded, nervous chuckle.

"Thank you," I tell them. "It means a lot."

We step out into the hallway and exchange hugs, and I have them put their numbers into my phone before we say our good-byes.

I fall into step with Sam as we hurry toward the front entrance, eager to put an end to this night. Since I didn't wear a coat, Sam tells me to wait inside while she gets the car and brings it around, but the moment she steps out, I notice...Axil. He's leaning against the door of his truck, wearing a long puffy coat that ends at his knees, his hands in his pockets, and his boot planted against the driver's side door.

He's here. I don't even care why. The sight of him brings tears to my eyes. I didn't know how much I needed him until right now. But there's nothing else I want more than his arms around me.

"Are you okay?" he asks as I run outside. He seems to notice my distress immediately because he pushes off the truck and runs toward me.

Then I'm in his arms, my feet no longer touching the ground as he holds me against his warm body, whispering encouraging promises into my ear. He pulls back to look at me and uses his gloved finger to wipe away my tears. "Let's go home."

I think I say yes, though it's hard to hear anything over the sound of my teeth chattering because I didn't bring a coat. Axil carries me to the truck, and Sam waves before heading to her car as Axil drops me in the passenger seat. He presses his forehead against mine and whispers, "It's okay. It's going to be okay."

The tears fall harder now, not because of my pain, but because I believe him, and for the first time in twenty years, I feel completely safe. He's all I need.

CHAPTER 18

AXIL

*V*anessa cries quietly the entire drive to my house. Seeing her cry feels like a blade being lodged into my side. It is horrible. But the one thing worse than that is seeing her make herself smaller so as not to bother anyone else with her tears. That makes my blood boil.

I am curious who is to blame for her sadness. Though I am certain I can guess: Trevor. Or it is her detestable former friend with the sharp voice and harsh features. I believe her name is Beth.

"Do you wish to tell me what happened?" I ask, keeping my voice soft. If I cannot yet offer her the comfort of my body, I must do so with my energy. I pull a peanut butter cup from the center console and silently hand it to her, hoping it will help.

She chuckles when she sees it but waves her hand. "No, thank you," she mutters while sniffling. She burrows deeper into the coat I placed in her lap once I got her settled in the seat. I will never understand why she attended this event without a coat on a night when snow was in the forecast. "And no, I don't want to talk about it."

I nod, putting the candy back in the console and returning my hand to the wheel. The snow continues to fall in wide, wet clumps, making it hard to see the road ahead.

"It's not that I don't trust you," she says, looking at me with her big, beautiful eyes bloodshot from the tears. "I just don't want to think about it anymore tonight. If that's okay."

"Of course, it is okay," I tell her. "Whatever you need, Vanessa. Tell me, and I will give it to you."

She offers me a small smile, then turns away, leaning her head against the window. We get back to my house within minutes, and when I help her down from the truck, I ask, "Would you like me to walk you home?" I do not want her out of my sight, especially with her being so upset, but I know I cannot push too hard, or she will run in the opposite direction.

"No," she replies quickly, and my heart sinks. "I'd like to stay... with you."

My stomach twists with excitement, not because I expect anything to come from her stay, but because holding her in my arms is all I have wanted to do since she discovered the truth about us. Now she is here, in need of support, and she is allowing me to give it to her. It feels as if I am floating.

"Yes," I reply, trying not to sound too eager. "Stay as long as you would like."

The house is quiet once we get inside. I do not know where my brothers are. Possibly asleep. I just know they are not here in the living room, which makes me happy as I want Vanessa all to myself.

"Whoa!" Vanessa jerks back as I hang my coat on the hook by the door.

Her eyes roam my body approvingly, and I never want them to stop. It is when I look down that I understand her reaction. "Ah, the suit."

"Yeah, the suit," she says as she pulls me in by the lapels on my jacket.

Well, Kyan's jacket that I borrowed.

"You look amazing!" Vanessa says. "I didn't think you owned anything that wasn't flannel."

"There is a lot you do not know about me, tiny human."

She steps back and draws a circle in the air with her finger. "Give us a twirl."

"You...wish for me to twirl?" I ask, surprised. It does not sound like a particularly masculine act, this twirling, but since she asked for it, I shall provide. I can deny her nothing. Taking off my boots, I use the smooth tiled floor to my advantage and spin around two full times before stopping. The room spins, briefly, but then my dizziness fades. "How was that?"

She is giggling, and the sound brings me immense joy. "Stellar twirl, sir." Bending down, she loosens the straps around her ankles and kicks off her shoes.

I take her hand and pull her into the center of the living room, moving the coffee table aside.

"What are you up to?" she asks, giving me a sideways glance.

"You shall see," I reply coyly. Taking my phone out of my pocket, I pull up my music app and find a generic romance playlist and press play. Then I bow before her. "May I have this dance?"

She offers her best curtsy and allows me to take the lead. I am not a skilled dancer, so we mostly sway while turning in a small circle, but I do not care because her body is pressed against mine and her hands are clasped at the back of my neck.

"You look gorgeous, by the way," I tell her, running a finger along her jaw. "This dress..." I trail off, lost for words. That is how exquisitely this dress fits her. It is molded to her body like a second skin, showing off the most delectable parts of her. I am just glad the only eyes on her right now are mine.

"Thank you," she says, dropping her chin. It is not something she usually does when complimented, and I am filled with rage that she is doing it now. It is as if she does not believe my words, when every time I have complimented her previously, she nodded in agreement while saying "thank you." This is not like her. I crook a finger beneath her chin and lift it. "A queen never cowers, Vanessa."

She smirks. "Is that so?"

"Yes," I tell her. "The queen of Sufoi lifted her chin so high at public functions that she was practically looking behind her. It is a sign of confidence. You have it, so do not hide it."

I lift her hand between us. "Is that not what this symbolizes?" I ask, pointing to the delicate crown tattoo on her finger.

Vanessa smiles. "I suppose I wanted it to remind me of my worth."

"Well," I say, putting her hand back around my neck, "when the tattoo fails to provide that reminder, I shall be happy to do so."

Her eyes dart back and forth between mine. "Tell me more."

"About the queen of Sufoi? Lovely female. Quite ruthless, actual—"

"No!" she shouts through laughter. "About you. About your past. I want to know everything."

The song ends, and it reminds me of something important. "Before I tell you every single thing about me," I say, stepping out of her embrace, and striding toward the kitchen island. I spot the object I bought yesterday in the hopes that she would change her mind and ask me to accompany her to the reunion, and quickly hide it behind my back before returning to her. "I would like to give you this." I hold it out for her and gauge her reaction.

"Is that a corsage?" she asks, her nose scrunched in a puzzled manner as she looks up at me.

"It is," I reply, opening the clear plastic shell. I drop the container on the coffee table and hold the band of the corsage out for her. "You see, Lady Norton had us watch many romantic movies to help us gain a better understanding of what human women want. Whenever there was a formal event at a high school, I noticed these flower bracelets were given to the females."

She slides her hand through the elastic band, then examines the flowers closely.

"I do not know if it is right," I admit, now feeling foolish. "I realize I was not your date this evening, but I thought you would enjoy it." Perhaps it is the wrong thing to give for a reunion. The flowers don't exactly match her dress, either. I should have listened to Kyan and given her a rose. This was a mistake. "You do not have to wear it, if you do not want to."

Her eyes lift to meet mine, tears mere seconds away from spilling onto her cheeks. "I love it," she says, her bottom lip trembling. "It's the sweetest gift anyone has ever given me."

That astonishes me. *This* is the sweetest gift she has ever received? "What about the pink candy?" I ask, half-joking.

Vanessa's mouth falls open as loud, uninhibited laughter comes tumbling out. She laughs so hard, she bends at the waist, putting a hand on my chest for support as she continues to howl. "No, the candy was good too," she eventually says upon catching her breath. "This is really thoughtful, though. Thank you."

I pull her back into my arms as the next song begins. "My pleasure. I enjoy giving you pretty things."

"Oh yeah?"

"Mmm-hmm."

"Well, you can certainly continue giving me pretty things," she says as if offering a generous piece of advice. "I won't mind. Not even a little bit."

I smile, knowing I should keep the next question to myself, but I cannot help it. "Does that mean you wish to continue spending time with me?"

She answers with her lips pressed against mine. Our feet stop moving as our mouths and tongues connect, doing a dance of their own. It is a kiss filled with hunger, but more longing. Slow and sensuous, I drink from her lips as if they are my only source of sustenance. My hands move from the small of her back to her hips, then down to her ample backside. I squeeze the soft flesh, loving how she feels in my hands.

"Oh, hello, there," a voice calls out cheerfully. I know before pulling my lips away from Vanessa's that it is Mylo interrupting us.

"Mylo," I say in a chilly tone. "So good of you to announce your presence."

"If I had not, what might I be watching right now, brother?" he asks as he continues down the stairs, leaning on the banister with a book in his hand.

"That's a good point," Vanessa says in agreement. Then turns to face my brother. "Hey, Mylo. Great to see you as always."

She takes my hand and tugs me along toward my room. The moment the door is shut behind us, Vanessa is clawing at my suit—well, Kyan's suit—trying to remove all the layers at once. We break apart long enough to undress ourselves, and just as Vanessa's zipper is all the way down, I pause, knowing what I am about to say cannot wait.

"Vanessa, there is something I must tell you," I begin, my throat getting dry already, and I have only just begun. She should know this before we proceed, though.

She turns to face me and flicks the straps of her dress off her shoulders, sending the whole thing down her body and landing in a pile around her ankles. Beneath the dress, there is nothing, just her glorious, tanned skin completely bare for me.

My breathing becomes ragged in an instant, just looking at her. She is incredible.

But no. I must share this with her first. "Um, Vanessa. What I wish to tell you is—"

"No," she says, stepping in front of me and pressing her fingers to my lips. "Please. I can't take any more negativity tonight. Can we just have this?" she asks, wrapping my arms around her, and placing them on her ass the way they were before. "And save the serious talk for tomorrow?"

We could, and god, do I want to. I have a hunch, however, that this is something she would prefer to know now. "It is just tha—"

"Axil," she says with a sigh. "Please. I'm begging you." She cups my face in her hands and stares deeply into my eyes. "Tonight, I just want you." She pushes up on her toes and kisses me, a needy, desperate kiss. "Please," she whispers against my lips.

I am powerless to deny her. If this is what she wants, then I shall give it to her, and I will be sure to discuss this important matter with her as soon as she wakes.

"I am yours, my love," I say before flicking my tongue against her thick bottom lip.

That is all the encouragement she needs, apparently, because as the words leave my mouth, her lips are there. I feel her hands moving deftly as she loosens my tie while I focus on removing my pants. Kicking them off my legs, I lift her into my arms and carry her to the bed. Her legs remain wrapped around my middle, even as I lay her on her back.

"I need you," she says, her tone raw and full of emotion as her chest heaves. A shudder rips through my body the moment her hardened nipples brush against my bare skin. My cock pulses against her belly, desperate for her wet heat. She wraps her fingers around the head, stroking me all the way to the base. With her other hand, she pulls me down for a kiss.

I groan into her mouth, the sight of her needy and writhing beneath me fills me with male pride. "I have missed you," I growl. "I do not think I can go slow."

She smiles at me wickedly as her hand drifts farther between us until she's cupping and massaging my sac. "I don't want slow," she whispers. Then her fingers circle my cock as she guides me toward her entrance. "Need you now."

"Wait," I say, sitting back on my heels. I reach over and pull out a condom from the drawer on my nightstand and tear into it.

"Good thinking," she says, spreading her legs wider for me.

These condoms are incredibly tight, uncomfortably tight. But Vanessa prefers to use them, so we shall.

I cover her with my body as I settle myself at the apex of her thighs, then I slowly push inside. I am not moving fast enough, however, because Vanessa presses the heels of her feet into my backside, causing me to thrust until I am fully seated inside her. She sucks in a breath when we are hip to hip, her light blue eyes never leaving mine.

"Okay?" I ask, checking in on the feel of her body as well as her mind. I still do not know what occurred tonight, but I want her under me without regretting a second of it tomorrow.

"Mmm," she nods, her blunt teeth sinking into her bottom lip.

Then I start to move. She moves with me. She is soaked, the

sounds of our sex echoing through the room. We never quite settle on a rhythm, and it is neither smooth nor particularly athletic, but that does not take away from her intoxicating scent as it fills my lungs, or the way her cunt flexes and flutters around my cock.

She whimpers as I pick up the pace, her back arching as her eyes roll back.

"You take my cock so well," I whisper into her ear, my tongue tracing the shell of it. "Perfect, Vanessa. You are so fucking perfect."

Her fingernails scrape along my back as her legs tremble. "Oh god. Oh my god," she moans.

"You are mine," I growl against her neck, letting my teeth graze the smooth skin of her throat. "Say it."

She moans, her thighs locked around my body.

My tongue runs along her jaw. "Say it."

There are so many things I want to do to her. So many parts of her incredible body I have yet to explore. But tonight is not the night for such things. We will have plenty of time for more adventurous pursuits.

"I'm…yours," Vanessa says as her breath catches. Her face twists into a look of pure ecstasy and anguish as I continue pounding into her. I reach down and rub her clit, and she shatters a heartbeat later, her entire body shaking with the force of her release. "Good girl," I whisper, pressing a kiss to her throat, before taking the skin of her neck between my teeth and biting down.

That seems to stretch her orgasm a little further. Just long enough so that when I come, she's coming with me. A loud, primal growl is ripped from my throat, and I feel her hands stroking the sides of my face as I come down.

I toss the condom into the small, steel trash bin next to the bed, then pull her body against me, her back to my front. We wiggle our way beneath the covers, chuckling at the clumsiness of it.

She falls asleep first, and the deep, even cadence of her breathing has me following close behind.

Several hours later, I awaken before her, sunlight streaming through the narrow gap between the blind and the window. Quietly, I pull myself out of bed, throw on a pair of black sweatpants, and head into the kitchen to make my mate breakfast in bed.

I go with chocolate chip pancakes drenched in maple syrup and fresh strawberry slices on the side. It does not take long to prepare enough for both of us, and on light feet, I tiptoe back into my bedroom carrying both plates. I even maintain my natural form, not bothering to mask, since Vanessa has already seen it. Besides, I want to spend more time with her like this, as I truly am.

Upon closing the door, I find Vanessa staring down at her phone, her brow furrowed, and lips parted. "What is it?" I ask, concern thick in my tone.

She doesn't answer me at first. It is as if she is frozen in shock. At some point, she notices my presence and lifts her gaze to mine. "Um," she says, her voice shaky as she puts a hand on her chest. "Sam just texted me."

"And?" I ask. "Is she well?"

"Yeah," she mutters, dazed. "She's fine." She rubs her forehead, then scoffs as she looks toward the ceiling. I have no idea what is happening, but her expressions are hard to follow. "But, uh, Trevor is dead."

CHAPTER 19

VANESSA

*a*xil doesn't say anything when I tell him Trevor is dead. I don't know what to make of that. Truthfully, I don't know what to make of Trevor's death either. It seems impossible that I saw him last night, and a few hours later, he was gone.

"How?" he eventually asks, walking slowly toward where I'm sitting on the bed.

He puts two plates on the desk. Pancakes covered in syrup with strawberries on the side. Normally, my mouth would be watering at the sight of pancakes, but right now, it feels like there's a rock in my stomach.

"Um, he crashed his motorcycle, I guess," I reply, my gaze dropping back to Sam's text. My eyes scan the letters again, making sure I didn't miss something like a "just kidding!" or an "almost" before the word "died" because this…doesn't feel real. "He was drinking at the reunion, so that could've had something to do with it. That's all she said."

"How do you feel?" he asks, sitting on the bed, facing me.

"I don't know," I reply honestly. How am I supposed to feel? Sad that a life was lost? Relieved that the man who raped me and one of my best friends is now gone forever? I'm not sure how I'm supposed to feel, but I know I should feel something, and it terrifies me that I don't. What does that say about me?

My phone rings, breaking through my thoughts. It's Sam.

"Hey, any more info?" I say as soon as I pick up.

"I mean, kind of. I can't exactly call Beth directly, so I'm getting the story through, like, four people," Sam explains. "Who knows if it's accurate, but I guess he went off the road on one of those sharp turns on the way to their lake house. His bike hit a boulder."

"Jesus, that's brutal."

"Seriously." We're both quiet for a long time, not knowing what to say. "Should we go to the funeral?"

I bark out a laugh. "What? Absolutely not. Why would we go to the funeral?"

"I don't know," she says, her tone sounding defeated. "Isn't it the right thing to do?"

I consider this. Maybe attending the funeral of your rapist is the *polite* thing to do, knowing his girlfriend (whom you also hate) is grieving the loss of her man. But given that Sam and I would be standing off to the side the entire time, wondering if our presence is appropriate as we listen to his friends and family go on about what a wonderful guy he was while in our heads we're screaming, "bullshit," it doesn't feel like the *right* thing to do.

"Seems dicey," I tell her. "I think we should skip it."

"Yeah," she agrees. "You okay?"

"Fuck, I don't know. Are you?"

She chuckles. "I don't know either. It's weird, right?"

"Very."

"All right, I'm going to spend some time with Mom as I try not to think about this. Call me later?"

"Sure thing."

After she hangs up, I find myself unable to move. I'm so confused that even getting out of bed seems like it would take far too much effort.

"Did she say what caused the explosion?" Axil asks, pulling out his desk chair and taking a seat. He uses his fork to cut the pancakes into smaller pieces before taking a bite.

"The explosion?" I ask, still dazed.

"The engine of his motorcycle exploded, did it not? That is what killed him?"

Sam didn't mention an explosion. I assumed he died from blunt force trauma when his bike hit the boulder. Where is he getting this? "No, Sam just mentioned the crash. Do you have superior hearing or something?" I ask, teasingly. "Could you hear Sam on the other end?"

He laughs. "Yes, I do, actually. But I must have misheard her. My mistake."

My eyes remain on Axil. I'm not sure why, but I feel compelled to watch him. He continues to eat his pancakes, and twice, I notice him look at me out of the corner of his eye. He seems nervous, though maybe he's trying to process the same thing I am. He did meet Trevor once, and the interaction wasn't pleasant.

He holds up my plate. "Would you like some?"

"No, thanks," I reply, my appetite completely gone. "Can that happen?" I ask, not knowing why, but letting the words come. "A motorcycle engine exploding when it hits something?"

My dad owned a motorcycle for a few years before my mom made him sell it, and I remember him talking endlessly about how safe they are if you're a good driver.

"Um," he says, still chewing. His eyes dart around the room as he speaks, never landing on me. "I would assume so. I do not know much about motorcycles, though, I am afraid."

Why won't he look at me?

"Axil," I say in a shaky voice. Fear, deep visceral fear begins to unfurl in my chest. "What did you do last night? Before you picked me up?"

His gaze goes to the ceiling. "Um, last night... Well, I had dinner with my mentor, Rick Olsen."

Relief washes over me. "Oh! Oh, good. That's great."

"And then I went to the gas station on the way home..." he adds, his words becoming slightly stilted at the end. "That, um," he says, rubbing his forehead. "That is where I ran into Trevor."

"What?" I ask, but it comes out more as a squeak. "You ran into Trevor?" The fear returns, jolting my heart into a lightning-fast rhythm. "What…what are you saying, exactly?"

His knee starts bouncing nervously. He remains quiet.

"Axil…"

He sighs, dropping his face in his hands. "I tried to tell you last night. I did. Do you remember? I tried and you said no. You begged me to tell you another time."

I hold up a hand, tears filling my eyes. "Are you saying," I whisper, my hands shaking, unable to believe what I'm about to say, "that you were involved in Trevor's death?"

He doesn't need to say it. His silence tells me all I need to know.

His eyes finally meet mine and then dart away. "Vanessa, I—"

"Nope!" I shout, refusing to listen to another second of this. Throwing off the covers, I grab a T-shirt and sweatpants off the chair in the corner of Axil's room since my only other option is the dress I wore last night. They're Axil's clothes, so they're huge on me, but that doesn't matter. Not compared to *this*.

Once I'm dressed, I grab my phone and stomp toward the door. "Come on," I shout, demanding that Axil follow.

"What are you doing?" he asks, following on my heels as I go out into the living room.

"Hey! Alien brothers! Come out here!" I yell through the house. "Code red! Dragon emergency!"

"Vanessa, stop shouting," he says, trying to calm me down.

Zev emerges from his wing upstairs, and Mylo emerges from the other side of the first floor, down the opposite hall from Axil's room.

"Come on!" I shout again. "We've got some serious shit to deal with here."

"Vanessa, please," Axil begs as his two brothers join us in the living room, sitting on opposite couches.

They look mildly afraid of me, which I would find funny if our current predicament wasn't so dire. "Were you planning on telling them?" I ask Axil.

"Telling us what?" Zev asks, crossing his arms over his chest.

I turn to Axil. "Do you want to tell them, or should I?"

Axil runs a hand through his hair. "Fine." He holds out his hands, and says, way too casually, "I killed Trevor."

"You what?" Zev asks the same moment Mylo asks, "Who?"

Zev's eyes don't leave Axil's as he says to Mylo, "Trevor is the nefarious human male that attacked Vanessa long ago. Axil and I had a minor confrontation with him at Tipsy's."

"He also attacked Sam," I clarify.

"Who is Sam?" Mylo asks.

Whew, we need to catch him up on a whole lot. Speaking of which, "Where's Kyan?" I ask.

"Probably at work," Axil mutters sarcastically. "Where he always is."

"Okay, well, someone please call him and have him come home. We need to get him up to speed." I grab my phone and turn to Axil. "I'm going to call Sam and have her come over too. She should be in on this."

"Sam? Why? She cannot be involved."

Dropping the phone to my side, I level him with a glare. "I don't think you realize the sheer volume of shit you've gotten us into. The cops are going to question everyone who knows him. Everyone who has a connection to him." I lower my voice. "He raped both of us. Sam and me. I don't know if anyone is aware of what he did to her, but they definitely know what happened to me. And we just so happened to have a confrontation with his girlfriend the night he died."

"But it looked like an accident," Axil says, trying to reassure me. "I was sure to make it look like an accident. Why would the police question you?"

"Maybe they won't," I reply, doing my best to think logically, though I'm finding that to be an impossible task. "You're right, maybe all they'll see is a guy who was drunk and driving too fast on a dangerous road and wasn't wearing a helmet when he crashed."

Officer Burton's face pops into my head. "Or maybe his uncle will be suspicious about the timing and circumstances of his death and will want to dig a little deeper. If that happens, and all of us aren't on the same page, we are fucked. Do you understand? Fucked."

He nods as his gaze drops to the floor. He seems very confused, which makes me feel guilty, in a way, because even though he and his brothers have been living on Earth for thirteen years and have found a way to blend in, that doesn't mean he understands every aspect of human life. They've done everything possible to hide among us thus far, and Axil just went and put a bull's-eye on his back.

Mylo pulls out his phone and starts talking to someone, presumably Kyan.

"I will call Luka," Zev says, walking out of the living room with his phone pressed to his ear.

I take Axil's hand. "I know this isn't ideal, having Sam here. It exposes you. All of you. But I promise, you can trust her. And she needs to know what's going on. If only to keep her safe." Squeezing his hand until he looks me in the eye, I add, "We can't let them think she had anything to do with this."

He blows out an unsteady breath, and says, "Very well. Call her. Get her here."

After an hour of trying to get everyone together in the same room, we end up with Kyan and Sam, but no Luka. He didn't answer when Zev called him and hasn't called back.

The moment Sam walks in, Mylo jerks back from where he stands in the kitchen. "You," he says, his tone mystified as he stares at her.

She looks equally stunned. "You...have glasses?"

What is happening? "Have you two met before?" I ask.

Simultaneously, they say, "No," but it's clearly a lie, based on the volume and tone of their voices. Hmm.

I lean down next to Sam's ear. "I'm gonna need to get that story from you later."

She dismisses me with a scoff, waves hello to the rest of the brothers, and takes a seat on the couch in the center. "So, why am I here?"

Kyan, Zev, and Mylo make their way from the kitchen to the living room and take their seats. Axil remains standing by my side. "Right," I begin. "I think the best way to do this is to lay it all out there at once." I look to Axil. "Yeah?"

He nods, chewing on the inside of his cheek.

I take a deep inhale, then launch into it. "So, Samwich, these fine gentlemen are actually aliens from a planet called Sufoi. Their space-ship exploded outside of Earth's atmosphere, and their pods crashed in the middle of the woods in the suburbs of Boston. They have the ability to change their skin color to any shade, and can hide their horns—yep, they have horns—at will.

"They can also shapeshift into these humongous dragon-type crea-tures that breathe fire. Several years ago, four of the five moved in next to my Aunt Franny, and they grew to be close friends with her. I, too, have gotten close to them," I nod in Axil's direction, "one of them, actually. Anyway, um, he's not a fan of what Trevor did to us, and last night he ended up killing him. Any questions?"

"Yeah," she replies. Her eyes dart between me and Axil, then she leans forward and rests her elbows on her knees. She lays her chin against her fist and sighs. "What are we planning on telling the cops?"

Mylo barks out a laugh. "That is your question? *That?*"

"Yes, why?" she replies with a serious face, looking somewhat offended.

"Out of everything Vanessa just said, your main concern is how we are going to handle the cops?" Kyan asks, narrowing his gaze at Sam.

"I mean, I figured there was something off about you guys," she says, shrugging. "I just assumed you were serial killers, or part of some incestuous orgy ring, or something."

"Um, you thought they were serial killers but didn't think to tell me about that theory?" I ask, mildly insulted that she would just let me continue banging someone she thought was a murderer. Although, I suppose he is, technically.

"Well, I didn't know for sure," she says quietly. Then she throws her hands up. "You think I didn't try to dig up more info on you all?" she shouts. "You're four insanely hot brothers who willingly live together despite clearly having enough money to afford your own homes. That's shady. None of you are on social media. Shady. And you chose to settle here in the middle of fucking nowhere," she counts off on her fingers. "Shady, shady, shady."

"Now that you know the truth?" Mylo says, his chin jutting forward as if eager for her response. Far more eager than anyone else in the room.

"Honestly, I'm relieved," she says, leaning back and sinking deeper into the couch. "Aliens, I can handle. Serial killing orgy bros, I cannot."

"That is fair," Zev says with a smirk.

Wow, she's taking this much better than I expected. Much better than even I did.

"Okay, so back to Trevor," she says, looking at Axil. "How and why?"

I wince. I'm pretty sure I don't want the answers to either of these questions. It feels safer to not know. Plausible deniability, and all that. "I don't think we need to get into the details. What we should really be—"

"Wasn't asking you, Vanilla," she mutters dryly. Her brows lift as she continues staring at Axil. "Well?"

"Uh," he begins, fidgeting with the button on the collar of his flannel. "I, uh, I do not wish to upset Vanessa, so…" he trails off.

I wait for him to expand on that, but when he doesn't, I proceed with the paper-thin version of a plan that I currently have. "Okay, so I think we shou—"

"Actually, I changed my mind," Axil declares, a muscle ticking in his jaw as he steels his spine. "I will tell you how. I will tell you everything."

CHAPTER 20

AXIL

I want to deny it, if only to remove the look of horror on Vanessa's face, but I cannot. The events of the previous night begin to play in my mind from the moment I left my mentor's house earlier in the evening.

Rubbing my palms together, I address Sam. "How, you ask?"

A smile tugs at my lips as I turn onto Route 106 in Loudon. Another excellent dinner at Rick's house. Upon finishing our root vegetable gnocchi, we went out to his shed and he showed me some new woodworking techniques he picked up from a recent trade show. He has been an invaluable resource when it comes to perfecting my work. He is also a generous, kind man. It is a shame he never got to meet Lady Norton. Perhaps they would have enjoyed each other's company.

I notice I am running low on fuel, and since there is a storm coming later, it might be best to refuel now while the roads are clear. Pulling into the nearest gas station, I go through the motions, still thinking about the gnocchi. I should get the recipe from him. Perhaps it is a dish Vanessa would like.

My chest tightens at the mere thought of her. She is currently at her school reunion, and I find it puzzling she chose to attend without me.

Why would she not want me by her side, protecting her from another confrontation with Trevor? It makes no sense.

A loud rumble catches my attention as a man on a motorcycle pulls up to the pump next to me. He is not wearing a helmet, which is extremely idiotic, especially on a night where the roads will be covered in snow, but I would expect nothing less from the rider in question.

"Well, well, well," Trevor says in a cocky tone as he climbs off his bike. "It's the gigolo."

"Trevor," I say without looking up from the gas pump in my hand. *I would prefer to avoid seeing his face, with his small nervous eyes and horrendous facial hair. He has a nose you cannot help but want to break.*

I hear him chuckle, the sound most unpleasant, as he strolls inside the food mart. He seems to be dressed somewhat nicely, or what I imagine is nice for him. His navy-blue pants are pressed, and he is wearing a white dress shirt with blue dots that seems to be tucked in. He comes out of the food mart with a pack of cigarettes in hand. "Missed you tonight at the reunion, bud," he says as he crosses the barrier between us and leans against the pump I am using.

I busy myself with cleaning the windshield of my truck, continuing to ignore him.

"We're having an after party for everyone, you know..." he says, his breath sour with the strong scent of alcohol. "I think Vanessa and Sam are on their way now, in fact."

My hand stills. No. There is no way they would willingly attend a function hosted by Trevor. He must be lying.

"Man, they sure looked good tonight," he adds, his tone wistful. "Especially Vanessa."

I will not let him goad me. I cannot. Things will turn ugly, which will lead to me causing irreparable harm to this frail human's body. I must remain calm to protect my family.

"That dress she was wearing. Wow," he says with a gleeful scoff. "It left nothing to the imagination."

Protect the family. I must protect my family.

"Though, you have to like big girls."

He says the word big *in a disparaging way with his cheeks puffed out. I do not understand it—why her size would be something to mock—but I know I do not like his tone. How easy it would be to wrap one hand around his throat and squeeze. And squeeze and squeeze until his small eyes grow big and bulge from their sockets.*

"Is that your thing?" he asks, tilting his head to the side as if he is genuinely curious about my response, and not simply mocking me. "You have a fat fetish or something?"

How long would I need to choke him before his face turned the same color blue as my natural skin?

Do not kill him this way, my draxilio notes. Take him to the edge of death, so he is forced to witness his entire, pitiful life flash before his eyes.

I cannot argue with how delightful that would be.

"Hey, no shame in chasing fatties, bro," Trevor continues. "I get it. In fact, I had a thing for Vanessa a long time ago."

Protect the family. Protect the family. Protect the family.

He leans forward and slaps his hand on my shoulder. "A word of caution from someone who's gotten a piece of that pussy..."

My gaze lingers on his small, weak hand as a growl rumbles inside my throat. He is testing every boundary I have. Every last shred of willpower is being used to keep myself from snapping his neck.

"She's kind of a bitch, you know? One of those wicked sensitive, high maintenance feminists, so just watch yourself," he says in a quiet voice as if offering me valuable advice and not slandering my mate. Such a foolish choice on his part. "One minute you're fucking her, and the next thing you know, she's crying and making up bullshit lies." He lifts his hand from my shoulder and shrugs. "Women, right?"

My hands begin to shake as Trevor smirks. I clench my fists to make it stop, but the tremors spread throughout my body. I feel sweat form on my forehead as I focus on breathing in and out through my nose.

End him, my draxilio growls.

He desperately wants me to shift so he can take over. His rage pulses through me like hundreds of tiny heartbeats.

Kill. Kill. Kill, he chants in my head. Protect our mate. Kill him. Kill him now.

No, I send back through our mental link. We cannot. We must keep our secret to protect the family. We must behave in the human way.

He grunts at my lack of action.

"Anyway, I've gotta get the house ready for the party," Trevor says, smacking me on the back. He returns to his pump and finishes paying. "I'll give Vanessa your best," he adds, laughing maniacally as he revs the engine. Then he is off, taking a left out of the gas station parking lot and speeding off into the night.

I make quick work of paying, then hop in my truck. My tires squeal as I pull out onto the road, taking a right. The inside of the truck is silent as I drive home, going as fast as I can without going more than five miles over the speed limit. My mind, however, is a funnel cloud of chaos and fury as I recall every horrific, insulting word Trevor uttered about Vanessa. My draxilio roars as he pushes me to avenge her honor.

Follow him. Hurt him. Kill him.

The chant is uttered inside my mind over and over until it is the only thing I want to do. I start thinking about what that monster did to Sam and Vanessa and who knows who else. He was not held accountable for his crimes. Now he walks through life as if he is untouchable. There is no other explanation for the sheer audacity he seems to possess, and the way he mocks and taunts not just me, but Vanessa and Sam too. His victims.

As if that were not enough, he seems to have convinced himself that he has done nothing wrong.

He is a danger to all, my draxilio reminds me.

And he is right.

By the time I pull my truck into the garage at home, I am convinced of one thing—he must be stopped.

I step into the front yard. Ours is a quiet road, and there is hardly ever traffic. Looking around, I am confident that no one but Vanessa could possibly witness my shift, and she is not home. I must do this now before I lose my nerve.

My draxilio purrs approvingly. Find him. Destroy him.

It takes mere seconds before my body transforms into the winged beast filled with fury and flames. Quickly, I launch into the sky, so I may cloak myself. I cannot cloak and become invisible while on the ground, so there is no time to stretch my limbs and shake out my wings. I must find my comfort in this body while in the air.

High above the trees, I follow the path I took back to the gas station. It is a twenty-minute drive, but since I am flying, it takes only four minutes. Then I follow the direction Trevor went. The scent of his oily scalp mixed with a cologne that smells like a chemical fire helps me track him instantly.

This part of the road is dark and desolate with dangerous curves every mile or so.

Snow begins to fall the moment I spot him. It does nothing to impair my vision, but it will make it more difficult for Trevor's human eyes to see me coming once I remove the cloak. Excitement fills my chest. I want to savor the terror in his eyes when he realizes what is about to happen.

I fly ahead of him, then flip around in the air to change direction. As he approaches the next curve, I dive, gliding just a few feet off the road. He leans into the curve, and I remove my cloak, lifting my lips to show off my many sharpened fangs.

A frightened shriek rips from his throat upon seeing me. He jerks his handlebars to the right in an effort to avoid colliding with my chest and hits a rock the size of a basketball on the side of the road, sending his body flying over the handlebars and into a boulder that sits between the road and the cliff below.

Shifting into my flightless form, I mask as I stride toward his crumpled body. When he lets out a choked moan, I sigh in relief. He lives.

"Hello, Trevor," I say, rolling him onto his back with my foot.

Blood pours from his nose, staining his lips and goatee, and there is a gash across his forehead so deep, I see bone. His knuckles are scraped and bloody, and a spot of red on his lower abdomen grows, getting wetter by the second.

That does not look good. Perhaps there is not a chance for Trevor to change his ways. Oh well. "It seems we do not have much time," I tell him with a sigh. "Shame."

"Y-y-you," he stammers, tears streaming down his face. He coughs, one hand reaching for his chest, the other completely still at his side. The closer I look, the more I notice that arm lying at an odd angle.

I know I am supposed to feel guilt for Trevor's current state, but I do not. If this is what it takes to prevent him from causing any more pain, so be it. His soul is as hideous as the patch of hair on his chin.

"Sh-sh-sh..." he whimpers.

"What is that?" I ask loudly, cupping my hand around my ear. "What are you trying to tell me, bro?"

He is not reaching for his chest after all, but his shoulder. He continues trying to get the word out, unsuccessfully, as he points to it with his other hand.

I step one foot over his body, straddling him. "Oh no, is your shoulder in pain?" I ask, crouching down. "Would you like me to help you?"

He nods as he continues to cry. But then his good hand drifts down below his shoulder, going lower, and lower, until it reaches the hem of his shirt at his waist. Is he reaching for his gun again? Did he take the weapon to the reunion?

Time to end this.

I rise to my full height, lift my foot waist high, and slam my boot down on his misshapen shoulder until I hear several cracks. He bellows into the night air as snow continues to fall.

"There is no one here to help you, Trevor," I tell him. "It is just you and me," I say, clearing my throat as I walk in a slow circle around his body.

He continues to wail through labored breaths as his hand shakes where it hovers over the decimated remains of his shoulder, the weapon in his possession completely forgotten.

I slowly let my mask evaporate, revealing myself in my natural state. I want him to know a monster defeated him.

His eyes widen as he takes me in, my blue skin, the horns, all of it. He shakes his head hastily, refusing to accept what he sees.

"I-I-cuh...I c-can't..." he chokes out. Then he continues to sob as he lies there. His left leg looks similar to his right shoulder, bent strangely, and the blood spot on his shirt has now grown to the size of a grapefruit. I must move this along.

"Here is the thing, Trevor Burton," I say, enjoying the feel of his full name on my lips, knowing that name will no longer carry the fear and pain that it has. "You are going to die today. It is not because you called Vanessa a bitch earlier. I feel I must make that clear."

I bend down until my face is just an inch or two above his. My draxilio bristles, wanting in on the action. I let him, but not before I say, "It is because you commit unspeakable acts of violence without facing any form of punishment."

Once the shift is complete, Trevor screams, and I can hear the gurgle of blood in his throat as the life begins to fade from his eyes. I cannot let him suffer much more, I decide, and use my front paw to lift his body off the ground until it is level with my snout. Then I let go, sending his body careening toward the pavement. And with a final crack of bone, I hear Trevor's heartbeat stop.

My draxilio is not satisfied. He wanted more. He wanted to play with Trevor, to torture him until his final breath left his body. But it is done. Trevor is dead, and the world is better for it.

Just to appease my beast, however, I lean back on my haunches, and tip my head back. The familiar warmth pooling in my belly makes me smile. Oh, how I have missed this. Taking a deep breath in, I stick my neck out and my jaws open wide as a stream of fire bursts from my throat, and up into the sky above. I hold my flames steady as I lower my head, and shoot a final blast toward his motorcycle. It hits the engine, causing an immediate explosion.

My draxilio is at peace, and strangely enough, so am I. The connection between us has never felt stronger.

Then I take one final look at the scene before me. This will look like a terrible accident caused by a man who refused to wear a helmet while riding along a dark, dangerous road in the middle of a snow-storm, after having consumed several drinks.

Satisfied with the result, I cloak myself and fly home.

It is only when I am in the shower, rinsing off any possible signs of where I have been that I realize Vanessa is probably getting ready to leave the reunion. Nerves tighten my chest as I wonder if I have done the right thing. What will Vanessa think? Should I tell her the truth? Either way, I need to see her. I don't know how she got to the reunion, given Lady Norton's car is still not running, but even if Sam drove her there, she will need safe passage home in this weather. I do not know what Sam drives, but it is unlikely that it is as stable on icy roads as my truck. I will show up and offer them a ride home. Yes, that is an excellent plan.

"And you wish to know *why*?" I ask Sam, without looking at her. I keep my gaze on my mate. "Because I love you, Vanessa. Desperately. I love you, and he caused you pain." I feel my bottom lip tremble. "I have loved you every moment of every day since we met, and I will not allow anyone to hurt you and get away with it. I wish I had a more sophisticated reason to give you, but I do not."

My heart thunders inside my chest as I watch Vanessa, hoping she feels as I do.

"Rapists on Sufoi die horrible deaths. A fitting judgment for such a heinous act." I lift one shoulder in a half-shrug. "That is how we see it, anyway. I know your laws are different here, but that does not mean I understand them. I could not let him live another day with such a strong sense of entitlement."

I take Vanessa's hand in mine. "I am not sorry. I killed him, Vanessa, and I am not sorry." I press Vanessa's hand against my chest above my heart. "You are *mine*. Too much of your life has been spent trying to forget what he did." I clear my throat, holding back emotions. "But you are still living in fear. Fear of even seeing him, or hearing his name, and I know it is because deep down, you worry he still has the power to hurt you without ever facing repercussions."

Vanessa's eyes look watery, and I cannot tell if it is because she is horrified by my words or feels them herself.

"Now, he cannot hurt you anymore," I whisper, pressing a kiss to her palm. "He cannot hurt anyone."

It looks as if Vanessa is about to say something, but the doorbell rings, and she pulls her hands from my grasp. Everyone freezes, caught off guard by the interruption.

"Could it be Luka?" Mylo asks. No one answers him.

When Mylo opens the door a second later, three officers are standing there.

"Axil Monroe?" the old male in the front says in a croaking, brittle tone as he looks around the room.

I step forward.

"Come with us, son. We'd like to ask you a few questions."

CHAPTER 21

AXIL

"I have told you this twice, already," I explain to the officers, as calmly as I can, considering they are asking me to repeat myself a third time. "I had dinner with Rick Olsen at his home in Loudon. He is a friend and mentor of mine. I stopped to get gas on the way home. It was there, at the gas station, that I ran into Trevor." There is no use trying to cover that up since I assume there are cameras that could easily confirm it. "I came home to change my clothes, and then picked Vanessa up from the reunion. We returned to my home after that."

Officer Burton, whom I gather is Trevor's uncle, who Vanessa spoke of, looks at his partner, skeptically. "Trevor didn't say anything to you while the two of you were pumping gas?"

"We spoke," I tell them. "He said something about the party he was having, and how eager he was for it to begin." Not a total lie, but not entirely the truth either. "Then he sped off on his bike. Though I did notice he was not wearing a helmet," I add, feigning concern.

"It's not required by law," Officer Burton quickly interjects.

"I understand, but surely, on a night when there is supposed to be a snowstorm, a helmet would be wise, do you not agree?"

Officer Burton purses his lips. "The motto of this state is 'Live Free or Die,' son, and since it's not required by law to wear a helmet, it's up to each individual to choose if they want to do so."

I raise my hands in surrender.

"Now, do you mean to tell me you made no other stops on your way home from the gas station?" he asks, again.

"No," I reply. My route from the gas station to home was direct, though I did go back after returning home, but that's not what he's asking. "I went straight home."

"Hmm," he says, scratching his chin. "Interesting."

My knee begins to bounce as agitation sets in. I know this is their strategy, to get me irritated until I slip up and change my story. I refuse to fall into their trap.

"You were seen just a few days ago at that new bar, uh, Tipsy's. Over there on the corner of Hobart Street," he says. "You recall being there?"

"Yes."

"Trevor was also there that night. Seems you two got into an argument of some kind. Can you tell us about that?"

I shrug. Is he expecting his nephew to sound like an innocent victim? And I am some kind of bully? "From what I recall, he was drunk and being disrespectful to the women I was with, so I asked him to return to his game of pool." Clearing my throat, I add, "I believe that was when he lifted his shirt and showed me the gun he had stuffed into the waistband of his pants. A nonverbal threat, I believe."

The other officer starts scribbling something on a piece of paper, much to Officer Burton's chagrin. He glares at the paper, trying to read it, but with the way he's squinting, clearly, he cannot.

"Are you charging me with a crime?" I ask just the way Vanessa told me to before I left the house in the back of the police car.

"Not at this time, no," the other officer says.

"Great. Can I go then?"

The other officer looks to Officer Burton for approval. Begrudgingly, he nods. They walk me out to the front area of the police station, and Officer Burton says, "You're free for now, Mr. Monroe, but this is just the beginning of our investigation. We may need to speak to you again, so I wouldn't leave the state, if I were you."

As if there was anywhere else that I would like to go. My mate is here. Nothing else matters. "Very well," I reply as I leave.

When I walk outside, I find Mylo waiting for me in his car. I was hoping Vanessa would be here too, but no. It is just Mylo.

"Thank you for waiting," I tell him as I get into the passenger seat.

"Of course, brother," he replies with an easy smile.

I knew this would not faze him. Hardly anything does. We spent too many years as the king's henchmen on Sufoi, slaughtering his enemies and fighting his wars for something as trivial as this to come between us.

Though, the same cannot be said for Luka. "Get in touch with Luka?" I ask Mylo as he turns onto the main road through town.

"No," he replies heavily. "We have all called him, texted him, left voicemails. Nothing yet."

"Where is Vanessa? Is she still at our place?"

"Uh, no," he says, slightly distracted as he changes lanes. "She and Sam went back to her house to discuss everything further."

My heart sinks into my stomach. I was hoping she would either still be at my house, waiting for me to return, or would want to be at the police station when I was done being questioned. And yet, she took the first opportunity to leave.

Telling her how I felt and why I did what I did was thrilling, a relief, even. I knew it was a risk, and that it might scare her, but I could not keep it from her a moment longer. She should know what kind of mate I will be.

However, now that she knows what I am capable of, perhaps her feelings have changed. Never toward her, of course—I would rip my heart from my chest before I would lay a finger on her in anger—but toward anyone who causes her pain. It does not seem to be the human way, and perhaps more intense than she is used to.

Does she think me a monster? Or worse, does she hold me in the same regard as Trevor? That would devastate me. During my confession, I did not notice fear in her scent. If anything, there was a hint of arousal, which was surprising. If she feared me, surely, I would know it.

Perhaps it is not fear that she feels around me now, but instead, disgust. It is unfortunate that the emotion of disgust does not change her scent at all, therefore I would not be able to tell. She will not agree to be my mate if I disgust her, of that, I am certain.

I should not have said anything at all. It was too soon, and the timing was atrocious. Vanessa will forever remember my declaration of love being tied to Trevor's death. The romance of that moment being completely negated.

What a foolish decision that was.

"All will be well, brother," Mylo says, looking at me with warmth in his silver eyes.

"That is kind of you to say, but I am not so sure."

"You assume the worst," Mylo adds. "This situation is certainly bad, but we will find our way out of it. We always do."

"I know that is why Luka refuses to speak to us, but we could really use him right now," I say, thinking about our time in Boston before we moved here. We found ourselves in a similar predicament when he was courting Harper, and though we were merely trying to protect her, the end result was the same as it is now: the death of a human and a frantic scurry to cover it up.

"He will come around."

I jerk my head in Mylo's direction. "How can you be so sure? What incentive does he have to help us at all?"

Mylo huffs a breath, a thoughtful expression flashing across his face. "I just know. We are a lucky bunch. We are lucky we survived the crash, and Luka is lucky he found Harper. Our luck has continued as long as we have been on this planet. I know it will continue."

Over the next twenty-four hours, Mylo, Zev, and Kyan are taken in for questioning, and I am taken in again, essentially to repeat what I already told them about the night at Tipsy's.

We continue calling Luka, but he never answers.

It feels as if our luck has run out.

CHAPTER 22

VANESSA

*I*t's been two days since the police questioned Axil, and one day since he was questioned a second time. I'm starting to freak out. What if they're getting closer to the truth? What if someone saw him out there with Trevor? What if someone heard Trevor screaming?

I can't bring myself to consider what could happen beyond them charging Axil with murder, because the moment I do, images of test tubes and needles flood my mind. I picture Axil lying unconscious, strapped to a bed while experiments are being done on him and his brothers. I would never forgive myself if they were discovered. Forget going to jail for murder. This would be so much worse.

And all because of me. Because Axil wanted to protect me.

Then my mind drifts back to *What the hell is wrong with me?* for wanting Axil as much as I do, considering he confessed to murdering Trevor. And then said he loved me in the same breath. My skin shouldn't have felt like it was on fire as Axil described what he did to Trevor.

I should've been afraid. Disgusted. Horrified. I should've booked it out of there as fast as I could and stayed far away from Axil. That's how a normal person would react, right?

Yet, even after a few days to process his revelation, I'm not afraid, disgusted, or horrified. Not at all. If anything, I'm in awe. His declaration of love stole my breath. No one has ever said such beautiful things to me before. I've heard "I love you" from guys I've dated, but it always felt flat and obligatory. Axil's was neither. It was real, and what I have with him feels like the kind of love I assumed didn't exist. The kind of love that was too good to be true.

So why is it so hard for me to say it back? To tell him that I love him, too, and that I want to spend the rest of my life with him? I should've said it. He should know how I feel. How I've felt since... since, well, I'm not sure when it happened, exactly, but somewhere along the way, I fell madly in love with Axil Monroe.

I wanted to tell him. I almost did too. But just as I opened my mouth to let the words out, the doorbell rang, and Officer Burton took Axil away.

Maybe I should just call Axil now and tell him what I couldn't in the moment. As I reach for my phone off the nightstand, it buzzes, causing me to jump.

Sam: *Funeral is today. You sure we shouldn't go?*

Me: *Yes, we definitely need to skip it. That's the number one thing I learned from crime shows. Murderers tend to show up at their victims' funerals. We can't be anywhere near there.*

Sam: *Okay, but we're not murderers. And it seems like the entire town is going. Wouldn't it look weirder if we were the only ones not in attendance?*

Me: *I see what you mean, but I still think it's a bad idea. I can't face Beth right now.*

Sam: *BTW, should we be saying all of this over text? Want me to call you?*

Me: *LOL, well, too late now.*

Sam: *Fair point. I don't even know what I'd say to Beth. I feel so bad for her daughters, though who knows what role Trevor played in their lives or how much he was involved.*

Me: *She said something in passing when I ran into her at the* *grocery store. Something about how she couldn't leave Trevor alone with the girls for too long.*

Sam: *Wow.*

Me: *Yeah.*

Sam: *How's Axil doing? Have you talked to him?*

Me: *We've had dinner the last two nights, but it's weird. I can't stop thinking about what will happen if they charge him. And what will happen to his brothers the moment they discover he's different? The vibe between us has just been tense. He goes to touch me, and I pull away.*

Me: *He keeps telling me there's nothing to worry about, but I don't think he understands how bad this could get.*

Sam: *That sucks.*

Me: *Ugh, I know.*

Sam: *How are the brothers holding up?*

Me: *By "the brothers" do you mean...Mylo?*

Sam: *I hate you.*

I'm tempted to call her a liar and continue teasing her, but I'm too tired. These last few days have been exhausting. I'm sure it's directly related to stress, but I've struggled to get out of bed, and even when I do, after a few hours, I lie down for a nap.

Sam suggested I distract myself with busy work—easy activities that will occupy just enough of my brain to keep me from worrying, but not so much that I actually have to think. So I've been making mood boards on Pinterest for how I'd like to redecorate the house.

I've also been writing letters to Aunt Franny. They're not drafts of my good-bye letter—I refuse to spread her ashes and let her go for good, which I know isn't great since the date I was supposed to spread them has passed—but more random thoughts that pop into my head. I write them down addressed to her, read them aloud, and throw the paper away. I just need the ability to vent to her, because I feel so alone right now, and I wish more than anything that she were still here.

At some point, I'll write my good-byes and go through the motions of spreading the rest of her ashes. I'm just not ready. Maybe when I'm less terrified about what will happen to my alien boyfriend, but I can't do it now.

Since I'm stalling on saying good-bye, I also haven't found the treasure. It seems silly to put off such a major task that I've been desperate to accomplish since I first arrived, but fear of the unknown has left me paralyzed and unmotivated.

My stomach drops when my phone starts ringing, but the tension fades when I see that it's Willa. She's been checking on me every few hours since she first heard of Trevor's death, and even though I can't have Aunt Franny here, I'm so happy I have Willa.

"Hey, kid," she says when I pick up my phone. "Doing okay today?"

I let out a sigh. "Yeah, I guess. You going to the funeral?"

"Ugh, I don't want to," she groans, "but Beth's daughters are in Jordan's class, so if I don't, it'll become a whole thing with the other moms."

"Yikes," I say, not knowing how else to respond.

"I'll swing by after, if you want?" she offers.

"Yeah, sounds good."

The funeral is set to begin in just over an hour from now. I can't imagine a more perfect time to close my eyes and let the world around me fade to black.

* * *

By the time I wake up, it's already dark out. It seems I slept right through lunch, which is very odd for me. I've never been one of those people to "forget to eat," and I've never understood the people who do. My stomach growls just thinking about catching up for the meal I missed as I get out of bed and pad to the bathroom to splash water on my face.

The moment I step out of the bathroom, the doorbell rings. It's probably Axil, checking in about dinner tonight, though he usually comes in through the back door.

Oh, Willa said she was going to come by after the funeral. It must be her. A smile tugs at my lips as I head toward the door. I'm very much in need of one Willa's too-tight hugs. But when I open the door, it isn't Willa.

It's Officer Burton.

"Good afternoon, Vanessa," he says stiffly. "I noticed you weren't at the services today for Trevor."

"Right," I squeak out. This is awful. Terrible. I want to scream for help, but what good would that do? "I, uh, wasn't feeling up to it."

He narrows his gaze, and I feel like a girl in high school again, sitting in his office after the worst moment of my life, silently begging him to believe me. "I'm going to need you to come down to the station to answer a few questions."

Then it's as if the world spins around me, and my hearing goes out like it does for people near an explosion. There's just a steady ringing in my ears as they lead me toward the police car and help me get in the back seat.

It's only once I'm in the car that I notice I'm still wearing slippers, which are now ruined from walking through the snow. The drive to the station is quick, but it feels like it takes hours, and part of me wonders if this is it. If when I enter the police station, I won't be coming back out.

I know *I* didn't kill anyone, but Axil did, so technically, that means I'm aiding and abetting, right? Or is it an obstruction of justice? Maybe both. All I know is I *cannot* blow Axil's cover.

Officer Burton leads me past his office, the same one he's had for over twenty years, and into a room with a table, three chairs, and a large mirror. It's exactly how I expected an interrogation room to look.

Thankfully, a second officer joins us at the table, so it's not just me and Officer Burton. I'm not sure I could handle that again. Not after last time, and certainly not under these particular circumstances.

"So, Vanessa," Officer Burton begins. "I had a chat with Beth today at the funeral."

He pauses, and I wait for him to continue. When he doesn't, my palms start to sweat. He's toying with me, and he knows it.

"She said the two of you had quite the argument at the reunion," he finally adds.

"Um, yeah," I say, nodding.

"This took place around nine-eighteen, the night of Trevor's death. Would you say that's correct?"

I shrug. "I have no idea what time it was, but that sounds right."

"Now," he says with a sigh, "since Trevor's time of death was approximately nine-fifteen, you're currently not a person of interest in this case."

I release the breath I didn't know I was holding. And I immediately regret looking relieved, hoping Officer Burton didn't notice.

"But what can you tell us about this man?" he asks, dropping a picture of Axil on the table. It's his license photo.

"He's, uh, my neighbor," I tell him, feeling the need to clarify further. "Or actually he was my aunt's neighbor, but she died, and now he's my neighbor."

"Right," Officer Burton says. "Is that all he is to you? Just your neighbor?"

Did Axil tell him we were together? Shit, I should've asked him so we could be on the same page. If he did tell them we're together, and I say we're just friends, that will look suspicious. But if I tell them we are together after Axil told them we're just neighbors, that will also look odd. The important thing is to avoid making Axil seem like a liar because then they'd have a reason to question him again.

See, now I'm getting in my head.

"Well?" Officer Burton asks with an irritated furrow of his brow. "It's a simple question."

"Um," I begin, feeling a drop of sweat run down my spine. I brush my bangs out of my eyes, nervously. "He's a friend. A friend and a neighbor."

"I see," he replies, unconvinced. "And you were with him the night of Trevor's death, were you not?"

"I mean, yes, but…" I stammer, my eyes darting back and forth between the two officers. What is he implying? That I helped Axil? "Why do you ask? I don't see how that matters."

"The reason I'm asking doesn't matter. I just need you to answer."

"Well, yes. He picked me up from the reunion and took me home."

He scribbles something on the paper in front of him. I lean forward, trying to read it upside down. I can't help myself. If whatever I'm saying is making Axil look guilty, then I need to give him a heads up. Officer Burton notices me peeking and snatches the paper away.

"Did he take you home? Or back to his house?" he asks.

"His house. I said that." But wait, did I? I can't remember. "He took me back to his house."

"No, you said he took you home," Officer Burton says, wagging his pen. "So which is it?"

My fists clench as I say "His house. I said we went back to his house" a bit louder than was probably necessary.

"Seems like you're having trouble keeping your story straight."

"No!" I cry out, as the walls of this tiny room feel like they're closing in around me. "I just got confused about that one thing!"

Officer Burton holds up a hand. "There's no need to get emotional. Just calm down."

Seriously? How is one supposed to act in an interrogation? Is everyone that comes in here perfectly calm?

I roll my eyes. I know I shouldn't, but I can't help it. "I am calm!"

"Listen, Ms. Bradford," Officer Burton shouts, "if you don't get a hold of yourself, you're in for a very long night."

I'm so screwed.

CHAPTER 23

AXIL

*W*hen I pass a police car the moment I turn onto my street, a shudder rips through my body. Who is being questioned now? Mylo again? Zev? What more information do they need? Or were they looking for me? Have they found evidence to link me with Trevor's death?

I rush inside the house and am surprised to find Zev and Mylo eating Chinese food and watching TV. "Was it Kyan?" I ask, tossing my car keys onto the table by the door.

"Was what Kyan?" Mylo asks with his mouth full.

"In the cop car," I tell them. "I just passed a cop car when I turned down our street. I figured one of you was being questioned again."

"Oh," Zev says, looking surprised. "No, the cops did not show up here. Kyan is still at work."

If they didn't come here, then...

I knock the front door off its hinges as I slam it open, running at full speed. I hear Zev yelling at me from the living room, but I do not stop. I do not stop until I reach Vanessa's back door and start pounding on it. I turn the handle, but it appears to be locked. Looking in the little window, the kitchen looks dark. I race around to the bedroom but cannot see anything since the curtains are drawn. I am panicking by the time I reach her front door, pressing the doorbell over and over in the hopes that she is still here, just asleep, or something.

Nothing. She does not come to the door, which means she is not home. There are only two other homes on this street, so if the cops came to collect someone, it had to be Vanessa.

Charging back around Vanessa's house, I almost collide with Mylo and Zev as they work on fixing the door. "Move!" I shout, skirting around them to grab my keys. Seconds later, I am back on the road and driving toward the station.

I send Vanessa several texts once I arrive, but she does not respond to a single one. When I go inside and ask if Vanessa is there, I am told I will need to wait until Officer Burton is done questioning her, so I go back to the truck and wait. An hour later, I spot movement at the entrance out of the corner of my eye. It is Vanessa, walking outside, still in her slippers, with puffy cheeks and swollen eyes. I leave my keys in the ignition and race toward her, gathering her in my arms as she continues to cry.

Officer Burton stands just inside the door, shooting me a lethal glare. He wants me to be afraid of him, which is quite humorous, given what I truly am.

Ignoring him, I take Vanessa's hand and guide her toward my truck. "You were questioned?" I ask quietly once we are both strapped in.

"Yeah," she says, sniffling. "It was awful. I tried to do well," she says, staring down at her hands, folded in her lap. "I tried to keep you from sounding guilty or suspicious, but...I–I don't know. Officer Burton kept tripping me up."

"It is okay," I tell her, trying to reassure her. "Do not worry."

"No, it's not okay," she says, dropping her face into her hands and crying harder. "I fucked up. I was nervous and it made me look guilty."

I put a hand on her back as I drive, gently rubbing. Seeing her like this is gutting.

"If they think I was involved or covering for you..." she trails off, not wanting to state the consequences.

"Nothing will happen to you, Vanessa," I tell her, my tone firm. "I promise you. I will not let you take the blame for my actions."

This is all my fault. I was selfish and impulsive, and I let my temper guide my hand. I still do not regret ending Trevor's life. The world is a better place without him. But if this hurts her, I will never forgive myself.

We drive home in silence as a plan begins to take shape in my mind. If Officer Burton suspects I am guilty, and that Vanessa had something to do with it, he will not stop until she and I are both behind bars. Given that Trevor was his nephew, I am certain he will refuse to accept this as a motorcycle accident and nothing more. He wants someone to blame. He is greedy for it. Because, otherwise, he will have to face the fact that his nephew was a reckless fool.

He also seems eager to link Vanessa to Trevor's death, obviously because of her previous accusations against Trevor. I am sure this all feels like justice to Officer Burton. I would almost respect his vengeful endeavors if he were not targeting my mate in the process.

What this feeble human does not realize is that I am no ordinary male, and when a draxilio finds their mate, nothing can stand between them. I will not allow anyone to blame Vanessa for this, and I do not care if I have to burn this entire town to ash to make my point clear.

She laces her tiny human fingers through mine once we get out of the truck and head inside my house. We eat some of the leftover Chinese food Zev and Mylo left on the counter, and immediately climb into bed.

We do not have sex. In fact, we do nothing but kiss as Vanessa is clearly too upset. I do not mind as long as I get to hold her in my arms. And I do. I press kisses along her cheeks and forehead, and when she falls asleep, I whisper, "Nothing will part us, Vanessa. You will forever have my protection. This, I vow."

Slowly extracting myself from her grip, I pull myself out of bed and take a seat at my desk. If I am going to do this, I need to make sure I leave things in order. Starting with Mylo, I write letters to all my brothers, including Luka, telling them where I have gone, and what I plan to do. I assure them that this will in no way complicate their lives. I will not allow my hasty decisions to ruin their futures here on Earth.

When I am done with the last letter, Kyan's, I pull out a blank sheet of paper and begin my letter to Vanessa.

My love,

At this very moment, you are soundly asleep in my bed right where you belong. You look so ravishing, the way your lips are parted—despite the steady stream of dribble that is now on my pillow. I jest, of course. Every part of you makes me hard, including your sleep dribble.

I am so sorry for the place in which we currently find ourselves. It was never my intention to cause you distress. You do not deserve to relive this particular pain over and over, and while I thought my actions would ultimately bring you peace, I see now that I have only caused more harm.

The only way to clear your name is to give them mine. I shall confess to taking Trevor's life while making it clear you had no involvement whatsoever. Officer Burton wants revenge, and to get that, he needs a criminal to charge. Once he has it, all of this goes away. You and my brothers will no longer be watched.

There is no reason to worry. While it will take some time for me to find a way back to you, I promise you, I shall find a way. We will not be apart for long. I refuse to exist without you.

You are the center of my universe, Vanessa. That shall never change.

I love you.

-Axil

I fold the letter and place it on the pillow next to her before I go. And I commit her shape and face to memory as the thought of her will be the only thing that sustains me over the coming days.

Taking a deep inhale once I am outside, I steel my spine. It is time to face my destiny.

CHAPTER 24

VANESSA

I wake up to the crinkling of paper beneath my chin. Confused, I look around, still half-asleep. I realize I'm in Axil's room, which makes me smile, but the smile fades when I reach over to his side of the bed and find the sheets cold. He's not here and hasn't been for a while.

Pulling myself up into a seated position against his headboard, I rub a hand down my face as I examine a piece of paper. It's a letter from Axil.

I'm halfway down the page when I leap out of bed and run down the hall, screaming for his brothers to join me in the living room.

Mylo and Zev are already there, their expressions somber and serious. "You got one too?" They ask, holding up their letters.

"Yes," I mutter. "Did you know he was going to do this?"

They shake their heads in unison.

"We called Kyan. He is on his way home," Zev says, holding up the letter with Kyan's name on it. "He has not read his yet."

I shift my weight between my feet, not knowing what to do. If Axil turned himself in already, there's not much I *can* do. Unless we figure out how to bust Axil out and then we go on the run. I'm not a huge fan of road trips, but maybe it wouldn't be so bad with Axil. My acting career was kind of going nowhere anyway. And if we're able to sell Aunt Franny's house, we'll have some cash to set us up for a little while.

Kyan bursts through the door, a welcome interruption from my anxiety spiral. He rips off his blazer and tosses it across the room in a ball, grumbling under his breath. "Stupid asshole!" he shouts.

Wow, he is terrifying when he's mad.

He paces back and forth across the entryway, his muscles taut as he runs a rough hand through his hair. It's longer than Axil's, but the same light brown color. I would describe it as shaggy in length, but not in appearance. It's always slicked back with gel, or whatever he uses, giving him a stern boss-man-from-the-eighties look.

"If he had just fucking waited two more days, I would have been able to help him," Kyan yells, shoving his fist into the back of the leather couch.

"How?" I ask, taking slow, cautious steps toward him into the living room.

He shakes his head as he stares at the floor. "I was working on something."

Mylo turns to me. "Don't mind the cryptic response, Vanessa. Kyan does not like talking about his very important job," he says."

"What are we supposed to do now?" Zev asks, crossing his arms over his chest.

"You are supposed to shut the fuck up and do exactly as I say," a loud voice booms as a man I don't recognize storms into the house.

"Luka!" Mylo shouts, leaping off the couch with his arms outstretched.

"No time for that," Luka says upon Mylo's approach. He looks around the room, and his gaze lands on me. "You are the mate?"

"Vanessa," I say, pointing to myself. "Nice to meet you."

He surprises me with a genuine, warm smile. "It is an honor." Then he claps his hands together as he takes a seat on the couch. "Let us free Axil, shall we?"

* * *

It takes three hours, four pizzas with pepperoni and banana peppers, and fifteen cans of orange-flavored sparkling water for us to come up with a solid plan.

"I shall go over it again," Luka says, taking the time to look each of us in the eye before continuing. "We take two cars. Kyan and, um, sorry, what is your name again?"

"Sam," she says, excitedly. I was worried when I called her that she'd refuse to get involved, but it turns out, Sam is quite passionate about justice for aliens. That, or she wanted an excuse to see Mylo again. Who knows?

"Sam, right. Kyan and Sam will drive. We park across the street from the station at the nail salon," Luka continues, going through the steps he jotted down in his phone. "Then Sam will go in and flirt with the officers at the front. There should be two. She will distract them with nude selfies."

Everyone in the circle nods in agreement.

"So you know which photo you are going to use, then?" Mylo asks Sam, his brow arched.

"Hmm, I think so," she replies casually. "There's so many to choose from, but I've got it narrowed down to three." She tilts her head to the side. "Maybe I'll just show all three."

Mylo nods, trying to keep it cool, as his eye twitches.

"When the officers are looking at that, she will give us the signal to sneak in behind her." He takes a loud sip of sparkling water, then points to Mylo. "Mylo, what is that signal?"

"She will scratch the back of her head, and give us a thumbs up," Mylo says for the second time.

"Very good," Luka claps. "Then Zev, Vanessa, and I will sneak in and locate Axil's cell, which should not be hard, since it is a small station. Zev will pick the lock..."

"Wait, how do you know it's a lock you can pick?" I ask. "What if it opens with a code or something?"

"Then I shall enter the code," Zev replies as if it should be obvious. Kyan, Luka, and Mylo are all giving me the same "duh!" look.

"Okay, but how will you know the code?"

"Do not worry your pretty human head about that," Luka says with a chuckle. "Zev does stuff like this all the time."

I'm not at all comforted by that, but I also know they won't let Axil rot in a jail cell, either so I guess I'll have to trust Zev knows what he's doing.

"Now," Luka says, clearing his throat, "if we run into trouble, aka another officer, specifically, Officer Dipshit, I will do what I do."

This plan is still so vague. I feel like I'm missing several important parts to it. But whenever I question something, one of the brothers shuts me down with a "don't worry, we've got this" type of response. I would take it as a sexist dismissal and bite their heads off accordingly, but I also wonder if it's because I'm human. Maybe they have more tricks up their sleeves.

While I appreciate their confidence, these are aliens trying to navigate the jumbled dysfunction of the human criminal justice system. I'm worried they're in over their heads.

"What happens when we get him out?" Sam asks. "Are you all just gonna come back here and see how long it takes for the cops to figure out what happened?"

"By the time we get him out, this will no longer be an area of concern," Luka replies. "But if, for whatever reason, we get him out before we can safeguard our futures, everyone will come to my house where we will lie low for about a week while we get things in order." He sighs, heavily. "Then we shall choose our next location and head there."

Wow. So I guess we would need to leave it all behind. I hate that as soon as I decide to stay in Sudbury, something happens that forces me to leave. But as long as Axil is free, I can adapt.

He's the one I want. I know that for certain now. Any doubts I previously had are gone. I know Aunt Franny won't love the idea of both of us leaving this patch of land behind, but I think she'd approve of the match. I know she would.

"Everybody ready?" Luka asks, eagerly rubbing his palms together.

There are head nods and sighs and an abundance of nervous energy as we get up and stretch our legs. I'm disappointed to discover that when we step outside, it's still light out.

"Shouldn't we...wait? Until later to do this?" I ask, checking the time on my phone. It's only two-thirty.

Everyone looks at me like I'm off my damn rocker.

"Why would we wait?" Luka asks, his nose scrunched up.

I suppose I don't have a good enough reason other than capers like this typically take place at night. "We can't exactly sneak around in broad daylight."

"We don't need the cover of darkness to get this done," Kyan says, placing his hand on my shoulder. He's been a surprising source of comfort since I met him. He shoots me a wink before getting into the driver's seat of his car, and the rest of us split into two groups with Kyan following Sam.

There aren't many cars in the parking lot, and luckily for us, the nail salon is closed today, so that lot is empty as well. We park next to each other, and through the windows, we all exchange a nod that says "good luck" before Sam heads inside the station.

Luka, Zev, and I follow about a minute behind, and duck behind a bush that's about seven feet from the station entrance, but still close enough that we'll be able to see Sam's signal.

I see her flip her long, curly hair over her shoulder as she throws her head back and laughs at whatever one of the cops up front said. It's clearly a fake laugh, but Sam's wearing a V-neck cut so low that I'm hoping they're too distracted by her cleavage to notice.

She leans over the front desk, showing off her ample assets as she hands them her phone. One of them starts choking on his coffee while the other stares at the phone with his mouth hanging open.

The one with his mouth open says something, to which she giggles and puts her hand on his arm. She asks for her phone back, swipes across the screen a few times, then turns to show them again, but before they get a peek at the screen, she fumbles with the phone, and it falls between them on the floor. The moment they both scramble to pick it up, she gives us the signal.

The three of us scurry inside but remain crouched, so they can't easily see us over the desk. Sam lays her top half on the counter as she points to the phone, still on the floor, and says, in a much higher voice than I've ever heard her use, "Oh, then there's the one of me eating a popsicle while my sorority sister tries to unhook my bra with one hand."

Genius. She was never in a sorority, but they don't know that.

At the end of the hall, we turn right, and find a locked door marked "Holding." Zev steps out in front of us, waving a hand at the cameras we pass, and each one's little red light immediately turns off. Amazing. My job is to keep watch as the caboose. Zev pulls two bobby pins from his pocket, then closes his eyes as he presses a hand flat against the lock. He opens his eyes with a fresh determination and gets to work twisting the pins together inside the keyhole.

Five seconds is all it takes for him to get the door open, and I suspect there's some kind of genetically modified dragon magic at play here.

We race down another hallway, and at the end, we find four jail cells, all empty except Axil's.

"What are you doing here?" he asks when he sees us. Then he notices Luka is here too. Axil's eyes turn ice cold. "I called you. Several times."

Luka turns to me. "Vanessa, keep an ear out for anyone coming down that hall."

"Do not order her around," Axil growls. "What are you doing here? You just decided you care about your family now?"

Even though I'm on high alert halfway down the hall, I still keep my eyes on Axil and Luka. Luka sighs and shrugs his shoulders. "I am here now, am I not? Also, it will be me who gets you out of this mess. A mess you never needed to be in, for the record."

"Yes, extremely dumb of you to turn yourself in, brother," Zev adds, entering that same meditative state as he presses a hand to the lock on the cell door.

"Why?" Luka shouts. "Why would you do this?"

"Guys! Keep it down," I remind them in a loud whisper.

Axil's face softens when he looks at me. "It was the easiest way for me to protect Vanessa." He drops his chin to his chest. "Perhaps it was rash, and I did not think it through, entirely—"

"No, you did not think it through entirely," Luka says with a sarcastic chuckle.

"Vanessa, I am so sorry," he says, ignoring Luka. His eyes are pleading. They draw me in, those eyes. My feet start moving before I even realize it, and soon my hands are wrapped around the bars of his cell. "Please, forgive me."

"I forgive you," I tell him immediately. "I love you. We are going to get you out of here, okay?"

"Wait," he says, shaking his head. "You love me?"

I lean my forehead against the bars. "Of course, I do. I'm yours, Axil. Always. I'm sorry I didn't tell you before." I thought he knew. It felt like I had made it clear that we were partners in this. I didn't run away when he admitted to killing Trevor. I stuck around. But still, I should've told him. "I know your eyes haven't turned, but I'd be honored to be your mate, if you still want me."

His eyes turn watery. He covers my hands with his. "There will never be a day I will not want you. You are my heart."

"Hey!" a voice calls from the end of the hallway. Officer Burton's stern, unpleasant face appears, and the moment he sees me, he groans. "Jesus Christ." Over his shoulder, I hear him mutter to his partner, "Cuff that crazy bitch. I'll deal with the others."

When I look back at Axil, his eyes are a bright, bone-chilling red color where they should be white. "Axil! Your eyes!" I shout. He backs up as far as he can inside the cell and ducks his head down.

Everything happens so quickly. Zev is still struggling to open the lock, and Luka is just standing there with a strange, narrowed gaze on Officer Burton. We've been caught. The jig is up, and we're all about to be arrested. Why isn't anyone reacting appropriately?

The only thing I can think to do is distract them. I don't have any nude selfies to share, and I wouldn't even if I did. Acting sexy doesn't come naturally to me. But I don't need to be sexy to hold their attention. I have other tools at my disposal.

They think I'm crazy? Might as well lean into it then. I open my mouth and let the chaos out.

CHAPTER 25

AXIL

I want to look away in an effort to hide my eyes, but I cannot. Vanessa is far too captivating to look away from. My draxilio is equally enchanted by her, letting out a steady purr as he watches in awe. I am not sure what she's doing, but it is very clearly a performance as she sounds nothing like herself. What is this called when a person delivers a long string of uninterrupted speech? Ah, yes, a monologue. Lady Norton told me about this.

The monologue Vanessa is reciting is unfamiliar to me, but now that I am hearing it, I am desperate to discover the source. It is a poem, and it is written for someone specific, that much is clear from her words. She begins to cry halfway through it, looking utterly heartbroken at the raw emotion she is revealing.

The authenticity is not the most fascinating part of this display, however. No, that would be her voice. A voice that is not at all hers, but an impression of someone else. Someone whose voice is lower, and possibly suffering from chronic congestion. It is a voice that also sounds a bit like a horn, with a hollow honking quality to it.

I decide I do not care what this is from or who she is doing an impression of. She is clearly trying to distract the cops with how ridiculous, yet earnest it is, and it is working. That is the level of her talent. If we ever do get out of here, I will offer to move to Los Angeles with her, so she can keep pursuing her dream. Her talent is too grand to be wasted.

At a certain point, Luka steps in between Vanessa and Officer Burton, not saying anything, just holding Officer Burton's gaze. Vanessa notices and quiets her voice as her monologue comes to an end.

I can tell the moment Luka has Officer Burton under his spell. The way Officer Burton's features soften, and the glazed look of his eyes is a dead giveaway.

"Officer Burton, is it?" Luka asks, smiling.

Officer Burton just nods, his movements robotic.

"A pleasure to meet you, sir," Luka says, his voice sickly sweet. "I am Axil Monroe's lawyer."

Vanessa looks at me, confused. I shake my head, indicating she shouldn't worry about it. This is the ability Luka carries as a result of his modifications and has used it more than once to get us out of trouble. It is why he was so reluctant to help us now. We have relied heavily on his ability to influence the decisions of others, and he grew tired of exploiting humans for our own gain.

Luka's gaze shifts to the officer behind Officer Burton, pulling him in. "And you are?"

"Officer Freeman," the man replies, his tone dreamlike.

"Wonderful. Now, my client here has been wrongfully imprisoned, and I am going to insist you let him go."

Officer Burton glances at me, then back at Luka. "He confessed to murdering my nephew."

"No," Luka replies flatly, "he did not. You misunderstood him. Isn't that right?"

"Right," both officers reply with a robotic nod.

"You do not have enough evidence to charge him, but regardless, there was no crime committed here, you see, because your nephew was a reckless, entitled little prick, and his death was an accident."

"Right," they repeat in unison.

"Trevor Burton was speeding down that curvy road, in the dark, at the beginning of a snowstorm," Luka says, leaning in close to Officer Burton. "He lost control of his bike and went off the road, where he died. There are also several witnesses who can attest to him drinking at the reunion before getting on that bike. And Trevor has a history of driving under the influence, right?"

"Right."

"Perhaps if he had been wearing a helmet, or sober, he might still be alive," Luka adds. "But I suppose we will never know."

"Right."

"So now, you are going to take your keys and open that cell."

"Right." Officer Burton pulls his keys from his pocket and unlocks the cell door.

"From this point on, Axil Monroe is innocent in your mind. He did nothing wrong. He is an upstanding citizen of Sudbury, and you are honored to have him and his brothers living in your town. And you are going to close this case, because you know it was an accident despite how badly you would like to believe otherwise."

"Right."

Luka steps to the side, but pauses, holding up a finger. "Another thing. You're going to leave Vanessa Bradford the fuck alone. Right?"

"Right."

I approach the open door, and Officer Burton quickly steps out of my way, ducking his head in shame. If only he could keep this wretched man under his trance forever.

Luka lifts his hand to awaken the officers, but I stop him. "Ask if there is a back door. We cannot just walk out front with them still in a daze."

"Ah," Luka nods, turning back to face Officer Burton. "You will let us out the back door. Upon hearing a car horn honk three consecutive times, you will awaken, and feel immediately compelled to close this case."

"Right."

"What the fuck?" Vanessa whispers conspiratorially as we follow the officers through another hallway and toward the back entrance.

We step outside and spot Sam back in the car with Mylo and Kyan in the other car. Luka tells the cops to go inside and turn away from the door, presumably so they cannot watch our getaway. The moment we see their backs, we race to the car.

I hop in the car with Sam and Vanessa, and Vanessa climbs on top of me in the backseat as Sam pulls out of the parking lot. My mate presses her lips to mine, and I feel her smile against my mouth. Then she whispers, "You're free."

I am free.

* * *

VANESSA

Oh my god, it worked. Axil is free. I can't believe it. "What was Luka doing in there?" I ask, still blown away by his ability to turn Officer Burton into a mindless zombie. It was beautiful.

"He has the ability to influence people's decisions," Axil explains. "And Zev has the ability to feel inanimate objects as well as alter them."

My mouth falls open. "You mean to tell me Luka could've come up here and done this days ago and didn't?"

"He is quite stubborn," Axil says, defending his brother. "It is an ability we took advantage of when we first arrived. He vowed to never use it again after the last time."

"What happened last time?" Sam asks from the front seat.

Axil scratches his beard as he looks out the window. "It is a long story. But it was used to protect his mate. I think that is why he made an exception for me, because he knew I was trying to do the same thing."

I press my forehead against his. "I'm your mate. It's official now, you blood-eyed beast." His eyes are no longer red, which I assume is a good thing.

"No turning back now, little human," he says, nipping at my bottom lip. He pulls back to look at me with wide eyes. "And what were *you* doing in there? What was that from?"

"Oh," I say, waving a dismissive hand, "it was just a monologue to distract them from seeing your red eyes."

Sam laughs. "You did a monologue? Which one?"

Suddenly I feel shy, having to explain it after the fact. "It was, um, it was the one from *10 Things I Hate About You*. You know the poem Julia Stiles reads?"

"Yeah…" Sam replies.

"Well, I did it in a Kermit voice."

Sam gasps. "You what!"

"And she cried!" Axil adds. "It was outstanding." Then he grabs my chin, pulling my face down toward his. "You are so talented. I could not look away."

I chuckle, rubbing my nose against his. "Thank you, sir."

"I fully support your acting career should you choose to continue on that path," Axil says, his tone genuine. "Whatever makes you happy."

"Well, I doubt I'll find many acting gigs out here, but I might meet up with the old Drama Club members once in a while to flex the old muscles," I tell him, surprisingly excited about that. "I need to find a job first, though."

"Why?" he asks, puzzled.

"Um, because…money?" I reply. "I know you're not from around here, but money is kind of key to survival."

"Fine," he says with a smug smile. "I have plenty of that for both of us. You do not need to work, if you do not want to."

I pull back to look at him. "Wait, are you serious? How much money are we talking about here?" He's made references to his wealth before, but I assumed that was all bravado.

Axil pulls my head down and whispers the number in my ear. I gasp instinctively. My alien is a damn billionaire. "Are you kidding me?" Then I attack him with my mouth. It's not as if I'm only into him for his money, but I've never known a life beyond living paycheck to paycheck, so I'm certainly looking forward to the ease that financial stability provides.

"Hey, you guys *cannot* have sex in the backseat, okay?" Sam scolds, glaring at us through the rearview mirror. "I'm not getting pulled over immediately after busting someone out of jail. That would be too pathetic."

We agree, begrudgingly, and I haul myself off Axil's lap and into my own seat. But the moment she drops us off at my place, Axil grabs my hand and runs full speed toward the door. "Your legs are longer!" I shout, trying to keep up.

He pulls me into his arms and lifts me across his chest, his arms beneath my legs and behind my back as he carries me across the threshold. "Home," he says with a contented sigh as he sets me on my feet.

I look around and nod. "Home."

Axil's arms wrap around me from behind as he presses a kiss to the top of my head. Then his hands begin to wander. One goes to my breast and squeezes while the other travels down my stomach and between my thighs. "Get these off," he groans, pulling at my clothes.

Our shoes come off in the dining room. Our shirts and pants land in the hallway. Just before we stumble into the bedroom, Axil breaks the clasp of my bra clean off, and before I can admonish him for it, he's pulling down my underwear.

"Cannot wait," he says in a husky voice. "Need you now."

He continues kissing my neck as he guides me down on all fours in the hallway. I look over my shoulder at him, standing behind me, stomach muscles rippling as he breathes, his hand wrapped around his giant throbbing cock. "So beautiful," he says, his eyes heavy-lidded as he looks down at me.

I hear him get on his knees behind me, but I don't feel him until he presses a kiss to my ass cheek. He kisses the other side and gives it a little bite, which sends a jolt of electricity up my spine. He put his fingers in my ass before. Does he want to do that again? Or does he want to use his cock this time?

I'm surprised by the thrill that races over my skin at the thought of it. It didn't seem like me, or a thing I'd even want to try before, but that was before Axil came into my life. I want everything he has to give.

His hand snakes around my stomach and dips down between my

legs. He presses his chest against my back as his tongue traces the shell of my ear. "You're so wet for me."

I'm already gasping, my hips jerking to meet his fingers, begging to be filled by him. "I've missed you," I moan.

"Mmm, I want to fuck this tight little ass," he whispers, using his other hand to massage the bite mark he left on my cheek.

"Please," I reply, breathy and needy, and in a voice I don't recognize.

He chuckles. "Not yet, little human. There is plenty of time for that. First, I must make you mine, body and soul."

I put my hand over his and push his fingers against my clit, refusing to wait another minute for him to give me what I want. The head of his cock brushes against my entrance, and he moves it up and down my slit, driving me wild with need.

"Please," I beg again, shifting my hips back to meet him.

He slams into me, not stopping until his thighs slap against my ass, and all the breath leaves my body. It stays that way as he starts to move, pounding into me relentlessly as if I were nothing but his little plaything. He crooks a finger beneath my chin, turning my head to the side so I can look at him. "Keep your eyes on me," he says. Then I feel his fingers move through my swollen, wet folds until he finds my clit. He rubs a slow circle around it, and my body lights up from the inside.

"Vanessa…" he groans almost as if he's in pain. "Fuck."

I try to keep my eyes on him, but it's impossible to keep them open when he's playing my body like it's his favorite instrument.

By the time he switches it up and starts moving his fingers side to side, I'm already gone. The combination of him fucking me hard and fast while his thick fingers caress my clit sends me over the edge as my hips move of their own accord.

Before I'm able to come down, I feel him pull out and his hand cups my pussy. I whimper at the empty feeling, but then I feel wetness followed by his cockhead moving between my cheeks as he presses against them, trapping his cock in the crack of my ass.

Through his ragged breaths, he says, "This ass is about to my mine." He nudges inside, slowly, and I tense. "Relax," he whispers.

I'm trying, but it feels like he's trying to push an entire tree through an olive. And then I'm annoyed by the terrible analogy and clench my jaw at the mental image.

"Breathe for me, Vanessa," he says, kneading my ass, encouragingly. "Just breathe."

I focus on the path of my breath, in and out, and once that steals my attention, my muscles loosen as he goes deeper. The deeper he goes, the harder it is to breathe, and just when I think there's nowhere else for him to go, he pushes farther inside me.

"You're too big," I moan, my nails digging into the thin rug beneath.

"You can take me, Vanessa. I know you can."

I cry out, my body unable to do anything else while so filled with Axil's cock.

"Yes," he hisses proudly. Then he pulls out and thrusts back in. "Good girl. So good for me."

This is unreal. To feel such intense stimulation in that particular area, I never knew it could be like this. Blinding, unrelenting pleasure shoots through me, bursting through every muscle, every nerve, every cell as I hold on for dear life.

Two thrusts later, and Axil comes too. He pulls out, hot jets of come streaming across my back. I hear him grunt appreciatively at the sight, then he bends down and presses a kiss between my shoulder blades. "I love you, Vanessa Bradford."

Using the last embers of my strength, I push myself up from where my face was pressed against the rug and turn to face him. "I love you, Axil Monroe."

"Axilssanai," he says. "It is my given name."

"Mmm," I say, pulling him down for a kiss. "Axilssanai. You healed me, you know."

The dimple in his cheek deepens as a wide smile spreads across his cheeks. "Yeah?"

I nod, thinking about how my body used to shut down when I even considered having sex with someone. He changed me. "Yeah."

Then, right before my eyes, he unmasks, letting me see him in his natural state. He's so stunning like this.

"Promise me something," I tell him.

"Anything."

"Whenever we're home, you stay like this," I say. "As you're meant to be. I want to see more of the real you."

His eyes fall closed as he presses his forehead against mine. "You honor me."

He pulls me to my feet, and we rinse off together in the shower. After I make him a peanut butter, jelly, and chip sandwich for dinner, we bundle up and head outside, but not before grabbing a shovel.

"You think we should do this now?" he asks, leading me to the top of the hill on the other side of his shed where the view is completely unobstructed, and the river and cornfields glow by the light of the full moon.

"Technically, I was supposed to do it the day after the reunion, at two in the afternoon," I tell him. "I feel like it's rude to wait any longer."

He tilts his head to the side. "That was your scheduled time too?"

"What?"

"That's when Lady Norton wanted me to say good-bye to her as well."

I chuckle, shaking my head. The woman set us up for an extremely morbid first date. That's so like her. "Do we dig first, or spread her ashes first?"

"I think we say good-bye and spread her ashes first," Axil suggests.

That does sound like the right order of events.

Axil clears his throat as I hold Aunt Franny's urn. He doesn't read from a letter. He speaks from the heart.

"Lady Norton, I am not sure the words exist in the English language to properly convey my gratitude," he begins, looking up at the moon.

At first, I find it odd for his gaze to land there since her ashes are in the urn I'm holding. But when he continues speaking about the power of her friendship, the way she used to laugh with her entire body, and her breathtaking generosity with the few people she truly loved, I understand. Aunt Franny was a force. She was magnetic and bold and never wasted a second worrying about what other people thought.

I don't know what happens when we die, but I know Aunt Franny's essence is not in the small pile of ash trapped inside a box. Whatever form she's taken, it's bigger than that. Way bigger. With how much she loved her people, and how vigorously she rooted for those people to find happiness, she might as well be the moon.

"I shall never forget the moments we shared," Axil says in closing. "Sweetest of dreams, Aunt Franny."

He takes the urn from my hands, and instead of spreading some on the ground, he takes some into his gloved hand and opens his palm, letting the wind carry her ashes away.

"Your turn," he says with a warm, gentle smile that makes me melt.

I've been dreading this moment, even before I found the last letter. I had no idea how to say good-bye, or where to even begin. How do you say good-bye to the person who, not only gives you a house, but a life you never dreamed possible?

I blow out a breath and lift my eyes to the moon. "My Dearest Aunt Franny," I start. "I didn't realize it until just now, but...this isn't good-bye. I know it was part of your plan to have me say good-bye so I could move forward with my life. I've learned that I don't need one in order to get the other. Because, with you, it's never going to be a good-bye. I'm going to keep talking to you, even when you don't want to listen. Even when you're too busy floating in a pool of chocolate with Bruce Lee," I say, giggling.

"What?" Axil asks, his brow furrowed.

"Never mind."

"What I'm saying," I continue, "is that as long as I live here, which will be a very long time, I think, I will still feel your presence. This place is not mine, and no longer yours. It's ours."

My eyes sting with tears, and I don't hold them back. I don't even try. I just let them fall. "I was too focused on my own misery, my own lack of success, to leave room for anything else. Until you brought me home. Thank you," I say, a sniffle breaking through my words, "for bringing me home, and for making it a place I never want to leave again."

Axil pulls me into his side, rubbing my back as I tell Aunt Franny how much I'll always love her. He holds out the urn, and I take it, turning it on its side, and letting the rest of her ashes fall from the box and into the wind.

I take one last look at the moon and turn to Axil. "Should we dig?"

"Indeed," he replies.

The steel box we discover is not buried deep. It's maybe two feet beneath the ground. Without Axil's inhuman strength, we never would've made it that short distance with the ground still very much frozen.

He grunts as he pulls it out and drops it next to the hole. I stare at the top of it, wondering if this is truly the treasure. If this is really the end of Aunt Franny's game. What if I open it and it's a bunch of animal crackers and a letter that says, "Ha-ha! Dumbass!"

That's not really her style, though.

"Open it," Axil nudges.

"Okay, okay," I say, more to myself than him. With shaky fingers, I use one of the faded, bronze keys on her keychain to undo the lock, flip the latch, and lift the top. There's no letter. And no animal crackers.

Just fifteen thousand dollars in cash.

EPILOGUE

VANESSA

A MONTH LATER...

"*H*ey, no running on the stage, guys!" I remind the group of seven-year-olds who are too focused on a game of tag to put their costumes on.

"Van! Look what I brought," Willa shouts upon entering the auditorium, carrying a giant cardboard box.

"What is that?" I ask, meeting her halfway.

"Aunt Franny's hats!" she says, opening the top flaps and pulling out a ridiculous-looking maroon top hat with feathers. "I thought they'd be good for the lost boys."

"And girls," I correct her, leaning forward, lowering my voice, "because we don't have enough boys to fill all the roles."

"Ah, good call," she says. "Thank you so much for helping, but shouldn't you be sitting down? Taking it easy?"

"I'm pregnant, not made of tissue paper," I tell her. Though sitting does sound nice. I've been chasing after kids for the last half hour.

"Oh my god, I'm so excited to be an aunt!" Willa says, clapping her hands together. Then she puts her hands on my belly and I almost slap her. Almost.

"Hey, I'm only a month along. That's still just me down there. Hands off the goods." My eyes drift to the emerald necklace Willa's wearing. "What's that?"

She looks down and her eyes brighten. "Oh! I found it in the box with Aunt Franny's hats. Isn't it pretty? I've been wearing it every day."

"It really is," I reply. I don't tell Willa it's the necklace Mom has been asking about. The one she was certain Aunt Franny stole from her because Willa deserves it more anyway. It suits her, and clearly Aunt Franny wanted her to have it.

My phone buzzes in my pocket, and when I pull it out, I find a text from Tia about an upcoming casting call.

Tia: This sounds perfect for you! Sorry, I know you're all settled and happy in NH, but I had to send it along. Miss you!

I smile as I type my response.

Me: Miss you too! Thank you for this, but I'm going to pass. Lots of stuff keeping me busy around here. I'll text you when I'm in L.A. next month! Gotta pack up the apartment and haul my stuff back here.

She sends back several emojis, most of which don't make sense to me, but at least three smiley faces with heart eyes, so I take it as a good sign.

Willa and I run through the rehearsal plan for the rest of the week, and just as we're finishing up, Axil and Mylo enter the auditorium. Axil's wearing a gray T-shirt with a red flannel over it, the sleeves rolled up to his forearms, and he's carrying a bouquet of flowers.

"My love," he greets me, kissing the tip of my nose.

"Hi, dear," I say, wrapping my arms around his middle and pressing my head against his chest. Then I turn to his brother. "Hi, Mylo."

"Vanessa, you are glowing," he says with that lopsided, boyish grin that I'm sure melts all the hearts at the library.

"Mylo, I'm not very far along, so that's probably just sweat," I explain. "But thank you anyway."

Axil looks down at me. "You ready?" he asks, handing me the flowers.

Inhaling deeply, I moan at the warm floral scent. It's not the same as buying myself flowers, but it'll certainly do.

I nod, then turn to Willa. "Do you mind finishing up here?"

"Not at all," she says brightly. "I got this." Then she pats Axil on the arm. "Pregnant ladies like foot rubs, just FYI, future brother-in-law."

"Thank you for the tip," Axil says, chuckling.

We haven't set a date yet, and I'm not in a rush to do so. He proposed again the day after we dug up Aunt Franny's treasure chest, and I said yes, of course, but he already feels like my husband. It's probably the whole *mate* thing. In Axil's eyes, we're already mated, and therefore, share an eternal, unbreakable bond. So why go through the fuss of planning a wedding?

Willa really wants to be a bridesmaid, and I certainly don't want to disappoint her, but Axil and I have talked briefly about eloping. Or having a simple ceremony at the county courthouse. For now, I like just being his mate.

We stop on the way home to get gas, and Mylo and I hop out of the truck while Axil fills the tank. It's finally spring in Sudbury, which means the snow has melted completely, and the jackets are light. There's rain, and lots of it, but after not having any rain in L.A., I'm desperate for it.

It's not raining now, though, which means it's just a calm spring day.

That is, until a cop car pulls into the gas station next to us.

Officer Burton groans as he gets out of the driver's seat, and his face sours the moment he sees us.

"Ah, nice day, isn't it?" he says, his tone the opposite of friendly.

"Very nice," I reply, eager to keep this interaction short.

The three of us stand there, saying nothing, silently urging the pump to go faster so we can get the hell out of here.

My skin crawls when I hear Officer Burton's low, hoarse chuckle. "You know, it's strange..." he says. "There's something about you people that gives me a bad feeling. Something I just don't trust."

The pump clicks, and Mylo lets out a relieved exhale as Axil goes through the payment prompts on the screen.

"Is that so?" I reply, not knowing what else to say.

He steps between the barrier between our pumps and leans against it. "You did something to me," he says, pointing to me. "I don't know what, but I'll find out, and when I do, I'm coming for you."

"And what is it you think I did?" I ask, honestly amused he thinks I'm the source of his hazy memories.

"Like I said, I don't know," he replies coldly. "A hex. Some kind of curse. Maybe you brainwashed me."

Laughter bursts through my lips. I can't help it. "Are you accusing me of being a witch, Officer Burton?"

"I'm going to find out what you did," he vows.

Maybe it's because I'm in such a good place, emotionally, or maybe it's because I'm flanked by two alien dragon shifters. Or, a third possibility, maybe the pregnancy hormones are making me act impulsively, but I take a step toward Officer Burton, watching his features tighten the closer I get. I lean toward him and say, "It's your word against mine, though. You really think anyone is going to believe you?"

He flinches at my words. The reaction is subtle, but I notice it, and it fills me with glee.

We get back in the car before Officer Burton can form words and continue on our way. Turning onto our street, Axil asks if Sam is still planning on helping us paint the nursery.

"Not for another two weeks, at least," I reply. "She left this morning on an assignment. When she gets back, though."

"Sam is gone?" Mylo asks, leaning his head forward between Axil and me.

"Yeah, but she'll be back soon," I reassure him.

His expression is hard to read, but if I had to guess, I'd say he's a bit sad. The two of them continue to be tight-lipped about whatever happened between them, and I've given up trying to needle it out of them.

Axil pulls into the driveway, and Mylo hops out, heading back to his place. We still spend time next door, and Axil still has his shed, of course, but for the most part, Axil has moved into my house, and we're making it our own. We just replaced the couch he broke and are figuring out the overall aesthetic we want.

The front door hasn't even fully shut behind us before Axil unmasks and is kissing my neck and unbuttoning my shirt. I don't protest. I can't seem to get enough of him. I keep expecting the honeymoon period to pass, but it hasn't. If anything, we've become more ravenous for each other with each passing day.

Axil pulls me against him, and I feel his hardness pressed against my belly. "Take off your clothes and get on the table," he orders me.

I come close to suggesting an alternative location as this table is so nice. He made it himself for Aunt Franny, and the wood carving in the center is so intricate and beautiful, but I decide against it when I can't think of anywhere else I want him to take me. We've had sex on every other surface in the house at this point.

He takes a step back and slowly undresses himself as he watches me. I can't be seductive when I want him this much, so I rip my clothes off as fast as I can and step on the chair at the end of the table before climbing onto it.

Axil's eyes gleam as he takes himself in hand. "On your back."

I obey, spreading my legs wide and watching him suck in a breath at the sight.

The ridges that cover his cock are a lighter shade of blue than the rest of him, and I can't take my eyes off of them. I'm still a little bit mad at him for not telling me that part of his masking includes the disappearance of those incredible ridges when he's trying to look like a human. But now that I know, we don't have sex unless he's my beautiful blue, horned, ridged alien mate.

"Are you ready for me, Vanessa?" he says, walking slowly toward me like a predator about to pounce.

I run my fingers through my folds, finding them soaked. "Yes. So ready for you."

Then he's on top of me, his cock nudging at my entrance.

"Fuck, yes!" I cry out when he pushes forward.

"My perfect mate," he says, kissing me so deeply that my toes curl.

He sets a brutal pace, and I match it as our bodies arch and lift to meet each other. "Harder," I beg, reaching out to grab the edge of the table for leverage.

Axil grunts as he grants my request, slamming into me until I can't form words.

A loud creaking sound is the only warning we get before the table legs buckle beneath us, and the table collapses with us still on top.

"Are you okay?" Axil asks, frantically checking me over.

But I start laughing, and suddenly I can't stop. "I'm fine," I manage to choke out. He looks around at the destruction around us and starts laughing too. "You broke my table!"

He leans down and rubs the tip of his nose against mine. "I shall build you a new one."

* * *

Thank you for reading HER ALIEN NEIGHBOR! I hope you loved Axil and Vanessa's story. Are you wondering how Sam and Mylo already know each other? What about their Happily Ever After?

Good news! You're about to find out!

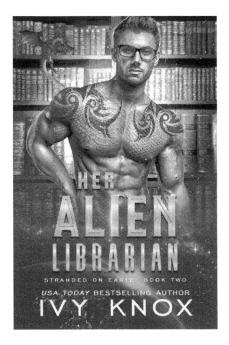

Mylo Monroe cares about three things: the library he runs, his brothers, and remaining single so he can continue his carefree lifestyle. But much to his chagrin, there's one woman he can't get out of his head no matter how hard he tries.

Samantha Rodriguez is an award-winning photographer and has spent her illustrious career traveling the world capturing breathtaking moments on film. She was certain her life would never change, but when her mother's Alzheimer's worsens, she hangs up her camera and travels to her hometown of Sudbury, New Hampshire, so she can remain at her mom's side.

Luckily, her best friend lives in Sudbury, but that friend is also married to the brother of the hottest one-night stand Sam has ever had. Since her divorce, Sam has vowed to remain single, but when she's unexpectedly invited to her ex-husband's wedding, she enlists Mylo as her pretend boyfriend for the event. He plays his role all too well, making them both question whether there's more to this heat between them than a casual fling.

Meanwhile, as her mother's condition worsens, a nefarious local cop from Sam's past threatens to expose Mylo and his brothers for what they truly are, making a happily ever after seem impossible.

How can she care for her mother and develop a relationship with Mylo when both could be taken from her at any moment?

Start reading HER ALIEN LIBRARIAN now!

ALSO FROM IVY

ENJOY THIS BOOK?

Did you enjoy this book? If so, please leave a review! It helps others find my work.

Get all the deets on new releases, bonus chapters, teasers, and giveaways by signing up for my newsletter.

FROM IVY

$\mathcal{W}$hile I love writing books that take place on faraway planets, dropping these giant, hunky alien brothers on Earth was an absolute blast. They do their best to blend in, but as soon as love enters the scene, their primal instincts take over and drama ensues.

The drama between Axil and Vanessa is pretty dark, rooted entirely in Vanessa's unprocessed trauma from her rape. Her pain is difficult for Axil to witness, because if he wants to keep his true identity a secret and protect his brothers, he has to sit by and do nothing. He can support her emotionally, but the man responsible for causing his mate pain remains free. And since Trevor is not held accountable for his actions, Axil takes it upon himself to see that justice is served.

This was a deeply personal story for me to write, because I, like many women, am a rape survivor. I think the weirdest, most devastating thing about being a rape survivor is the moment you learn just how big of a club this is. There are so many of us that have experienced this particular horror. You feel the comfort in the solidarity, but also overwhelming rage. It's one thing when it happens to you, but to learn it has happened to almost every woman you know…it guts you.

The lack of justice and accountability for rapists in this country, in this world, is abhorrent.

That's why Trevor dies—because in the worlds that I create, the bad guys will always lose. I had fun killing him off too. Like, a whole lotta fun. Maybe too much fun? I guess that's for my therapist to decide.

Trevor is not the only villain in this story, though. His uncle, Officer Burton, is the one who allows his harmful behavior to continue by keeping him out of jail. His decision to bully Vanessa into not pressing charges all in an effort to preserve Trevor's "potential" (gag) is what silences Sam when it happens to her years later.

Now, let's move on from the villains and get back to our heroes, shall we?

Vanessa was such a dream to write. In the beginning, she's where she wants to be (in Hollywood), but struggling, bitter about her lack of success, and very much alone. The last place she would ever expect to find happiness and a sense of community is in her hometown of Sudbury, New Hampshire—which is not a real place, by the way. There's a Sudbury, Massachusetts, so I took that town's name and put it in NH—but when she gets there, she has no choice but to face her fears and her trauma, and everyone around her helps her do that.

And then there's Axil. He was a lot grumpier in my head than he ended up on the page, but that's mostly because of how his friendship with Aunt Franny, aka Lady Norton, evolved as I wrote. I pictured him sitting in Aunt Franny's living room as she made him watch *Bridgerton,* and him asking questions about human mating customs with genuine curiosity in his eyes, and I just fell in love with their unique teacher-student bond. She was their unofficial guide to humans without ever asking them about their true identities.

Everything about Aunt Franny warmed my heart. Her letters, the treasure hunt, the love she had for Vanessa and the boys—all of it. I hope you enjoyed it too!

Next up, we find out what really went down in Boston between Luka and Harper, and we get to see the boys use their unique powers to go from rags to riches after they land.

Stay tuned!

Love,

Ivy

P.S. - I would be nowhere without my team of brilliant, bad-ass editors: Tina, Mel, and Jenny, who turn my words into something lovely. They work so hard and give me such incredible support. I'd be lost without them.

And to my parents, my husband, my friends, and my dogs for the love they showered me with the moment I first shared my rape story years ago—thank you for keeping me steady through all the ups and downs. Healing is not a linear journey, but you've certainly softened the bumps along the way.

RESOURCES

SAMHSA (Substance Abuse and Mental Health Services
Administration Hotline)
1-800-662-HELP (4357)
TTY: 1-800-487-4889
samhsa.gov

RAINN (Rape, Abuse, & Incest National Network)
1-800-656-4673 (call or chat)
rainn.org

National Suicide Prevention Hotline
1-800-273-8255 (call or chat)
suicideprevention.org

National Domestic Violence Hotline
1-800-799-SAFE (7233) (call or chat)
thehotline.org

ABOUT IVY

Ivy Knox has always been a voracious reader of romance novels, but quickly found her home in sci-fi romance because life on Earth can be kind of a drag. When she's not lost on faraway worlds created by her favorite authors, she's creating her own.

Ivy lives with her husband and two neurotic (but very cute) dogs in Chicago. When she's not reading or writing, she's probably watching *Bridgerton, Ted Lasso*, *New Girl,* or *What We Do in the Shadows* for the millionth time.